Rita Bradshaw was born in Northampton, where she still lives today with her husband (whom she met when she was sixteen) and their family.

When she was approaching forty she decided to fulfil two long-cherished ambitions – to write a novel and learn to drive. She says, 'the former was pure joy and the latter pure misery,' but the novel was accepted for publication and she passed her driving test. She has gone on to write many successful novels under a pseudonym.

As a committed Christian and fervent animal lover, Rita has a full and busy life, but she relishes her writing – a job that is all pleasure – and loves to read, walk her dogs, eat out and visit the cinema in any precious spare moments.

Also by Rita Bradshaw

Alone Beneath the Heaven
Reach for Tomorrow

Ragamuffin Angel

Rita Bradshaw

First published in 2000
by HEADLINE BOOK PUBLISHING

First published in paperback in 2000
by HEADLINE BOOK PUBLISHING

9

ISBN 9780747263265

Printed and bound in Great Britain by
CPI Group (UK) Ltd, Croydon, CR0 4YY

Typeset by CBS, Martlesham Heath, Ipswich, Suffolk

HEADLINE BOOK PUBLISHING
A division of the Hodder Headline Group
338 Euston Road
London NW1 3BH

www.headline.co.uk
www.hodderheadline.com

In memory of Hannah Eley, a very special little girl who had the face of an angel and a spirit to match Connie's any day! In spite of all the pain borne so bravely in her eleven years on this earth, she was sunshine and laughter and everything that is good in the world, and we all miss her more than words can say.

Part One
1900
The House In The Wood

Chapter One

The January night was raw and cold, the sort of mind-numbing cold that only the biting winters of the north produce, and the thin splinters of ice in the driving wind caused the man emerging from the dark cobbled street to tuck his muffler more securely into the neck of his thick cloth coat.

He glanced back the way he had come as he paused, pulling his cap further down on to his forehead, but there were no running footsteps, shrieks or cries disturbing the frozen streets, in spite of the scene he had just endured. And he knew who had been behind that, by, he did. He'd known immediately he'd stepped through the front door that her mam had been round to see her the day.

He began to walk swiftly now and with intent, not, as one might have expected, past Mowbray Park and towards the hub of the town centre of the rapidly growing Bishopwearmouth, where the countless pubs and working men's clubs provided a brief haven from the daily grind for hundreds of Sunderland's working men. He turned in the opposite direction, entering Mowbray Road, towards Tunstall Vale, and when he was hailed by two other men as they emerged from a side road he merely raised an abrupt hand in response, his walk checked in no way.

'By, Jacob's in a tear the night.'

It was said laughingly, even mockingly, and the second man answered in the same tone, shaking his head the while. 'It's fair amazin' what some women'll put up with. Now, my Bertha'd break me legs afore she'd consent to what his missus allows.'

'Aye, well likely Jacob's lass don't have too much say in the matter, eh?'

'Aye, man, you could be right there. Damn shame though, I call it. They've not bin wed six year an' she's a bonny lass when all's said an' done. Aye, it's a shame right enough.'

The men didn't elaborate on what was a shame, but now there was no laughter softening the rough Sunderland idiom as the two of them stared after the big figure, which had long since been swallowed by the freezing darkness.

'Makes you wonder though, don't it, what goes on behind locked doors? Aye, it makes you wonder . . .'

The lone form of Jacob Owen was walking even faster now, in spite of the glassy pavements and the banks of frozen snow either side of the footpath, and before long he had left the last of the houses bordering Tunstall Road far behind, passing Strawberry Cottage and then, a few hundred yards further on, Red House. The sky was low and laden with the next load of snow, and with no lights piercing the thick blackness the darkness was complete, but it would have been obvious even to a blind man that Jacob had trod the path many times before as he strode swiftly on, his head down and his shoulders hunched against the bitter wind.

Just past Tunstall Hills Farm Jacob turned off the road, climbing over a dry stone wall and into the fields beyond, where the mud and grass were frozen hard. The going was more difficult now; the ridges of mud interspersed with snow and puddles of black ice were treacherous, and the blizzard forecast earlier that day was sending its first whirling flakes into the wind, obliterating even the faintest glow from the moon, but Jacob's advance was faster if anything.

When he turned into a thickly wooded area some minutes later, he emerged almost immediately into a large clearing in which a tiny ramshackle thatched cottage stood, a small lean-to attached to the side of it enclosing a large supply of neatly sawn logs piled high against the wall of the dwelling place.

Now, for the first time since leaving the sprawling outskirts of the town of Bishopwearmouth, Jacob stopped dead, drawing in a deep hard breath as he ran his hand over his face, which in spite of the rawness of the night was warm with sweat. His eyes took in the thin spiral of smoke coming from the cottage chimney, and, as though it was a welcome in itself, he smiled and exhaled.

He was across the clearing and its freshly dug vegetable patch in a few strides, the thickly falling snow just beginning to patch the spiky winter grass at the edge of the plot of land with ethereal beauty, and he opened the cottage door without knocking or waiting.

For a moment he stood outlined in the glow and warmth of the cosily lit room beyond, and then the sound of voices drew the dark silhouette inwards, the door was shut and all was quiet again.

It was some two hours later that the lone hoot of an owl was disturbed by a band of men – five in all – moving stealthily into the clearing from the exact spot Jacob had emerged from earlier. The snow was now a thick blanket muffling any sound they might have made, and the whirling curtain of white provided extra cover as they approached the cottage, their big hobnailed boots marking the virgin purity with deep indentations.

The first man, who was small and stocky, paused at the side of the curtained window, gathering the others around him in the manner of a general marshalling his troops. 'We're all agreed with what needs to be done then?'

'I don't like this, John.'

'For crying out loud, Art!' The first man rounded on the much taller man who had spoken, his voice a low hiss. 'He's making our name a byword and you know it. Mam said Mavis was beside herself again this morning when she called in. You know what folk are saying as well as me; why, when Mavis Owen has got five brothers, does her man think he can get away with keeping a fancy woman in the house in the wood? And they're right, damn it. We should have stepped in months ago when Mam first found out what was what.'

'I know Mam would have it that's what people are saying. I'm not so sure myself.'

'Don't talk daft, man.'

'Aye, well supposing you're right, how does tonight solve anything? If Sadie Bell has already given him one bairn he's not likely to walk away just because we tell him to, now is he? And there's talk she's expecting another.'

'I don't care how many bastards his whore drops, he'll do what we tell him and finish it. And who says this third one is Jacob's anyway? Her stomach was already full when she came snivelling back from Newcastle years ago, so that's two bastards to two different men as we know of. She's likely got blokes visiting here every night of the week.' The smaller man's tone was pugnacious, his voice a low growl.

'I don't think she's like that.'

'I've heard it all now.' The smaller man turned his head as though in appeal to the other three, who all shifted uncomfortably. 'She's a trollop, the sort who'd open her legs for anyone, and what really sticks in my craw is that she hooked Jacob when she was working at the firm. You think she doesn't laugh up her sleeve at us all? Oh aye, I know her sort all right.'

He didn't doubt it. Art Stewart looked at his oldest brother – whom he had never liked – and he had a job to keep his thoughts to himself. He had shared a bedroom with this brother once the twins, Gilbert and Matthew, who were four years younger than him, had been weaned, and he knew John had had women from puberty onwards and that he had paid for them most of the time.

'What are you going to say to him, John?'

This last was spoken by Dan who, at fourteen, was the baby of the Stewart family, but although his face had the look of a young boy, his physique was already that of a man, and he towered over his oldest brother by a good three or four inches. He was a good-looking lad – all the Stewart boys were, and their sister, Mavis, who at twenty-five was the second born, was also far from plain – and like Art and the twins he was tall and lean; it had been left to the eldest two, John and Mavis, to inherit their mother's small, chunky stature.

'I'll tell him all this is finished.' John's hand made a wide sweeping motion towards the cottage.

'And . . . and if Art's right and Jacob won't listen?'

John brushed the snow from his shoulders, taking off his cap and shaking it before pulling it back over his thick springy hair, his actions slow and deliberate. It was a full thirty seconds

7

before he responded to the question, and then his voice carried a grating sound when he said, 'Then we'll have to make him listen, lad, won't we. We're here tonight so's his whore can see we mean business and her meal ticket's finished, all right? Mam said it's the only way and she's right. Gilbert, Matt, you with me on this?'

'Aye.' The twins spoke in unison as they mostly did. Along with Dan they were still living at home, John having married a year after Mavis, and Art the year after John. The twins were bright enough to know on which side their bread was buttered however – you didn't argue with their mother and get away with it, nor John if it came to that.

'Right.' John's eyes flicked over them all again but he avoided direct contact with Art's steady gaze. 'Let's get on with it then, we're turning into blooming snowmen out here with all this jawing.'

John's first knock at the gnarled shabby door of the cottage went unanswered, but as his hand was lowering for the second time the door was wrenched open and Jacob himself stood framed in the aperture, minus his coat and cap and muffler. John watched his brother-in-law's eyes narrow, and after a quick, 'Stay where you are, I'll deal with this,' to the occupants of the room, Jacob stepped down into the snow, pulling the door shut behind him whilst keeping his hand on the latch.

'Evening, Jacob.'

John sounded as though he was enjoying himself, and his small stocky frame seemed puffed up with importance, but it was to Art that Jacob said, 'Aye, well what's all this about then, man?' after he had glanced at them all in turn.

'You know damn well what it's about so don't play that game.' John cut in before Art could open his mouth.

'Is that right?'

'Aye, it's right.' John was fairly bristling now.

'And if I say I don't?'

'Look, Jacob, don't make this any more difficult than it needs to be.' There was a conciliatory note in Art's voice. 'We've come to talk to you, that's all.'

'Oh aye?' Jacob's narrowed eyes swept over the five men in front of him before coming to rest on Dan, and he continued to look into Dan's worried face as he said, 'And you had to bring the lad with you, did you? I thought better of you, Art.'

'He's old enough to work and he's old enough to be here.' Again John's voice brought Jacob's gaze his way. 'And who are you to say what's right and wrong anyway?'

'Meaning?'

'Meaning you stand outside your fancy woman's cottage and then have the gall to criticise us? You're a cool one, I'll give you that, Jacob Owen, but your days of visiting here are over.'

'I work for your father, John, and when we're there you have the authority to give me any orders he tells you to, but outside is where it finishes. When I step out of those doors of an evening I'm me own man. I don't interfere in your marriage and I don't expect you to interfere in mine.'

'I don't keep a whore on the side.'

He was spoiling for a fight. Jacob looked at the small man in front of him, who had all the aggressive tenacity of a bull terrier, and something in the other man's eyes told him how this was going to end. Whatever was in Edith Stewart had been passed down in the genes to her eldest all right, and he'd bet his last penny it was his mother-in-law who had instigated this little visit. She controlled John, she controlled them all, even the old man. His thoughts prompted him to say, 'Does Henry know you're here the night?'

'You leave our father out of this.' Gilbert had summoned up the courage to speak, and the answer and the manner in which it was spoken told Jacob his father-in-law was ignorant of the nocturnal visit. He was glad of that. He had always liked Henry Stewart and he knew Edith's husband liked him; indeed, he had always suspected that Henry had almost anticipated his daughter's marriage being a troubled one in view of the fact that Henry had lived with her mother for nigh on thirty years. *Thirty years.* And from what Mavis had sobbed at him on their wedding night regarding her mother's instructions to lie perfectly still and endure what had to be borne, Henry's married life could not have been easy.

'Go and get your coat and cap.' John thrust his chin forward as he spoke. 'You're coming with us, and you can tell her' – he jabbed towards the cottage with a fierce finger, his eyes screwed up – 'that you won't be back.'

'Over my dead body.'

'And that can be arranged an' all.'

They were staring at each other now, and although the rage in Jacob was high there was fear there too. John was a belligerent individual and could be vicious, and he was never so nasty as when his mother had stirred him up about something or other. John by himself he could possibly handle – at five-foot-ten he was a good four inches taller than his wife's eldest brother – but all five of them . . .

'Jacob, come back with us now.' Again Art was the peacemaker. 'You're our brother-in-law, we don't want bad blood between us any more than you do, but Mavis is our sister. Surely you can understand how we feel? And when

10

all's said and done you've only been married six years come next month.'

'I know how long I've been married, Art,' Jacob said heavily, and there was such bitterness in his tone that it caused the five faces in front of him to stretch slightly. 'If anyone knows, I do. And I'll tell you something else an' all while I'm about it; if it wasn't for that woman in there – the woman you call a strumpet and a trollop and worse – there might have been murder done before this day. I was reeled in by your mam, do you know that?' His angry gaze took in each man in turn but no one said anything, not even John.

'When I came to work for your father as his accountant and chief clerk she looked me over, although I didn't know it at the time, and decided I was eminently suitable as her future son-in-law. I was an educated man, and with my father being a schoolmaster and my mother involved in various good works, I was a darn sight more suitable in your mam's eyes than some of the lads who were sniffing about. Oh she reeled me in all right, same as your sister did, although with Mavis she was only following orders. Your mam thought I'd be malleable, that once I became part of the family and had my security and daily bread tied up with Henry Stewart & Co., Oil Merchants and Importers, I'd be happy to take orders, keep my mouth shut and feather my own nest.'

'What are you griping for, you've done all right,' John challenged roughly. 'There's not many as well set up as you and Mavis in your own place, and bought and paid for at that. Granted it's not Ryhope Road but me and Art aren't complaining and our places are no bigger than yours.'

'This isn't about the size of the house, man.' Jacob swore softly, shaking his head before repeating, 'It isn't about that,

that's nothing. Dammit all, what do you take me for?'

'What then?' Art's voice was low and steady and he took a step forwards. 'What's really eating you?'

'You want to know, Art?'

'I've said, haven't I?'

'Aye, you've said, but it strikes me the lot of you just want to hear what you want to hear.'

'I've had enough of this.' John's glare took in Art as well as Jacob, and the smaller man's hands were bunched fists at his side. 'The plain facts are that that whore in there has two brats already and a stomach full of the next one, and she's making a fool of all of us—'

'You shut your filthy mouth!' Jacob's face was drained of colour. 'You don't know the first thing about her. She's a good woman, a warm woman, and meeting her helped me keep my sanity after I'd lived with your sister for two years. I was ready to top meself when I met Sadie and I tell you that straight.'

'You—'

As John's fist struck out, Art caught his brother's arm and held on to him as Jacob continued, a spate of words flowing out of his mouth now. 'I should have known on the wedding night how it was going to be but I thought she was just frightened, being a young lass of nineteen and all, and that she'd come round. Come round!' He made a guttural sound in his throat. 'Your mam had done too good a job for that, damn her. How would you feel if your wife was physically sick with fear every time you came near her, eh? You answer me that. I've taken Mavis five times in six years of marriage and each time I felt I'd raped her. The things your mam had drummed into her . . .' He swore again. 'She's not normal,

12

she can't be, and she's made her daughter worse than she is. You don't know how many times I've thanked God the rest of you were lads.'

'You dirty liar.'

The blizzard was ferocious now, whipping the snow into a mad frenzy, but it was nothing on John as he wrenched himself free of Art and flung himself on the man in front of him, Gilbert and Matthew adding their weight to his as the three of them began to rain punches on Jacob's tottering form.

The speed with which the cottage door opened indicated that the inhabitants within had been listening to the proceedings, but as Sadie Bell, heavily pregnant and screeching like a banshee, made to hurl herself into the mêlée, Art caught hold of her, shouting for Dan, who was standing transfixed by the violence in front of him, to help hold the distraught woman.

Dan would have obeyed, but out of the corner of his eye he'd become aware of another figure, that of a slight, golden-haired child darting after its mother, and when the small girl of around six or seven tried to go towards the fight he reached out and caught her, lifting her off her feet as she began to struggle and add her cries to those of her mother.

Jacob was on the ground now and he was screaming as John's thick hobnailed boots belted into him again and again with savage intent. Twice Gilbert and Matthew tried to pull John away, shouting the while for him to stop, that Jacob had had enough, but each time John flung them aside and returned to the blood-soaked figure on the red spotted snow like an enraged animal that, having scented blood, was determined to go for the kill.

In the end, and only when Jacob was limp and unmoving,

Gilbert and Matthew wrestled John to the ground, urged on by Art and Dan's frantic shouts, holding him down by brute force for some thirty or forty seconds as he continued to resist.

And then a silence came upon them all, even Sadie, as, Art having released her, she stumbled across to Jacob's still form and knelt down in the snow by his side.

'Sadie?' A bent old woman was standing in the doorway of the cottage, her arms around a small toddler who was clinging to her tattered skirts but making no sound. 'Is he breathin', lass?'

''Course he's breathing.' Art was frightened; it sounded in his voice.

'Just about.' Sadie lifted her head towards her mother and the fruit of Art's voice was reflected in her white face and streaming eyes. 'But he's awful still, Mam.'

'Get him inside.'

'No.' John was standing now, Gilbert and Matthew either side of him, and unlike the rest of them his face showed no fear and his voice was cold and weighty when he said, 'He'll never set foot in this brothel again, I'm telling you.'

'It's not a brothel.' The old woman's voice was loud and indignant. 'An' you know it, I'll be bound, but it suits you to say otherwise, don't it, you evil-minded so-an'-so.'

'Don't, Mam.' Sadie spoke to her mother but her gaze was on John, and his eyes, as hard as black marble, stared back at her through the curtain of snow. She knew this man. When she had first started work in the most menial of jobs at his father's warehouse in William Street she had been warned about John Stewart almost immediately by the other girls. He was an upstart. The other sons were all right the girls had said, and the father, Henry Stewart, was reportedly just the same as when he had started the family business some thirty years before a few hundred yards away in Norfolk Street. But John Stewart was like his mother – he fancied himself a cut above ordinary folk. Not that that stopped him trying it on, one of the more attractive women packers had warned Sadie. Hands like an octopus he'd got, and he'd talk dirty given half a chance. You had to watch your step with John Stewart, but it didn't do to get on his bad side either; he could be a nasty bit of work. And from day one he had wanted her – the lust in his eyes had made her flesh creep at times and she had had to repulse him over and over again.

'That's right, Sadie. You tell the old crone to mind her tongue.'

Again John seemed to be enjoying himself, but then his gaze snapped from the woman who had been a torment to his flesh and who'd haunted his dreams from the first day he had set eyes on her four years before, as the child still held within Dan's grasp said quite clearly, 'You're a very nasty man you are, a wicked man, an' you'll burn in hell's flames.'

'Hush, Connie.' Sadie rose as quickly as her bulk would allow and hurried to take the child from Dan. 'Go in with your granny an' Larry, go on,' she implored on a hiccuping sob.

'No, Mam.' As Sadie made to push her daughter towards the cottage door the child resisted, and then, as Gilbert and Matthew hoisted Jacob's unconscious body upwards and on to Gilbert's back at a sign from John, with Matthew supporting the limp frame, Connie caused further consternation as she said, 'Me Uncle Jacob's a grand man, he is, an' I'm goin'a tell of you. I'm goin'a tell you hurt him an' that you made me mam cry.'

'None of that.' As John stepped forward, his arm rising and his face ugly, Dan's voice was not the voice of a fourteen-year-old boy but that of a man, as he moved the child behind him. 'You leave the bairn alone, you've done enough here the night.'

'Me?' John's face was mottled with temper. 'That's good, that is. You were all on for this tonight, so don't come it, Dan.'

'You said we were just going to frighten him.' Dan pushed the child into her mother's arms as he spoke, his voice losing its harsh note as he added, 'Take her inside, Mrs Bell. This is not something a bairn should see.'

'Aye, an' whose fault is that?' The old granny cut in again, but she was looking straight at John. 'You'll rue this night's work afore you're finished, you see if you don't. God won't be mocked an' He knows a black heart when He sees one.'

'Mam, *please*.' Sadie's voice was agonised as she bundled the still resisting child into the cottage, turning in the doorway as she looked towards Dan and Art, who were standing together and apart from the other three, and said, 'You'll look after him? Jacob? He needs a doctor.'

Her concern for the other man seemed to inflame John still further, and his features were contorted as he said, not in a loud tone but with deadly intent, 'You! You might fool the other poor sots but you don't take me in, Sadie Bell. You set your cap at him from the first day you laid eyes on him, didn't you, and all the while acting the virtuous widow. You don't think you fooled anyone with that tale? A man's only got to look at you to see what you are—'

'That's enough.'

Dan and Art spoke as one but as Dan pushed John

backwards, away from the white-faced figure in the doorway on whom the smaller man had been steadily advancing, John swung his body up and round on his youngest brother as though he was going to strike him. And the intention was in his furious face for some seconds before Dan's steady, quiet stance seemed to check it.

'By, you make me sick, the pair of you. Soft as clarts.'

Neither Dan nor Art answered John but their unity caused the smaller man to grind his teeth before he turned away, gesturing violently at Gilbert and Matthew to follow him. And it was like that, without another word, that the five men left the clearing and made their way back across the fields to the road with their unconscious bundle, there to begin a grim-faced procession back to the lights of Bishopwearmouth.

Chapter Two

Poverty is relative. As she opened her eyes to the dim light of morning, Peggy Cook's weary gaze took in the packed bedroom, in which there wasn't a spare inch of space unoccupied. Aye, it was relative all right. She remembered her Seth saying that more than once and he hadn't been a man to waste words on idle chatter. She thought she'd died and gone to heaven when he'd married her and brought her to this cottage, and she still thanked God that she wasn't ending her days in the East End where she'd lived her first fifteen years. Lived? By, she hadn't lived – existed more like.

She shut her eyes again – Sadie and the bairns weren't awake yet; the longer they could sleep the better after the horror of the night before – and allowed her mind to drift back over the years.

She had been born fifty-five years before, in 1845, one of seventeen children born to her Irish immigrant parents, only seven of whom had survived to adulthood. Her home, a two-up, two-down back-to-back hovel in the East End, had been a place where foul language, brawling, drunkenness and thriftlessness was rife, the cockroaches, rats and bugs vying for food and space along with the human residents.

She'd met Seth hop-picking when she was a young lass of

19

fifteen and he a grown man of twenty, out for a walk on his day off from the newly opened Ryhope Colliery with some of his fellow miners. They had married as soon as they were able. He had brought her to this cottage on her wedding day, and although they had shared it with his old mam at first – his da being dead – she had cried tears of thankfulness that night. And in spite of her only giving him the one bairn, their Sadie, he had loved her till he'd been killed in a fall at the pit five Christmases ago.

Peggy opened her eyes again, glancing over at the sleeping forms of Sadie and the two children lying in the double brass bed that had been hers and Seth's for all of their married life. Their Sadie had kicked up a fuss some months before when she'd insisted on moving to the rickety, wooden bed in the corner of the room that had been Sadie's before she'd left to get married, but to tell the truth it wasn't just because Sadie needed the room, her being with child again. Her arthritis gave her gyp these days and it was more comfortable in her single berth without any stray elbows or knees catching her unawares; the bairns were restless sleepers like their mam, especially Connie.

Connie . . . Peggy's gaze softened as it took in the small form of her granddaughter curled beneath the scant covers like a tiny animal trying to conserve all its warmth. In spite of Sadie having banked up the fire the night before in the sitting room cum kitchen – the other room the tiny cottage boasted – the bedroom was icy-cold, although the interconnecting door was ajar. She was glad her Seth had had two years with his granddaughter before he'd died; he'd fair worshipped the bairn. Her eyes misted over. Aye, worship wasn't too strong a word for how he'd felt about Sadie's bairn. She'd often thought that the countless miscarriages she had suffered all her married life, one after the other, had pained him more than her. He was a man who should have had a quiverful of bairns, her Seth, and certainly his grandchild was more like him than anyone else. By, the way Connie'd gone for that John Stewart last night . . .

The thought of the small stocky man with the gimlet eyes and hard mouth made Peggy move restlessly, and as though her unease had transmitted itself to Connie, her granddaughter stirred and stretched. But today there was none of the usual yawning and snuggling down again that characterised Connie's reluctant starts to the day. Instead, the small golden-haired child sat bolt upright, her big blue eyes looking straight across at the wrinkled, grey-haired figure of her grandmother as she whispered, 'Gran? What's the matter?'

'Nothin' me bairn, nothin'. Don't fret yourself.'

'Is it that man? Has he come back?'

'Heaven forbid, lass.' Peggy crossed herself quickly. As a staunch, died-in-the-wool Catholic she was nevertheless full of myriad superstitions, not the least of which being the foolhardiness of speaking out your deepest fears.

'He hurt Uncle Jacob, didn't he,' Connie said, and then as Larry, Connie's two-year-old half-brother and Jacob's son, grunted in his sleep beside her, she slid from under the covers on to the bare stone flags, squeezing between the side of the bed and the massive wooden chest and two orange boxes that held their spare clothes to reach her grandmother's pallet at the foot of the brass bed.

As her grandmother drew back the sparse brown blankets and hitched herself against the wall to make room, Connie climbed carefully into the space provided. She had learnt at a

21

very early age that her grandmother's twisted limbs and swollen knobbled hands must be treated gently and with respect, and now, as she wriggled herself into position, she whispered again, 'Gran? That man hurt Uncle Jacob, didn't he.'

'Aye, hinny. Aye, that he did.'

'An' he don't like me mam, does he?'

Would that he didn't. Peggy looked down into the sweet face of her granddaughter and the pure loveliness wrenched at her heart. Her Sadie had always been beautiful – a rose on a dung-heap, Seth had teased laughingly – and that beauty had caused her bairn nothing but sorrow in the long run. Now it looked as though this flesh of her daughter's flesh was going to be even more lovely than her mother.

Peggy swallowed deeply. 'No, he don't like your mam, hinny.'

'Father Hedley says we have to pray for them that don't like us.'

'Aye, well the Father is a good priest, a holy man.'

'I don't want to pray for that man, Gran.' Small lips curled back from straight white teeth. 'I hate him, he hurt me Uncle Jacob.'

Peggy's mouth worked for a moment, but for the life of her she couldn't come up with an answer to satisfy her granddaughter.

'An' the Father says we shouldn't be hyp— hypo— We shouldn't tell lies an' all, an' if I prayed for him that'd be the same as lyin' wouldn't it?'

Two enormous deep-blue violet-tinged eyes surveyed Peggy and again the old woman swallowed. This child of her heart, this child who was so like her Seth in nature, had a way

22

of going straight for the kernel of the nut. For a moment the weight of this present worry that had come upon them was made the heavier for fear of how her granddaughter would fare in the future. The world didn't like truth – truth could be stark and uncomfortable, it could reveal things that were better left hidden – and it was better by far to cope with your lot and keep your mouth shut.

'Perhaps the good Father was sayin' it's our duty, as devout Catholics, to forgive, hinny?' Peggy suggested softly.

Connie surveyed her grandmother unblinkingly. She didn't think that was what the Father had been saying at all. She knew her mam had forgiven her father when he left them when she'd still been in her mam's belly. Her da hadn't wanted to be married, her mam had told her. It was nothing to do with her; her da would have loved her if he had seen her, but he hadn't been able to think of that when he had left. And so he had gone, with the lady of the house where her mam and him had been lodging in Newcastle, and her mam had come back home to the house in the wood. And then her mam had heard the ship her da and the lady had been on had sunk and they were dead. And she had cried. Her granny had told her that her mam had cried buckets, and then that had been that.

But this, this with her Uncle Jacob, was different. A pain like earache came into her small chest and she wanted to press her hand against her heart to ease it.

The man who had hurt him was nasty, bad, like the thief who had been crucified next to our Lord and hadn't asked for forgiveness even though he had been suffering something awful. And the way he had looked at her mam had frightened her, and she knew it had frightened her granny. She, herself, hadn't been able to get to sleep for a long time after they had all gone to bed, and even when her mam and Larry had been fast off she'd known her granny was still awake. She'd known.

'I hate him.'

It was an answer in itself and Peggy sighed inwardly.

'Aye, that's as may be, but you remember what your mam said last night, hinny? You don't tell no one what happened here or it might cause trouble for your mam, an' we don't want that, eh? Your Uncle Jacob works for that man, or his father leastways, an' their arm is long, lass. Aye, their arm is long all right.'

Connie had a sudden vision of a long curling tentacle – like the freshwater snake Joe and Len Potts had caught and brought to school in a bucket – with a hand attached to the end of it reaching out all the way from Bishopwearmouth, and she shivered.

'I'll go an' put the kettle on, Gran.' She slid out of bed again, reaching for her red flannel drawers and petticoat which she pulled over her rough wool vest and the linen smock she slept in, followed by her brown wool dress and calico pinafore.

In spite of the layers of clothing Connie was shivering as she padded through into the other room, there to pull on her stockings and thick black boots which had been drying overnight in front of the range, having got soaked through the day before.

This room was also crammed full of furniture, but the damp musty smell that pervaded the bedroom in the winter months was not so strong in here and therefore Connie liked it best. The room was small and square, the front door leading straight into it, and the fireplace was an open black range enclosed in a steel fender, in front of which was a small clippie mat set on stone flags. Under the window on the side of the cottage an old battered table stood, with two high-backed wooden chairs set under it, and next to that a five-foot wooden saddle with flock cushions. A large oak dresser, holding plates, dishes and cutlery, and a small casket on which stood the tin bath and within that the washing-up bowl completed the sum total of furniture, but every item had to be edged round such was the lack of space.

The lavatory was nothing more than a small stone outhouse some twenty yards from the cottage, with whitewashed stone walls and a scrubbed wooden seat extending the breadth of the lavatory with a round hole in the middle of it. It was kept fresh with ashes from the fire and raked out once a week by Sadie, and was a cold lonely place in winter and somewhat smelly in the summer.

Fresh water was carried from the small beck some fifty yards behind the cottage come rain, hail or snow. But the kettle was full this morning, as was the rain barrel just outside the cottage door, and within moments Connie had poked the fire into a blaze, mashing the tea a few minutes later and carefully carrying a pint mug of the black liquid in to her granny.

'Ta, me bairn.' Peggy knew that Sadie didn't normally approve of the child handling the big iron kettle for fear Connie would scald herself, but today was an exception, and so now she added, her voice soft, 'Bring your mam a sup, eh, lass?'

An hour and a half later Connie had fetched a can of milk from Tunstall Hills Farm, piled the sides of the range high with logs and fed Larry his breakfast of bread and dripping, and she was now attired in her coat and hat ready for the walk across the fields to the road. At the junction of Belle Vue Road, some two-thirds of a mile further on, she would meet Miss Gibson, a teacher from St Patrick's school in the East

End which she attended, and would be escorted along Tunstall Vale to the tram stop just before St Bede's Park where the two of them would board the tram and ride the last half of the journey in comfort.

Connie didn't mind the walk in the summer, in fact she enjoyed it when the birds were singing and the air was warm, but she hated it on dark winter mornings. However, all her pleas to attend a school nearer to their home had gone unheeded. Due to her connections with the East End Peggy had sent Sadie to the Catholic school there, and so, it was reasoned, Connie must go too. The fact that Sadie had never learnt to read or write was neither here nor there. But this particular morning it wasn't the thought of leaving the blazing fire for the bitter winter's day outside, or the fact that it was inspection day, when all the children's heads were combed for lice and their necks scrutinised for boils, that was causing Connie to dawdle as she cut herself two chunks of bread and dripping and wrapped them in her handkerchief for lunchtime. She didn't want to leave her mam today, she had a funny feeling . . .

'Connie, get a move on, hinny. You'll miss Miss Gibson if you don't hurry.'

She didn't care. Connie wandered to the bedroom door and stood in the doorway looking at her mam and Larry snuggled in the big bed, and her gran still lying in the pallet bed. Her mam was always up first as a rule, but she'd felt tired this morning she'd said, and she still looked white and peaky, her eyes all red-rimmed.

'Mam—'

'You're goin', Connie.'

'Aw, *Mam.*'

'An' less of the aw, mam.' For a moment Sadie was tempted to give in to the unspoken entreaty in her daughter's deep-blue eyes but then she hardened her heart against the silent supplication. This child of hers was as bright as a button – look at how she was already reading a bit and writing, and her only a bit bairn – and if she was going to get anywhere in the world she needed education. Education was the key to rising out of the mire; that's what Jacob had said time and time again and she believed him. Jacob was educated and he was wise and clever. *Jacob*. Oh, oh, Jacob . . .

'It's not *fair*.'

'Neither is a blackbird but it still sings.'

It was Sadie's stock response and normally brought a reluctant smile, but today Connie wasn't having any of it.

'I didn't take me penny yesterday, Mam,' said Connie hopefully, 'an' Miss Gibson paid me tram fare.' There had been no money in the house the day before, Sadie having spent their last few pennies at the weekend on flour and yeast, twopennyworth of peas, beans and barley, and threepennyworth of scrag ends to make the stews and bread that would hopefully see them through a few more days. Connie had shuddered at the scrag ends – the lungs and intestines were black with congealed blood and had sawdust sticking all over them – but she had nevertheless cleaned them in the tin bowl and chopped them into as small pieces as she could manage.

'Aye, I know.' Sadie knew all her daughter's manoeuvrings. 'Your Uncle Jacob's seen to that. Take what you need out of the jar an' make sure you give Miss Gibson what you owe her.'

Connie's heart plummeted. Her mam hadn't liked Miss

Gibson having to sub her the day before and she'd known she
wouldn't have let it happen again. You could make out you'd
forgotten once, as she'd done the day before, both with the
tram fare and her penny for the week for school, but no one
would swallow the same story twice. 'An' Mrs Johnson said
it's tuppence if we want to bring our sewin' home.'

'Do you want to?'

Connie thought of the crumpled, creased apron she had
laboured to make which was spattered with blood drops from
pricked fingers, and now her face said one thing and her lips
another. 'Aye, Mam.'

Tuppence. By all that was holy them teachers lived in a
different world. Tuppence would buy enough fish at the
dockside for a good couple of dinners. 'Well take that an' all
then,' Sadie said heavily, 'an' don't lose it, mind. Keep it in
your glove not your pocket.'

'All right, Mam.'

Sadie pressed her teeth into her lip and shut her eyes for a
second before she said, 'An' for goodness sake take that look
off your face. Miss Gibson'll think you've got the bellyache
or somethin'.'

Connie continued to look at her mother for one more
moment, her azure eyes reproachful, and then she turned and
walked back into the sitting room. She dragged one of the
hard-backed chairs across to the fire, before climbing on it
and reaching up for the blue and white pottery jar on the
wooden shelf above the range. There were a collection of coins
inside now; several farthings, halfpennies and pennies, along
with the silver glint of a sixpence, one shilling and two bright
half crowns. Connie's eyes widened. Coo, her Uncle Jacob
was rich. He must be to give her mam all this money, mustn't

he? Nevertheless, she only took the penny for school and what she owed Miss Gibson, along with the tram fare for that day. She didn't want the silly old apron, she had just thought it might put her mam off sending her if she thought she'd got to pay for that as well.

''Bye, Mam.'

Once more Connie was in the doorway, surveying her mother's pale drawn face, and such was her expression that it caused Sadie's countenance to mellow and her voice to be soft as she said, ''Bye, me bairn, an' don't fret now. We'll be all right here until you come home, lass. I promise.'

Connie nodded, the weight that had been on her heart since the scene outside the night before lifting at the note in her mother's voice. They would be all right, and her Uncle Jacob would be back soon – hadn't her mam said that very thing when Larry had cried so much he had made himself sick?

Her Uncle Jacob loved them and he loved her mam. Sometimes, when she saw her mam and Uncle Jacob look at each other, their faces seemed to sort of shine and it made her feel all nice and warm and safe inside. She wanted to laugh and jump up and down and hug herself on those occasions, like when she saw the first snowdrops in the wood or watched a field of golden corn turn and wave in the bright sunlight. Her mam was beautiful, she was the most beautiful person in the whole wide world, and Uncle Jacob would be back soon. He would.

Two weeks later and Jacob Owen had still not returned to the house in the wood, but when Connie heard the knock on the door followed by the sound of Father Hedley's voice calling,

'Hallo there! Is anyone in?' she knew that one of her prayers, at least had been answered.

She had been to confession twice in the last fortnight, straight from school on a Thursday night, when they were marched into the church by the teachers and made to sit in the hard wooden pews whilst they reflected on the sins they had to confess when it was their turn for the penitent box.

Connie didn't mind confession and she never tried to get out of it like some of the other children by pretending to be sick or having stomachache; at least she didn't mind it when the priest was Father Hedley. Father McGuigan was different. He was tall and stiff, with eyes like pale-blue ice, and the last time he had come to the cottage in the autumn and she and her mam had come in from gathering wood to find him talking to her granny, he had just stared at her mam for ages. And then her granny had sent her and Larry outside to play, and when the priest had left and they'd gone indoors her mam had been white and she'd kept saying, 'It isn't fair, Mam, it isn't an' you know it. Some of 'em have had more men than I've had hot dinners an' got away with it, an' I *love* him.' And then her granny had stuck up for Father McGuigan and her and her mam had had a row and everything had been horrible for a few days.

But Father Hedley was lovely. And this last Thursday in confession she'd told him all about the men hurting her Uncle Jacob, 'cos everyone knew that the second a priest stepped out from the confessional box his memory was wiped clean of everything he'd been told. And the Father had said everything would be all right and she wasn't to worry and she hadn't . . . until she'd got home again. Her mam had been poorly since the weekend and she hadn't gone into school yesterday, and she had been praying Father Hedley would come and talk to her mam and take the frightened look out of her eyes. And now he was here.

'Good morning, Peggy.'

'Good mornin', Father.' Like her granddaughter, Peggy had sent up a swift prayer of thanks that it was Father Hedley who had called. How they would have coped with Father McGuigan the day she didn't know. 'Can I offer you a cup of tea, Father?'

'That would be most welcome.' The bedroom door was open and Sadie was lying with the old feather bolster wedged behind her, and now the priest's voice was softer still as he said, looking straight into the pale beautiful face, 'Not too good the day, Sadie?'

'No, Father.'

'Not this influenza I hope?'

'No, Father. I'm . . . I'm just a bit tired, that's all.'

'Aye, well, better that than influenza, eh? I hear there are fifty a day dying in London and we're not too far off that here. The grave-diggers are working day and night, and the London hospitals can't cope with the epidemic. You just make sure you keep well away from anyone who might have it if you're not feeling yourself.'

'I will, Father. I . . . I don't go out much with the weather bein' so bad.'

'Quite right, quite right.' The priest smiled at her before turning to the fire in the living room and holding out his long bony hands to the blaze. 'By, Peggy, it's a fair walk from the last tram stop and with the wind trying to cut you in two.' Peggy held out a mug of tea to him without replying and he took it from her with a nod of thanks, smiling at Connie as he pulled one of the straight-backed chairs close to the fire, and seating himself before he said, 'Well, and how are you feeling today, Peggy?'

He hadn't come to talk about her health. Peggy looked straight into the kind, thin face of this elderly priest she had known most of her life, and she knew he knew. Somehow, he had found out about the happening of two weeks ago. Could it have been the bairn? She glanced at Connie and the clear bright eyes stared back at her without any hesitation or evasion. No, it hadn't been the bairn. But then the priests knew everything so she shouldn't be surprised. 'I'm all right, thank you, Father.'

'Good, good.' Father Hedley was looking at the frail, crippled figure on the hard-wood saddle but he wasn't really seeing her as his mind grappled with how to get round to the main purpose of his visit. After the child had spoken to him on Thursday night he had made it his business to find out all he could, and in the process he had become deeply disturbed.

This was a nasty business, a very nasty business, and it could well get nastier. He knew of the Stewart family; not intimately, they were not of the true faith but of Protestant persuasion so he understood, another thing which had sent Father McGuigan into a holy frenzy when he'd discovered Sadie's association with the brother-in-law. The Stewarts' housekeeper's aunty was in his parish and she had told him her niece, Kitty McLeary, was a Catholic of sorts, or had been in her native Ireland. Apparently, the wife, Edith Stewart, ruled the family with a rod of iron, but there was no doubt they had a fair bit of influence in the town, and their prestige over the last few years had grown considerably since Henry Stewart had moved his central and commodious warehouses and offices to William Street. This night-time visit the child had spoken of had been hushed up right enough, but the outcome of it was sending ever widening ripples in its wake.

'Can I offer you a shive of sly cake, Father?'

'Aye, you can, Peggy. I'd have to be six foot under to refuse a piece of your sly cake, now wouldn't I?'

'I made it, Father.' Connie had just taken a mug of tea into her mother, and as she emerged from the bedroom with Larry perched on her hip, the toddler having woken from his morning nap, her voice was shy as she continued, 'Me mam's been feelin' poorly an' Gran's hands have been bad, so I've been doin' the cookin'.'

'Is that so?' Father Hedley smiled at the fine-boned, fairy-like child as he reflected, and not for the first time, that this delicate-looking little lassie was stronger than she looked. Which was just as well all things considered. 'Then I'll enjoy it all the more, eh? But don't let on to your granny mind.'

'Oh, Father.' Connie smiled her sweet smile before glancing at her grandmother, who was also smiling, and saying, 'I'll see to it, Gran.'

'Ta, me bairn.'

The sugared pastry, rich with currants, having been disposed of, and the big brown teapot having been refilled and then emptied twice, Father Hedley sat forward slightly and cleared his throat three times.

To anyone who knew him – and Peggy certainly knew him, indeed it could be said she even loved him, if her reverent adoration could be couched in such disrespectful terms – this meant the priest was coming round to the real purpose for the pastoral call. And when Father Hedley hesitated, clearing his throat yet again, Peggy's apprehension increased tenfold.

'I was attending Mrs McClough's mother on Saturday night, her that lives in St Bede's Terrace,' Father Hedley began quietly. 'The old lady hasn't been able to get to mass for some weeks now and Mrs McClough mentioned she was fretting. And while I was there she happened to mention that one of her neighbours, Jacob Owen, had had a fall at work and been hospitalised for some days.'

Peggy sat stiff and rigid staring at him, but when Sadie, her hand pressed to her mouth, made a little noise between a moan and a sigh from the bedroom, the priest turned in his seat and looked directly at her.

'Now through the years I've heard of a good few in Jacob's position having a "fall", along with normally sensible and clear-sighted women walking into doors the night their men get their wages and visit the public houses. You get my meaning?'

Sadie, her hand still pressed to her mouth and her eyes wide, nodded slowly.

'And this looks to be a nasty fall; there's talk of him being confined to a wheelchair.'

'Oh no, Father. No, not that.'

'Do you find it so surprising? Didn't you ever think—' Father Hedley stopped abruptly. This wasn't the time for recriminations, but for a moment the old priest was irritated and weary, infinitely weary, of human folly. The pair of them – Jacob Owen and Sadie – had taken the Almighty's laws and trampled them in the dust and then they expected what? That He would turn a blind eye to their fornication? That the great Creator would allow the flouting of the sacrament of marriage to go unrebuked? But what was he saying here? This evil deed was man's doing, not God's, and only he who was without sin could cast the first stone . . .

'Oh Father, Father.'

Sadie was crying now, great choking sobs that shook her frame, but it was noticeable to Father Hedley that it was the child and not the mother who went to comfort her, and when Peggy said, her voice low and pained, 'What's to be done, Father? Oh, what's to be done? I told her no good would come of this,' he knew Peggy's thoughts had moved along a similar line to his own.

'When is the child due?'

'In two months' time, Father. At the end of March.'

Two months. Dear God, two months in the depth of winter and with no means of support; do You intend to let it be the workhouse?

'Father?'

There was more, much more, he had come to say, but with the old lady staring at him with haunted eyes and the child with her arms round the shaking figure in the bed, Father Hedley felt it was enough for one visit. He had told them Jacob wouldn't be back and that was all they could cope with; he'd tell them the rest when he came next time.

But life was going to be hard, there was no doubt about that, and stuck out here without any neighbours to lend the odd helping hand they really were on their own. Mind, perhaps that was a blessing in disguise in the long run. How Sadie's association with a married man would have been viewed by any neighbours was questionable. Only last week he had had to break up an angry scene between a woman in the same position as Sadie and a group of red-faced housewives who fancied themselves annointed to tar and feather the unfortunate young lass. As it was the girl had got away covered from head to foot in soft filth and with the loss of her hat, but he didn't like to think what might have occurred if he hadn't happened along. The self-righteous frenzy of a mob was a dangerous thing, and in that particular case he had a nasty suspicion the cronies of the wife had been encouraged to show their displeasure by Father McGuigan. In fact half of the problems he encountered every day seemed to be incited – if not caused – by his compatriot in arms.

Father Hedley sighed inwardly. Only a few days ago Father McGuigan had read out the newspaper report stating that at the turn of the new century Britain's imperial power had never been greater – 'The empire, stretching round the globe, has one heart, one head, one language and one policy' was how it had gone if he remembered rightly – followed by more pieces declaring this century would see more compassion and understanding than any other man to man. How he could do this and then go and stir up certain of their congregation to all but murder some poor girl in the name of God was beyond him. By, it was. But then, they would never see eye to eye on matters like this, and perhaps that was why the good Lord had decided to place them together in this corner of His vineyard? Saint Paul had had his thorn in the side, and who were Father McGuigan and himself to expect anything different?

The thought of the other priest, who was more of a trial than the rest of his flock put together, caused Father Hedley's voice to be thin as he said, 'I must be away, Peggy. I'll talk with you again soon.'

'Can I come with you to the road, Father?'

He was about to refuse Connie as the child appeared at his side but there was something in the small face that checked his response, and instead he nodded abruptly. 'Wrap up warm, it's very cold outside.' He turned and glanced through the bedroom doorway but Sadie was now huddled under the thin blankets, Larry sitting in a disconsolate heap at her side, and she was still crying.

Once outside the air cut his throat with its coldness, but the child seemed oblivious to the bitter chill as she marched along at his side, her small face set in a frown.

'Father?'

'Aye, Connie?' He knew the tone. Almost from when she could talk – and that had been exceptionally early if he remembered right – this little mite had engaged him in conversations that had at times fair amazed him with the depth of her inquisitiveness and intelligence. It was a sin to have favourites among the flock – the good Lord had spoken about that very thing Himself – but this child was different somehow. She touched something deep inside him that he hadn't known was there, and it had been that way since the first time, as a bairn of three or four, she had reached up and taken his hand when she had walked to the road with him, very much like she was doing now.

'Uncle Jacob isn't going to come back, is he.'

It was a statement, not a question, but nevertheless Father Hedley said, 'No child. He isn't.'

The pure brow wrinkled some more, but then the priest missed his step and almost went headlong as the clear tone said, 'Then who is going to fill up the money jar?'

Father Hedley cleared his throat several times. 'The money jar?'

'Uncle Jacob fills up the money jar on the mantelpiece when he comes. It was empty the last time an' me mam was

37

worried; I hadn't even got me penny for school or the tram fare, but then Uncle Jacob put in lots of money, even a shillin' an' two half crowns, an' we got a sack of taties an' other things.'

Father Hedley gave a short cough. 'And have you got much left in the money jar?'

'A bit. Me gran made Larry a vest of brown paper rubbed with a tallow candle for his chesty cold last week 'cos she said we couldn't afford to get the onions an' black treacle an' stuff to make a syrup, but when he got worse me mam got sixpence an' I fetched everythin', an' some ipecacuanha wine an' squills from the chemist an' all. Me gran played up a bit but mam said we'd pay out more in the long run if he was took real bad.'

Father Hedley thought of the undersized, puny little boy who always seemed to be ill and nodded slowly. 'Your mother was right, Connie.'

'Me gran didn't think so. They had a right do an' me mam cried a bit.' There was a brief pause and then, 'Me mam's cryin' all the time now, not like when me Uncle Jacob comes an' they have a talk in the bedroom an' me mam comes out all happy.'

Father Hedley almost missed his step again, and now the childish tone was faintly reproving. 'You've got to look down at the ground all the time, Father. It's the puddles of black ice you see.'

'I'll remember that, child.' Father Hedley felt in his cavernous black pocket and brought out a small bag of bullets. 'Here, I forgot to give you these earlier, but share them with Larry, mind.'

'Oh I will, Father. Ta, thanks.' Another pause, while a

boiled sweet was tried and tested, and then, 'So who will fill up the money jar then, Father?'

'God will provide, Connie. God will provide.'

They were coming to the road and Father Hedley had never been so relieved in his life.

'Will He, Father?' It was doubtful.

'Aye, in one way or another, but you must do your part and pray now mustn't you.'

'Oh I do, Father. I do. But . . .'

'Yes?'

'Does God still strike people dead? Like He did in the Bible? If you pray *really* hard would He do that for you?'

'*What?*'

'Bad people,' Connie hastily qualified.

Father Hedley peered at her for a long moment and then he said, 'Who would you want striking dead, Connie?'

Well that just showed Freda Henderson was wrong when she'd said that priests were like everyone else and remembered everything you said in confession. She'd told Freda it was wicked and that she'd go to hell for saying that, and she was right. She'd told the Father in confession all about them men and that she hated them, and here he was looking at her all blank like.

Connie gave a little skip as the doubts that had assailed her since Freda's remark were laid to rest. 'Just bad people. Goodbye, Father.'

'Goodbye, Connie.'

Father Hedley stood and watched the small figure as it made its way back towards the trees in the far distance, and now his face was even more troubled than when he had come this way a couple of hours before. That little body held a greater capacity for feeling than most of the men and women he knew. Where Connie loved she loved unreservedly, but where she hated she hated with equal determination. She had seen something no child should see that night two weeks ago, and he didn't like to think how it was going to affect her in the future. No, he didn't like to contemplate that at all.

Chapter Three

Ever since Father Hedley's visit earlier that day, Sadie had seemed possessed of a nervous energy that wouldn't let her rest.

When Connie had returned to the cottage her mother was up and dressed for the first time in days, and wiping over the oil cloth which covered their battered wooden table. From there she had progressed to the oak dresser and hard-wood saddle, polishing and cleaning and carrying the flock-stuffed cushions outside to give them a good beating before replacing them on the gnarled wood. Then she had been on her hands and knees scouring the stone slabs, despite Connie's protests, and would have taken the clippie mat the same way as the cushions but for Connie wrenching it out of her mother's hands and lugging it outside herself.

Connie had already prepared a pan of broth for their evening meal that morning, with twopennyworth of pulses and vegetables and a meaty ham bone the farmer's wife had slipped her when she had fetched a can of milk the day before, but Sadie had insisted on fetching out her baking tins and making a batch of dough with the last of their flour, saying that they needed a round of stottie cake to eat with the broth.

It was now four o'clock, but the sky was so low and heavy that it was nearly dark outside – they had lit the two oil lamps at three that afternoon – and a fierce wind whipped the bare branches of the trees making them moan like poor lost souls in purgatory. So it was all the more perplexing that Sadie was determined to go and gather wood for the fire.

'Mam, *please*.' Connie was beside herself. Her mam looked bad – strange, funny; she ought to put her feet up, her granny had said so and she was right. It wasn't often her grandmother said anything like that – certainly not to her mam – so it made it all the more portentous. 'I'll go to the farm tomorrow an' get one of the lads to deliver a load of logs.' She didn't suggest their buying coal; she knew the money jar couldn't run to that. They hadn't had coal on the fire for weeks.

'We can't afford it.' Sadie's voice was dull. 'An' that's the last of the logs you brought in earlier.'

'They'll last until tomorrow, Mam.'

'An' if we get snowed in?'

'Stanley or Thomas or Percy from the farm will come to see if we're all right. They did last year, didn't they?'

'Listen to it, Sadie.' Peggy added her weight to that of her granddaughter. 'It's blowin' up for a blizzard, lass. Now have some sense. You know they love the bairn at the farm an' they'll let her have a load of logs on tick. They know we're good for it.'

'But we aren't, Mam, are we. Not any more. Not if we want to eat, an' we shan't soon be able to do that.'

'The good Lord will provide—'

'*Mam!*' Sadie made them all jump, and when she said in a harsh voice, 'Me da always said that God looks after them as looks after themselves,' Peggy's mouth set in a straight thin line. She reached for Larry, and, setting him on her knee, remained silent.

'I'll get the wood, Mam. You stay here,' said Connie anxiously, after a swift glance at her grandmother's angry face.

'We'll both go, lass.' Sadie was pulling on her old boots, which needed soleing and heeling, as she spoke, and the weariness in her voice emanated all through her heavy swollen body. Was it possible Jacob wasn't coming back? She didn't dare think that, she couldn't believe it. They had been making plans the last few months, plans to move away down south, where no one knew them, and start afresh. His wife wouldn't give him a divorce, Jacob had known that without asking. The mother, Edith Stewart, would rather see her daughter dead than divorced, he'd said, and Mavis was completely under her mother's thumb. But she wouldn't have minded about him not being able to marry her, legal like, if they could have been together. Well, she would have minded, but with Jacob beside her she could stand anything. Oh, Jacob, Jacob. A *wheelchair* . . . No, she wouldn't believe that. He would get better, he *had* to get better. For all their sakes.

'Here's your coat, Mam.'

As Sadie took the coat Connie was holding out she glanced at her daughter's worried face, and a fresh surge of anguish brought the weakening tears pricking at the backs of her eyes again.

Jacob had loved her little lassie like she was his own. When she thought of the difference between him and Michael Bell . . . He'd been all mouth and trousers, Michael Bell. A charming ladies man who had swept her off her feet and had her married and installed in lodgings in Newcastle, where he worked, before she could say Jack Robinson, but that hadn't stopped him carrying on behind her back with all and sundry. She had been so blind, so stupid. And then she'd fallen for

Connie, and the bigger she'd got the more he'd been repulsed until he'd off and skedaddled with Mrs Grove, their landlady. And Mr Grove had gone mental and thrown her out the same day. But then, later, there had been her Jacob.

'Do you want your gloves, Mam?'

'Thanks, hinny.' The threadbare gloves were more holes than wool, but as Sadie pulled them over her red, rough hands she wasn't seeing them, her thoughts returning to Jacob. He had cried the first time they'd come together, sobbed like a child and all the time murmuring loving endearments the like of which she had never heard before. He had been so grateful, so amazed, so broken that she had let him love her, *wanted* him to love her, accepted his body into hers with pleasure and gladness. And his wonder had revealed more about the hell of his marriage than any words could have done. She wouldn't let him stay trapped in that diabolical existence, even if he *was* crippled. If he never walked again, she would take care of him. Oh . . . The futility of the thought brought her head swaying as she stood to her feet. How could she? With the bairns, her mam? *What was she going to do?*

'Shall I bring the sack, Mam?'

'Aye, there's a good lass.'

The force of the wind nearly took the door off its hinges as they stepped out into the clearing, and after Connie had battled to close it the two of them walked further into the wood, gathering pieces of kindling along with some heavier chunks of fallen branches as they went.

It was just after they had ventured across the wooden bridge over the beck – constructed by Sadie's grandfather when he had first built the small stone cottage several decades before – that Sadie slipped on the raised root hidden by damp, partially frozen leaves and undergrowth. She tried to save herself, twisting her body as she fell, but only succeeded in falling on her back rather than her stomach and with enough force to drive the breath from her body in a great gasp.

'Mam! Oh, Mam, Mam.' Connie was kneeling at her side in an instant but it was a moment or two before Sadie could speak, and then her lips were white as she said, 'Help me get back to the cottage, lass. It'll be all right. Don't fret,' only to find that the pain made her cry out as she tried to rise.

'I'll go an' get Gran.'

'No, no, Connie.' As the child went to dart away Sadie clutched hold of her. 'Your granny can't help, not with her arthritis. I'll be all right if we can just get back, hinny.'

'All right, Mam.'

The pain was like a red-hot needle now, or rather hundreds of them, and they were all stabbing deep inside her stomach, in her womb. Was she going to lose the baby? She could feel Connie's arms tight round her and she leant against her child for a moment, a feeling of nausea competing with the needles which were growing and sharpening by the moment. It might be the best thing rather than being born into this. And then the thought was fiercely contested. This was Jacob's baby. *Jacob's*. And he had been so proud of Larry and so excited when she'd broken the news about this one. She couldn't lose it, she couldn't.

The pain was filling every part of her, squeezing itself into the core of her being and radiating out in unbearable waves that had her sweating despite the icy air. She had to get back to the cottage, she had to.

'Come on, Mam.' Connie's voice was soft but her little arms were surprisingly strong as she helped her mother to her feet, and it was like that – with Sadie bent double and Connie taking most of her weight – that they lurched and stumbled back to the cottage.

The child, a little girl, was born just before midnight and it never drew breath. Connie had stayed with her mother all the time – Peggy's distorted hands were little more than useless when it came to handling hot water or bearing any weight – and so it was she who cut the umbilical cord and wrapped the tiny perfect body in a piece of rough towelling before placing it gently in her grandmother's arms. Connie was aware she was crying, she could feel the tears running down her face and there was a salty taste on her lips, but she also knew she had to be strong for her mam. Her mam was poorly, very poorly. This wasn't like when Larry was born. Her mam and her granny had seen to things between them then, and although her mam had grunted and moaned and cried out a bit, she'd been sitting up straight after, laughing when Larry'd yelled his head off until he'd been put to the breast. But there was no laughing tonight. And no yelling.

The babby was dead. That tiny, doll-like scrap that had eyelashes and little nails and everything was dead. Its little face had been beautiful but there had been nothing she could do. And she was frightened, so frightened, her mam was going to die too, but until the storm stopped she couldn't even go for help.

The blizzard had started almost as soon as Connie had got her mother back to the safety of the cottage, and the howling wind was still driving the snow against the stone walls of the dwelling place with enough force to batter them down.

Connie eased the blood-stained bundle of old sacking, with

its jelly-like substance which had followed the baby, from beneath her mother, so that Sadie was lying on the lumpy bare mattress. She pulled the thin blankets over the inert figure in the bed and lifted her gaze up and out through the doorway to check on Larry – fast asleep on the makeshift bed she'd made earlier for him on the saddle – before turning back to her grandmother who was sitting on the pallet bed.

'Oh me bairn, me bairn.' Her grandmother raised her grey head from the minute bundle in her arms, and the old woman's streaming eyes made Connie even more frightened. Her granny never cried. Her mam maybe, and their Larry often, but her gran . . .

'Shall I heat up some broth for me mam, Gran?'

It was a moment or two before Peggy could speak, and then she said, her voice quivering, 'Aye, you do that, hinny. That's a good idea. Your mam needs somethin' nourishin'.'

The morning brought its own set of problems. The snow was deep – three or four foot in places, even deeper where it had drifted – and although the wind had abated slightly the air was a good few degrees colder. They had no wood for the fire which meant no hot food or drink, and Connie knew her granny was worried about her mam. Her mam was hot and sticky despite the icy chill in the bedroom, and she didn't seem to recognise any of them, not even Larry when he clambered on the bed and hollered in her mam's ear before Connie could get him away.

'I'm goin' to the farm, Gran.'

'No, lass. The snow's too deep an' them drifts are treacherous. You remember old Sam Mullen? I've told you about him, haven't I. Two weeks it was afore they found him

47

an' old Sam knew these parts like the back of his hand. One of the lads from the farm'll be along shortly.'

'Will they come today, Gran?'

Straight for the jugular, as always. Peggy stared at her granddaughter as she struggled to keep the panic and fear from showing. The cottage was like a block of ice; Larry was already blue with cold, and from the look of her Sadie had a fever. They could die waiting for help and the bairn knew it, young as she was. Dear Mary, holy mother of God, what should she do? If she let the bairn go and something happened to her she'd never forgive herself, but if she didn't . . .

And then the decision was taken out of her hands as Connie said, with a maturity far beyond her tender years, 'I have to go, Gran, you know I have to go. The farm'll send one of the lads for the doctor an' I'll see if they'll let us have some coal or wood or somethin' to tide us over for a bit. Shall I take me grandda's walking stick?'

'Aye, you do that, lass, an' stick it in the snow afore you to test how deep it is, eh? An' it's Doctor Turnbull we want, all right? An' . . . an' tell 'em to say to be quick.'

'All right, Gran.' Connie glanced across at the tiny towelling bundle lying in a makeshift cot in one of the dresser drawers, and the lead weight in her chest became heavier. This was all them men's fault, it was, and she hated them. She hated them all, and she wished they'd go straight to hell and burn in everlasting torment without a drop of water to quench their thirst, like that story about the rich man and Lazarus and Father Abraham they'd had at school the other week. She sighed heavily, picked up the walking stick from the side of the cold range and, after saying goodbye to her grandmother, opened the front door and stepped into a white frozen world.

* * *

Dan Stewart hadn't slept properly for nights on end – fifteen nights to be exact, ever since he had accompanied his brothers on their mission to the house in the wood and their lives had been changed for ever. He wished with all his heart he hadn't listened to John. By lad, he did. When he thought about what had happened because of it . . . His stomach heaved and it was in answer to that he told himself, No more, no more. He had been physically sick several times in the last two weeks, his stomach so knotted up that even trying to eat produced acute nausea, although none of the others seemed so affected.

They had originally planned to take Jacob back to his wife that fateful night, but when he had started the terrible blood-curdling groaning they had left the road and cut across the back of Ashbrooke Hall and Hendon Hill, approaching his parents' secluded detached residence in Ryhope Road as quietly as they could with John's handkerchief stuffed in Jacob's mouth to stifle his moans. He'd gone in first, to make sure that Kitty – their housekeeper-cum-cook-cum-maid of all trades – was abed, and then once the others had brought Jacob into the room his mother liked to call the morning room, he had gone up to his parents.

Dan shut his eyes tightly for a moment and then opened them again as he glanced at himself in the full-length mirror attached to the back of his wardrobe door. He saw a soberly dressed young man in a suit and tie – a black tie, the colour his mother had insisted they all wear from now on.

If he lived to be a hundred he would never forget the look on his father's face when he saw what his lads had done to his daughter's husband, or the pandemonium that had followed seconds later when his father had had the seizure.

Apoplexy, the doctor had called it. A sudden inability to feel and move due to a rupture in the brain. And this pronouncement with Art and John keeping Jacob quiet in one of the bedrooms upstairs, and his mother already planning how her son-in-law's multiple injuries came about by a fall down the steep stone steps leading from the canned and dry goods warehouse to the cellar below. His mother was a cool one all right. Dan clenched his teeth together. The thought had been neither laudatory or cheering.

His father had lingered for a full week before he had died, although the doctors had assured them he was aware of nothing. Jacob, on the other hand, was going to linger for a lifetime, trapped in a body that was useless but with his mental capabilities unimpaired. Damn it all ... Dan felt himself begin to sweat. And all because one of John's rages had got out of control. But no, no. He had to be honest with himself here. John was merely the bullet in the gun. The hand that pressed the trigger was his mother's. It always had been, Art was right in that respect, and it had only been misguided loyalty on his part that had prevented him seeing it clearly before. But he saw it now. By all that was holy he saw it now.

He left the large, well-furnished bedroom quietly and stepped on to the landing, which showed highly polished floorboards either side of the blue carpet running down the middle of it. This carpeting continued down the wide staircase and into the spacious hall, but here the carpet reached the walls on all sides, which were of a dark brown and hung with many fine pictures.

Kitty had just closed the door to the breakfast room and the middle-aged housekeeper was dressed, as his mother had demanded, in a black alpaca dress over which she wore a starched white apron. She smiled at him now, raising her eyebrows slightly as she saw him reach into the alcove to one side of the front door for his overcoat. 'She's waiting for you to go in and join her,' she whispered softly, inclining her head towards the closed door. 'Gilbert and Matthew are already down.'

'I don't want any breakfast this morning, Kitty. Tell her I was in a hurry, would you.'

'Now, lad, you know you'll get it in the neck when you come home tonight. Just go in for a minute to appease her.'

Dan was aware it was concern for him, and not his mother, which prompted Kitty's coaxing. The large rotund housekeeper had been part of his life for as long as he could remember, and from a very small boy he had known it was Kitty's strong and deep respect and affection for his father, and her unconditional love for himself and his brothers and sister, that enabled the forthright Irishwoman to tolerate his mother's fussy pedantic ways and sententious attitude. Certainly it was the only thing that had her clothed in the black dress and apron, he reflected wryly.

It had been eight years ago when his mother had made the decision that their social standing now made it desirable for Kitty to be so attired, but he could recall the announcement as though it were yesterday, and the squall that had followed which had rocked the household for days. But there had only ever been one possible outcome, and so Kitty had consented – albeit grimly – to the uniform, balking only at the starched cap with the long ribbons that tied under her chin. 'I won't be looking like a badly made Christmas cake that needs covering up for no one, now I do put me foot down about that.' And so, with his father acting as gentle arbitrator, an uneasy peace had fallen again.

'Kitty . . .' Dan shook his head at the big Irishwoman who, if the truth be known, had a bigger place in his heart than the woman who had given birth to him. 'I really don't think I can face going in there this morning.'

'You'd be surprised what you can do if you need to, lad.'

No he wouldn't. Not any more he wouldn't. 'I'll make it right tonight, bring her a bunch of flowers or something.'

'Do it for me then. You know what she can be like, she'll make me life hell all day. And she loves you, lad. Whatever else, she does love you.'

He knew that. His mother's love had always been like a thick blanket, suffocating him, weighing him down and filling him with enormous guilt because he had known, right from a bairn, that he couldn't reciprocate the feeling. She didn't give a fig about the others, not deep down. Oh, she went through the motions, made the appropriate noises and so on, but they all knew it was as though she had only had the one child. Art, he knew, felt sorry for him; perhaps Mavis did too as she'd had her share of being smothered, although in a different way. The twins had each other and didn't care much about anyone else, but it was John who bitterly resented the favouritism. John, who was so like their mother and so ached for her approval.

The thought of his brother brought Dan's mouth into a hard line and he said, opening the front door as he did so, 'I'll talk to her tonight, Kitty. I'm sorry.'

'All right, lad. All right.'

His father's funeral the day before had been a nightmare, and the empty places belonging to Jacob and Mavis a constant reproach, but it wasn't that, or the harsh words he and his mother had exchanged when her calm composure had driven him to voice his disgust at her lack of emotion, which had prevented him from joining his mother and the twins in the breakfast room. He hadn't wanted to walk to work with Gilbert and Matthew this morning, he had other matters to see to, and Art, bless him, was providing him with the necessary cover by saying he'd sent him to oversee a consignment of marine engine, cylinder and burning oils being given speedy shipment down at the railway, should anyone enquire of his whereabouts.

He hadn't allowed for this wretched snow though. Nevertheless, in spite of the conditions Dan walked swiftly, almost at a trot, cutting through the Cedars and then across the open ground away from the built-up area of the sprawling outskirts of Bishopwearmouth to avoid seeing anyone he knew. He skirted round the edge of the Old Quarries and into the road bordering Tunstall Hills Farm and then the fields beyond where he found himself wading knee-deep.

He could have missed her. That was the thing that haunted him for days afterwards. As it was he ignored the thin, reedy cry at first, putting it down to the solitary call of a bird if it registered on his consciousness at all. It was only when he had walked some ten yards past the great bank of snow that bordered a dry stone wall that something – a second cry, the disturbance of the smooth, lethal white coverlet behind him – caused him to swing round and retrace his steps.

And then he saw the tip of a small gloved hand sticking out of the pale silver tomb, and the beating of his heart filled his ears. His face blanched, turning as ashen as the beautiful frozen world around him, and he sprang forward, digging at the snow frantically and all the time babbling that it was going to be all right, that he was here now, he was here . . .

When he uncovered the small white face he thought for a moment that she had gone, that he had been seconds too late, but then the eyes opened and two orbs of a startling deep violet-blue stared at him. 'Me feet are stuck.'

'What?'

'I think I've slipped in a ditch an' me feet have gone through the ice an' they're stuck in the mud,' said Connie matter-of-factly.

'Right.' He didn't have time to marvel at her stoicism, that came later, but once he had dug and dug and uncovered most of the small form he found that her feet were indeed stuck fast in the glutinous mud beneath the ice, and that she had sunk to above her calves. It was her instinctive raising of her arms in front of her face that had saved her and formed a pocket between the suffocating white mass and her upper arms, but she was cold, very cold. She wouldn't have lasted much longer.

Once he had pulled her free and lifted her up into his arms her tininess became all the more poignant, and he found himself raging in his mind against the adults who had allowed so small a child to venture forth in such dire conditions. These people! You wouldn't send a dog out in this. Something his mother had said recently when she'd been on her high horse with his father came back to him. A family had been begging for bread at the back door, and the mother's and children's feet had been bare and bleeding and the lot of them clothed in rags. His father had happened in the kitchen as Kitty had been sending them away with a loaf and some cold brisket and cheese, and he had fetched some old clothes and a couple of pairs of boots that he, Dan, had outgrown, and handed them to the snotty-nosed little urchins. His mother had been furious, absolutely furious, insisting that they would immediately be taken to the pawnbrokers and the money used to buy beer and tobacco for the man and woman.

'They don't want to rise above their squalor, that's what you don't understand, Henry,' she had stated coldly. 'They wallow in it, their hands forever stretched out as they shun honest toil. They don't think like us.'

It was one of the rare occasions he had heard his father raise his voice to his wife, and in the heated exchange that had followed, when his father had reminded his mother that both he and she had come from working class stock and he – for one – was proud of the fact, Dan's sympathies had all been with his father and the destitute family, but now he wondered if there hadn't been a grain of truth in his mother's declaration.

He glanced down at the child in his arms. 'Right, we'd better get you back to your mother and get you warm.'

'I can't go back home yet, I haven't bin to the farm.'

The small figure wriggled but the last had been said through fiercely chattering teeth and Dan didn't relinquish his grip. 'Nevertheless, home it is.'

'You put me down, you!' A small part of Connie's brain was acknowledging that she wouldn't have got out of the ditch without this lad helping her, but a larger part was telling her he was one of them – one of them that had caused all the nasty things that had happened – and now her struggles became frantic as she began to beat her small fists against his chest and yell, 'You! You! It's all your fault. It is. Me mam's bad an' the babby's dead an' it's all your fault.'

By the time Dan got to the cottage he had got the gist of what had happened, but nothing had prepared him for the freezing cheerless interior of the tiny dwelling place, or the sight of that drawer with its pitiful package, and he was to remember the feeling, as though burning coals had been heaped upon his head, for the rest of his life.

Raw emotion was tearing at him as he ran as fast as he could to the farm, thrusting a handful of coins into the farmer's wife's hands and telling her to get fuel and food to the cottage while he went for the doctor, and it was still with him in all its searing intensity when he struggled into Bishopwearmouth, his chest on fire from the exertion and the breath rasping in his throat.

No, Doctor Turnbull wasn't here at present, the small neat maid informed him when he reached the practice in High Street East in the East End. Peggy had been adamant that only Doctor Turnbull would do – she had been treated by his father as a child and later, when the son had inherited the practice, had found him as understanding about such matters as payment by instalment as his predecessor. Some of the more highfalutin of the medical fraternity wouldn't turn out before you had greased their hand with a half crown, and what good was that when you were faced with an empty purse and a sick child or whatever? Peggy had challenged Dan bitterly.

If the matter was as urgent as it appeared, the maid continued, perhaps the young gentleman would like the address of the patient Doctor Turnbull was attending? It wasn't too far.

Yes, the young gentleman would like it very much indeed, Dan assured her quickly, and so it was that he found himself running the twenty or thirty yards into Hartley Street and then along into Northumberland Place where he banged at the door of one of the houses.

Dan knew this area; his father's business stretched from William Street to more warehouses storing heavy goods such as tar, pitch and resin in East Cross Street, while ships' provisions, consisting of mess beef and pork, together with the overspill of canned and dry goods from the central warehouse in William Street, were catered for in another two-storey warehouse overlooking the river in Sunderland Street, so in spite of living in the seclusion of Ryhope Road he had, to some extent, seen how the other half lived. He and his brothers, without their mother's knowledge, would oft times escape the house to the old market in the East End of a Saturday night, which would be full of people from the collieries and shipyards round about. Besides all the stalls holding second-hand clothes and such, there were barrels of nuts and raisins sold at ha'penny a bag, sweet stalls, buskers playing accordions, a roundabout – like a fairground – at the top of the market, even boxing most Saturdays.

Dan had always loved the Saturday nights, from drinking at the tap in the centre of the market which had a lead basin and a lead cup attached to it with a very heavy chain, to the walk home when they would spend their last pennies on fish and a halfpennorth of chips, and finish off with a quarter of brazil nut toffee from the large sweet stall at the bottom end of the market. Everyone always seemed happy on Saturday nights and – in a childlike fashion – he had never questioned the poverty that was apparent under the jollity.

But now, as the door was opened by a young child of indeterminate sex who stared at him warily, it was the smell that hit Dan first; the smell of unwashed humanity, of decay and rot and mould and a hundred other things besides, and he found himself wanting to retch.

57

'Is—' He had to take a deep breath and try again. 'I've come for Doctor Turnbull. Is he here?'

'He's seein' to me da, he's had his leg smashed right bad at the docks the day,' the child replied without much interest.

'Can I talk to your mother then?'

'Me mam's deliverin' the washin' down near Mowbray Park with our Gertie an' Jimmy.' The child sniffed wetly, catching a drip from the end of its nose on the back of its hand. 'You can come in if you want,' it offered apathetically.

'Right . . . Thank you.'

Dan found himself stepping into a narrow hall, devoid of wallpaper, where the encrusted floorboards spoke of years of dirt.

'You want to come in the kitchen?'

'No, no thank you,' said Dan hastily. 'I'll wait here if I may?'

'Please yerself.'

It seemed like forever to Dan before Doctor Turnbull emerged from the first door on his right, but within minutes they were back at the surgery and shortly afterwards bowling through the snowy roads in the good doctor's horse and trap.

The scene which met their eyes at the cottage was fractionally better than earlier in as much as the farmer's wife had been true to her word and sent a good supply of logs and a sack of coal, along with another sack containing a whole ham, fresh milk, eggs and some other foodstuffs which were spread out on the table by the window. However, in spite of the roaring fire now blazing in the range the two rooms were still cold, and when Doctor Turnbull walked through to the bedroom, after a cursory glance at the drawer, his voice was sharp when he turned to Peggy – ensconced in front of the fire with her shawl pulled tight around her and her arthritis deepening the wrinkles of pain on her face – and said, 'How long, exactly, has she been like this?'

Peggy shrugged wearily. 'The bairn gave her a bowl of broth once she'd cleaned her up just gone midnight, but after that . . .'

The doctor glanced at the golden-haired child standing just within the bedroom, her brother perched on her hip, and his voice was tinged with the sense of failure and frustration he always felt in such situations when he said, 'You looked after your mother, did you? That's a good girl. You were quite right to give her the broth, she needed something inside her to fight the fever.'

'Is . . . is me mam goin'a be all right?'

'Of course she is.' It was too hearty, and as Doctor Turnbull's eyes met those of Dan – who was standing by the front door – he swallowed deeply, moderating his tone as he added, 'But not for a few weeks I'm afraid. Do you think you can take care of her?'

Connie nodded vigorously. Of course she could. It was her mam, wasn't it!

'I'll give you some medicine for her, and you carry on giving her the broth several times a day, eh? And milk. Lots and lots of milk.'

Hark at him. Lots and lots of milk. Peggy's thoughts were bitter. And where would the money come from for this milk and broth he was rabbiting on about? That's what she'd like to know. The doctor was a good man, oh aye, she'd give him that, but he lived in a different world to half his patients, and wasn't that the truth. When had he and his good wife ever been so desperate for coal that they had sent their bairns out following the coal carts for the loose pieces of coke which rolled into the road when the wheels of the carts bumped and shook? Bairns as young as three and four darting under the wheels at risk of life and limb, and dragging their sack home at the end of the day, often with lacerated, bleeding feet.

And how often had they seen the inside of a pawn shop? Aye, she'd like to know the answer to that one. When she'd been a bairn, come Monday morning, regular as clockwork, anything worth pawning would be wrapped in a parcel and taken to the pawn for a few pennies to see them through the week. If they'd been lucky it might be out on the Friday night, but by the end of the weekend the whole scenario would be repeated.

And she dare bet he didn't get his fruit down at the market like some of a Saturday night, scrabbling under the stalls and in the gutter for dirt-encrusted, mouldy bits that were perhaps all they'd eat that day. No, his maid would go out to see the fruit man in the back lane when he called, choosing this and that and having it on account most likely. And would one of his bairns be down the mines from as young as seven or eight? Twelve it was supposed to be, legal like, but who could afford to take notice of the law when it was either sending the bairns out for any work they could get or the workhouse?

And now here was her bonny lass, as near death as dammit. The gates of the workhouse were opening in front of Peggy's eyes and filling her with dread. But her Sadie wouldn't die, not now, not with the doctor to see to her and the cottage warming up. But if it wasn't for the young lad standing here there'd be no fire in the hearth and no food on the table. Mind you, he'd been part of this trouble that had come upon them, although – and she glanced at Dan now – he was of a different stamp to the rest of them fiends. Beneath that lanky, gangling exterior he was nowt but a stripling.

When Doctor Turnbull shut the bedroom door in order to examine his patient it was this last thought of Peggy's that made her say, her voice low, 'Look, lad, don't think I'm not grateful for you helpin' our Connie the day, an' for takin' the trouble to come, an' for the coal an' food an' all, but them brothers of yours will take it out of your hide if they know you've come here.'

'Art wouldn't,' said Dan uncomfortably, aware of Connie's eyes tight on him as she stood, still holding the toddler balanced on her small hip, just outside the bedroom door. The bairn didn't like him but then who could blame her? he reasoned silently. 'I discussed it with him yesterday and he understood.'

'Well I dunno about that, lad, but that little one – John, is it? – now he's right dangerous if you ask me, an' we've enough on our plate without havin' another visit from the likes of him, an' that's what it'd mean if he found out you'd been consortin' with Jacob's other family.'

Jacob's other family. Dan stared at the old woman. He had never thought of them in that light but that's clearly what they considered they were.

'So's it's best all round if you don't let on about all this an' you don't come back. I don't want the bairns hurt.'

'John wouldn't—' Dan stopped abruptly, shocked to discover that he couldn't say, in all honesty, that he was sure his brother wouldn't hurt Sadie Bell's children. His mouth was slightly agape and after closing it he swallowed twice before saying quietly, as though to himself, 'I don't understand how all this has happened. Everything, everyone, has changed.'

'I don't think anyone's changed, lad. It's just that life has a way of bringin' the scum to the surface.'

They said nothing more until Doctor Turnbull left the bedroom two or three minutes later. After placing a large bottle of medicine on the mantelpiece with instructions that Sadie be given a dose every four hours, he carefully lifted the tiny bundle from the drawer and made his goodbyes.

Dan followed the doctor to the door, but turned on the threshold and looked at Peggy again. 'I'll see to his bill.'

'Aye, all right, lad.' She didn't thank him and Dan did not expect her to, but they both knew that because of the things of which they had spoken, this was, of necessity, his last visit to the house in the wood.

'Goodbye, Connie.' When Dan transferred his gaze to the child he saw her small chin lift slightly and the rose-bud lips tauten, but she said nothing, merely eyeing him with a hostility which was more than a little daunting in so young a child. But he had seen the dart of anguish crumple her face when the doctor had picked up the body of the baby and the movement – instantly checked – that she had made towards the man.

He stared at her for a moment more, his heart going out to her, and she stared back, not giving an inch, and then he turned, stepping out into the bleak cold world outside, and shut the cottage door behind him.

Chapter Four

'Mam, I know exactly what you're sayin', 'course I do, but we don't have any choice. Surely you see that?'

'What I see is that you might bring that madman down on our heads agen an' that won't help us or Jacob.'

'Larry is Jacob's child an' he knows that, an' if I have to create a scene the like of which they've never seen before I shall make sure I see him, however ill he is. I *have* to see him, Mam—' Sadie stopped abruptly, her hand to her chest as she gulped at the air for some moments before saying more slowly, 'I have to.'

'You're not well, lass,' said Peggy pleadingly, her eyes on her daughter's ashen face. 'It's only bin three weeks since the— since you were took bad, an' Doctor Turnbull said—'

'Doctor Turnbull said a lot of things,' Sadie interrupted wearily, 'but we've only enough food for today an' the coal an' logs are all gone. You know how things are, Mam. Don't make it worse.'

'Well, leave the bairns with me then. Don't drag them along.'

'I'm goin' with Mam. Larry can stay here but I'm goin'.'

Connie's voice had been fierce but now Sadie lifted her

hand for her daughter to stop. 'You know full well why I'm takin' 'em, Mam.'

'Aye, I do an' all, an' no good ever come out of blackmail.'

'That remains to be seen, but they're comin'.'

'Eee, I don't understand you no more. You're me own, but I don't understand you. Your da must be turnin' in his grave with the shame you've brought down on our heads. I told you at the beginnin' they never leave their wedded wives, now didn't I? But you knew best.'

'He would have left her,' said Sadie dully.

Connie hated it when her mam and grandma fought like this and they were doing it all the time now, her grandma's voice low and bitter and her mam's sort of dead sounding. Connie looked at them both before she turned to Larry who was sitting on the hard-wood saddle and said softly, 'Come on, I'll get your coat on.' He nodded at her, scrambling down at once, but he didn't speak. He hardly ever spoke, and when he did it was in a baby gibberish of his own devising, even though he was well past his second birthday. But he sensed how things had changed in the last few weeks, she was sure of that, and she'd noticed that more and more it was her he came to when he was tired or he'd hurt himself. And her mam was so thin and peaky. Beautiful still, she assured herself quickly in the next moment, as though the thought had been a criticism. Her mam was still the most beautiful person in the whole wide world and always would be, but she did look poorly.

There had been a thaw over the last week, a gradual thaw which meant the severe flooding of the year before had not been repeated, but still the ground outside the cottage was a quagmire. Walking became easier once they reached the road but already her mam was as white as a sheet and making little gasping noises with each breath.

'Give Larry to me, Mam. I'll piggyback him.'

Connie looked up at her mother as she spoke and when Sadie made no reply, but simply stopped and positioned the toddler on to Connie's small thin back, her anxiety increased.

Connie's legs were aching long before they reached St Bede's Terrace off Mowbray Road, but although she had stopped a few times and humped Larry up further on her back – even persuading the reluctant toddler to walk a little way once or twice – she said not a word of complaint. She liked the look of St Bede's Terrace. It was a tidy street, and it had front gardens too, not like near her school.

The thought of school brought Connie nipping at her bottom lip. She had found, much to her surprise, that she'd missed not going to school over the last three weeks. It wasn't like when she was on holiday, not with the other children still going, and now Ethel Miller would be crowing she was in front of her with her reading and she wouldn't be top of the class any more. Normally her mam went on and on about how she had to go to school and be educated, but since that night when her mam had got sick she hadn't mentioned her going back.

The memory of that night with all its attendant horror was held fast in her mind, and however much she tried to think about something else she only had to shut her eyes to experience it all again. She wished she could talk to her mam or her grandma about it but somehow she knew she mustn't. It would only make their quiet fighting worse if she said anything; her grandma knew she was still upset about it, and her mam had been different since that night. She couldn't say anything to her mam. But once she was back at school she'd go to confession and tell Father Hedley. Aye, that's what she'd do.

'Connie?' Her mam's arm across her small chest brought her to a halt. They were standing on the pavement in front of one of the neat thin gardens now, and unlike most of its neighbours – which were quite devoid of snow – this one still had a remnant left here and there. 'I want you to stand here with Larry – put him down now, that's it – an' say nothin', you understand me? Not a word, mind.'

'All right, Mam.' Connie felt a little hurt. Her mam had talked as though she was telling her off about something, she thought a mite resentfully, as she watched Sadie pick her way carefully down the path to the front door and knock twice with the brass knocker.

After what seemed like a long time to Connie, her mother knocked again, and then, after another wait, a third time.

'Who is it you're wanting?'

Connie saw the next door neighbour's head emerge from the bedroom window but Sadie didn't answer at first. And then Connie saw her mother straighten and answer, very evenly, 'Mr an' Mrs Jacob Owen. I understand they live at this address?'

'Not any more, lass.' The woman peered down at Sadie, her gaze moving to the children at the gate and then back again before she said, 'Who is it that's enquiring?'

With a touch of asperity Sadie replied, 'A friend of the family. I understand Mr Owen was involved in some kind of accident recently.'

'Aye, that's right. Nasty it was. The poor devil'll never be any use again, that's what my Cecil says.'

'Really.'

Connie wriggled a little. She didn't like it when her mother spoke in that cool thin tone, and she could tell the neighbour didn't like it either when she said, 'I'm surprised, if you're a friend of the family, that you expected to find them here anyway. Mrs Owen's been staying with her mam since the accident and when he come out of hospital that's where he went. Didn't no one tell you?' The woman's tone was tart.

There was a longer pause this time and then Sadie said, 'No, no one told me.'

'Aye, well that's where you'll find them. Ryhope Road, you know it? The Stewarts have got a right canny house just down from Backhouse Park. Big stone place it is, with pillars either side of the front door. It's nowt but ten minutes or so.'

'Thank you. Thank you very much.'

Her mother's back was very straight when she turned and walked up to the pavement, and she bent and lifted Larry into the crook of one arm before taking Connie's hand in a firm grip. They didn't pause in their brisk walk, not even when they entered Mowbray Road, and it wasn't until they had reached Ryhope Road that Sadie suddenly leant against the high stone wall that bordered this very pleasant, affluent street and set Larry on his feet. There were huge trees bordering all the gardens; in some places they reached over the road on both sides forming an arch, and Connie was just thinking this must be a very nice road to live in when she noticed her mother's face. 'You all right, Mam?'

Sadie had her hand pressed to her chest and her face was white, and it was a moment or two before she said, 'Aye, I'm all right, hinny, but hold Larry a while, would you, lass.'

They passed the gatehouse to Backhouse Park and within a few minutes were looking through substantial wrought-iron

67

gates set in a high stone wall at the house the neighbour had described. The house was not the largest in Ryhope Road, nor did it possess a great deal of land, but it stood aloof and proud in the bitter chill of the winter's morning and it was very imposing. The short pebbled drive was immaculate, the large, gracious, horseshoe-shaped steps to the front door numbered six or seven, and there were ten windows along the front of the house alone. Moreover, it was surrounded by giant oaks at the back and sides which increased the air of grandeur.

'Do you want me an' Larry to wait here, Mam?'

Sadie hesitated. She didn't know how this was going to go except that it would not be pleasant. She found herself wringing her hands and stopped abruptly, glancing down at the two children. The whole point of bringing them was for them to be seen, and what with this great wall and the gates they might not be noticed. 'No.' Sadie opened the gate as she answered. 'You come with me an' put your brother down now. He's bin carried all the way here, he's got to walk a bit sometimes.'

They walked along the drive with Larry between them swinging happily on their hands, and then Sadie went up the steps and pulled the bell before returning to stand with the children.

The door was answered by a pretty, plump woman wearing a black dress and an apron, and whatever she had been about to say never left her lips as her mouth fell open in a gape. She darted a glance behind her before pulling the door partly to and venturing down two of the steps. 'What do you want? You must be mad coming here. Get yourself away now, go on.'

'I'm—'

'I know who you are, lass. There's nothing that goes on in this family that I don't know about, even if certain members of it would like to think differently. Aye, I know who you are all right. I nursed Jacob when he come out of the infirmary and he described you to a tee.'

The woman's tone wasn't hostile – flustered would have described it better – and Sadie stared at her for a moment before she said, 'I . . . I have to see him – Jacob. I need to talk to him. *Please.*'

'Lass, I'm telling you—'

Whatever she had been about to tell her Sadie never knew, because in the next instant the door was opened fully and another woman stood in the aperture, her voice sharp as she said, 'Kitty? What on earth do you think you are doing skulking out there, and who are these people?'

This must be Jacob's mother-in-law. This was her, Edith Stewart, the matriarch. Sadie's heart was pounding and her legs felt weak as she looked at the small, smartly dressed woman in front of her. Edith Stewart's plain, dark-claret brocade dress was deceptively simple, but the material which fell in deep folds to the top of her neatly shod feet was beautifully cut and the exquisite gold fob watch pinned to the ruched bodice of the dress was clearly expensive. Everything about the crisp, eagle-eyed woman spoke of wealth and authority. Her hair was still very black with merely a touch of grey, arranged high on her head in a loose bun, and her eyes – which were of the same gimlet hardness as her eldest son's – were looking straight into Sadie's terrified blue ones.

'Well? State your business,' the irritated voice continued coldly, 'but if it's a handout you're looking for we have nothing to spare. I know you people, the word soon gets about, doesn't it and—' And then, like a steel trap snapping shut, the words were cut off and the ebony eyes opened wide for a moment. '*No.*' It was a hiss. 'No, it can't be. You wouldn't have the sheer affrontry.'

'Mrs Stewart?' Sadie's voice was shaking even as she told herself she couldn't afford to show any weakness in front of this woman. 'I need to know . . . I have to see Jacob. I—'

'You filthy, dirty trollop! You brazen huzzy, you. You think you can come here, *here*, to my home, with your ragamuffin brats and your whining! I'll have you horsewhipped.'

'Madam! Come back inside, please.'

As Sadie took a step backwards from the enraged woman Kitty actually caught hold of her employer's arm, only to be shaken off so violently that a less heavy or well-endowed woman would have been thrown to the ground.

'Did you know? Did you know it was her?' Edith asked her housekeeper, white flecks of spittle gathering at the corners of her mouth. And then, without waiting for an answer, she swung back to Sadie who had both children clinging to her skirts, and bit out, 'I'll see you rot in hell before you get your hands on my daughter's husband again. They've gone, do you hear? Gone far enough away so you and your flyblows will never find him, and I'll make sure they never come back.'

Sadie was aware that Edith Stewart was showing her working class roots and that the genteel façade had been blown apart, but there was no victory in the realisation. The woman was dangerous – it was there in the narrowed eyes and snarling mouth – and she had no idea what she would do next.

Kitty must have been of the same opinion, because again she caught hold of Edith saying, 'Please, Madam, please. Don't do anything rash.'

'*Anything rash?*' As Edith jerked her arm free her voice rose still higher. 'I'd like to string her up by her thumbs and display her as the loose piece she is. Scum! The lot of them, scum! And flaunting her guttersnipe brats in front of my face when she was the means preventing Mavis having any by her legal husband—'

'That's not true.' Sadie spoke through trembling lips, her voice low but clear. 'You know that's not true. She wouldn't sleep with him, she went hysterical if Jacob went near her.'

'Lies! All lies!'

Larry was crying now, wailing into Sadie's skirts, and as Kitty said, 'Madam, I know you're upset but when all's said and done they are only bairns, this is not their fault, let's leave it for now,' Edith seemed as though she was going to have a fit.

'Only bairns? *Bairns?* They are little animals born of a bitch on heat, that's what they are, and Henry is dead because of that woman. Don't forget that, Kitty.' And then, as she advanced another step towards Sadie, 'Did you know that, eh? Did you know you've got a man's death on your conscience besides another being crippled? My husband was too decent a man to be able to stand your association with his daughter's husband and it killed him.'

'Mrs Stewart—'

'You're scum, girl. *Scum.* Not fit to draw the same air as decent folk—' And then Edith's words were cut off and her breath ejaculated as a small missile hit her stomach.

Connie hadn't understood half of what was being said, but she knew the lady from the big house was being nasty, really nasty, to her mam, and she had stood it long enough. As her head hit Edith's midriff her legs and arms were kicking and lashing out, and such was Edith's utter shock and surprise that she was frozen for a good few seconds as the screaming child battered at her.

Sadie, impeded by Larry still clinging to her skirts, only succeeded in dragging her daughter off the staggering figure when the couture dress was ripped beyond redemption and the bun hanging in dishevelled disarray halfway down Edith's back, and it took both her strength and that of Kitty to hold the child back.

They left in the midst of a tirade the like of which Ryhope Road had never heard before, and which was far more in-keeping with that of a fishwife down at the docks, and Sadie didn't stop or let go of Connie until they had passed Barley Mow Cottage and then Ivy Cottage, and turned into the Cedars. She walked swiftly for some few yards down the tree-lined street, still hauling both Connie and Larry – the latter having lost his footing numerous times – violently by their arms, and then she stopped, letting go of Larry and hitting Connie a resounding slap across one ear followed by a second across the other ear that took Connie clean off her feet.

Connie couldn't see or hear for a moment such was the swirling of her head, and then when the darkness receded and she saw her mother's face and heard Larry's crying, she managed, 'Mam, oh, Mam. I'm sorry, Mam. I am, I'm sorry.'

And then she felt her mother's arms about her and realised her mam was sitting in the mud alongside of her, the tears streaming down her face, as she murmured over and over again, 'Oh me bairn, me bairn, me bairn. May God forgive me. Oh me bairn. I'm sorry, hinny. I'm sorry.'

How long they sat there in the sludge and dirt Connie didn't know, it was enough that when they eventually rose to their feet her mam was kind with her again and her voice was soft when she said, 'Come on, me wee brave bairn, let's go an' tell your granny she was right after all, eh? That should please her,' and funnily enough it was at that moment that Connie wanted to cry.

Chapter Five

The sky was a transparent silver expanse and of such a brilliant hue that it hurt the eyes to look upwards, but Sadie wasn't looking upwards as she stumbled along in the bitterly cold afternoon, picking her way through the bulging sacks, barrels, crates and miscellaneous bundles that were strewn all over the wharf. It had been a long shot, applying for work at the grain warehouse, and she knew her physical appearance had been against her. They wanted big strong females – on the limited occasions when jobs for women were available at all – and she was too thin and slight, too pale and fragile-looking after losing the baby, to inspire confidence in future employers.

Every day for the last week, ever since the visit to Ryhope Road, she had trudged the three miles into Bishopwearmouth, enquiring at all the warehouses, the shops, the factories, even the fish quay and the curing houses, but to no avail. She had sent Connie 'on tick' to the farm, and the bairn had managed to secure enough logs and food to tide them over to the present time, but now there was no fuel and no food on the table, and the farm would want payment before they obliged again.

She had even gone to see Father Hedley a couple of days ago, in desperation, but although the priest had been sympathetic he hadn't been able to hide his condemnation of the circumstances that had brought her to this point, and the two or three jobs he had known about had been ones she had already been turned down for. *What was she going to do?*

Of necessity they were all going to bed once darkness fell and rising with the dawn, there being no money for oil for the lamps, and the long nights seemed endless as she tossed and turned and racked her brains for a way out. But there wasn't one – saving the workhouse. And that wasn't a way out; she would rather see them dead than incarcerated in that soulless prison where the children were separated from their mothers and fathers on entry; and someone like Peggy would end her days in the infirm ward. It was her mother's secret fear that she would be consigned to the workhouse in her twilight years, and she couldn't let that happen.

Sadie pulled her worn felt hat – cleaned that morning with salt and flour – more securely over her golden hair as the fish-tainted air froze her ears, and turned into Long Bank away from the quays. The Bank joined Low Street and High Street, and she had just passed a kipper-curing house and stepped round a horde of children – most of whom were in dirty tattered clothes and with bare legs and feet, or old cracked boots that were falling off their feet – who were playing in and around a small fishing boat at one side of the road, when she heard her name being called.

'Sadie! I thought it was you, lass.'

As she turned she recognised one of the female packers from her days of working at Henry Stewart & Co., a large, jolly, red-haired girl with whom she had struck up a friendship for a time. 'Hallo, Phyllis.' She didn't really want to talk to anyone but she forced a smile.

'What you doing round these parts then?' the other girl

asked as she reached her side. 'It's been ages since I've seen hide or hair of you, lass.'

Sadie hesitated a moment. Phyllis had been a convivial companion at the warehouse, but she remembered the redhead had also been somewhat ribald and suggestive on occasion, especially when there were men about. But there weren't any men about now, she told herself in the next instant, and besides, after her affair with Jacob who was she to judge anyone? Nevertheless, her voice was strained when she answered, 'I'm lookin' for work. Do you know of anythin', Phyllis?'

'Nay, lass. There's nowt goin' I know of, but I'm a married woman now, expectin' me first bairn end of May so me workin' days are over.'

Sadie nodded slowly. She was feeling most peculiar, faint and sick, and it must have shown in her face because the other girl said, 'You all right, lass? You look all done in. Look, I'm just off to get me an' Frank's mam's dinner – we lodge with her 'cos he's away on the boats most of the time – so why don't you come an' have a bite an' a sit down for a while?'

'I . . . I don't have any money with me.'

'Oh, don't worry your head about that, lass,' the other girl said breezily. 'I can stand you to a meat pie or faggots an' peas, whatever you like. Frank's mam always has cow-heel an' tripe, she's a one for her tripe, she is.'

Sadie hadn't had anything in her stomach except one slice of bread and dripping first thing and she knew there was nothing to eat when she got home; the temptation was too much. 'Ta, thanks, Phyllis.'

Once in the pie shop the smell brought the saliva running

in her mouth. She hadn't eaten properly for days – what food there had been she had tried to save for the children – and now the hunger was threatening to overwhelm her. So when Phyllis, after a long look at her white face and thin frame said, 'I always have a couple meself, same for you, Sadie?' she could only nod her thanks weakly and swallow hard.

She watched Phyllis order four meat pies and her mother-in-law's cow-heel and tripe, and present the can for the peas which was duly filled, and then they were out of the dilapidated shop and making their way back along Long Bank to Low Street and the harbour.

Sadie was holding the pies which were wrapped in a piece of newspaper, and the smell and heat of them were filling her senses so much it hardly registered when Phyllis opened a door in one of the houses and pushed her inside.

Phyllis's mother-in-law's house was filthy but there was a blazing fire in the hearth and it was lovely and warm. From what Sadie could make out the two women did nothing but sit and talk all day, certainly there was no evidence of any housework or cooking, but the old lady was friendly and insisted Sadie join her and Phyllis in a glass of stout from the grey hen – the large stone-ware bottle she fetched from the scullery. Sadie had only tasted stout once before in her life, and she had thought she didn't like it then, but after a couple of glasses with Phyllis and her mother-in-law the grimy room seemed brighter and more appealing, Phyllis's conversation more quick-witted and amusing, and the world in general a more benevolent place. For the first time in weeks Sadie found herself relaxing. She was replete after the big meal, as warm as toast in front of the roaring fire, and as the women chattered and dozed the winter's afternoon away – aided and abetted by several more glasses of stout – Sadie lost all sense of time and purpose.

So it was with a sense of shock that she heard Phyllis say, after what Sadie thought had only been an hour or two, 'It's gone five, Mam. I'll light the lamp, shall I? It's nearly dark outside.'

'Five o'clock?' Sadie jumped up from her flock-stuffed chair only to find she had to hold on to the table for a moment or two as her head spun. 'Phyllis, I should have bin home hours ago. Me mam an' the bairns'll be worried out of their minds.'

'Oh, don't you worry, lass,' said Phyllis comfortably. 'You've got to have a life of your own an' all. Stay an' have a bit of supper, eh? There's some chitterlings with bread an' cheese, or a pig's trotter if you'd rather?'

'No, no I have to go. But thank you.'

'As you like, lass. As you like.'

She wished she hadn't had all those glasses of stout. As Sadie pulled on her coat and hat her head was whirling. And what was she going to say to her mam? It would be seven o'clock before she was home.

When Sadie stepped out of the front door after further goodbyes to Phyllis and her mother-in-law – both of whom were a little the worse for wear after the stout – the freezing air hit her like a solid wall and made her gasp. It must have snowed a little at some time during the afternoon because a light layer was lying on the ground and the frost was making it sparkle like diamond dust. But night was falling rapidly now, it was dark already and the temperature was a good few degrees colder than earlier in the day. Sadie thought of the long walk home and her shoulders drooped, but what was even more disheartening was that she had no good news to impart at the end of it. Suddenly all the pleasure and cosy enjoyment of the afternoon was gone and reality was back with a vengeance, made all the more stark by the serenity of the hours she had enjoyed at Phyllis's.

Sadie hurried along Long Bank, cutting into Silver Street from High Street East, and then into Prospect Row from whence she was intending to take a short cut across the town moor into Hendon, before striking westwards past the Hendon Ropery and towards Mowbray Park.

It had been years since she had been out on the streets after dark – four years to be exact, ever since she had taken up with Jacob and left her job at Henry Stewart's – and although the lamplighter had already lit some of the streetlamps the back lanes and alleyways were dark, unknown places, places where things were sometimes done that were . . . not nice.

She had just stepped on to the path that would lead her across the moor, past the bandstand and the Trafalgar Square almshouses and on to Hendon Junction, when she was conscious of someone just behind her, and with the knowledge came the realisation that this someone had been there for a few minutes. She was being followed.

'What do you want?'

Her voice was overloud, and almost immediately a man stepped out of the shadows, shushing her as he said, 'Quiet, lass, quiet. I was just wonderin' if you're doin' the business the night, that's all.'

'Doin' the business?'

'Aye. I know it's a bit early but when I saw you turn on to the moor . . . I like it private like, always have done. Can't be doin' with visitin' houses meself, too much chance of bein' seen.'

He was a tall man, and burly, but his manner wasn't threatening – indeed it could be said to be sheepish – and now Sadie stared at him for a long moment before she said, 'You think I'm a . . .'

'Look, lass, don't get on your high horse. If I've made a mistake I'm sorry, all right? But I'm prepared to offer a couple of bob if you're game.' And then, when Sadie continued to stare, 'All right, two an' six then, but I'd want to see you for that, mind, up top. An' you won't get a better offer the night, I'm tellin' you.'

Two and sixpence? He was willing to give her two and sixpence? That was nearly a week's rent in some places, and a half crown would mean she could pay the farm what she owed and get the lads to bring a load of logs and maybe a sack of taties on tick.

Whether it was the stout, or the memory of how it had felt to be snug and full to bursting, or yet again the recollection of the occupants of the cottage all huddled in the brass bed for warmth as she had left that morning, their faces pinched and hungry and Larry crying because his stomach was empty, Sadie didn't know. But when she found herself nodding and walking deeper into the blackness of the moor it was as though it was happening to someone else. It wasn't real, the whole afternoon hadn't been real.

And so it had begun.

Part Two

1905

The Workhouse

Chapter Six

How do you measure time? In the last five years England had seen the creation of the Labour Party by the trade unions, the death of Queen Victoria, a state of emergency declared in Ireland, along with the crowning of Edward VII. 1903 saw the formation of a new militant movement – The Women's Social and Political Union – whose fiery and determined leader was a Mrs Emmeline Pankhurst. Two years later, an MP who stated that 'men and women differed in mental equipment with women having little sense of proportion', whilst emphasising that giving women the vote would not be safe, succeeded in seeing the Suffrage bill fail, and the first suffragettes were sent to prison for their beliefs.

But to hundreds of northerners the electrification of Sunderland's tram service and the boom in the shipyards was the only news worth talking about, signifying, as it did, the steady and determined progress of the north into the twentieth century. And when the most famous escapologist of all time appeared in the Avenue Theatre, Sunderland, in May 1905, crowds flocked to Harry Houdini's appearances, stating it wasn't only London that could command the stars to perform. That, *that*, was news, man.

But for Sadie Bell, caught in a downward spiral that had

begun that evening on the town moor five years ago, time was measured only by the night hours. Wet mouths, grasping hands, oftentimes foul breath against her face, and the thrust of a stranger's body as it penetrated her flesh summed up this eternity known as time. She didn't know or care about the events beyond Sunderland's dark backstreets, it was enough that she survived the next twenty-four hours, a night at a time. The indignities, the humiliation, her mother's silent reproach even as she held out her hand for the night's takings, had ceased to call forth a silent protest deep within her. This was life. And life had to be endured. It was as simple as that.

Now, as she glanced across the small living room which was warm and sticky in the airless June evening, there was no animosity in her dull gaze as she took in Father Hedley sitting with her mother and the two children.

'Hallo, Sadie.' Father Hedley's voice was without expression.

'Hallo, Father.' She hadn't known he was here. She was rarely home before three in the morning and consequently slept most of the day away, usually rising about five to a meal Connie had prepared and cooked. After washing and tidying herself, Sadie would then leave the cottage for the walk into Bishopwearmouth where she would make for the East End and the docks. There was business done along the quays most nights, and in the labyrinth of bars and gin shops, brothels and seedy eating places of every description, there was also safety in numbers. Sadie didn't go to the town moor any more; there had been the odd girl disappear – one of whom had ended up floating in the black water of the docks – when they had gone there.

'Well, Peggy, I'd best be going.'

As the priest rose Connie darted a sidelong glance at him. Father Hedley always did that – got up to go as soon as her mam appeared, even if he'd only arrived a little while earlier. And he never laughed with her mam these days, he was always sort of stiff. The only good thing was that Father McGuigan didn't come at all. She had asked her granny why it was that the priests didn't approve of her mam being on the night shift at the laundry where she worked, and her granny had said it was because the priests believed she should be home with her children at night. Which was stupid, really stupid, when you thought about it, because even her granny admitted that if her mam hadn't got the job when she did it would have been the workhouse for the lot of them. And since her mam had been at the laundry they had never been short of food or coal and logs for the fire, and they'd even had some money spare with which to purchase the hens and cockerel and the goat from the farm two years ago. She could understand Father McGuigan playing up – he would argue with the Pope himself as Freda Henderson would say – but not Father Hedley. It had saddened her to know that Father Hedley could be dogmatic like that. It still did. Which was one of the reasons she hadn't walked to the road with him of late. But tonight was different. She needed to talk to him tonight.

'Larry, you get the baked herrings on the table an' the bread an' butter,' Connie instructed as she too rose and followed the priest to the door, and then to her mother, 'I won't be long, Mam.'

'Aye, all right, pet.' Sadie hadn't raised her eyes since that one glance at Father Hedley, but now she looked at Connie and smiled and her eyes were soft. She was bonny, her lass. As bonny as ever she'd seen, and with her bust developing and her hips losing their flatness she was growing up fast. Pray God Connie would never find out about the whoring. Aye, pray God, but at least it had provided for her schooling. And her bairn was bright. As bright as a button. She had often thought it strange that Michael's child should be so intelligent, whilst Jacob's – and him a learned man and all – should border on the dim-witted. Even now, at seven years of age, Larry still had a job stringing a sentence together and he was no nearer learning his letters than when he had first started school two years ago, in spite of Connie's patience with him. By, how that bairn loved her brother, and him her.

Outside the sticky confines of the cottage – where the smell of the baked herrings soused in onions, cloves and vinegar which Connie had cooked earlier was strong – the air was sweet and full of the scents of summer, even though the smoky pall and oppressive staleness of the steelworks and dark gloomy factories of Sunderland were but two or three miles away. The town's expanding economy and the resulting population growth meant Bishopwearmouth was rapidly devouring its outlying districts, but as yet the house in the wood remained untouched. For how much longer, though? Father Hedley questioned as he breathed the woody air deep into his lungs, and for how much longer could this child at his side remain untouched by the darkness that was within her own family? It troubled him, it troubled him greatly, this affair of Sadie Bell.

'Father?'

'Aye, Connie?'

For a moment Father Hedley felt he had gone back a few years in time. Since the mother had succumbed to temptation, Father Hedley had been aware that the running of the household he'd just left had fallen wholly on the slim shoulders of the child at his side. He knew Connie rose at the crack of dawn to deal with the grandmother who was now quite infirm, as well as doing the washing and cleaning, and preparing and cooking the meals for the family. The girl was mother and father to her brother, cook, housemaid . . . It was too much. How many times had he told himself it was too much, whilst reminding himself in the next breath that there were others just as worse off – ten times, twenty times worse off – in the wretched decaying tenement slums of the East End, where unimaginable depths of squalor reduced whole families living in one room to nothing more than animals? But he couldn't get away from the fact that his sorrow and pity was more profound where this child was concerned. It was grieving to the Almighty that he should favour one of the lambs of his flock in this way, but there it was. Somehow the thought of this child's spirit being crushed was unbearable. And now here she was, speaking in that certain tone experience had taught him meant trouble.

'Father, you don't like me mam goin' into town at night, do you?'

'*What?*'

'Me granny says you think she oughta be here with us, but if she stayed at home there'd be no money comin' in.'

Dear God, dear God. Father Hedley blew his nose on a large white handkerchief, but even with this prevarication no words came to him.

'The thing is, Father, me mam's bin workin' at the laundry for years now an' she's not well. You know she's not well, don't you?'

Father Hedley nodded, his black-clad figure straight as he

forced himself not to sag with relief. So Connie still believed the story she had been told about the laundry. Thank God. Aye, thank God.

'An' she won't get any better till she gives up workin'. So you don't think she ought to work, an' I don't think she ought to.' Connie glanced at him as though the last statement was an explanation.

'What are you saying, child?'

'Me mam says I've got to stay on till at least next year, an' she wants me to perhaps train in an office, somethin' like that, but that'll take ages till I'm earnin' proper.'

'I think I get your drift. You are saying you wish to leave school and obtain employment so your mother can give up her job working at . . . Ahem!' The Father cleared his throat somewhat violently. 'At the laundry. Is that it?'

'Aye, yes, Father.'

'Well, I agree with your mother.' The priest's voice was crisp now. 'You should stay on at school and finish your education, Connie. You are a bright girl. A very bright girl and—'

'But, Father' – Connie cut him short – 'that won't help me mam *now*, will it, an' I've learnt everythin' I can learn already.'

'We've never learnt all we can, child. I am over sixty years of age and I am still learning. It's only the good Lord who is truly wise.'

He was avoiding the issue, and Connie's face and voice stated this when she said, 'Aw, you know what I mean, Father.'

He knew what she meant all right, and like he had said, he was with her mother on this. Everything in him rebelled at the idea of Connie in domestic service, or working in a factory, or some other dead-end employment. It was too late for the mother but not for the daughter. Father McGuigan had what amounted to an obsessive fear of their parishioners seeking education and enlightenment, maintaining that once ordinary people were taught to think and question, the first thing they questioned was the existence of heaven and hell and God Himself. Personally he believed that his God was greater than any questions that could be put to Him, but this avenue of argument had not been well received by Father McGuigan; neither had his pointing out that Pope Leo XIII, who had died two years ago, had worked unstintingly to reduce class warfare and provide equal opportunity for all men. No, that hadn't gone down well at all with Father McGuigan, Father Hedley reflected ruefully.

'Father, please, listen to me.' Connie's voice was a little too shrill and a little too quick to be natural, and now, as he glanced down at the ethereal, golden-haired child at his side, he met the full force of the great sapphire-blue eyes under their fine curving brows, and the appeal in them drew him to a halt. 'Me mam . . . Me mam's not well. She's not, Father.' Connie's voice was passionate in her desire to make him understand. 'She has these turns, pains in her chest an' she looks awful, an' they're gettin' worse. She tries to make out she's all right but I know she's not, Father. An' I could work. I could, Father.'

'Child, you're not old enough. Now you know that.'

'But lots of 'em do it, you know they do, Father.'

'That does not make it right.'

'Oh, Father.'

When her voice broke and she lowered her head her face was not clearly discernible but he knew she was fighting back the tears, and after a long pause, during which he drew his lower lip into his mouth and shut his eyes for a few moments, Father Hedley said, 'What do you want me to do, Connie?'

'Just . . . just to tell me if you hear of anythin' goin', Father, an' . . . an' maybe tell them you know me?'

'You want me to recommend you for employment when you should be attending school?'

Put like that it sounded awful. Connie rubbed her nose and fiddled with one of her plaits, but then she raised her eyes to his and answered simply, 'Aye, yes. I do, Father.'

He should have known better than to ask. Where her family was concerned there was nothing she would not do or say. And then he was further reminded of this when she prompted urgently, with scarcely a blush, 'Will you? Will you, Father?'

The righteous disapproval of Father McGuigan was like a sword probing his conscience but he ignored it for the moment. 'What sort of thing did you have in mind?'

'Anythin', Father, I don't mind. I'm as strong as a horse.'

They looked at each other, the old priest and the slim young girl, and the thought flashed through his mind that if half the men and women he knew had this sort of loyalty and love his life would be a lot more tranquil. And then he nodded slowly, and, her hand slipping into his, they continued their walk to the road.

Sadie was later than normal as she hurried along the cobbled alleyway which led from the High Street to the quayside. There were numerous small boats moored at the water's edge and several upturned along the quay, and she could hear the sound of the 'Keel Row' being sung with the accompaniment of a fiddle in the Earl of Durham. There was a pair of constables standing outside the Old Custom House – owing to the many nefarious and rough and rowdy characters frequenting the riverside no policeman was so foolish as to walk alone – and so, although she had arranged to meet one of her regulars in that pub, she slipped into the merry din of the Earl of Durham.

The song changed to a popular hit of a couple of years before, 'Bill Bailey won't you please come home', as the door closed behind her, and through the murky light, thick with a film of smoke, she saw the normal seething crowd of sailors and dockers interspersed with steelworkers, miners, fishwives and – like herself – dock dollies. She had been indignant when that term had first been applied to her, she remembered now with a bitter twist to her lips. That had been when she could still feel and react. Now she felt nothing, it was as though a paralysis, a slow deadening of her mind and emotions had choked the life inside her leaving just an empty shell. But it was a shell that men were still prepared to pay for and that was all that mattered.

And then, as though someone had heard the thought and offered a direct challenge, she saw him. John Stewart. He was standing with a group of men at the bar, and just as he spat down on the sawdust-covered floor his eyes glanced across the room and met her shocked gaze. She saw him stiffen, and then watched his hard black eyes take in her loose hair, the low neckline of her dress which was now exposed after she had dropped her shawl over one arm on entry in to the public house, and the paint and powder she had hastily applied in the alleyway a moment or two before. They were the marks of her trade and he recognised them as such, and slowly, very slowly, a smile slid across his good-looking face.

And Sadie knew she could still feel.

Should she go? Now? Quickly? The thought was there

through the surge of blinding hate that was making her ears ring, but such was the force of her emotion that Sadie found she couldn't move. She was aware of a big man at the side of her – a Swede or Dutchman by the sound of his accent – asking her if she wanted a drink, but still she couldn't take her fascinated gaze from the satisfied dark one across the room. And it drew her. Like a lemming towards a cliff, like a moth towards a flame, it drew her, and then she was standing in front of him and listening to him say, his voice cocky and sure of itself, 'Sadie. Sadie Bell isn't it? It's been a long time, lass,' and she knew he still wanted her. The lascivious desire was plain to read in his face.

'Hallo, John.'

She had never called him by his first name before – at the warehouse he had been Mr Stewart, the eldest son and someone to be instantly obeyed – and his eyes narrowed for a second. But then they cleared and Sadie knew what he was thinking. She was a whore. One of the dockside scum and brazen with it by the look of things, and he was going to have her tonight.

Over her dead body.

'What you drinking then?'

There was a note in his voice that told her he was pleased she'd been seen searching him out. She was still beautiful; she hadn't yet been reduced to having to accept any and every customer, and she still charged more than most and got it.

For a moment Sadie didn't trust herself to speak, and then she said, her voice low and steady, 'Port and brandy.' She had progressed to that from stout and golden ale after just a few months, finding the strong liquor helped what followed.

'Port and brandy it is, lass.'

That John was aware of, and relishing, the covert nudges among his group of companions was evident in the lilt to his voice when he turned and ordered the drink, and then he swung back to her, his voice overloud as he said, 'How about you and me taking a little walk this evening, eh? There's money in me trousers and something else you'll like.'

She didn't have a chance to answer before the barman tapped John on the shoulder and handed him the glass, but as John passed it to her he said again, 'How about it then?', his eyes making no secret of the fact that he was already stripping the clothes from her body.

It was a waste of a good drink but it couldn't be helped, and never had she got so much pleasure and gratification from a measure of wine and a measure of spirit as when she watched it hit John Stewart's grinning face. He was absolutely still for a good three seconds and then he shook his head violently, drips of deep red liquid flying in all directions, as she hissed, 'I'd have to be dead before I consented to scum like you touching me.'

The torrent of foul abuse that sprayed out of his mouth coincided with the punch at her face, and although she had been expecting the blow she wasn't quick enough to avoid it altogether. His clenched fist struck her on the right side of her head, making her ear ring, but she was still on her feet when she saw his friends grab him and restrain him as he struggled to get free.

'Here, come on, I'm havin' no rough stuff the night.' The landlord was there like a shot. 'I've had the law pokin' around twice this week already an' that's twice too much. Out, the lot of you. You an' all, Sadie. Go on.'

It was taking four of his comrades to hold John, and now

he was screaming unintelligibly, enraged at being prevented from reaching the object of his fury. He was fighting mad, they could all see it, and the brief moment of enjoyment his friends had felt at seeing the bumptious little upstart – as they all privately thought of John Stewart – being brought low by a whore, *a whore*, was swallowed up by their concern at what he might do if they let go of him.

'Get yourself away! Go on! We can't hold him forever.'

In spite of the shouts being directed at her Sadie remained stiff and silent as she continued glaring at John, and then said, her voice a deep growl as it came from her throat, 'You're a big nowt, John Stewart, an' there's not a person alive'd say different if they spoke the truth. It was you an' your mam that killed your da an' you know that, don't you. Deep inside you know that. You killed him as sure as if you'd taken a knife an' slit his throat.'

'For crying out loud, woman! Get yourself away before there's murder done. We can't hold him much longer.'

'I'm goin'.' Sadie drew herself up as she spoke and her tone could have been described as disdainful as she added, 'I wouldn't stay in his company for a hundred guineas, the gutless swine.'

Once outside the Earl of Durham Sadie found she was shaking like a leaf and the pain in her chest, which had first made its appearance in the weeks after the miscarriage and which had got steadily worse over the intervening years, was choking her breath and sending pains radiating out down her arm. She had to get away, they might let John loose in a minute. It was the one thought in her mind and it enabled her to stumble along the quay, her hand pressed to her heart, and into the passageway at the side of the Crown and make her way up into the High Street where she leant against the wall of a terraced house for some minutes before continuing on her way.

How many times she had to rest she didn't know, but when she finally reached the house in the wood the sky was lightening and the dawn chorus just beginning.

She was dying.

She had fought against it with each laboured breath, but as Sadie sank down on to the wooden settle she couldn't fight the knowledge of her imminent demise any longer.

'Mam?'

It was still a little early for Connie to be up but her daughter was beside her in a moment, and she saw Connie's face was white with horror which indicated how bad she looked.

'Mam, what's wrong? What is it?'

'Listen to me, lass. Listen.' Sadie reached out and gripped the young hands, her lips blue and her face ashen. 'The Stewart family have done this. You hear me, lass? The Stewart family. I'm not a bad woman, I've only ever loved two men in me life. One was your da an' the other one was Jacob, an' he'd have married me if they'd let us alone. Oh aye, he would.' But the pain was hitting with renewed ferocity and a steel clamp had seized her chest, cutting off the words and bringing rushing darkness.

Oh no, Lord, not like this. Please, God, not now, not with the bairns still so young. And then, as she hovered between two worlds, You forgave Mary Magdalene and her no better than she should have been. Forgive me, Lord.

Chapter Seven

Father McGuigan sat very stiffly on one of the straight-backed chairs under the open window, his cup of tea steaming gently on the table in front of him as he gazed across the room at Peggy. What were things coming to? he asked himself silently. As if it wasn't enough that Sodom and Gomorrah had visited the world in the form of that salacious and promiscuous dancer, Mata Hari, who had been so highly acclaimed for her degenerate prancing in Paris the month before, here was one of his flock – and a good, devout Catholic, in spite of the shame of having had such a daughter – daring to try and justify the unjustifiable.

'I repeat, Mrs Cook, there is no excuse for the dissolute lifestyle which Sadie adopted some years ago,' he stated grimly, his thin nostrils twitching. 'You would have been clothed and fed in the workhouse, and the children would have received an education. To my mind that is far better than opening the door to the devil.'

The priest hadn't taken his cold opaque eyes off Peggy as he had spoken, and after a pause – during which the pale-blue stare seemed to penetrate right into Peggy's skull – the old woman mumbled, 'Yes, Father,' as she thought, There speaks one who is sure he'll never end his days there. And then almost immediately the superstition of centuries stepped in and she mentally crossed herself, seeking God's forgiveness for venturing to criticise one of His chosen ones. It was the shock, that's what it was. If she lived to be a hundred she would never forget waking up this morning to the sound of Connie's agonised crying, and finding her granddaughter cradling Sadie's body in her thin arms, all the while raining kisses on the beautiful lifeless face. Thirty years old. Her bonny bairn had been but thirty years old. And now there was only purgatory if Sadie had departed this life in the grace of God, or – heaven forbid – eternal damnation. And there was no doubt where Father McGuigan placed her.

Oh, why did Father Hedley have to be ill in bed with bronchitis? she railed in the next instance. If ever they had needed the presence of the wise kind priest she had known for over forty years it was now. And look at Connie. Making Father McGuigan a cup of tea and then disappearing outside with Larry instead of sitting quietly and respectfully as was the custom. But then the bairn was beside herself. When Connie had returned home from Bishopwearmouth where she'd informed the authorities and the priest about Sadie's death there had been no prising her from her mother's side; sitting there stroking her mam's face and talking to her as though she was going to answer . . . Dear God, dear God. Where was it all going to end?

'God won't be mocked, Mrs Cook.' Father McGuigan, having taken a good swallow of the tea, returned to the attack. 'He is righteous in all His ways – *all*, Mrs Cook – and I shouldn't have to remind you of the fact. I—'

There was a sudden skirmish outside – they heard it quite distinctly through the open window – and when the door of the cottage burst open a moment later and Peggy saw the look on her granddaughter's face she closed her eyes for an instant. Connie had been listening. She might have known.

'My mam was a good person.' Larry had followed Connie into the cottage a second or two later and now Connie put her arm about the young child's shoulders, drawing him into her side, as she approached the disdainful priest. 'She was, she was a good person.'

There was a pause during which Father McGuigan and the red-faced girl stared at each other, and the priest's voice was both dismissive and cutting when he said, 'Do not speak of things of which you do not know.'

'I *do* know!' Connie's voice had risen and again Peggy closed her eyes for an infinitesimal moment. To shout at a priest! Of all the things that had happened that day this filled her with the most alarm and foreboding. What was the lass thinking of? She'd bring down the wrath of the Almighty on their heads. 'Just 'cos me mam worked in a laundry it doesn't make her bad!'

'Worked in a . . .?' Father McGuigan turned to Peggy and his lustreless eyes were pitiless. 'Is that what you told her?'

'Father, *please*.' Peggy was wringing her hands now.

'Is it, Mrs Cook?'

'Aye, yes, Father.'

'He that speaketh truth sheweth forth righteousness, but a false witness deceit. Proverbs twelve, verse seventeen,' Father McGuigan stated coldly.

'Rejoice not when thine enemy falleth, and let not thine heart be glad when he stumbleth, lest the Lord see it and it displease Him.' Connie had little idea of what she was repeating but the verse she had learnt at school the previous

101

week somehow seemed apt. Father McGuigan didn't like her mam, he had never liked her. And priest or not she *hated* him.

The effect of her words on the priest was electrifying. Father McGuigan stared at her, his eyes nearly popping out of his head, and then his voice was like thunder as he bellowed, 'You dare, you *dare* to quote scripture at me, you insolent girl?'

'She's just a bairn, Father, she doesn't know what she's saying.' Peggy had never been so horrified in her life. 'She means no harm, really. Please, Father—'

'I know what your granddaughter means, Mrs Cook, and she is your daughter's child all right.' Father McGuigan kept his eyes on Connie's defiant face as he spoke. 'The sins of the mother . . . Your mother was a prostitute, girl, a woman of the streets. She did not work in a laundry and the money she earned was not by honest toil. Do you understand me?'

Connie believed him instantly. A hundred little things which had puzzled her over the years fell into place and completed a giant jigsaw in her mind. And it was in that moment, at twelve years of age, that Connie left the realms of childhood behind for ever.

Her face had gone as white as lint, but to Peggy's petrified gaze her granddaughter seemed to grow in stature as she faced the dour old man and shouted, 'Out! Out of this house! An' don't you dare set foot here again.'

'*What?*'

Peggy was past speaking now, she just watched the drama unfolding in front of her eyes with dumb disbelief.

'You heard me, you . . . you horrible man. My mam did what she did because she loved us an' because she had to. She knew me granny was frightened of the workhouse an' she wanted to keep us all together, that's all, but the Church didn't help her, did it. You come here, sayin' she was bad an' all, but you'd have left us to starve, wouldn't you. It's your fault she had to do what she did.'

Neither of them noticed Peggy as she slid silently to the floor in a dead faint.

The tall, angular figure of Father McGuigan was bending over slightly, his hands like claws, and in that instant no one would have looked upon his dark countenance and said he was a man of the cloth. The content of his words, along with the manner in which they were spoken, matched the furious rage contorting his thin face. 'Repent of this wicked rebelliousness whilst there is still time,' he ground out slowly, 'or you will surely join your mother in eternal damnation. Come to the Lord's holy mass and make a good act of contrition.'

'My mam's not in hell!'

'What? What did you say?'

'She's not.' And then, as Peggy raised her head and attempted to sit up, Connie said to Larry, 'Help your granny, pet,' before walking with quiet deliberation across the room and opening the door. And as Father McGuigan comprehended the gesture his lean, skeletal frame seemed to swell and expand, stretching the contours of his face, but he said not another word until he was outside in the bright afternoon sunlight.

'Your mother chose the wide path of corruption and dishonour.' He glared at Connie and she, in turn, glared back. Her heart was so sore that the priest's displeasure seemed like nothing in the enormity of this trouble that had fallen upon them. Her lovely mam was dead. *Her mam*. They had come to take her away just half an hour before Father

McGuigan had called, and they had spoken of an examination, something called a post mortem, to determine the cause of death. She could have told them what had killed her mother, she thought bitterly. The Stewart family. *She hated them, she hated them all.* And then the memory of a tall, lanky lad with kind brown eyes and gentle hands flashed into her mind before she resolutely pushed it away, feeling that just the memory of Dan Stewart was a betrayal of her mother.

'I shall pray for you, for you all,' Father McGuigan snapped tightly, swinging round and marching out of the clearing like an enormous black crow.

'Connie?' Larry was tugging at her blouse, and she turned to see her grandmother on her feet. Peggy was clutching at the back of a chair and she suddenly looked a very, very old woman.

'Connie?' Larry spoke again, drawing her attention back to his small face.

'Aye, hinny?' said Connie heavily.

'Mam?' he asked hopefully.

Connie felt a great weight descend on her. She had known for a long time that this little brother wasn't like other children, although by unspoken common assent the matter had never been discussed at home. But now she met her grandmother's rheumy, pink-rimmed eyes and their look held for a long moment.

'Mam's not here, hinny,' she said at last. 'Mam's . . . gone.'

'Workin'?'

'Aye. Aye, she's workin'. She's had to go away for a time but you'll be a good lad with me an' Gran, won't you.'

'Larry good lad.' The small head nodded. 'Me spice cake, Connie?'

'Aye. Just one, mind.'

Connie watched her brother as he trotted across the room and took one of the currant teacakes Peggy had put out for the priest. Larry had been here all day, he had witnessed her sorrow and that of her grandmother, the weeping and agonising, and he'd cried too. He had watched the strangers come and carry his mother's body away, and he'd listened to what had been said, and yet, somehow, it hadn't really touched him at all.

It had been after the attack on Jacob that Connie had first noticed Larry's strange ability to shut out the bad things in life and only to see what he wanted to see. It might have been there before, she wasn't sure, but from that harrowing night she felt Larry had changed. It was as though her brother had retreated into a world of his own – a world of his own making – since that time, and whenever things got unpleasant or difficult or confusing he simply blotted them out of his consciousness. It worried her, it worried her very much, but perhaps in this instance it was a blessing. Certainly it had been clear to them all that the only time the small boy got upset or concerned was when she, his sister, was distressed. Even this morning Connie had had the feeling that Larry's weeping was solely a reflection of her own sorrow, and once she'd dried her eyes and forced herself to smile and converse with him, his happy demeanour had seemed to bear this out.

'Spice cake, Connie?' Larry was making his way back across the room, a teacake in his outstretched hand.

'No, no thank you, hinny. You eat yours, I don't want one.'

'Aye, Connie. Spice cake.' The little face frowned up at her as he reached her side, and his voice was insistent.

Had he noticed she hadn't eaten anything the day? It would

appear so. Connie suddenly felt an overwhelming surge of love for this damaged little person and, bending down, she hugged her brother to her as she whispered, 'I love you, Larry. I love you very much.' They were going to rise above all this – the humiliation and the degradation – and she wasn't going to let Father McGuigan or anyone else say anything about her mam or the rest of her family, she told herself fiercely. She would fight the whole world if she had to, and she'd win.

It was another four days before Father Hedley was well enough to make the journey from the East End, and it so happened he met Connie returning from the farm with a half side of bacon, in the field approaching the wood. He immediately noticed the change in the girl, who he had – until that moment – thought of as a child. It wasn't just the fact that Connie had put her hair up – gone were the childish plaits and in their place was a thick shining coil on top of her head – but the new maturity was in her stance, her attitude, even the way she greeted him, her voice controlled and circumspect as she nodded and said, 'Good afternoon, Father Hedley.' And then, before he could reply, there was a trace of the old impetuous child he knew as she added, 'You don't look too good, Father. Are you supposed to be out yet?'

'Out yet' was very appropriate, Father Hedley thought with a touch of dark humour. The week's confinement in bed with no avenue of escape from Father McGuigan's presence had seemed like prison, and after their difference of opinion – which had escalated into a full-scale clash – regarding the burial of Sadie Bell, things had been unbearable. Still, he had held out and got his own way on that, and there was no need for the family to ever know that Father McGuigan had

intended for Sadie to be buried in a common grave and without
the rites of the Catholic church.

'I'm middling, Connie, if the truth be known, and much as
I'm thankful for the good Lord's sunshine this heat is taking
it out of me. But I'm glad I've seen you like this. Perhaps we
could sit a while and have a little chat before I go and offer
my condolences to your grandmother?'

'Aye, yes, Father.' It was not said with any enthusiasm,
and the reason for this became clear after they had seated
themselves on a fallen tree trunk conveniently situated in the
shade of a spreading oak tree at the very edge of the wood,
and Connie said, 'I suppose Father McGuigan told you what
happened when he came to see us? Well, I'm not sorry, Father.
I'm not. I don't care what my mam did, she was a good person,
and for him to say what he did—'

'There, there, child. Don't upset yourself.' Father Hedley
couldn't tell her that he had secretly applauded her courage
whilst being amazed at her temerity, and he had no intention
of being hypocritical either, so he passed over the incident
with a wave of his hand and a muttered, 'I didn't come to
discuss that, Connie. That's over and done with.'

'Oh. Oh I see, Father.'

'No, it was what you mentioned to me last time we met,
about work of some kind. I suppose the need is all the more
great now?'

Connie nodded. The funeral would take every penny they
had but she was determined her mam would have a proper
send off, especially after what Father McGuigan had revealed.
It was only the heathen or the lowest of the low that didn't
provide for such; everyone knew that even the poorest of
families would beg, borrow, steal or pawn every item they

had – the clothes off their backs – in order to have 'a good do'. Never mind the bairns were running around with raggedy backsides and they were weeks behind with the rent, proprieties had to be observed and folk knew that the payment for a special mass and a good wake for the newly departed meant dividends in the hereafter.

'I'll do anythin', Father.' She looked up at him as she spoke, and the warm creamy tint to her clear skin, the deep violet-blue of the heavily lashed eyes and the mass of shining golden hair brought fresh fear into the old priest's heart. He didn't want her to have to do anything; that was exactly what had happened to the mother and already Connie showed signs of a beauty that would eclipse Sadie's. Mind, from when she was knee-high to a grasshopper Connie had had something Sadie didn't have. He would have liked to have called it her faith, and perhaps her inner strength could be attributed to that in part, but she was a fighter too and he had recognised the Boadicea spirit very early on.

'Well, work isn't easy to come by, Connie, not for a young lass just leaving school, but I understand there's a job as a paid helper in the workhouse laundry if you're interested. Somehow' – and now there was a twinkle in his eyes – 'the matron is under the impression you are fourteen years of age.'

Connie stared at him, her eyes widening and her stomach swirling. The workhouse. Just the words had the power to create a dread that was more than legitimate if only a quarter of the stories she had heard were true. On the few occasions she had passed the extensive series of buildings between Hylton Road and Chester Road which accommodated over nine hundred people and had its own hospital, mortuary, farm and so on, she had, ridiculously, she admitted to herself, averted her eyes and hurried past as fast as her legs would carry her. And now Father Hedley was suggesting she *work* there. But what else was there? Nothing, absolutely nothing. And with her being so young, and the stigma attached to her mother's name following her . . .

'Thank you, Father.' She forced a smile even as her blood curdled and made herself ask, 'Who do I have to see?'

'I'll take you along there the day after your mother's funeral, which I've arranged for Wednesday incidentally, but we'll talk with your grandmother about that in a minute or two. You'll be having an interview with the matron – Matron Banks – in the morning, and if she is satisfied you will begin work the next day. I see no problems.'

'No, Father.' No problems. No problems in voluntarily walking into the place that haunted young and old alike? 'Thank you, Father.'

The post mortem recorded that Mrs Sadie Bell of West Wood Cottage died of a heart attack on Monday 19th June, 1905, and the day after the funeral, on Thursday 29th June – the same day the House of Lords rejected the bill for compulsory Sunday trading, much to the delight of the fervent church faction – Connie entered the grim confines of the Sunderland workhouse with Father Hedley.

They were shown to the matron's office by a female inmate clothed in the ugly workhouse uniform of grey shapeless dress, white apron, starched cap, and big, stout, hideous boots, and Connie was immediately aware of the faint odour that seemed to permeate the air. It was unpleasant but as yet she couldn't put a name to it, and it had the effect of sending the butterflies in her stomach into a further frenzy.

'Ah, Father Hedley.' Matron Banks was sitting writing at a large, solid-looking oak desk as their guide opened the door after a respectful knock, and as she raised her head and smiled, her rather dour features mellowed somewhat. When she rose to her feet Connie saw that although the matron was dressed in a uniform of a kind, the beautifully cut, if severe, black dress was of the finest material and the small buttons that fastened the bodice were mother-of-pearl. 'And this must be Miss Bell? Do please be seated.'

The only smell in the matron's office was the perfume from a large vase of freshly cut flowers on one corner of the desk, and with the sunlight streaming through the window which took up most of the facing wall, and the other two walls lined with bookcases, the room was not unappealing. But it didn't quieten Connie's unease, and when Father Hedley said, with a reassuring pat on her shoulder, 'I'll leave you to it. I have an appointment at The Little Sisters of the Poor Home shortly, I'm on the board you know and we need to finalise the old people's summer outing,' she felt like the last friend she had in all the world was leaving her.

Connie was still standing in front of the great desk when the door had closed behind Father Hedley, and when Matron Banks said again, with a wave of her hand, 'Do be seated, Miss Bell,' she sank down on to one of the two hard-backed chairs placed strategically three feet apart from each other and eighteen inches either side of the corners of the matron's desk.

'Father Hedley speaks highly of you.' There was a long pause and Connie was aware that she was being scrutinised intently; it was with some effort that she resisted the impulse to fiddle with the collar of the plain blue serge dress she was wearing. It wasn't a summer dress, and with the high neck and long sleeves it was stifling in the fierce heat of the June day, but it was the only garment she possessed that was nearly new and smart, having been bought at a fraction of the original cost from one of the second-hand stalls in the Old Market for her mother's funeral.

Oh, her mam ... Connie swallowed hard and tried to answer the matron's questions as clearly and succinctly as she could, but all the time the knowledge of where she was – the very place her mother had fought so hard to keep her family from entering – was making her stomach churn.

'And I understand your birth certificate is missing? That your late mother lost it?'

Connie nodded. If she had spoken the truth she would have said she wasn't even sure Sadie had ever registered her birth; the fact that her mother had been unable to read or write and the remoteness of the house in the wood made that eventuality all too probable, in spite of the law stating that all births had to be registered within forty-two days.

'Do you want to ask me any questions?' The matron's tone had softened somewhat in the last ten minutes or so. She knew this girl's background and she had been more than a little wary of employing her – she already had enough trouble among both the inmates and her officers with regard to discipline and standards being upheld, and she couldn't afford any looseness or immoral behaviour to infiltrate the ranks – but the slim and quite startlingly beautiful girl in front of her was not at all what she had expected. In fact she was a pleasant surprise. Matron Banks prided herself on being a good judge of character, and from what she could ascertain the mother's profligacy had not tainted the daughter.

'I don't think so.'

'I don't think so, Matron Banks.'

Connie coloured and repeated quickly, 'I don't think so, Matron Banks.'

'Then let me tell you a little about the workings of the institution. The accommodation is for 938 persons, and the children are lodged and boarded apart from the adults and educated at neighbouring schools. The same wise principle which has caused the Guardians to keep the children apart from the adult inmates, and the consequent contamination, has made them discard the uniform for the children so that they are spared the stigma of a special workhouse brand. The Guardians feel they are breaking new frontiers in this liberal approach.'

The matron paused, obviously expecting some appreciative comment, but Connie merely nodded quietly. The poor children, and the poor parents. It was awful.

'On a Saturday, and of course with permission and with an officer present, the inmates may receive visitors. These may be family or friends from outside the confines of the institution, or perhaps a husband from the male side visiting his wife, or a parent visiting a child. It is doubtful that you would be asked to perform this duty as you will be working in the laundry, but occasionally it might be necessary to stand in for an officer who is ill. You understand me?'

Connie managed a 'Yes, Matron Banks,' this time.

'In a moment, Mrs Wright, the assistant matron, will get someone to show you round the officers' mess and sitting room, the recreation room, kitchen, and the officers' accommodation which consists of individual bedrooms. All this is quite separate to the inmates. Then you will see the inmates' kitchen and dining hall, the hospital and the infirm wards, the nursery, the chapel, the laundry, the dormitories and so on. The laundry staff have every Sunday free from eight in the morning until ten in the evening, one Saturday a month off, and every other evening from half-past five to ten o'clock. You will be paid two and fourpence a week which will be reviewed in six weeks if you prove satisfactory, and given four meals a day.'

Another pause and a hasty, 'Thank you, Matron Banks.'

'I understand you wish to take up employment as from tomorrow?'

'Yes, Matron Banks.' After the funeral they had been left with just a couple of shillings and their vegetable patch, plus the odd egg or two from the hens and the milk from the goat, on which to survive.

'Then you may still take the Sunday leave this week.'

This last was spoken in the manner of one bestowing a great concession as the matron picked up a large brass bell from the desk in front of her and rang it. The door opened immediately to reveal Connie's previous escort, who must have been waiting outside for the summons, and as the girl shuffled into the room the matron's voice changed to one of cold authority when she said, 'Show Miss Bell to Mrs Wright's office, Maud.'

Once outside the matron's office Connie followed the shambling figure in front of her down the narrow corridor to a door some fifteen feet on the right, and there Maud stopped, her voice nasal as she turned and said, ''Er's in 'ere,' before continuing on her way, head and shoulders bent and looking with every step as though she was going to trip over her own feet.

Oh, what was she going to do? What was she going to do? She'd never be able to stand working in this place. Connie stood looking at the brown-painted door as her mind raced and the smell assailed her nostrils again. And then she wet her lips rapidly, her back straightening as she breathed in deeply and lifted her hand, knocking sharply on the wood.

Mrs Wright turned out to be a large, stout personage who looked more like a man than a woman, but under the iron-grey scraped-back hair and bristling moustache her manner was not unfriendly. Within moments one of the young junior officers Mrs Wright had summoned to conduct Connie arrived, and so the tour of the many areas of the workhouse and its grounds, which consisted of endless corridors, confusing sections leading one into another, iron staircases and door after door after door began.

Connie thought the officers' communal areas and the small individual bedrooms were nice enough, if a little stark and austere, but it was when she and her guide left the staff quarters and progressed into the workhouse as a whole that the smell got stronger and the atmosphere became one of gloom and doom.

The laundry itself was a huge barn of a place, and the machinery was old and noisy and worked by line shafts and endless leather belts clicking above the vulnerable heads of the workers. A massive mangle with several cylinders stood in the centre of the room, and either side of this machine there were big tables piled high with wet washing waiting to be squeezed and pressed.

Behind the mangle at the far end of the room stood enormous wicker baskets containing the dirty and soiled linen waiting to be soaked in the poss-tubs and beaten with the poss-sticks – great wooden beaters on four legs which measured four feet high. To the front of the mangle were lines of long wooden benches, above and to the back of which ran big metal frames. These supported the flexible gas pipes leading to each individual flat iron of which there were five per station.

Apart from the roof lights and long narrow windows every six feet down the left-hand wall, the only lighting looked to be provided by six gas mantles, which on a dull day would make the dangerous working conditions twice as bad as the workers struggled in the dim flickering light. Connie noticed that even now, on a sunny June morning, the army of mainly female workers consisting of inmates with a few officers supervising, all wore the same dead expressions. And this was going to be where she would spend every day, apart from Sundays, from now on. It was a daunting thought.

But there was worse to come. The inmates' kitchen showed the presence of cockroaches and the food, which was being dished up ready to be taken through to the dining hall, made Connie feel sick, but it was the infirm wards that presented the cause of the smell that had seemed to permeate into every nook and cranny to a greater or lesser extent. The stench of urine and other strong objectionable odours was so acute that Connie found she was holding her breath, and yet she could see the place was kept scrupulously clean and the green-painted walls and stone floors scoured daily.

Nevertheless, the thought of her granny being confined in such surroundings – as Peggy undoubtedly would be if she ended up in the workhouse, due to her arthritis making her virtually helpless – was unthinkable, and for the first time Connie truly understood her grandmother's inordinate terror

115

of the place. It was the end of hope, of dreams, of love, even life itself. A living death.

'Here, you all right?' The officer who had been consigned to show her round – a young girl called Mary O'Donnell – was peering into Connie's face and took hold of her arm, almost manhandling her away into the main hospital, as she muttered, 'Eee, come away out of it, lass, I'd forgotten how it affects you the first time. I've bin workin' here a year an' more an' I hardly notice it now.'

'Don't you?' Connie didn't know if she found this comforting or disturbing, but she tended towards the latter. The thought that she might become anaesthetised to such conditions was frightening.

'You won't see over much of this side anyway,' Mary continued cheerfully as she led the way towards the nursery annexe where the babies and very young children were housed and cared for. 'You might be asked to relieve one of the infirm ward attendants when you're on duty on a Saturday, but it'll be once in a blue moon. The worst duty, I always reckon, is Saturday visitin' in the hall, although it don't bother some of 'em. But I tell you, lass, some of the sights are pitiful, especially when it's an old married couple that's been split up an' they cry like babies. You feel like cryin' with 'em, or I do anyways.'

Connie glanced at the small mousy figure as a warm feeling of relief pierced the oppression. She could like this girl, she told herself silently. She hoped she would see something of her; it would be good to have a friend – someone she could talk to – in these depressing surroundings. As she caught Mary's warm, kind eyes she asked, 'Where do you work?', her manner a little shy.

'Me, lass?' Mary blinked her eyes and adjusted her spectacles – thick, hornrimmed monstrosities – which seemed to slip down her small snub nose every two seconds. 'Same as you, in the laundry for me sins, but it's not so bad when you get used to it. An' we have some right good cracks on the quiet like, an' of an evenin' there's a group of us walk into town an' have a look in the shop windows in High Street West or pay a visit to the Palace.' They have some good shows at the Palace. Course, some of 'em are just on the lookout for lads; there's a couple of 'em here who'd drop their drawers for anythin' in trousers.'

And as Connie laughed – something she would have thought impossible just minutes before – Mary grinned at her, revealing a set of beautifully even white teeth, and whispered conspiratorially, 'I tell you, lass, if old Battle-axe Banksy or the Wardress Wright knew half of what we get up to once we're clear of this place, they'd split their corsets for sure. An' what a sight that'd be, eh?' she added gleefully as she dug Connie's ribs. 'Don't bear thinkin' about, does it?'

Oh yes, it would be very good to have a friend like Mary . . .

Two hours later Connie was home again and sitting at the table, Larry on her knee, sipping a cup of tea whilst telling her grandmother all that had transpired, but in spite of making much of Mary's quips she couldn't raise a smile from her.

It was the same the next morning only more so, and a stranger would have presumed Connie was leaving for two months rather than two days, such was the intensity of the family's farewells.

'I'll be back on Sunday mornin', Larry, I promise. You

look after Gran for me, all right, pet?' Connie knelt down and took her brother in her arms, the pressure of his thin little arms as he hugged her causing a massive lump in her throat. 'An' you know your jobs, don't you? You have to see if the hens have laid every mornin' an' milk the goat, an' Gran'll tell you which vegetables to water the most. An' don't forget to put the bucket by the back door ready for when you need to fetch water the next time.'

'Connie, Connie . . .' In stark contrast to the way the child had behaved when his mother had been carried out of the cottage Larry was distraught, and it was only after prolonged hugs and kisses that Connie could extricate herself from his grip, and then the little boy's face was wet with tears.

But was it any wonder? Connie asked herself silently. Their mother had been a fleeting shadow in the child's life after the vicious beating of his father, seeing him only for an hour or so each day. It had been his sister who had bid him rise each morning, dressed him, fed him. Her hands that had mopped his tears when he'd hurt himself, tucked him into bed at night, talked to him, played with him.

'Connie? Mo-mo.'

Connie swallowed deeply when she saw what Larry was offering her. Mo-mo, a ragged piece of cloth that the boy had clung on to and treasured from when he was a baby, was his prize possession. It was his friend and his comforter, and he always went to sleep with the piece of frayed linen beneath one cheek.

'No, Larry. You keep Mo-mo.' She tried to smile but it was beyond her. Oh, Mam, Mam, you should be here! It wasn't her mother's fault, she emphasised in her mind as though her thoughts were a betrayal, but she – his sister – had had to take the place of mother and father in the boy's life, and that was making this doubly hard for both of them. And then, when Larry thrust the tattered piece of cloth at her again, she took it. It was his way of making sure she would be back, she realised suddenly, as she bent and hugged him again. 'Two days, Larry. Two days and I'll bring Mo-mo home. All right?'

He nodded slowly, the tears stopping, and she acknowledged that a promise had been made as she looked into the small face that was so like Jacob's. Nevertheless, Connie's eyes were moist when she turned to Peggy, and she found she was unable to speak.

'Eee, lass, it fair makes me blood run cold to think of you in that place, even as a paid helper. I can't help it, lass, I can't. Your grandda'll be turnin' in his grave an' no mistake,' said Peggy tearfully.

'Now come on, Gran.' For a moment Connie felt she was dealing with two children instead of one, and with Larry clinging to her skirts and her grandmother's wrinkled, sweet face all crumpled up she felt like howling herself. 'We've been through all this a hundred times, an' we've decided there's no other way, now haven't we? I'd never get set on anywhere else, it's only Father Hedley who's got me in as it is. Some girls of my age might pass for fourteen but I look twelve, you know I do, an' there's scarcely any work for grown women let alone bit lasses.'

'You watch yerself, lass. Just watch yerself.'

'I will, Gran, I promise. An' the matron said I can have a sub on me first week's wage an' bring home some bits, so I'll get a nice piece of brisket an' a half-stone of flour an' some yeast, an' some scrag ends an' cheese . . . Oh, it'll be all right, Gran. Don't cry.'

Connie left quickly – it was either that or not go at all – and walked swiftly along the narrow path at the side of the vegetable patch, and past the wooden hen coop to which the goat's lean-to was attached which the lads from the farm had constructed for them two years ago when her mother had bought the livestock. She paused at the edge of the clearing, turning to wave, and when she saw her grandmother's bent, frail frame and trembling lips and the way she was hugging Larry tight with her poor, distorted hands, she almost didn't follow the path through the trees. Almost.

But like she had just said aloud, there was no other way, she had to go. And she would soon be home again, two days wasn't all that long, and she'd bring a bag of acid drops and juju's for Larry as a surprise, and some of the soft liquorice sweets her granny liked to suck. The thought of the rare treats gave her the strength to smile and wave and then turn into the trees, emerging moments later in the field beyond, where she made for the road, leaving the house in the wood and its two occupants to the gentle warmth of the lovely summer's day.

Chapter Eight

Kitty was troubled. There was something afoot, she knew the signs – her holiness and John ensconced in the morning room for an hour or more with the door shut and their voices low always meant bother for some poor soul. The last time it had been Matthew – or rather the lass he had been courting for a few months – who had come under fire. John had gone in with a tasty titbit about something in the girl's family's past and within hours Matthew had been told to finish the relationship or suffer his mother's wrath. Exit the lass.

Kitty was frowning as she stood with her ear pressed against the morning room door. The twins were currently courting two sisters whose family was one of the leading lights in the town, but a plainer pair of lasses she'd never seen, and if either Gilbert or Matthew were in love she'd eat her hat. But their mother would get her own way, she'd be bound, and it wouldn't be long before a double wedding was in the air. Edith had organised John's wife for him so this wasn't the first time; it was only Art who had gone his own way up to now. By, the damage Edith Stewart could do when she opened her mouth; she fair terrorised the lot of them.

Why stick it then, feeling as you do? The voice in her mind was sharp and confrontational and she answered it almost immediately with an irritable shake of her head. Because even with Henry gone she was still tied into this family through bonds of love. She felt like Henry's bairns were her own – oh, not John, not him, he had always been a sly, cruel child with a vicious streak that was pure Edith, but the others she loved. Oh aye, she loved them, as fiercely and as passionately as she had loved their father, God bless his soul.

She had been nowt but a bit lass of thirteen when she had come over the water from Ireland to live with an aunty in Sunderland's East End. Her own family, consisting of mother, father, and six younger brothers and sisters, had been wiped out with the cholera within weeks of her father – a seaman – first bringing the disease home. Her mother's younger sister had been kind but harassed; her own large family were eating her out of house and home and she hadn't needed another hungry mouth to feed, so within days of her arrival in Sunderland Kitty had found herself applying for the job of nursery-maid to the Stewarts.

Kitty shook her head again as she thought of that interview with Edith. John had been two years of age and his sister, Mavis, barely one, and their mother had completely duped the homesick, bewildered Irish lass she had been then, when she had said Kitty's main duties would be to care for the children. Caring for the children, cooking, cleaning, waiting on table – she had been doing the whole lot within six months. But by then it had been too late to leave. She had fallen in love with Henry Stewart almost from the first time of meeting him, and her love had told her that Henry was desperately unhappy with his tartar of a wife. And so she had stayed, and their love – something purely of the mind and never of the body, much as she would have wished it differently – had continued until the day Henry had died. She had had his heart, his wife had had his name and their children. Kitty doubted if one of them loved their mother. Respected her maybe, feared her almost certainly, and in John's case craved her approval with obsessional single-mindedness, but love? No, not love.

The sudden scrape of a chair within the morning room told Kitty she better make herself scarce, and she hurried along the gleaming, thickly carpeted hall into the drawing room where she left the door slightly ajar and stood behind it, listening. She felt no compunction at all about spying on her mistress and John – it had served both herself and the rest of the family well in the past – but this time she heard nothing she could make head or tail of as the two of them emerged into the now deserted hall.

'Be a man, John, for once in your life.' Edith's voice was low but of a biting quality that carried quite distinctly to Kitty in her hiding place. 'You say you recognised the woman when she was carrying out her trade and she was quite brazen about it? She needs teaching a lesson. How dare she assume she can proposition you!'

'I sent her packing, I told you.'

'I should hope so, I would expect nothing less of a son of mine, but that is not the point. The mere fact that she had the gall to approach you and think you would receive her kindly is scandalous. She should be drummed out of town, that is the truth of it. The woman is gutter material.'

Some poor lass the two of them had got their teeth into for one reason or another, Kitty told herself silently. It didn't take much to get on the wrong side of John, and the mother was a bigger upstart than the son. Look at how she had gone for Dan two or three months back when the lad had said he approved of the bill aimed at giving miners under eighteen a maximum eight-hour day, when it was having its second reading in the Commons. It had ended with Dan slinging down his newspaper and storming out of the house before he'd finished his breakfast, after Edith had started on her tack of the working class knowing their place and being prepared to work all hours for the privilege of receiving a wage packet. She would push Dan too far one day soon if she wasn't careful. He was easy-going all right, like his father, but Edith didn't seem to recognise that he wouldn't be led with a ring through his nose like the twins and John. He was more like Art, Dan was, but whereas Art's manner had always been abrupt and defensive, Dan's lazy affability could fool you into thinking he was going along with things until he blew up and said what was what.

John had been mumbling something or other whilst Kitty's thoughts had wandered, but now Edith brought the housekeeper's mind back to the matter in hand when she said, 'Then see to it, John. Do what needs to be done.'

'What needs to be done?' John's voice was agitated. 'What do you mean? I'm not sure what you mean.'

There was a pause for some seconds as if Edith was weighing carefully what she was about to say, and Kitty found herself leaning forward, not daring to breathe, her hand pressed to her throat. Then Edith's voice sounded, curiously flat and emotionless, as she said, 'I'm sure you will think of something, John. Some act of . . . persuasion. The community needs cleansing of such women and you would be doing the town a service. Look at it like that.'

Landsakes, what was she provoking the lad to do now? Kitty let out a shuddering breath, but the front door had been opened and John and his mother had stepped out on to the drive, and she could hear no more. All the troubles in this family could be laid at Edith Stewart's feet, Kitty told herself bitterly, peering out into the hall before walking quickly through to the kitchen at the back of the house and from there into the scullery beyond, where the sheep's head and the two rabbits the butcher's boy had delivered earlier were waiting to be dealt with.

Kitty lifted the sheep's head from the big copper pan where it had been soaking for the last hour, having been ready dressed by the butcher. After placing it in the deep stone sink, she split the head open and removed the tongue and brains to cook separately. She filled the pan with three quarts of fresh cold water, positioned the two halves in it and carried it carefully through into the kitchen, setting it on the range to bring to the boil while she prepared the vegetables laid out on the kitchen table, ready to add them to the saucepan once the scum from the meat had been removed.

Her hands moved swiftly and adeptly and anyone observing her would have thought she was fully concentrating on the task in hand, but nothing could have been further from the truth.

Why did she have the feeling that whatever John and his mother were planning boded ill for all of them? she asked herself worriedly. There had been an inflexion in Edith's voice at the beginning of the conversation, a virulence, that suggested this was something more than her usual meddling. But who was the object of her wrath?

The scum skimmed off and the vegetables added, Kitty left the broth to simmer and walked back into the small stone-floored scullery to skin the rabbits. She always insisted the rabbits were delivered with their fur on; there had been cases of butchers passing off dead cats to the gullible, and she had no intention of being fooled. But through all the cleaning and jointing and preparation of the humpty-backed rabbit pie, her brain continued to worry at the question in her mind like a dog with a bone.

She had felt this same sense of acute unease five years ago if she thought about it, but she hadn't known why until it was too late, and the whole family had been blown apart. So much misery . . . She clenched her teeth against the pain, which was still as raw as ever. First Henry dying, then poor Jacob taking his own life three months later. 'Course, her holiness had insisted the overdose was accidental, but that was a story and a half.

Kitty's hands became still, and she found herself staring back down the years. Jacob's face when he had learnt he would never walk again, never be free from the pain which made him cry out if he was touched . . .

She shivered, shutting her eyes tight. Jacob had told her on the quiet – before his mother-in-law had had him and Mavis shipped off – that he would go mad if he had to be confined twenty-four hours a day with his wife. Aye, and maybe he had gone mad at that, poor soul. And another poor soul was Mavis, her wee bonny lass that she'd dangled on her knee. Jacob's death had sent her over the edge all right, and there she was spending her days incarcerated in a lunatic asylum which her dear mother had made sure was in the back of beyond somewhere down south, far enough away for any scandal to be kept under lock and key.

But she was rambling here; Kitty brought her mind back to the matter in hand. All that was in the past and finished with. Jacob was gone and they had never heard another word from his lass after she had turned up on madam's doorstep that day with her two ragamuffin bairns in tow. Aye, it was finished with.

So why – and now Kitty's stomach turned over and the palms of her hands began to sweat – why was she feeling like she did? Her sixth sense, that Irish intuition that Henry had always made fun of but which was very real, was telling her that some insidious tentacle from those days was curling about her family again. She had no firm foundation for her suspicions – save that deep malignant note in Edith's voice – but she could almost smell the dark, decomposing matter beginning to ooze up from where it had been buried. She wasn't worried about her holiness, or John either if it came to that, but the twins and Art and Dan, her precious Dan who was more her bairn than any flesh and blood child could have been, mustn't be hurt. She'd have to keep her wits about her. She nodded in answer to the thought. Aye, she would, and do a bit of careful snooping on the quiet.

There was something going on, and it was more than Edith disapproving of some lass one of the twins had got involved with, or a petty irritation concerning the business. Kitty had promised Henry on one of her visits to his bedside in the Infirmary during that last week that she would take care of his bairns. Never mind that they all said he couldn't hear or respond to anything; he had heard her. She knew he had. And that's why she had kept quiet about the lads and Jacob, although she would carry the guilt with her to her dying day, and why she kept her mouth shut about other things too.

Kitty glanced round the large and very pleasant kitchen. The shining, blackleaded hob with its two ovens – one solely for bread – and the steel-topped and brass-railed fender which was five feet long, the massive brightly coloured clippie mat either side of which sat two comfortable rocking chairs with flock-stuffed cushions, the large kitchen table with its leather-covered top around which were positioned four high-backed chairs, and another two poorer tables set along the far wall under a window, all suggested wealth and abundance. As did the row of shining copper pans, the flounced and full curtains at the window in the same material as the cushions, and the tall, wide and ornate wooden dresser against a second wall in which stood assorted crockery and glasses. The general opinion of folk would be that she should consider herself lucky to be working for Edith Stewart in such surroundings. An easy going-on they'd say, especially now the bairns were grown up and off her hands. Aye, that's what they'd say, sure enough.

But then people didn't know the half of it. Even her aunty, in whom she confided most things on her weekly visit to the East End, when she'd take a bag of groceries and the odd joint of meat, was unaware of the true facts concerning the affair of Jacob's 'accident'. And how could you explain to someone unconnected with the family what it meant to live with Edith Stewart? The manipulation and manoeuvring to achieve her own ends, the control she exerted? And the frighteningly cold-blooded lack of remorse? She never seemed to doubt herself, and even her vindictiveness was of a nature that was all the more powerful for its frigidity.

Kitty sighed deeply, her shoulders slumping. What she would give to tell someone all of it, to get it off her chest. How many times in the last five years had she regretted allowing her faith to lapse? Hundreds, thousands. But Edith had put pressure on her when she had first come into the house to work, making it difficult for her to get to mass and being awkward for days if she attended church. And then, once she and Henry had admitted how they felt she had been overcome with guilt . . .

Kitty sighed again and then straightened up before walking through to the scullery, where she washed her hands and changed her apron in preparation for serving the coffee and little cakes and fancy biscuits at Edith's coffee morning for the Christian Women's Guild of Fellowship, of which Edith was president. Christian Women . . . Her lip curled and her eyes were bitter, but at the sound of the doorbell she wiped her face clean of all expression and went to answer the door.

Chapter Nine

Had she only been working in this terrible place for one day?

It was Friday evening, and Connie couldn't believe she had still been with her granny and Larry first thing that morning. It felt as though weeks – months – had elapsed since their tearful farewell.

When she had arrived at the workhouse carrying her few personal possessions and meagre clothing wrapped in a brown paper parcel under one arm, an inmate had escorted her to the officers' quarters and her small, square room. It held a narrow iron bed, an ugly battered wardrobe, a two-foot square table and straight-backed chair, and the window was covered by a paper window blind which, when raised, showed a depressing vista of a brick wall directly opposite. Her uniform was laid out on the surprisingly thick grey blankets on the bed, and once she had changed the same inmate led her directly to the laundry.

She found her work as a laundry checker consisted of checking in all the soiled washing from the main hospital, the male and female mental blocks and the infirm wards, and entering each article into a massive ledger which covered most of her large desk. When the laundry had been washed and ironed it had to be noted in an adjoining column and sent out again. Some of the dirty washing smelt to high heaven – especially from the mental blocks and the infirm wards – and although Connie had two female inmates to do the actual sorting the stench was sickening and for the first couple of hours she actually felt quite faint. At five o'clock she had to total up both columns, check that each block and ward had its requirements for the night, make a separate list of items that needed mending or replacing, and then ask the head laundress to check her work.

At various times during the day, due to her two inmate helpers being great lumps who bordered on the mentally deficient themselves, and who stared at her vacantly if she asked them to do anything outside the actual sorting, Connie found herself humping heavy piles of clean and ironed washing to their collection points, sorting out the clothing from the sheets and blankets where necessary, pulling enormous wicker baskets of dirty laundry from one place to another, and doing a hundred other little jobs that had her head constantly spinning and her arms and legs aching.

'You all right, lass?'

She had just had her work signed off by the head laundress, a big, buxom woman who looked nice and jolly but who had a tongue like a knife if anyone got anything wrong – as Connie had on various occasions throughout the day – and was standing somewhat disconsolately in the now empty laundry realising she didn't have the faintest idea how to get to the mess room, where the staff were having tea, by herself.

'Mary!' She had to restrain herself from falling on the other girl's neck but she had never been so glad to see anyone in all her life.

'They had a panic in the nursery, several of the bairns have got gastroenteritis accordin' to the doctor, so a couple of us have bin helpin' out. Bedlam it was,' said Mary cheerfully. 'Fast as you shovelled in milk an' food one end it come out the other an' the whole lot were screamin' with the bellyache. Puts you right off havin' bairns, not that I ever wanted any in the first place. Here, come on.' She dug Connie in the ribs, something Connie was to learn was a familiar gesture. 'The others'll eat the lot if we don't get a move on, like bloomin' vultures most of 'em, an' them that are after gettin' a bit of refeenment' – she parodied the word with a ludicrous caricature that had Connie giggling – 'are the worst of the lot. Tight as a duck's arse when it comes to passin' the cake round.'

Mary had come to look her out specially. The warm glow that this knowledge gave Connie carried her through the evening meal at the long refectory table in the crowded, noisy mess room, and enabled her to chat and laugh afterwards – the mess room also doubled as the staff's sitting room – as though her stomach wasn't still turning from the smell of the laundry, which seemed to have been absorbed into her clothes and her skin, even her hair.

'You coming up the moor the night, Mary?' one of the other officers asked as several of them began to dwindle away. 'There's a travelling show up near the bandstand and they've got performing ponies and all sorts.'

'Performin' ponies?' Mary wrinkled her snub nose which caused her glasses to wobble dangerously. 'Can't compare to old Buffalo Bill's Wild West Show. Did you go an' see that last year, Connie?'

Connie shook her head. She had heard about the two-day show at Lands End Farm in Hylton Road in July of the year before, and the three special trains it had taken to transport the 800 people and 500 horses needed to re-enact the Battle of the Little Big Horn and Custer's Last Stand, but Larry had been ill at the time and she hadn't been able to go to the show which had been touring the provinces.

'Great it was,' said Mary dreamily.

'Oh you, you'd just got your eye on one of the Rough Riders,' the other girl said teasingly.

'Not me, I've got more sense than to get mixed up with a travelling man,' Mary responded smartly.

The banter was light and Mary was smiling as she turned fully to Connie, but there was something in the other girl's face – a shadow, something deep in the soft brown eyes hidden behind the spectacles – that caused Connie to say, 'What's the matter, Mary?'

'The matter, lass? Nothin', nothin' asides I'm back in that nursery tomorrow. I could do without it, I tell you straight, but I'm only doin' one day more an' then someone else can have a turn.'

Connie nodded, but she didn't think it was the prospect of the nursery duty that had caused her new friend to look that way. Still, whatever it was Mary clearly didn't want to discuss it, and that was her own business after all.

For a moment Connie had a fierce desire for the house in the wood and all that was familiar. The fire in the blackleaded grate and her granny ensconced before it whatever the weather outside, the comforting womb of a bedroom where they were all together, hearing each other's sighs and snores and breathing, the clucking of the hens and the taste of fresh warm milk straight from the nanny goat, Larry's arms tight around her neck when she tucked him in at night, and her mam . . . Oh, her mam.

Whatever her mam had done she had done for them, and she loved her more now than ever. She would give the world to be able to tell her that, to hold her close, to state that her mam could stay at home and her daughter would provide for them. But it was too late. Too late. But not for Larry, or her gran either, and that was why she couldn't give in to this childish impulse to gather her things and fly home. She had to be strong. Her mam would have expected it of her and it was the last thing she could do for her.

'You got the blues, lass?'

She hadn't been aware of Mary watching her, but now Connie forced a smile and nodded; speaking, just at that moment, was impossible with the lump in her throat.

'Aye, well it's not surprisin', this bein' your first day an' all, but you'll get used to it. Everyone does.' And then Mary leant closer, shutting out the sight and sound of the others as she said, her voice low, 'You aren't really fourteen, are you, lass?'

Connie stared at her, but behind the outward façade of calmness her mind was racing. If she told this girl the truth and Mary reported her all would be lost. Far from being a paid helper in the workhouse she could find herself working as an inmate for the next two years until she was fourteen, and her granny in one of the infirm wards and Larry separated from them both. But some instinct stronger than her fear was prompting her to trust this funny, nondescript-looking girl, and it was this that enabled her to answer, her voice even quieter than Mary's. 'I'm twelve.'

Mary said not a word, but they looked at each other in full understanding, and it was in that moment that their friendship was really born.

* * *

His mam was right, he should have done something like this years ago. She'd got away with murder, Jacob's whore, if you thought about it.

It was four in the morning, the day after Connie had entered the workhouse and John had had the conversation with his mother which had further inflamed his rage and burning resentment, and like the night five years before he was making his way to the house in the wood, but this time he was alone.

What was Sadie Bell after all but a stinking whore? She had put it on offer at the warehouse, oh aye, she had, but Jacob had got there before him, that was the truth of it. He could have had her; like Jacob he could have had her all his life on the side, but he'd just waited a mite too long in making his move. He ground his teeth, the image of the woman who had been like a canker eating away at him from the first second he had laid eyes on her, who he had wanted more than he had ever wanted anyone in his life, there on the screen of his mind. She had put a curse on their whole family, and moreover she had made him a laughing stock with that stunt in the pub. The word had spread quicker than a dose of salts. By, what he'd give to take it out of her hide. He swore, softly but profoundly, the profanities foul, and they seemed to propel his small stocky body along even more swiftly in the balmy moonlit shadows.

The cottage was in darkness when he came into the clearing but he had expected that, it was what he had planned for. The trollop would be back from her whoring now, however good a night she'd had.

He moved stealthily past the goat's lean-to and the hen coop, skirting round the vegetable patch and right up to the cottage door before he eased the sack which had been slung over his shoulder to the dusty, baked ground.

An owl's hoot almost over his head made him jump violently and then freeze, but the cool mugginess of the summer night enfolded him once again and he began to breathe more easily, the faint odour from the stone outhouse wherein the nettie was housed causing his nose to wrinkle. Animals, they lived like filthy animals, his mam was right on that count too. And like cleaved to like – aye, water found its own level right enough, and after tonight she perhaps wouldn't be so high and mighty when she was forced to take herself and her brats to her whoremaster – whoever that was – and live where she worked.

The thought excited him, and he stood for a moment, relishing his contemplation of the time when Sadie would be broken and desperate and he would make her crawl on her knees for him. And he would. Oh aye, he would. He wasn't finished with her yet, not by a long chalk. She was going to pay and keep on paying for what she had done to him.

He was smiling as he extracted the can of oil and the rags from the sack, but his expression turned to one of faint surprise when he tried the handle of the cottage door and it opened. Better and better. He had prepared himself for it being bolted, her being on her own out here with the bairns and her old mother, if the crone was still alive. An oil-soaked rag wrapped round a stone through the window followed by another lighted one would have done the trick, but this was easier. He could make sure the fire got a good hold now and he didn't want her salvaging much; the more destitute this left her the better.

It was absolutely black inside the cottage and it took a minute or two for his eyes to adjust, but there was a full moon and soon the dim shafts of light from the window allowed him to pick out items of furniture within the small room. He moved furtively over the stone flags to the clippie mat in front of the range, opening the can and sprinkling a good amount of oil from one end of the mat to the other, before doing the same over the table, the ancient, flock-stuffed cushions on the saddle and the thin curtains.

He could hear snoring from the other room, the door being slightly ajar, but such was the adrenalin rushing through his blood that he felt invincible as he lit first the curtains, which flared immediately, and then the cushions. He threw a match on to the table before adding another to the clippie mat, but as he stepped backwards he kicked over the can of oil which clattered on the stone flags as it expelled its remaining liquid in a stream towards the bedroom door. This seemed to light by itself in a flash from the clippie mat, and in the same instant, as there were stirrings from the bedroom, John dived for the door of the cottage, banging it behind him as he left.

Far from being exhilarated he now felt unnerved by the ferocity with which the fire had taken hold, and expecting the occupants of the cottage to come tumbling out of the door at any moment he ran across the clearing, ploughing over the vegetable bed and getting entangled in the runner bean canes in the process, before reaching the cover of the trees.

And then the screams started. Terrible screams, screams that caused his blood to freeze and the hairs of his head to rise up and prick his scalp. Damn it, why weren't they getting out? Sadie was able-bodied and that girl of hers must be twelve or thirteen by now. He was actually halfway back across the clearing when he stopped, his eyes wild, as the reality of what it would mean if he was seen hit him. He'd go down the line for this, sure as eggs were eggs. Even if he got them out he'd be facing a hefty prison sentence or worse.

The unearthly cries were reaching new hideous heights and again he took a step or two towards the cottage which was now clearly ablaze, before stopping once more. Whatever was happening in there they were as good as dead now; what good would it do if he got hurt too? And he hadn't meant it. He hadn't meant for them to get caught like this. It wasn't his fault, dammit, they should have moved quicker.

He clapped his hands over his ears to shut out the harrowing noise, swinging his head back and forth and shutting his eyes as he let the sound of his own moaning fill his mind, and it was some time later – he didn't know if it was seconds or minutes such was his panic and fright – that he became aware that the screaming had stopped and the thatched roof was sending a great pall of smoke into the sky.

He had to get out of there, but for the moment he couldn't act on the thought. His stomach felt loose, his bowels had turned to water, and he had to fight the desire to be sick.

He ran his hand over his face, scrubbing at his flesh which was damp with sweat, and glanced about the flickering clearing. He must right those bean canes and extricate the vegetables he'd crushed when he trod on them. It wouldn't do for anyone to think someone had been there. The oil can he could do nothing about now. He had meant to bring it away but when the place had gone up like that, like a tinderbox, there'd been no time for anything. Still, if it was found at all they'd most likely think it belonged to the family. He closed his eyes as the bile surged into his throat and swallowed hard, and then, as the crackling and heat reached new heights, quickly set about tidying up.

Once that was done the heat from the blazing building sent

him to the far side of the clearing where he glanced back once before moving, not towards Tunstall Road and the more direct route into Bishopwearmouth, but westwards, towards the Hetton Colliery railway and Silksworth Lane where he could join the Durham Road and skirt eastwards into Kensington Road.

As he walked the sky became lighter, dawn breaking in pastel shades that promised another glorious summer's day in this year of our Lord, nineteen hundred and five. It was Saturday 1st July, unmomentous to many, but it was the day on which the great philanthropist and founder of the Salvation Army, General William Booth, bought 20,000 acres of land on which to settle poor immigrants in Australia, and a revolutionary by the name of Albert Einstein proposed his startling new 'Theory of Relativity' to stunned fellow physicists. But in the north-east community of Sunderland these historic events passed unnoticed. The fresh new morning heralded the start of just another working day in which they endeavoured to hold body and soul together.

To Connie, still fast asleep in her dismal room in the benignant confines of the Sunderland workhouse, the 1st of July, 1905, was a date that would become seared on her memory as though inflicted by a branding iron. A day that would haunt her in dark nightmares for years afterwards, when she would see the flames and hear the heart-rending cries, watch grotesque stumbling figures turn into balls of fire and reach out to help, only to find that they crumbled into ashes at her feet. But as yet she was blissfully unaware of the tragedy which had befallen her grandmother and beloved brother, and such was John Stewart's ability at self-justification – a trait he had inherited from his mother – that he actually began to whistle as he strode across Broad Meadows to join Kensington Road, the first rays of golden sunshine warm on his face.

Father Hedley was tired. He had been called to a house in Stafford Street in the East End, close to the barracks, at three in the morning to perform the last rites on one of his elderly parishioners, only to find that the old lady was chary of being ushered somewhere she hadn't yet made up her mind to go. As well as the old granny there were two aunties, eight children and the daughter and her husband living in the two-up, two-down terrace, and when he'd arrived most of them had been squeezed round the desk bed in the kitchen where the old woman lay.

He liked this family. Although they were one of the poorest of his flock, they were good, decent, kind-hearted folk and the granny was a character. So he stayed on chatting, even when it became clear that the old lady had fooled them all again by reviving, and only left after he had shared the family's breakfast of pot boiley – crusts of bread mixed with milk and oats.

However, Father Hedley was finding that the bronchitis he had suffered two weeks previously was still taking its toll, and once back home he groaned out loud when, having settled himself in a comfortable armchair and put his feet up on the cracket in preparation for a doze, there was a banging on the front door, followed by the mention of his name.

'Father?' When the long-suffering Mrs Clark, who kept house for the two priests and generally looked after them, popped her head round the study door she spoke in an undertone. 'There's a constable in the hall asking for you. He says the farmer's wife at Tunstall Hills Farm sent him.'

'Oh aye? You'd better show him in then, Mrs Clark.'

So saying, Father Hedley lowered his feet and stood up, but within moments of the constable opening his mouth the priest found he had to sit down again. 'You're saying Peggy Cook and the little lad are dead?' Father Hedley's face was screwed up, his brown eyes lost behind his narrowed lids.

'Aye, I'm afraid so, Father.' The constable shuffled his feet before he said, 'Looks like the girl, Connie isn't it? had a lucky escape by all accounts.'

A lucky escape. Father Hedley was staring at the policeman but not seeing him; at that moment he was capable only of visualising Connie and her face when she heard this terrible news. It would break her. Dear God, it would break her. Hadn't the bairn stood enough in her short life? Why this, and why now?

The last thought prompted him to say, 'Has she been told? Connie, has she been told yet?'

The constable shook his head. 'They said at the farm that there's no other relatives, not that they know of leastways, and that you've had a bit to do with the family over the years? I understand you were responsible for getting the lass the job at the workhouse?'

Father Hedley nodded.

'I thought it might be better if you broke it to her, Father. They said she's a nice little lass and thinks a bit of her granny and brother, and the mother's only just died.' The constable made an uneasy movement here; he had been surprised when he'd discovered the lass's mother had been Sadie Bell. Not that she'd ever caused any trouble, Sadie, and she hadn't been foul-mouthed or abusive to the police when they'd tried to do their job, but nevertheless a whore was a whore.

142

The priest nodded again. 'How . . . how did it happen?' he asked heavily.

'Oil can got knocked over or dropped from what we can make out. Perhaps the lad was trying to fill the lamp, something along those lines, we can't be sure. Anyway, they got trapped in the bedroom and once the fire got a hold . . .' He drew his chin in, his voice soft as he said, 'Bad business. Bad business.'

Father Hedley inhaled a sharp breath. It was a bad business all right. And then he surprised himself as he asked, 'There was no jiggery-pokery then?'

'Jiggery-pokery?' There was a different note in the constable's voice now and his eyes had narrowed. 'Why? Do you know of any reason why that might be the case, Father?'

Did he? Father Hedley stared at the man and after a moment, during which he pulled in his lips and pressed down hard on them, he answered quietly, 'No, I know of no reason, Constable. I was merely enquiring, that's all.'

'I see.' The policeman kept his eyes on the priest as Father Hedley rose slowly to his feet. 'You sure about that, Father?'

'Quite sure.'

Quite sure. By, the constable thought, he'd like a shilling for every time he'd heard that one! And these priests, they were the worst of all. The power they wielded and the influence they had would be fine if it wasn't used just to scare the wits out of people regarding their immortal souls. He knew of deep, dyed-in-the-wool villains who would go to mass and light a few candles and such like and emerge with a smile on their faces, convinced they were right with God and man after ten minutes in the confessional box with a bloke like this one. No matter they had half killed someone the night before

– they had been given their penance and received absolution so all was well.

'Well in that case, Father, we'd better make tracks if you're ready?'

Father Hedley had never been less ready for anything in his life, but he inclined his head, drawing in a long hard breath before following the constable out of the room.

Connie was surprised to be summoned to the matron's office and not a little alarmed. The head laundress was in a foul mood and had already ripped strips off all the officers that morning, and as she walked the corridors with the inmate who had been sent to fetch her Connie wondered if she was in trouble for some misdemeanour or other. Nevertheless, she wasn't altogether sorry to escape her glass-screened corner of the laundry. Moments before she had been sent for, the stench had become overpowering when linen from the isolation ward – a ward which frequently treated those suffering from venereal diseases as well as infectious ones – had arrived covered with pus and discharge.

The smell was still in her nostrils when she reached the matron's office and knocked once, her heart pounding, before opening the door. And then, as her eyes went to the two men standing to one side of the matron's desk, that same heart seemed to want to jump out of her chest.

'Come in, child.'

The matron's voice was very soft and low as she rose to her feet, and as Connie's eyes flashed to her face before returning to Father Hedley's she felt as though her fear was strangling her. 'Is it me granny?' She stepped fully into the room as she spoke, and her voice became urgent and rapid.

'Is it, Father? Something's happened to me granny? Where is she?'

'Sit down, lass.'

It was the constable who spoke, but Connie didn't even acknowledge his presence as she reached out to Father Hedley, and he, taking her hands between his own, said, 'Connie, you've got to be brave. Very brave, lass.'

Oh no, no. Not her granny. And where was Larry? He'd be frantic without her or her granny. She must go to him . . .

'Connie? Look at me, lass.'

She hadn't been aware that her eyes had been moving wildly round the room, but now, at the sound of Father Hedley's gentle voice, she became still, her lips mouthing, 'Oh, Father, Father,' but without any sound.

As he began to speak, the priest saw his words register like blows in the large azure eyes now fixed on his, and never had he so desired to take another human being's pain and make it his own. But that wasn't possible and he knew it, and then he had said it all, and there followed a silence so profound not one of the adults felt able to break it.

Connie's head was buzzing. She wanted to speak – poor Father Hedley was looking so sad and holding on to her hands so tightly; she ought to speak, to show him she understood what he had been saying, but she couldn't. If she spoke, if she acknowledged it, it became real and it mustn't be real. *Larry couldn't be dead.* Her grandmother she could have understood, her granny was old and frail and in pain all the time. But Larry? The screen of her mind was filled with their parting, the way her brother had clung to her, his arms tight around her neck. He had such baby hands still, dimples instead of knuckles . . .

'Connie? Connie, sit down, dear.' It was the matron, and Connie wasn't to know that Matron Banks had just broken her cast-iron rule by addressing one of her officers by their Christian name. 'This dreadful accident must be a terrible shock for you, and coming so soon after your mother's demise . . .'

Her voice continued but Connie couldn't hear it. The buzzing was steadily becoming a hammering that was filling her head. Larry was dead. And her granny. *Burnt, they had been burnt.* And she hadn't been there; she had been lying in her bed, safe and secure in the officers' quarters, while they had been dying. How could they have been dying and she hadn't sensed something? She should have known . . .

'Listen to me, lass.' Connie found she was sitting on a chair although she had no recollection of seating herself, and Father Hedley was now kneeling in front of her, still with her hands clasped in his. 'You'll come through this. It might not seem like it now, but you *will* come through this.'

Connie blinked at him, and the priest found it difficult not to avert his eyes from the agony in her strained white face. She attempted to speak several times before she said, her voice very low, 'They . . . they burnt, Father?'

'No, no.' He swallowed hard. 'The smoke would have overcome them, I'm sure of it. They wouldn't have known anything, Connie.'

She wanted to believe him. More than anything in the world she wanted to believe they had simply gone to sleep and not woken up, the alternative was too horrific to contemplate. 'Are you sure, Father?' she asked pitifully.

Father Hedley took a deep breath and lied like he hadn't done since he was a wee bairn and in for a pasting from his father for stealing taffy from old Ma Blackett who ran the village shop. 'Absolutely sure,' he said firmly.

Connie slowly straightened her body, staring for some moments more into his worried face before she cast her eyes on the matron and the policeman, and then back to the priest. 'Thank you, Father.' She didn't question whether she believed him or not, at the moment it was impossible for her to think clearly, but in the deepest recess of her mind there was a gnawing sense of futility for all their struggles over the last months and years, and that was adding to the bitterness of her grief.

Why couldn't she cry? The thought sprang into her mind and challenged her dry eyes. They would think it odd, unfeeling that she didn't cry. They would assume she didn't care.

The priest and the other two occupants of the room did not think it odd, neither did they think the white, shocked young girl in front of them didn't care, but each in their own way wished that the safety valve of weeping could be released. They continued to speak soothing words of comfort for some minutes more until, in the middle of a kind but weighty discourse from the constable, Connie rose abruptly to her feet. 'I . . . I'd better get back.'

Her voice had been jerky and tight, and now it was the matron who said, very softly, 'Why don't you go and rest a while, dear? At least until lunchtime.'

'*No.*' And then more quietly, 'No thank you, Matron Banks. Goodbye, Father,' and with a nod at the constable, 'Goodbye.'

It was for all the world as though Connie were the adult and the three watching her the children, and each grown-up was aware of this but at a loss to know what to do or say.

Once in the dismal, deserted corridor outside the matron's office Connie realised she was shaking as if with a fit of the ague, but she took several deep breaths, her hands clenched fists at her sides, as she told herself she mustn't think. It would be all right if she didn't think. She would go back to the laundry and work, that's what she'd do.

Once back behind the glass screen the smell that had been so obnoxious and overpowering earlier now barely registered on her consciousness. She went about her work automatically and her helpers, frightened by her white face and stiffness, said not a word, even to each other.

At twelve o'clock she sent the two inmates for their meal but continued working at her desk, and at ten past Mary walked round the partition and simply took her in her arms, but even then Connie didn't cry. She simply stared at the other girl wordlessly as Mary murmured, over and over again, 'Oh, lass, oh lass,' before saying, 'Come on, you're comin' for a bit of a lie down, lass. Old Banksy herself suggested it.'

It wasn't until they reached Connie's room and she saw, there on the bed where she had lovingly placed it that morning, Larry's precious piece of rag, that her eyes sprang wide and she let out a long shuddering moan that rose and rose into a shrill cry.

It frightened Mary half to death but she didn't show it, and when the storm of weeping came she held Connie close until the front of her uniform was soaked with tears. Mary herself couldn't speak because of the enormous lump clogging her throat, but she made little noises, deep and soft, that needed no explanation.

It seemed aeons later when Connie spoke, and then the words were dragged out of her. 'How am I going to bear it?

Me mam, an' now me gran an' Larry. He . . . he was only seven years old, Mary. How can that be fair? He hadn't done anything to anybody, an' me gran was a grand woman.'

'Aye, I know, lass.'

'We were happy, we were so happy before they came. Why couldn't they have let us alone?'

Mary didn't have the faintest idea what Connie was talking about but she nodded anyway. It was better if Connie talked. That's what her own mam had said to her after— A door slammed in Mary's mind. But you couldn't always talk, not always, however much you wanted to. She, of all people, knew that. But Connie was talking now and that was good; the lass'd looked so bad when she'd first seen her.

'I hate them, Mary.'

'Who, lass?'

'The . . . the Stewarts. The Stewart family, them that live in Ryhope Road.'

It wasn't the time to ask the whys and the wherefores, but Mary made a mental note of the name before she said, 'You think you could manage somethin' to eat, lass?'

'No, no, I don't want anything.' Connie gulped deep in her throat as she fought the flood of tears that was rising again. 'I'd better get back to the laundry.'

'All in good time, lass. All in good time.' They were sitting on the edge of the narrow bed and now Mary rose to her feet saying, 'Look, you stay here an' I'll go an' see if there's a bite of somethin' in the mess room an' bring it along, all right? No matter if you can't eat it, it'll keep till later. Some cake or somethin'.'

Connie nodded. She didn't want anything, but Mary was trying to be kind and she appreciated the other girl's concern.

Once she was alone again she rose slowly and walked across to the window, pulling up the paper blind and gazing out on to the brick wall in front of her. This room was now all the home she had. She shivered, turning and surveying the dingy surroundings with new eyes. But it wasn't always going to be like this – by all that was holy it wasn't. She was going to make something of herself – for her mam, her granny, and for Larry. *Oh, oh . . . Larry.* She was the only one left now, but the Stewarts weren't going to have the satisfaction of winning, of destroying them all.

When they had crippled her Uncle Jacob that night it had started something, she couldn't explain it, but things had never been right since. All the bad things that had happened had their roots in that night, in that family.

But she would see her day with them. She nodded to herself, the autocratic figure of Edith Stewart standing militantly outside the big house in Ryhope Road clear in her mind. And the leader of the brothers, John Stewart, he was horrible, but she would show him too. Aye, she would. She wasn't going to let them beat her.

And the young lad, Dan? Immediately the thought came she pushed it away, angry that it had intruded this day of all days. But ever since he had rescued her from the snow she had found it difficult to banish his image from her mind, and it intruded at the oddest moments. He had helped them that day, given them food and logs and such, and paid for the doctor, but then all their trouble had been caused by his brothers so he should have, shouldn't he? Connie couldn't quite justify this conclusion and she brushed the confusion it brought to one side. He was a Stewart. And she hated *all* the Stewarts. End of story.

The tide of hate rose in her throat, seeming to choke her, and then she glanced down at the tatty piece of rag still clutched tight in her hand. *They were gone and nothing could bring them back.* She sank down on to the bed, the pain of her loss swamping her afresh and bringing a desolation so great it made her gasp at the air as though she were drowning.

Part Three
1913
New Beginnings

Chapter Ten

Connie had blossomed into a full-grown woman of unusual beauty in the last eight years, and as her grandmother had suspected many years before, her loveliness had even eclipsed that of her mother. At twenty years of age, she carried her five-foot five-inches very straight, and wore her thick, golden-blonde hair, which reached to her tiny waist when loose, high on the top of her head in a shining coil which made her appear taller than she really was. Her skin had the smoothness of warm cream, her lips were red and finely shaped, and her eyebrows curved naturally above the eye sockets and were of a delicate light brown. But it was her eyes – the deep blue of a violet shade and heavily fringed by brown lashes – that people really found arresting. They had just missed being too big for her face, although they still dominated it, and their liquid appeal was riveting.

But most of all Connie was determined and intelligent, two things which had proved – and were continuing to prove – a mixed blessing in the narrow confines in which she found herself living. The desire for knowledge which Sadie's sacrifice in sending her daughter to school had engendered, had been satisfied in part over the years. But only in part. Connie was a frequent visitor to the library in the Extension

Park just off Borough Road, at the rear of which was a large conservatory called the Winter Garden which housed tropical plants, cages of foreign birds and a pond well stocked with goldfish.

Until a couple of years ago she had had to consult a list to see which books were available for borrowing, but then 'open access' to the shelves commenced for Sunderland's working class and she liked nothing better than to browse amongst the thousands of books and choose her quota, which would be eagerly devoured in the privacy of her little room at the workhouse, much to Mary's frustration as she hadn't the slightest inclination towards books or learning. Mary couldn't understand Connie's interest in current affairs either, or why her friend spent precious pennies each week on such boring items as newspapers when she could have spent them on little luxuries. And Connie's avid following of the fortunes of the suffragette movement was quite beyond Mary.

This last passion of Connie's had come into being not long after Larry and her grandmother had died. In the midst of those caustic days she had come across an old newspaper and read, for the first time, about the militant battles in the war to get women the vote. The article had stated that the Prime Minister, Sir Henry Campbell, had advised a deputation of the Women's Suffrage Societies that, 'It is more likely you will succeed if you wait rather than act now in a pugnacious spirit', to which a Miss Annie Kenney, wearing the stamp of working-class clogs and shawl and standing on a chair, had retorted, 'We are not satisfied!'. She'd said that to the Prime Minister! Connie had been intrigued, especially when she'd read that on that same day the women's leader, an Emmeline Pankhurst, had addressed a 6,000 strong crowd in Trafalgar

Square and stated, 'We have been patient too long. We will be patient no longer.' It was fighting talk, and it touched something deep in Connie's angry, troubled heart.

During the next few years Connie had been horrified when she'd read of the brutal force-feeding of the suffragettes in the prisons, and the way they were treated by those in authority, but it was in 1910, when the fight for the vote for women came to Sunderland, that Connie and many others realised the sheer animosity of those who were against giving women their rights. On the 14th of February of that year three women were addressing a crowd at the corner of John Street and High Street West and were being continually heckled by men in the assembly. When things began to get out of hand the suffragettes were chased by a mob, one escaping into the High Street whilst the other two took refuge in the Arcade at Broadbent's Oyster Saloon. By this time the crowd had swelled to over 2,000, and although the women made their getaway at the St Thomas end of the Arcade they were badly shaken, and continued to suffer abuse and taunts from the mob before effecting their escape down Frederick Street.

It was a nasty incident, but far from intimidating Connie and other sympathisers when they read about it in the local paper the next day, it made them all the more passionate about the moral justice of the women's cause.

Even Mary was impressed when in June of the following year 60,000 women from all walks of life and all classes – factory girls and aristocrats, actresses and university graduates – marched through the streets of London in a five-mile-long procession dressed as Boadicea, Joan of Arc and other courageous women. And when Emmeline Pankhurst visited the Sunderland branch of the Women's Social and Political

Union for a meeting in the Victoria Hall in February, 1912, she accompanied Connie to hear Mrs Pankhurst appealing to the women of Sunderland to help the suffrage campaign, although most of the arguments went right over her head.

All she had to remember, Connie would explain patiently, was that with the vote women everywhere could start making a difference and the Government knew that and that's why they were afraid of the challenge. The awful riots in London, when thousands of pounds' worth of damage occurred in the East End and the windows of No. 10 Downing Street were shattered, would never have happened if the Movement hadn't been driven to such extreme action by the Government not only refusing the demands of women but taunting them with the accusation of not expressing themselves forcibly enough.

Why not women solicitors and managing directors and members of parliament? Why not a woman *prime minister* one day?

'A woman prime minister?' Mary's voice had been high when Connie had voiced that one. 'Never, lass. Never. The men'd never allow it.'

'Then women will have to make them,' Connie had answered with a twinkle in her eye, which had faded somewhat as she'd continued, 'Look at it like this, Mary. Can you see a woman prime minister refusing to accept the miners' unions' demands for a minimum of five shillings a day for men and two shillings for lads? *Two shillings* for young lads working in lethal gases and floods and fire in the pits. And would a woman send in the cavalry against men, women and children supporting striking miners like they did in Wales? And what about female shop assistants working ninety hours a week for a pittance, and all the women who bring bairns into the world in conditions that aren't fit for animals? Look at how your own mam and da are forced to live.'

'It's a man's world,' Mary would answer stolidly. 'It always has been. It's not right, but there it is.'

'Then women'll have to change it, won't they.'

Normally at this point in the proceedings Mary would nod thoughtfully, her eyes half closed as she said, 'Aye, you're right, you are that,' and then follow almost immediately with, 'Right, lass, you comin' to the Palace the night?' or something similar. And Connie would catch her friend's eye, and the two of them would laugh and escape into the world outside the harsh walls of the workhouse for an hour or two.

But Connie wasn't laughing tonight, and neither was Mary. It was a Sunday, and the February day had been raw with a cruel cutting wind and frequent snow showers, but in spite of the freezing conditions Connie had waited around for nearly an hour after the last mass for Father Hedley that morning. She had wanted everyone to leave, she needed to have the Father all to herself, and not for a rushed confession either. No, she had needed to talk to him. Really talk to him. And it had been an angry and bitter young woman who had poured out her heart to the old priest once they were alone in the vestry.

'It's not fair, Father, it's not. I've proved myself there over the last eight years, you know that as well as I do, and at twenty-two – well, they think I'm twenty-two anyway – I'm more than old enough to start training as a nurse. I don't want to stay in the laundry' – here Connie dismissed the back-breaking hours she had worked to claw herself up from laundry checker to second assistant laundress, and finally to assistant head laundress – 'any more, I don't. I want . . . oh, something more.'

'Are you sure of what you heard, Connie? You couldn't
have been mistaken?'

'I'm sure.' It was said with a great deal of asperity. 'They
didn't know I was there of course, Mrs Wright and the matron,
but the door was slightly ajar and because I heard my name
mentioned I didn't knock straightaway when I was delivering
the time sheets. They said—' Connie swallowed hard, the
conversation she had overheard still like an open wound. 'The
matron remarked it was a shame about the Bell girl and that
she didn't doubt I would be a good nurse, but of course the
idea was quite out of the question in view of my "unfortunate"
background. There . . . there was no possibility of them
recommending my application to train as a nurse when my
mother had been known to the police as a woman of ill repute.
That's what they said.'

Father Hedley nodded slowly. This had cut deep and he
was aware that the anger was covering a whole host of
emotions Connie had battled with during the years. He had
watched her fight back against circumstances which would
have crushed many others, and not only fight but gain ground.
Her efforts to improve her mind had not been without success;
she was now an articulate and well-versed young woman and
he knew she had read widely of the classics as well as modern
literature. Nevertheless . . . The old priest sighed inwardly.
Society was narrow-minded, especially where a young and
beautiful woman was concerned. She would be termed an
upstart by her peers and possibly a threat to those in authority
above her. This latest development surprised him not at all.

However, it wouldn't help Connie to speak his thoughts
out loud, and what he did say, as he gave her a reassuring pat
on the shoulder, was, 'When the good Lord closes one door

He invariably opens another, child. Life has taught me that if nothing else. But sometimes it's necessary to push with both hands. You understand me?'

And she had nodded, biting her lip in much the same way she was doing now as she finished telling Mary what had transpired.

'They're barmy, the matron an' Mrs Wright. Clean barmy. You'd make a canny nurse, lass, an' I'm not just sayin' that,' Mary declared stoutly.

'Maybe.' Connie looked back into the plain, bespectacled face in front of her and even managed a small smile as she said, 'But it's not going to happen, Mary, and I'm not going to waste time crying over spilt milk, neither am I going to apologise for my mother to anyone. She was a good mam and she did what she thought she had to do. I'm not going to have anyone sitting in judgement on her and then give them the opportunity to tell me about it.'

Mary stared at her. 'What are you goin' to do, lass?' she asked anxiously. She had been frightened she'd lose Connie when her friend had told her she was putting in the application to train as a nurse, but she was even more perturbed now. She had never thought she'd have a friend like Connie – she was more than a pal, even more than a sister, in spite of them being so different. Mary knew she wasn't half as bright but that didn't matter, not a jot, because Connie didn't care – Connie didn't judge people like that.

She would never forget the day, some few months after Connie's family had died, when she'd told Connie about her uncle and his friend and what they had done to her when she'd been a bairn. It had been the first time she'd talked about it to anyone besides her mam, and then that had been only the once when she'd come stumbling into the house with her knickers and clothes torn and blood trickling down her legs. It had been her da setting about his brother – half killing him so her da was put away for six years – that had caused her two oldest brothers to have to go down the mine when they were only nine and ten years old so the family could eat, and then their Ruby had died at four with the fever because her mam had no money to call the doctor.

They'd lived hand to mouth for years, and her mam had had to take in washing, as well as the cleaning jobs she had taken when she could get them at the big houses, but still there had been no money for clothes or boots in the winter.

She had been seven years of age when her uncle and his friend – a big, meaty docker with a huge pot belly – had raped her, and she had felt responsible for the family being torn apart from that moment on, right until she and Connie had talked things through. Connie had let her cry and rage, over and over again, and had kept talking to her until she had found some semblance of peace inside. That had been when she'd been fifteen years old.

Since then her fear of men – all men – had lessened to a degree, as long as they made no move to touch her in any way. Even when she took her wage home to her mam every Sunday morning she was careful to make sure she was never alone with her da. She didn't think he'd do anything, not her da – she knew he loved her and that he was heart sorry about what had happened – but she just couldn't help how she felt. And she never stayed more than a few minutes, she couldn't help that either, but it seemed as though since her da had come out of prison her mam had had a bairn every year, and the crowded, dirty house with its army of bugs and insanitary

162

conditions disgusted her. Yet she felt awful inside – *terrible* – for feeling that way, especially when her da had been locked away because of her.

'What am I going to do?' Connie repeated Mary's question and moved restlessly, rising from the straight-backed chair where she had been sitting to look out of the window at the swirling snow, which for the moment obscured the ugly brick wall beyond. As she turned back to Mary, who was sitting on Connie's bed, she said, 'I'm getting out of here, Mary. This has made up my mind. I've been thinking of going for ages, you know that. I was just hanging on to see if this nursing idea bore fruit, but if they don't want me I'm not going to beg and plead.' She raised her head, with its swathe of golden hair, proudly.

'Oh, Connie.' Mary's fingers went uncertainly to her mouth and immediately Connie understood, and her voice was warm as she said, 'I mean together, us going together, you daft hen. Here, look at this.' She reached over to the small table which was covered in books and pulled a newspaper from beneath the pile. 'The Grand has been advertising for an assistant housekeeper and there are two maids wanted there as well. That's where I went last night, once I was off duty, to see if the posts are still available.'

'The Grand Hotel in Bridge Street?' And now Mary's, 'Oh, Connie,' held more than a shred of awe. 'You didn't, lass, did you? What did they say? Do they still want two maids?'

'I'm not applying for one of the maids' jobs,' Connie said gently after a pause. 'It's the assistant housekeeper I'm going for. And yes, that's available, and there's still one maid's position to be filled.'

'Oh, lass.' Mary clasped and unclasped her hands. To be

free of the workhouse. She had started work in its dark confines nine years ago when she was fourteen and her da had been out of prison twelve months. He had been unable to get any regular shifts at Austin's shipyard in Wear Dock Yard where he'd been a welder, and the conditions he had endured in the prison, added to the years of working in the cold, wet, and in winter, freezing environment in the shipyard, had given him chronic arthritis in his hands and legs as well as welder's lung. So Mary had started work as soon as she was able and had taken home all her wage each week, keeping only thruppence at the beginning for herself. Her contribution, along with that of her two older brothers and later her younger sister, Beattie, who was a year younger than Mary and in service in a big house in Hendon, had enabled her parents – and the new family that was added to each year since her father's return – to survive.

'It will be all right, Mary.' Connie's voice vibrated with the depth of her feeling, and as always she seemed to understand what Mary was thinking. 'You want to leave don't you, and you'll be coming out with as much as you get here to give your mam, I promise.'

'Are you sure?' Mary wanted to escape the workhouse, of course she did she assured herself in the next moment, as the thought of leaving the grey confines she had hated for so long – and which were only made bearable by her friendship with Connie – brought a pang of fear at the unknown in its wake. Here she was fed and housed and secure, and her weekly wage was certain. There would always be workhouses, everyone knew that, but out there in the streets beyond the workhouse gates life was much more uncertain.

'Listen.' Mary's head had been averted but now she looked

directly into Connie's violet-blue eyes as Connie knelt down on the cold cracked lino and took the other girl's twisting hands in her own, stilling their agitation. 'You'd be getting what you do here, five shillings a week, I've already checked, and the hours are shorter, the work's lighter, and you get paid extra if you work at weekends.'

Mary's eyes opened wide – it sounded too good to be true – and then the reason for this became apparent when Connie continued, 'But it's not live-in. Now you know I've got a bit saved . . .' Her voice lowered here; only Mary knew about the laboriously saved nest egg hidden at the back of the rickety wardrobe which had accumulated over the years. On finding herself suddenly with no dependants and with her food and board provided for, Connie had determined to save a portion of her weekly wage, especially when her promotions at the laundry had resulted in modest but welcome pay rises.

Admittedly there were her clothes and toiletries to be paid for, and since Connie had discovered Mary's home situation she had insisted on paying for her friend whenever they enjoyed a night out. The Empire Theatre, with its cupola topped by a revolving steel globe surmounted by a statue of the Greek goddess of dance, was their favourite place. It was even fun whilst they were waiting in the stalls queue – different categories of patron entered by different entrances to avoid any social embarrassment – as they were entertained by buskers and tempted to buy hot potatoes and hot chestnuts, and in the interval they always had a cup of hot Bovril to see them through the second half of the show. They visited the Palace too, or sometimes the Cora at the bottom of Southwick Road which was originally the Wheat Sheaf Hall, and not at all grand and imposing like the other two theatres. Other times

Connie would treat Mary to a cream tea at the tea-rooms in Fawcett Street, or a pleasure trip by ferry round the harbour when they'd eat ice-creams and hold on to their hats.

'But you can't pay for yourself an' me an' all, lass, not rent money. It's too much.' Mary twisted her thin buttocks worriedly, causing the ancient bed to creak and groan. 'An' that money's yours.'

'It won't be like that, listen.' Connie straightened, seating herself on the straight-backed chair again before leaning forward and speaking in a low voice as she said, 'If I get the assistant housekeeper post I'll be earning eleven and six a week to start with, that's over two shillings more than I'm getting now.' And then, as her voice dropped even lower, 'I've a tidy bit put away, lass, going on forty pounds, and there's a small house for rent in Walworth Way off Union Street that'd do us proud. It's a twelve-month lease, and once I've paid the deposit we can sub-let the two rooms upstairs with shared use of the kitchen, and that'll mean we live there virtually rent free. But we'll be answerable to no one, think of it. We can come and go when we like, eat what we want, we'll be *free*. Independent.'

Mary's mouth had fallen open in a wide gape but she seemed quite unaware of this, her eyes like saucers behind her thick spectacles as she stared at Connie's flushed, animated face. The amount of Connie's painstakingly acquired riches had momentarily stunned her, but it was her friend's single-mindedness, rather than the thrift of the plan, which was rendering her dumb. *Connie really meant to go.*

'It's furnished mostly, but we'd need to get a few bits and pieces. Perhaps move a couple of the chairs upstairs if people are going to live in the rooms, and that'll give us more space for what we need in our room downstairs. But we can sort it out when we're in.'

'But . . .'

'What?'

'Just supposin' you don't get the housekeepin' job? What then?'

Connie made no reply for a moment, and then her voice was quiet and level as she said, 'I'm still taking that house in Walworth Way, lass. I'm going, I've made my mind up. I can't stay here now, not even another month or two. Something changed when I didn't get the nursing job, and this is my time for going. And anyway' – her voice became light and buoyant again – 'I shall get the housekeeping post. I'm determined I will. I'm going to push with both hands and keep pushing until I get what I want, and I shan't take no for an answer. That's what Father Hedley said after all.'

It wasn't exactly what the good Father had said but Mary was too dumbfounded to argue.

'I want more than this, lass. This . . . existence. All the years I've been saving have been for this moment, I feel it in me bones. Mrs Wright and the matron, they'll always see me as my mam's daughter. And I'm not ashamed of that,' Connie added swiftly, her colour high, 'I'm not ashamed of *her*, but I won't get a fair chance here. And that's all I want, lass. A fair crack of the whip.'

'Aye.' There was an expression in the violet-blue eyes that said far more than the mere words and made Mary want to cry, and it was that more than anything else that made her say, her voice firm, 'Well, I'll be crackin' me own whip alongside of yours, lass, you know that, an' one thing's for sure, we don't owe this place nothin'. By, we don't. I've seen enough hacky sheets an' stuff to last me a lifetime an' that's the truth. They say pigs are dirty, but there's nowt compared to folk for sheer filth in my book.'

'So you're with me then?'

'Aye, lass. I'm with you. An' mind you flutter them eyelashes when we go to the Grand, for both of us.'

'It's a woman we've got to see, the manager's wife I think.'

'Well, in that case you'd be best puttin' a paper bag over your head in case her husband's got a rovin' eye an' she knows it.'

Mary grinned at her, and then they both giggled at the picture her words conjured up in their minds, but as Mary walked back to her own room some minutes later there was no smile on her face and she was thinking, The Grand, by, the Grand. Trust Connie to start at the top.

The Grand Hotel in Bridge Street was a handsome and commodious establishment, centrally situated within one minute's walk of the railway station, and with an imposing front elevation of five storeys. Visiting dignitaries and stars appearing at the Sunderland Empire would frequently stay at this leading hotel on Wearside, and its restaurant was the place to be seen, so it was with some secret trepidation that Connie, Mary trotting along obediently at her side, approached the arched entrance on the Tuesday evening following her conversation with her friend.

Now the moment was here, with the huge building looming in front of her, she actually felt physically sick at her temerity.

It had been a wild idea, her applying for the assistant housekeeper's job, but if only she could get it it would show them. Quite who – besides the matron and Mrs Wright – it would show Connie didn't question, but there were definitely others there all right. All the veiled slights and covert whisperings by the other officers regarding her family background – which had begun with her first promotion – had gradually, over the years, become like a solid ball in the pit of her stomach, and she knew she was the focus of speculation and not a little jealousy. She would like it not to matter, she would really, *really* like it not to matter, but it did. And she was angry with herself that it did, but there it was. However, it had urged her to keep saving and saving, even when the temptation to go out and buy some grand new clothes or fancy shoes like some of the other girls had been almost overwhelming, and so her means of escape had mounted with the steady input into the old sweet jar hidden in the wardrobe.

Her legs were trembling as she entered the hotel and she could see Mary was totally overawed and speechless, but as the slim, smart hotel porter approached them Connie swallowed hard, put her shoulders back and smiled. 'Good evening.' It was a bit squeaky but she couldn't help that. 'We have an appointment for half past six with Mrs Alridge.'

'Right you are, lass.' The young man, who looked to be about Connie's age, smiled back at them both, before saying, 'Wait a minute an' I'll let her know you're here.'

'Thank you.'

They barely had time to glance around the very comfortable reception area before the young man was back again and gesturing for them to follow him through a green baize door. 'Mrs Alridge said she'll see you separately.' He pointed to a heavy oak door along the small corridor in which they were standing. 'Miss Connie Bell first.'

'That's me.' And then, as the porter nodded before stepping

forwards and knocking on the door, Connie said in a quick aside to Mary, who hadn't uttered a word, 'Now don't worry, lass, don't. You'll be all right.'

'Oh, Connie.' It was a whimper, but a voice had called from inside the room and the young man was opening the door, and all Connie had time for was a reassuring pat on Mary's shoulder before she entered what was clearly an office. It was not an excessively large room, and although the two leather-topped desks at one end and the filing cabinets and other office equipment were a little intimidating, the blazing fire burning in the grate and the square of carpet on which she was standing leant an air of cheer to the official surroundings.

'Miss Bell?' Mrs Alridge had been sitting behind one of the desks and she now rose to her feet, indicating the upholstered straight-backed chair which had been placed in front of it. 'Please be seated. I understand you are applying for the post of assistant housekeeper? Is that correct?'

'Aye, yes, that's correct.'

Mrs Alridge was not at all as she had imagined. The woman in front of her was younger than Connie had expected, probably in her early thirties, and beautifully groomed. The pale-blue dress she was wearing was very plain but cut in such a way that it fitted the manager's wife's slim body perfectly, and Mrs Alridge was very attractive, even beautiful, in a contained, cool way. Her wide grey eyes were now skimming over Connie, taking in every aspect of her, from her hair to her feet, and she seemed to reflect Connie's own thoughts as she said, on a light laugh, 'You are not quite what I expected, Miss Bell.'

'Oh.' Connie's face, which had been smiling politely, now became straight. She wasn't at all sure what the elegant creature in front of her had meant by that.

'It was a compliment.' Mrs Alridge answered her as though she had spoken out loud. 'I thought . . .' And then she flapped her hand at what she had thought as she said again, 'Do sit down.'

'Thank you.' Slowly she sat down on the chair as Mrs Alridge took her own seat, and then there was a moment's pause before the manager's wife said, 'The details you left with my book-keeper yesterday are quite sketchy. Perhaps it would be a good idea if, in your own words, you filled in the empty places. I understand you have no family?'

'No, that's right.' Connie made herself speak quietly and calmly but her heart was thudding. 'My mother died a week or so before I took the job as laundry checker at the workhouse, and . . . and my grandmother and my brother died in a fire the day after I started work, which also destroyed the family home.'

'How dreadful.' Lucy Alridge leant forward slightly but other than that barely perceptible action she didn't betray the interest that had gripped her about this strikingly beautiful girl with the great sad eyes. 'And your father . . . ?'

'My father was already dead,' Connie said evenly.

'I see.' Another pause and then, 'In your own words, go through your work history and present responsibilities, would you, Miss Bell?'

Somewhat stiffly now, as she tried to remember all the details, Connie began to speak, and it was some five minutes – with just the odd interruption here and there from Mrs Alridge – before she finished. They were silent again, and once more Connie waited, but this time the pause was even longer.

'Why have you decided to leave the workhouse at this present time, Miss Bell?'

Connie hesitated, and then she looked into the lovely expressionless face in front of her. She had been a few minutes in this woman's company but that had been sufficient time to understand that the manager's wife was no fool. She could prevaricate now, or tell the bare truth – that she felt it was time to move on to further her career and so on – but Mrs Alridge would know there was more to it than that. 'I wanted to train as a nurse but my application was turned down,' she said flatly.

'On what grounds?'

'I wasn't given an explanation.'

'Did you ask for one?'

Connie raised her head a little higher and now her tone was not at all how one should address a prospective employer as she said, 'No, I didn't, because I had already overheard that I would be unsuccessful and made up my mind to leave.'

Curiouser and curiouser. There was more here than met the eye, and perhaps more tragedy in those incredible violet eyes than even the loss of her family eight years ago could engender? 'I understand, if you should be offered the post, that you have no wish to live in, Miss Bell?' the manager's wife asked quietly.

Connie nodded. 'I'm renting a house in Walworth Way,' she said quickly. 'After all the years of being confined to the workhouse I would like to be independent.'

'Independent.' Lucy Alridge repeated the word. 'Yes, I can appreciate that. It must have been a very constricting lifestyle. I was born in the south of England and my father was the headmaster of a private boarding school. We lived, my mother and father and I, in an apartment at the top of the institution, and my timetable, like that of the students, was a very rigid one. Yes, I can understand your desire for independence, Miss Bell.' And then, with a mercurial change of conversation that Connie was to learn was habitual, the other woman said, 'Are you confident you could undertake the post of assistant housekeeper if it was offered to you? Mrs Pegg, the housekeeper, is often tied up with office administration or liaising with guests; it would be your job to oversee the staff – the waiters, porters, cook and seven kitchen maids, the two tea maids and the housemaids. Do you think you could do that? You have to be in three, four places at once a lot of the time, have eyes in the back of your head, and be arbitrator, dictator, friend or mentor depending on the situation and person involved. It is quite possible you will not be liked if you do your job properly, but you should be respected. Can you handle all that, Miss Bell?'

Connie stared at her. She didn't have the faintest idea if she was up to this but she was prepared to die in the attempt. 'Yes I can,' she said firmly. 'And I am not interested in being popular, Mrs Alridge.'

What an unusual young woman. Lucy Alridge made one of the lightning decisions that her instinct had prompted her to in the past and which had always served her well. 'Then how would it be if we agreed to a trial period of say . . . six weeks? And then if we are both satisfied we can draw up a permanent contract. How would that suit, Miss Bell?'

'You're offering me the job?' Connie's eyebrows shot upwards as her eyes opened wide, and now Lucy Alridge allowed herself a small smile as she said, 'You find that surprising?'

If Connie had answered truthfully she would have said she found it absolutely amazing, but what she did say was, 'I'll endeavour to do my best at all times, Mrs Alridge, I can promise you that.'

'If I thought anything else I would not have offered you the post.' And then her future employer further surprised Connie when she stood up and leant across the desk, her hands flat on the leather surface as she said quietly, 'I like ambition, Miss Bell, especially in a woman. My father considered boys more intelligent than girls, but I have not found that to be the case. It is just that most girls do not get the same opportunities, would you not agree? Now, I understand your friend, who also resides at the workhouse at present, is applying for the post of housemaid. Is that right? If she is successful in her application are you sure you could treat her in the same way as the rest of the staff under your jurisdiction?'

'Definitely, Mrs Alridge. Mary . . . well, Mary relies on me you see, but she would never do anything to make things awkward and she would be happy just to do her job and keep out of any internal politics.'

Internal politics. Yes, this was a very unusual young woman all right, and she would be interested to learn more about her, Lucy Alridge told herself silently. But for now there was the other girl to see and then she had to have a word with Cook about the menu for the function the Bowling Club were having on Thursday, before Harold came back from his club no doubt ravenous for his supper. 'Good.' She straightened, her tone dismissive as she said, 'Shall we say a week on Monday, Miss Bell? Will that give you sufficient time to get your affairs in order? And of course this is subject to your references being satisfactory.'

'A week on Monday will be fine, and thank you. Thank you, Mrs Alridge.' Connie was trying hard not to let her bemusement show, but inside she was singing, shouting, *laughing*! Assistant housekeeper at the Grand! They hadn't thought her good enough to train as a nurse and now she was going to be assistant housekeeper at the Grand. This was going to be a new beginning, *a new life*. If she could do this she could do anything.

And her face reflected her exhilaration as she stepped into the corridor again and said to Mary, whose hands were clenched nervously against her stomach, 'Go on in, she's waiting for you, Mary, and she's nice. She's really nice. Don't worry. We're on our way, lass. We're on our way.'

Chapter Eleven

It was the third Saturday in December, exactly one year to the day that the British Medical Association had voted against providing a service under new National Insurance laws, and only four days after a report had been published stating that 500,000 children in the United Kingdom were ill-fed and diseased. The working classes could have told anyone that that was only the tip of the iceberg.

But for Connie and Mary the year had been a good one. Exhausting and frequently challenging – there were times when Connie fell into bed too tired to even wash or clean her teeth, but it was *her* bed in *her* house and she was happy. Happy as she hadn't been for a long, long time.

She and Mary had taken up residence in number fourteen, Walworth Way, three days before they had started work at the Grand, and for the first four weeks they had had the house to themselves. After fumigating the bedrooms, which had been hopping with fleas, and getting rid of the old mattresses and tattered curtains, Connie had bought new mattresses for the two single iron beds in each room, along with new curtains for the windows and fresh bedspreads for each bed. It had eaten into the resources of the sweet jar but she had bought frugally and was satisfied the outlay had made the two rooms pretty and habitable, especially after she and Mary had added a small table – bought from the pawn shop – and two of the hard-backed chairs from the sitting room to each room to supplement the aged wardrobes.

Connie's advertisement in several shop windows, and for two evenings in the *Sunderland Echo*, for 'rooms for respectable gentlewomen, clean and with use of kitchen' saw the upstairs occupied by the middle of April, one room being let to an elderly widow and her middle-aged working daughter, and the other to two spinster sisters who worked at the Corn Mill off Queer Street. All four women were quiet and pleasant and paid their rent on the dot every Friday evening, and with the additions and alterations Connie had made to the two bedrooms she had had no compunction in asking half as much again to what she had originally planned.

The front room, which had become Connie and Mary's living space, had been a cheerless place when they had first looked at the house. But with the window cleaned and fresh thick red velvet curtains replacing the previous moth-eaten remains, the floorboards scrubbed and polished and a big bright clippie mat placed in front of the deep-set fireplace, it had begun to look better. The four straight-backed chairs out of the way upstairs, Connie and Mary had carried the table into the kitchen. This had given them more room for their new beds, Connie's being situated under the window which overlooked the street, and Mary's on the opposite side of the room against the wall adjoining the kitchen. The only other furniture the room had boasted had been a five-foot wooden saddle complete with mangy old flock-stuffed cushions and a wooden rocking chair with a broken arm.

Connie had re-covered the flock-stuffed cushions with the

same material as the curtains, as well as making two huge cushions – again covered in the curtain material – for the rocking chair, whilst Mary had mended the broken arm on the chair before re-papering the walls in a flower-patterned design that was bright and pretty.

By the time the room had been completely finished at the end of May it had thrilled the two girls every time they entered it, and with the rent for the house more than provided for by the four lodgers upstairs, the sweet jar was soon making a rapid recovery.

Workwise, Connie had struggled at first, not least because the housekeeper, Mrs Pegg, appeared to have taken an immediate dislike to her and had proved uncooperative at best, and at worst downright obstructive. It had been some weeks before one of the other housemaids had revealed on the quiet to Mary that Mrs Pegg had had her daughter lined up for the job as assistant housekeeper, but that Mrs Alridge had had other ideas, and although that hadn't made the difficult situation any easier it had helped Connie to understand the reason for the older woman's animosity.

But if she was held in disfavour by Mrs Pegg, Mrs Alridge was one hundred per cent behind her, and following several incidents when this was made crystal clear by the manager's wife, the housekeeper's attitude was moderated and an uneasy peace ensued. Connie made sure the housekeeper couldn't find fault with her work, often putting in twenty or so hours of unpaid overtime a week, which left her little time to indulge her love of reading, or anything else for that matter. But she didn't care. She was happy, happy and fulfilled, and as time went on and Mary told her that the staff – who had been somewhat chary at first – now held her in high regard, a

179

heightened sense of self-worth and contentment made the heavy responsibility and strenuous days enjoyable.

Now it was just five days before Christmas and the hotel had never been busier, most of the fifty rooms occupied and the restaurant full each night, both with guests and Sunderland inhabitants who were enjoying festive outings. And, wouldn't you know it, as she'd said herself to Mary the night before, half the staff were down with influenza, which necessitated the other half running round like chickens with their heads cut off.

By rights she and Mary should both have had this Saturday off, but they had worked all day before popping home for their tea – they could have eaten all their meals at the hotel but preferred the cosiness of Walworth Way, as well as the break from the frantic pace – and now the two girls were slipping and sliding along High Street West, which was frozen solid, replete after toasted muffins oozing with butter and jam.

It had been snowing heavily for days, and although the main roads were being kept clear the icy conditions made walking treacherous, but Connie and Mary giggled as they held on to each other, first one, then the other, nearly falling headlong on the glassy pavements.

'Oh, Mary . . .' Connie suddenly stopped dead, gazing up into the black velvet sky from which the first desultory snowflakes of the evening were beginning to whirl and dance. 'I can't believe how I feel right at this moment. I feel . . . I feel like a bairn on Christmas morning, like the whole world is mine and nothing can go wrong. I'd forgotten you can feel like this.'

'Aye, lass, we both had a short childhood.' And then, on a less sober note, 'But as for nothin' goin' wrong! By, that's temptin' fate, that is, with the bedlam that's goin' to hit us when we walk through the door. Old Ma Pegg was all for me an' Flo makin' the beds with a broom stuck up our backsides so's we could sweep up as we went this mornin', I'm not funnin'.'

They were giggling unrestrainedly again now, their breath forming white clouds in the icy air, but they were both to remember the conversation before the night was out and wonder what quirk of fate had been at work.

Lucy Alridge practically jumped on Connie as the two girls walked into the hotel a minute or two later, drawing her to one side as she whispered urgently, 'I'm so glad you're back, it's chaos, Connie, absolute chaos. Poor Harold is beside himself.'

Any formality between the two women had long since fallen by the wayside; Lucy Alridge held Connie in high regard, and more than that, as a close friend, and it was in that capacity that she addressed her now saying, 'Mrs Pegg has virtually collapsed and another of the waiters is ill. This dreadful flu just won't let up, Connie. Would you, *could* you, wait on tables tonight? We've already got two of the housemaids coming in for two of the kitchen maids who are ill as you know, because Cook can't cope. I wouldn't *dream* of asking you normally—'

'It's all right.' Connie put her hand on Lucy's arm as she said soothingly, 'Of course I'll help out, that's what I've come back for, isn't it.'

'You're an angel. And, Connie' – Lucy now leant closer and whispered softly – 'your efforts over the last months have not gone unnoticed by Harold and your Christmas box will reflect this, but keep it to yourself, will you?' By this Connie rightly assumed Mrs Pegg was not going to be treated as generously and she nodded quickly. Since her daughter had been refused the position of assistant housekeeper Mrs Pegg had become something of a thorn in Lucy's side, often declining to work any overtime and keeping rigidly to her allotted hours, as well as causing the odd spot of mischief now and again. It was unfortunate, because the woman knew her job inside out and was a very good housekeeper, but it did make Connie wonder now if Mrs Pegg's 'collapse' was totally genuine. It would be just like the housekeeper to flee a sinking ship and then stand back and criticise everyone else's efforts.

Connie was still mulling the matter over when she walked into the restaurant a few minutes later. She was wearing one of the housemaids' aprons, hastily acquired from the linen cupboard, over the plain blue dress that was her normal garb. Due to their managerial positions she and Mrs Pegg were not required to wear the frilled apron and cap which was the additional uniform for the rest of the female staff.

The restaurant looked to be running on oiled wheels as usual. Only the staff knew of the feverish activity in the kitchen and the fact that they were two waiters short. There was an air of subdued gaiety among the diners sitting under the Christmas garlands strung across the ceiling, and for a moment, as Connie stared at the scene, it was impressed upon her how profoundly life had changed in the last year and how much she had to be thankful for. Then she was drawn into the thick of it and there was no time for further reflections.

At half past eight, having been on her feet for two and a half hectic hours, Connie had a swift cup of tea in the kitchen and washed her face and hands in the large stone-floored scullery in preparation for the second half of the evening which would continue until well after eleven o'clock. Mary was up to her elbows in suds and conversation with one of the kitchen maids, and after quickly checking that her friend would wait for her so they could walk home together, Connie made her way back into the buzzing restaurant.

What drew her eyes across all the other tables to focus on one at the far end of the room Connie didn't know – it could only have been a sixth sense or some other inexplicable phenomenon – but there they were, the Stewart family. There was no mistaking them. She could only see their top halves, they were all seated, but the elegantly dressed figure of Edith Stewart was holding court, along with the five brothers who had come to the cottage that night and what looked to be four younger women, probably the brothers' wives or sweethearts.

The emotion attacked her first in the chest, causing her heart to thud so hard it actually hurt, and then it flowed up into her throat, causing her face to bleach and her ears to ring. Why hadn't she considered that this might happen? They were a wealthy family, the sort who considered it providential to be seen at all the right places, she should have *known* their paths might cross again one day. But no, they wouldn't have, would they, if she hadn't been helping out in the restaurant. Oh, what was she going to do?

And then, as if in answer to the unspoken cry, one of the heads turned. Connie recognised the young man immediately – it was the youngest son, the one who had held her the night they had attacked Jacob and then later rescued her out of the snow drift – and across the room and over the space of the intervening years their eyes met, the eyes of the smartly dressed, wealthy young man and those of the waitress.

During the time it took for her to gather her wits and move

she watched Dan Stewart's mouth fall open slightly, his eyes narrowing in disbelief, and then she had whirled round, retracing her steps out of the restaurant doors and coming to a halt outside where she took great gulps of air to quell the feeling of faintness.

He had recognised her. She leant against the lobby wall, her head pounding. But then she was so like her mother so perhaps that wasn't surprising? And he had hardly altered at all. A bit heavier perhaps, but then he was older. Thirteen years older. *Thirteen years*.

When she heard the doors to the restaurant open a second or two later she knew, without looking up, that he would be standing there. And when she did raise her head he was a yard away and staring at her, and then she realised he *had* changed. The boy was gone and it was the man who was fixing her with his gaze. And the man was tall and broad and – she felt a stab of betrayal at the thought – very handsome.

'You're . . .'

'Connie Bell.' Her head was well up now, her chin straining, and the stance was aggressive.

Dan Stewart acknowledged this and understood the reason for it, but such was his bemusement that for the moment he was at a loss as to how to deal with the situation. This was the person who had haunted his dreams for years. As a tiny elfin child she had plagued his night hours with remorse for what his family had done to hers, and even as recently as a year ago she had come to point an accusing finger in his sleep. He had suffered because of this young woman, this stunningly beautiful young woman who was so like her mother. He had suffered the torments of the damned since John had told them that the family had been killed in a fire at the cottage.

'I heard . . . There was a fire?' He had to pull himself together, she would think he was simple. 'I thought there had been a fire at the house in the wood?' he managed fairly succinctly.

'There was.' It was pithy.

'We thought you had all died, your mother and your family?'

'And of course you were devastated.' The bitterness was tangible, and now his eyes narrowed and his voice was terse when he said, 'Now that's not fair, I—'

'*Fair?!*' Her voice cut him off and as she took a step towards him, her eyes flashing blue fire, the thought came from nowhere – totally inappropriate in the circumstances, he conceded in the next instant – that this young woman was quite magnificent. She knocked all the other women of his acquaintance, including those his mother paraded before him at regular intervals under the excuse of dinner parties and the like, into a cocked hat.

'You ruined our family that night you and your brothers came for Jacob,' Connie hissed furiously, her body bent slightly forward in her rage. 'My mother had to—' She stopped, choking on the words. 'And then the fire took my granny and my brother. I hate you, I hate you all, do you hear?'

And then she saw the stricken look in his eyes and stopped speaking, and there was a long moment of silence before Dan said, 'I was fourteen years old at the time and I had no idea what I was getting involved in. That doesn't excuse what we did, I know that, but there hasn't been a day gone by since that I haven't regretted it.' There was a longer pause. 'I've wanted to say I'm sorry for years, Miss Bell. Please believe me.'

It was the 'Miss Bell', that and the way the broad shoulders were hunched, that enabled Connie to take hold of herself and check further hot words. She nodded tightly, drawing herself up straight. She vaguely remembered, that night he had been holding her back from the fray, that he had been shouting for them to stop hurting Jacob. And it had been this Stewart who had lifted her out of the snow and gone for the doctor for her mam. She supposed she owed her life to this man. There was a feeling inside her that made her want to press her hand to her chest bone to ease its ache. The feeling was filling her, confusing her with the myriad emotions contained in it, and it was to check what she perceived as weakness that she said, her voice flat now, 'You had better get back before they come looking for you. You might be sorry but I doubt if any of the others are.'

'Art is,' said Dan quickly. 'He's always felt bad about that night.'

'As well he might.'

'Aye, yes.' There was an awkward silence before Dan said, 'You . . . you work here then?' as he glanced at the apron.

'I'm the assistant housekeeper.' It was very quick and very sharp. 'I'm only helping out waitressing because a number of the staff are off with flu.'

'Yes, of course. I didn't think . . .' His voice trailed away. 'How long have you worked here?' he asked quietly after a full ten seconds had ticked by without either of them saying a word to relieve the tense atmosphere.

'Nearly a year.'

He made a small movement with his head as he said, 'You've a very responsible job for such a young lass. Not that I don't think you're capable of it,' he added hastily, before she could say anything, 'it's just that most girls are more interested in enjoying themselves, having fun, than . . .' He was making a right pig's ear of this, by, he was. Her face would have told him that if nothing else.

'I had to grow up quickly.' It was said without any vestige of self-pity. 'I was employed in the laundry at the workhouse before this for eight years.'

'Eight years?' He whistled softly. 'You couldn't have been more than a child.'

Connie shrugged slender shoulders. She had seen the house where he had been brought up and it was a world apart from how she had lived. No doubt he had been spoilt and cossetted from when he was a babby, mollycoddled and overindulged. Her mother had said that Jacob's in-laws came from ordinary working stock originally, but the Stewart children would have been taken everywhere by horse and carriage when they were bairns for sure, escorted by their mother or maybe a nursery maid.

Connie had seen such children dressed in their bonny little white suits and shining shoes, who, on dismounting from the carriage, would have been hurried past ragged, snotty-nosed urchins huddled on the pavement. The grown-ups would invariably ignore the ragamuffins especially if they were begging, putting a scented linen handkerchief to their noses as though to protect themselves from something contagious. But sometimes their precious charges would peer at the dirty gamins in much the same way they would stare at an oddity on view at the fair, or some strange apparition that wasn't quite human, their plump, well-fed faces displaying curiosity oftentimes flavoured with childish distaste. How could she explain to someone like Dan Stewart that at twelve years of age she had been far from being a child?

'Miss Bell—'

'Look, Mr Stewart, I've work to do and your family will be waiting for you.'

Again Connie cut him short, but in the same instant the doors to the restaurant opened and John Stewart was walking towards them, saying, 'There you are, man. What do you think you're playing at? She's going mad in there, you know how she is. What's the—' And then his voice was strangled in his throat and he started so visibly he seemed to give a little jump into the air before freezing, his mouth falling into a wider gape than Dan's had.

'It's all right, I'm not a ghost.' Connie's voice was full of icy disdain. John Stewart's face had gone quite white and for a moment he had looked terrified. 'Your brother was just about to join you, Mr Stewart.'

'What the hell . . .' And then, as he stared at her, he relaxed, swearing softly but forcefully which brought a terse 'John, *please*' from his brother which John totally ignored. 'You're the daughter. I see it now! You are the daughter, aren't you. How did you get—' He stopped abruptly, swearing again as he swayed and steadied himself with a hand on the wall.

'Cut it out, John, I'm warning you.' Dan's voice was cold but there was hot colour in his face as he turned to Connie and said, 'I'm sorry, Miss Bell.'

'Miss Bell.' It was said slowly, and with a relish that made Connie feel sick. 'Well, well, well.' The black eyes were moving all over her now, their light seeming to strip the clothes from her body and penetrate right through to her skin. 'You've grown into a beautiful woman, that's for sure. Like mother, like daughter, eh?'

'You leave my mother out of this.' Connie's voice was steely, and strangely – considering how she was feeling inside – without a tremor. If the younger brother had changed then so had the eldest, but with John Stewart it looked to be for the worst. The face she remembered as good-looking was now of a mottled complexion, the nose red and faintly bulbous indicating a more than average penchant for drink. And he had gained weight, lots of weight, in fact he was flabby. Flabby and unattractive. Her nostrils flared with distaste. 'You're not fit to speak of her.'

'Ah ha.' The hard beady eyes were gleaming. It was for all the world as though the slender young woman glaring at him had just paid him a compliment. 'Fiery little piece, aren't you, but a bit of spirit can make life interesting. What say you, Dan, eh?'

'I say you've already had enough to drink the night,' said Dan tersely, his face flaming. 'Why you had to start at home before you even got here I don't know. Come away out of it before you make a bigger fool of yourself than you have already.'

'What?' John peered at his sibling, his head on one side. 'Oh, so that's the way of it, Dan, lad? By, it'd take more than you've got to handle this one.'

'I suggest you go back to the restaurant *now*, otherwise I shall be forced to call for assistance and have you forcibly removed from the hotel for causing a disturbance. *Now*, Mr Stewart.'

'Eh?' John's head swung back to Connie who was standing as straight as a ram-rod and eyeing him with unconcealed contempt. For a moment it looked as though he was going to turn nasty, his face flushing turkey-red and his mouth curling into a sneer, then he took a visible breath before making an exaggerated bow that almost had him stumbling drunkenly forward. 'It's been a pleasure to renew your acquaintance, Ma'am. A very real pleasure,' he drawled slowly before giving a wide smile. 'Is that better?'

'I'm sorry.' Dan gave Connie one last desperate look before he hustled his now unresisting brother back into the restaurant, but even after the doors had closed behind them Connie didn't move for some moments.

She found she was taking deep draughts of air as though she had been running or partaking of some other strenuous exercise which had pushed her to the limit, and she was silently talking to herself, warning herself to do nothing hasty, to be calm, to *think*. Nothing had changed, not really. She had known they were here, in Sunderland, hadn't she? Of course she had. And, now she was free of the rigid confines of the workhouse, it wasn't unlikely that some day she would have run into one or other of the Stewarts. It was just unfortunate that it had been all of them, in one fell swoop like that, and especially – *especially* – that hateful beast of a man, John Stewart.

She continued to breathe in and out for some seconds more until her racing heartbeat was under control, and then, as the doors to the restaurant opened to emit a laughing party of guests – one or two of whom stared at her a little curiously as they passed – she forced herself away from the wall against which she was leaning. She hadn't let herself or her mother down, that was the important thing. She had conducted herself with sobriety. She hadn't given in to the desire to strike John Stewart; she had behaved like a well-bred young lady. So why, knowing that, did she wish she had torn into him, kicking, biting, clawing at his face with her nails? Because she did.

She did. The way he had looked at her . . . It had made her flesh creep.

She adjusted the collar of her dress and smoothed down her hair, willing her fingers not to tremble, before walking swiftly in a semi-circle towards the other entrance to the kitchen. She really couldn't go back into the restaurant, not tonight. She just didn't trust herself not to empty a bowl of soup over John Stewart's head.

A cup of tea. That's what she needed, a cup of tea to steady her nerves and deal with the quivering in her stomach.

In the organised bedlam that was the kitchen no one noticed her entrance at first. She walked across and sat on a stool to the side of one of the ovens, and it was Mrs Merry, the cook, who glanced her way, caught, no doubt, by the rarity of a stationary human being in the midst of the hullabaloo. And then, at Mrs Merry's exclamation of concern, several others turned to look at her, and within moments she was surrounded by friendly faces expressing sympathy.

'Take a breather for a minute, lass, that's the ticket.'

'Eee, another down with this flu. Can't say I'm surprised.'

'White as a sheet, she is. She should never have come back the night, Mary. You should've told her.'

'Death warmed up. You can't fight this flu, that's the thing.'

The comments swarmed about her but Connie, although comforted by the overt sympathy, found it easier to say nothing, accepting the hot drink that was placed in her hands some moments later simply with a nod of thanks.

'Connie?' Once the pandemonium was back in full swing Mary sidled to her side, speaking in a whisper as she said, 'What's up, lass? It isn't the flu, is it. You had a gliff or somethin'?'

'Aye.' Connie had to stop herself slumping but she wasn't going to let John Stewart win. 'You could say that, Mary. It's him, John Stewart, the one I told you about. The one who hurt Jacob. He's eating here, with his mam and the rest of the tribe.'

'Eee, no, lass.' Mary's head dropped to the side and she screwed up her eyes behind the spectacles before saying, 'But he didn't see you? He didn't recognise you, did he?'

'Aye, he did.' It was bitter. 'I look like my mam you see. I look just like her, and . . . and he liked me mam in a funny sort of way. You know.'

'Oh, lass.'

Mary went to put her arms round her but Connie stopped her with a lift of her hand as she murmured, 'No, don't, lass. It's best they think I've got the flu, least said soonest mended. I'm going to go home, I don't want to run into him again. I'm not sure if I'll be able to control myself twice in one night. I'll . . . I'll see you later. All right?'

'Aye, all right. I'll get away as soon as I can. But are you sure you feel up to going home by yourself?'

Connie straightened, and her voice was soft but firm and brooked no argument when she said, 'I'm perfectly all right, Mary. It'd take more than scum like him to worry me, but this is a good job and I don't want to spoil it by going for him, he's not worth it. And he might try to provoke me to do just that. I don't trust him. There's something, well, sinister about him. It sounds far-fetched but there it is. I remember the way he looked at my mam all those years ago, it's sort of stayed in my mind somewhere, but I didn't realise what it meant until he looked at me in the same way tonight. He's . . . dirty, mucky.'

'An' the others?'

Connie shrugged, lowering her head. 'There was only one other I met tonight, the youngest one.'

'The one that pulled you out of the snow?'

Connie didn't look up as she nodded, saying, 'Aye, him. He's . . . Oh, I don't know. He's not like his brother at any rate.'

'Perhaps he hides it better than t'other 'un?'

'No, he's—' Connie raised her head, but stopped abruptly, her eyes leaving Mary's and travelling over the kitchen before she said, 'You'd better get back to the sink, lass, and I'll see you later. Let Wilf walk you home, you know he'd jump at the chance.'

Wilf was the young porter who had conducted them to the office on their first visit, and he had made no secret of his pursuit of Mary from almost the first day of their arrival. The fact that Mary had rebuffed him at every turn and laid into him with her tongue nearly as often hadn't seemed to concern him in the least, and there had been times lately – just the odd one or two – when Connie had suspected that her friend wasn't as averse to his attentions as she maintained. His wry, wicked sense of humour and cheerful demeanour was very entertaining and he made Mary laugh. That, Connie considered, was a very good sign.

'Wilf?' The distraction worked and now Mary forgot all talk of John Stewart's brother. 'Not likely. I might be daft but I'm not that daft, lass.'

But she blushed scarlet and Connie determined to have a word with Wilf on her way out and let him know Mary was going to walk home alone. If the terrible attack by her uncle wasn't going to ruin Mary's chances of being a wife and a mother it would need patience and perseverance, and Wilf had already displayed those attributes in abundance. Furthermore, Connie knew from little remarks that several of the staff had let slip that he was really smitten with her friend. The two of them seemed to strike sparks off each other, both being quick-witted and amusing, but on Wilf's side Connie had detected a certain covert tenderness that underlined the young porter's dealings with Mary.

'You could do worse, a lot worse, lass.' Connie got to her feet as she spoke. She just wanted to get home now, home to the little oasis she had created where she was her own mistress and answerable to no one. But Walworth Way was just a stepping stone. She hadn't mentioned it to Mary yet, she knew her friend found change difficult and only accepted it when it was thrust upon her, but she had plans. Plans to work for herself in some way, a little front-room shop maybe, or something similar. That was what she wanted. And her own home, bought and paid for – yes, that too. Why not? she asked herself fiercely. She could do it. And scum like John Stewart would be forced to acknowledge that she couldn't be pushed around like her mother had been. Her poor mam hadn't stood a chance against the likes of him, but her daughter had had opportunities her mam's generation hadn't, and, by all that was holy, she'd make them work for her. And if ever the chance came to rub John Stewart's nose in it she'd take it. By, she would. And glory in it.

Chapter Twelve

'You know we've got to go, now then, so give over, Art. Put up with it for the bairns if nothing else.'

'The bairns? They'd as soon stay here and *you* know *that*.'

'No, no I don't. They like playing with their cousins, and bairns always enjoy family get-togethers.'

'Huh. There's families and families, lass.'

It was Christmas Day morning, and all over Sunderland folk were celebrating. In the tenement slums of the East End there were a good few children who had woken up to a stocking filled with one present – if they were lucky; the rest of the brown paper parcels consisting of turnips or cabbages and the like would end up in the pot before the day was out. When empty flour sacks on flea-infested mattresses were bedding for whole families, even the bread knife had been pawned, and men were doing ten-hour shifts unloading iron-ore boats, their trousers wet to the thighs and their flesh raw for less than four shillings a shift, Christmas Day was simply a day on which there was no possibility of work.

In Bishopwearmouth too, there were houses where bread and dripping was the Christmas dinner, although the man of the house could be found still sleeping off the carousing of the night before, having arrived home mortallious in the early hours, and yet others where hard-working, decent parents had struggled to make something of the festive season on starvation rations.

Art Stewart's wife, Gladys, had come from the latter, and the thought of her beginnings was with her when she said to her husband, her voice sharp now, 'Stop your griping, Art. You don't know you're born half the time. If the worst you've got to put up with today is your mam and the rest of them you won't do too bad. There's plenty who'd give their eye teeth to be sitting down to the sort of meal you'll enjoy come one o'clock.'

'Aye, aye, I know, lass. Don't take on. Come here, come on, we're not going to fall out today of all days.' Art's voice was deflated and as he took his wife in his arms she rested against him for a moment, her head falling on his chest.

She knew she was lucky to have a man like Art and certainly, if his mother had had her way, they wouldn't have been wed. Edith had already had a lass lined up for her third eldest child when he had met her, Gladys, at the Avenue Theatre. She and two of her friends had gone to see a staging of *Richelieu*, one of her friends having been given free tickets by her uncle who was the stage manager.

There had been ructions when Art had first taken her home, but he'd stood his ground, even when it had rocked under his mother's fury, and once they had been wed Edith had made a show of accepting her into the fold. But it was only a show. Art's mother never missed a chance to belittle her if she could, and Gladys knew it was that, more than anything else, that got under her husband's skin. But family was family, and Edith was his mother, and they couldn't not go on Christmas Day. They'd never hear the end of it.

Nevertheless, Gladys's thoughts made her voice soft as she raised her head and looked into her husband's big, good-looking face, and as she touched his cheek with the palm of her hand she said quietly, 'It'll only be for a few hours, love, and Dan will be glad you're there.'

'Aye.' Art rubbed his chin thoughtfully. 'That's true enough. I don't know how Dan puts up with it day in, day out. But he was never one for causing a scene, Dan. Anything for an easy life.'

'Maybe.' Gladys inclined her head but her voice was at variance with the action when she continued, 'He's a gentle soul, your Dan, and he thinks a bit of Kitty as well as feeling responsible for your mam now the twins are married, but still waters run deep, Art. There's times . . . well, when I think he doesn't like your mam much.'

'That makes two of us.'

'Oh, Art.'

'I'm not pretending, lass, not with you. You know what I think, and I tell you there are times when I feel sick to me stomach that I haven't had the guts to make a break with the whole lot of 'em – 'cept our Dan of course. The way John struts around the warehouses at times . . . But there it is. The wage packet can't be ignored, eh?'

The last was bitter and Gladys's voice was even softer when she said, 'It's not that and you know it. Your da would have wanted you to stay in the family business, it would have broken his heart if you'd split from the boys and your mam, now wouldn't it? And you and Dan are a good influence in there. I reckon John would have gone down the line before now with some of the shady deals he'd have got involved in if you and Dan hadn't put your foot down.'

'Perhaps it'd have taught him a lesson.'

'No, not John.' Gladys could have said much more but this was not a day for honesty, more for glossing over Art's brother's strange dark nature, and now, as two small children, a boy and a girl, came hurtling into the room, the boy carrying a brightly painted toy steam engine and the girl a big flaxen-haired doll, she said brightly, 'Come on you two, go and get your coats and hats ready to go round your granny's.' And to the heated chorus of protest which immediately ensued – and which their father made no effort to check – Gladys said firmly, but without any real conviction, 'That's enough of that, you'll enjoy it when you get there.'

Kitty had almost finished the last elaborate table setting in the tastefully decorated dining room when Dan found her just before eleven that morning, and she squealed before covering her mouth with her hand as he tweaked her playfully in the ribs.

'Eee, you! You're not too old to have your backside smacked, me lad,' she warned him, her eyes bright, and then, as her gaze fell on to the small, gaily wrapped package he was holding out to her, 'What's this? You've already given me me present.'

'Chocolates and stockings?' He dismissed the earlier present with a scornful wave of his hand. 'That wasn't your present, not really, but I wanted to give you this . . . privately.'

He had intended his tone to sound airy, but when Kitty looked into his eyes and said, 'Why, lad?' he didn't know how to express himself. How could he say that he had wanted this moment to be special for her, that he knew of everything she had to put up with from his mother and that he often felt for her, especially because he knew she stayed to make life easier for him, and even for the rest of them although they were married and not so close to his mother's authority. And he loved this big plump woman in front of him, he loved her in a way he'd never done his natural mother. He should have been Kitty's child, that was the way he felt.

Kitty watched his Adam's apple move up and down as he swallowed and searched for words, but whatever she read in his face seemed to satisfy her because she made a little movement with her head as she said, 'Oh, lad, lad. Thank you,' and she took the present from him, opening it carefully.

The little ruby and diamond pin was exquisite and worked in fine gold, and at her gasp of delight he removed it from the box and pinned it, very tenderly, on the lapel of her black alpaca dress.

'Eeee, no, I can't wear it there. She'll ask me where I got it,' Kitty protested tremblingly. Edith had always been jealous and resentful of the regard in which Dan held her and she didn't want a scene on Christmas Day.

'And you tell her.' His voice was firm and cold as he spoke of his mother, but that wasn't unusual. 'I bought it for you to wear, Kitty, not to hide away; I just wanted to give it to you when we were by ourselves, that's all. I'm not ashamed of giving it to you.'

'An' I'm not ashamed of wearin' it, don't think that, lad,' she said softly, her eyes moist. 'It's just that she gets a bit . . . upset like, at times.'

His mother's tyrannical rages and rapacious quest to control and manipulate every area of all of their lives couldn't be termed 'getting upset', Dan thought wryly, but looking into Kitty's troubled face he made himself smile. 'Don't worry,' he said softly, 'I've thought of everything, you know your lad.' It was said to make her laugh, and when she did, he added, 'I've bought her a pendant, all right? I'll give it to her in a minute.'

'Oh, thank you, lad, thank you.' Kitty patted his arm gently, and such was the strangeness of the atmosphere they had lived in for so long, neither of them considered it odd that Kitty should be so grateful Dan had bought his mother a gift too.

It was two o'clock. The first course of dressed crab had been served and eaten, and John had just carved the enormous turkey and they were all helping themselves to vegetables from the heaped dishes in the centre of the table. There were seventeen present in all, although the youngest three children were in high-chairs. Edith, seated at the head of the table, was smiling and almost gay for once, Dan's heavy gold pendant resting against the silk of her grey frock. Next to her sat John and his wife, Ann, and their only child, Sidney, who was fifteen years of age and like his mother in appearance. They were making conversation with Art and Gladys and their two children, Catherine who was ten and David who was two years younger, the youngsters comparing presents and the adults laughingly bemoaning the state of their bank balances.

The twins and their wives were either side of Dan, and their children, girls of six and two for Gilbert and Doreen, and twin girls of three for Matthew and Ruth, were clearly overexcited and on the verge of becoming tearful.

It looked to be a jolly family gathering, the festive table, laden with food and bottles of wine, adding to the air of prosperity and overall lush ambience, and Edith felt a deep satisfaction as she surveyed her possessions – her children and grandchildren being the most rewarding. She was even sufficiently mellowed to include Gladys in the thought today, although normally the mere sight of the big, strapping woman who looked what she was – a nice, ordinary, working-class northern lass – was enough to set her teeth on edge.

She would make sure Dan didn't make the same mistake Art had at any rate. Dan would marry well, very well, she was determined of that. She touched the pendant at her throat, a small smile playing about her mouth as she glanced down the table at her youngest son, her face serene and content.

John caught the gesture – it was the same one his mother had made several times during the two hours they had been with her – and his jaw set tightly. You would have thought no one had ever given her anything before, the way she had rammed that damned bauble down all their throats the minute they'd got in the door. There were the twins, they'd given her the silver cutlery set which must have cost a pretty penny, and Art and Gladys had stoked up for the monogrammed leather luggage, nice bit of leather too. And his gold and mother-of-pearl jewellery box would have cost more than all the rest put together. And what does she bill and coo over? A tuppenny-ha'p'orth of nowt. Damn her.

But he knew something that would put Dan in his place, aye, and he wouldn't be the blue-eyed boy then, would he. A few words from him and he'd wipe that look off his mother's face all right. The thought warmed him, relaxing his jaw. He'd been going to tip her the wink on the quiet but maybe this was better with them all here; he could pass it off as a bit of a joke if he played his cards right. But his mam wouldn't laugh. Not his mam.

He enjoyed his dinner after that, and once Kitty had served

the plum pudding with a rich brandy sauce and they had all got their spoons dug in, he began to hum a popular hit of the year, 'Hello! Hello! Who's your lady friend?' in-between mouthfuls.

'What's the matter with you?' Ann cast him a surprised glance after a moment or two, at the same time as Edith, on his right, her tone irritable, said, 'John, for goodness sake, what are you humming?'

'Dan knows. Eh, man? 'Tain't that right?' He slurred his words slightly as he spoke, which wasn't altogether acting; he'd drunk a good few glasses of wine during the meal, and his mother only bought the best.

'What?' Dan, at the other end of the table, had been occupied with his youngest niece who had been endeavouring to stick a stray pea up her nose and hadn't heard what had been said.

'"Hello! Hello! Who's your lady friend, who's the little girly by your side?"' And at Dan's blank look, 'Sorry, man. Have I spoke out of turn?'

'I don't know, have you?' Dan asked coolly.

Oh, so that was the tack he was going to take? Well, he'd fix him right enough. John forced a hick of a laugh, but in spite of his flushed face there were three people in the room who knew he was not as intoxicated as he'd like them all to believe. Dan was one of them, John's wife, Ann, was another, and Art had been set up too often in the past when they were children by this particular brother not to know when John was following some hidden agenda of his own.

'Oh, I get it.' John turned his eyes from Dan to his mother before shrugging his shoulders. 'Enough said, sorry I spoke.'

'What's all this about?' Edith cast a swift look at Dan's

tight, closed face before nudging John sharply. 'John? I'm talking to you. What's going on?'

'Not for me to say. I just thought he'd have told you, that's all.'

'Told me?' And then, as Edith put two and two together, 'It's a girl, is that it? That *is* it. Who is she and how long has this been going on?'

'Now don't take on, Mam. He's not a bairn—'

'Cut the hypocrisy, John. You've said what you intended to say; at least be man enough to come out into the open.'

Dan's voice silenced even the chatter of the children. Not one of them had ever heard Dan speak in this way, or seen his face so hard and angry. This was not the easy-going, affable, quiet soul they all knew and – apart from John – liked and loved. This was someone quite different.

'Wha . . . what do you mean? Nowt wrong in having a bit of fun is there? You should've said something if you wanted it kept quiet.'

Dan ignored John's blustering after one cutting glance at his brother and spoke directly to Edith as he said, 'John was trying to tell you, in his own inimitable way, that he saw me talking to a girl a few evenings ago. And not just any lass either, this one is known to you – or at least her name is.'

'Her name?'

'She is the daughter of Sadie Bell.'

'*What?*'

Edith's voice was not loud but the quality of the one word was enough to cause the twins' wives to start gathering up the children and ushering them out towards the drawing room. It was only Sidney, John's boy, who remained at the table with the adults, and his thin face was not the face of a youngster as he moved closer to his mother, putting a hand on her arm.

Ann, for her part, was half turned in her seat and staring at her husband with something approaching hatred on her face, and she spoke next, saying, 'Whatever this is about you had it all planned, didn't you, for maximum effect. How could you? How could you on Christmas Day, John, with the bairns and everything?'

'Shut up you.'

It was quiet and savage, and as their eyes caught and held for a moment the look that passed between them was chilling. Did they know what he was like, the rest of them? Did they have any idea what he was *really* like? The bitter feeling of aloneness, which had begun the day she married John Stewart and was only eased by her son's love and companionship, flooded Ann now. How many times had she sat with them all like this? she asked herself silently. Joining in the conversation, smiling, acting a part, the part of the contented, quiet wife? Hundreds, thousands probably by now. In the early days of her marriage she had been in the habit of watching Mavis and Jacob, and then Art and Gladys when they had wed, and she'd used to wonder if those women were suffering the torments of the damned too. But they hadn't been, of course they hadn't been. Not like her anyway.

She had thought she'd landed in hell on her wedding night.

Nothing, *nothing* her mother had told her on her wedding day morning or the odd conversation she'd overheard between her married sisters had prepared her for what he had demanded and what he had done. She had known men laid great store by this thing that happened in the intimacy of marriage, and she had been nervous and not a little anxious to please him that first night. She was plain, she knew that, and until John had come courting she had never had a lad look the side she was on, and so when John Stewart – and him handsome and quite a catch – had made it clear he was interested she had been in seventh heaven.

She had been as innocent as they come on her wedding night and he had treated her worse than a hard-bitten whore. It had been two hours before she had managed to crawl, quite literally, into the dressing room attached to the bedroom of the suite at the hotel in Seaham where they were residing for their week's honeymoon, and her legs had gone into spasms for an hour or more.

The next morning, when the state of her distress had been such that she had threatened to walk home to her mother if he didn't call a carriage, he had blamed his bestiality on the wine and brandy he had consumed at dinner, and had used all his persuasive powers to prevent her leaving. When that hadn't worked he had made the visit to her parents' home himself, promising to bring her mother back with him, but instead he had returned with a letter.

Exactly what had passed between her mother and John she had never found out, but the letter had been short and to the point. Her parents would not be made a laughing stock by having their daughter – who should have been married years before – returning after one night of marriage, it had stated coldly. She would grow accustomed to the state of marriage and all it entailed, all women did, and she would learn how to please her husband. There was no question of anything else. Her parents would forget this had ever happened and it would not be mentioned again. She was a married woman now and her husband's responsibility. They were saddened – deeply saddened – by her lack of delicacy and sense of wifely duty, but they trusted that her husband would forgive her and, therefore, so must they.

She had wanted to die. But she hadn't died, and later, after endless months of mental and physical torture, she had begun to change and find that the shy, gentle creature who had married John Stewart was gone for ever. And from that point she had begun to fight back.

'Where did you meet this . . . this whore's brat?'

Edith's voice intruded into Ann's thoughts and brought her back from her dark memories to the scene in front of her, and now she saw Dan's face was white except for two slashes of red colour across his cheekbones.

And then they all jumped visibly as Dan shot up, sending his chair shooting backwards to clatter against the ornate, gold-leafed chiffonnier before falling on its side.

'Any more talk like that and I am leaving.'

Dan saw his mother's face contract and her eyes narrow, and for a moment she appeared stupefied, but then her voice came low and icy, saying, 'You dare to talk to me like this? Your own mother?'

'This is all getting out of hand, I'm sure there's a simple explanation if we all act sensibly and keep our heads.' Art, as peacemaker, threw his hands wide, and appealed to Gilbert and Matthew as he said, 'Eh, lads? Perhaps a cup of coffee or a glass of port?'

'All the coffee and port in the world won't make any difference to the facts, Art.' Dan continued to stand over the festive debris of the table and his voice was cool, very cool, as he said quietly, 'I ran into Connie Bell that evening we went to the Grand and I talked to her. That is the extent of my crime.'

'But I thought—'

'Aye, so did I.' Dan nodded at what Art had begun to say. 'I thought they'd all gone but not so; it appears she escaped the fire that took the others.'

'The Grand?' Edith's eyes were screwed up as she tried to understand the meaning of what Dan had said. 'She was there? In the restaurant?'

'She's a waitress, Mam.' The sneer in John's voice was reflected in his face.

'She's the assistant housekeeper,' Dan corrected grimly, 'and a fine young woman.'

'*Fine . . . ?*' Edith's face, which had been white, now flushed with ugly colour, and her voice was a low hiss as she said, 'I forbid you, *I forbid you* to associate with that girl, Dan. Do you hear me? I forbid it!'

'I am twenty-seven years of age, Mother. You can't forbid me to do anything.'

'Oh yes I can! You are living under my roof, my boy, and don't you forget it.'

'That's soon rectified.'

'Dan? Dan, man, what are you doing?'

Art caught hold of his brother as Dan walked past him making for the door, and now everyone was standing, apart from Edith and John.

'I'm doing something I should have done a long, long time ago, Art,' Dan said bitterly. 'But duty and misguided pity and, aye, and lack of guts if the truth be known, stopped me. But no more, I've had enough. I've had a bellyful, man.'

'If you walk out of that door don't think you can come crawling back when it suits you.'

Dan looked at his mother and his voice, in stark contrast to her own, which had been incensed, was even and almost expressionless as he said, 'I won't be back, rest easy on that,' and after shrugging off Art's hand from his arm he walked out of the room without another word.

'Satisfied?' Art's eyes had followed his youngest brother but now he swung round on John angrily. 'You're a damn menace, that's what you are.'

'Oh aye, that's right, take it out on me,' John ground out, with a quick glance at the others. 'Dan's running after that trollop's brat and he's still whiter than white, is that it?'

'By, man, you'll open that big mouth of yours once too often one of these days.'

'And you'll shut it for me? Is that the idea?'

'Leave him, Art. He's not worth it.'

As her husband lunged across the table at John, Gladys caught hold of his arm, pulling him back, only for Edith to turn on her, her voice bitter as she said, 'You dare to criticise my son when you used every trick in the book to get his brother to marry you? Don't think I don't see through you, madam, because I do. I've been on to you from day one.'

'Right, that's it, get the bairns.' Art practically manhandled Gladys to the door where he turned, glancing back at the remaining few round the table as he said grimly, 'And a merry Christmas to you an' all,' before banging the door hard behind him.

They were ushering the children into their coats and hats in the hall, Kitty flapping about as Gladys tried to explain what had happened, when Dan came down the stairs carrying a small portmanteau and with his outdoor clothes on.

'Dan, Dan, lad.' Kitty was beside herself, the tears streaming down her plump jowls as she all but threw herself in front of the door. 'Don't go like this, lad, please. You know what she's like, she'll calm down when she's had a chance to think. If you go like this, you'll always regret it.'

Dan came to her now, and taking her hands in his bent forward and kissed her before straightening and saying quietly, 'I won't regret it, Kitty. We both know I'd have gone a long time ago but for you, but I can't stay another night under this roof. I'll get lodgings in town somewhere so don't worry.'

'It's Christmas Day, lad, there'll be nowhere open.'

'He's coming home with us, Kitty, all right?' Gladys glanced across at Art as she spoke, and as her husband mouthed, 'Thank you, lass', she smiled before continuing, 'We've plenty of room since we moved to the square and I don't think Art's used his study above once, you can have that, and there's already a fold-down bed in there.'

She was speaking to Dan now, and as he shook his head saying, 'No, no, Gladys, I couldn't impose like that,' Art's voice came back loud and strong saying, 'Don't be daft, man. How could my own brother impose? And the bairns will love it, you know they will. They think the world of you as it is. Now that's the end of it, it's settled. You'll be as snug as a bug in a rug in there, and like Gladys said, the room's never used. You'll be doing us a favour, keeping it aired like.'

'She'll look at it like sticking the knife in, you know that, don't you? You won't get any thanks from her.' Dan gestured with his head towards the dining room – the door of which was still closed – as he spoke.

And now the likeness between the two brothers was accentuated as Art looked at Dan, his face grim as he said, 'Between you and me, little brother, that won't worry me a great deal.'

* * *

Edith heard the front door open and close, and she was aware that the murmur of voices which had penetrated the dining room from the hall had ceased, but she still couldn't believe that Dan had actually left until Kitty came into the room moments later. 'Well?' She raised her eyebrows at her housekeeper, and it was the expression on Kitty's face – because the younger woman couldn't bring herself to speak – that told Edith he had gone.

The two women stared at each other for a second, one with her eyes swimming with tears and the other with a face as hard as iron, and then Edith nodded sharply, as though in answer to something which had been voiced, and said, 'We are ready for the hot mince pies, Kitty. Please inform Miss Doreen and Miss Ruth that their presence is required in here, and once you have served coffee I would like you to take my four youngest grandchildren to the nursery for a nap. Is that understood?'

Edith did not wait for an answer, her attitude dismissive as she turned to John and engaged him in conversation regarding some extraneous matter connected with the business, and after a pause Kitty left the room as quietly as she had entered. But behind Edith's unruffled exterior she was boiling with rage. That Dan, Dan of all people, *her* Dan, had dared to defy her like this and in front of everyone. After all she had done for him, the sacrifices she had made. She could have expected such ungratefulness from Art – her third born had always been a difficult child, unmindful and rebellious even before he had met that common-born huzzy who had become his wife – but Dan? No, not Dan. Right from the first moment she had seen his face, seconds after he had been born, she had loved him.

It had surprised her, the depth and quality of the love she had experienced for her youngest child. Until then she had thought herself incapable of loving anyone.

Her father had been employed in building the North Dock in Monkwearmouth in the 1830s, but by the time she was born, in 1854, he hadn't worked for years. They had lived in one of a row of foul-smelling hovels opposite the abattoir, and she'd loathed and detested the dirt and stench of her childhood. The walls of their two-roomed cottage had always been damp, and the stone flags on the floor had oozed water and thick slime. It had been cold and dark and detestable, and she had bitterly resented her beginnings and despised her parents and siblings. At the age of fourteen she had put herself into service with a wealthy family in Bishopwearmouth, and from that first day she had never gone home again or even acknowledged to anyone that she had a family.

She had met Henry Stewart one January evening in 1872. It had been her half day off and she had gone to the Assembly Hall in Sans Street for a levee featuring the 'Two-Headed Nightingale', Miss Chrissie-Millie – billed as an astonishing freak of nature possessing two heads, two sets of arms and legs but all blended into one body – and she had pursued him with relentless determination from that night on. She had recognised in Henry an ambition to rise above his surroundings that almost matched her own. By 1874 she had contrived for him to marry her – John being on the way – and from that point she had driven him and herself onwards and upwards, with a single-mindedness that allowed no room for sentiment or finer feelings.

The physical side of marriage she had used as a means to an end, although she found it deeply repugnant. It produced heirs, necessary to build the Stewart empire, and it also kept Henry dancing to her tune.

Her children had proved a great disappointment. Mavis and the twins she considered spineless and uninteresting, Art an ingrate, John . . . John she disliked whilst giving him a grudging respect for the ruthlessness he could display when necessary. She never allowed herself to reflect on why she did not like her first born; the reality, that John was in effect a mirror image of herself, would have been too disturbing to contemplate.

When, six years after the twins were born, she had found herself with child again at the advanced age of thirty-two, she had been beside herself with rage and mortification. Working-class women, the society she had clawed her way out of, went on having bairns like rabbits, ladies did not. She'd vowed this child would be her last and had prepared to tolerate it as she did the others, whilst locking her bedroom door for good against her husband. But then something hitherto unknown had happened to her heart when she had held Dan in her arms nine months later. She had fallen in love.

And now he had dared to throw her love back in her face! As Doreen and Ruth and her grandchildren joined them again, Edith forced herself to smile and converse naturally, but her mind was racing. It wasn't Dan's fault – it was important she saw this clearly. It was that ragamuffin brat, that *guttersnipe*, who was to blame. She blinked as she glanced down the table at the empty places where her family should have been.

She had felt a great sense of well-being, even pleasure, when John had come to her that morning years ago and told her what he'd done and the result of it. The death of that huzzy and her family by fire had been a clean end – purifying even

– to something which would have continued to fester if it hadn't been dealt with. Atonement had been needed for Henry's death – didn't the Bible itself claim an eye for an eye and a tooth for a tooth? – and there was Jacob's suicide and Mavis losing her mind. And she had been right to think like that, by, she had. This last episode proved it if nothing else. One of them had escaped and now look at the trouble that strumpet was causing. Assistant housekeeper! And how had a wanton creature like that got such a position? On her back with her legs open no doubt. Men were fools! The whole lot of them.

But it wouldn't end here. No, oh no, not if she had anything to do with it. She would see her day with Sadie Bell's flyblow and teach her a lesson she'd never forget. But she'd tread carefully; there were more ways of killing a cat than skinning it, and if the baggage was aiming to sink her claws into Dan, this required some thought. Did those responsible for maintaining the Grand's superior reputation know they were employing the results of a trollop's whoring? Possibly not. Very possibly not.

Edith raised her head suddenly, glancing round the table with something approaching a benevolent smile as she said, 'I think we'll have our mince pies and coffee in the drawing room. How does that sound? And once Kitty has taken the children you'll find the envelopes containing your Christmas boxes on the bureau.'

And to the chorus of thanks – Edith's cheques on such occasions reflected her approval, or otherwise, of their obedience and acquiescence to her authority, and she could be very generous – she inclined her head, her smile widening. This Bell chit would soon be dealt with, her days of masquerading as a respectable woman were numbered, and when Dan returned home duly chastened she would be gracious with him, gracious and forgiving. If she handled this right it might even persuade him to look favourably on Miss Isabel Rotherington, the magistrate's spinster daughter, who would make an excellent wife, being quiet and pliable, if a little old at twenty-eight. Yes, she would have no trouble with Isabel Rotherington if Dan could be induced to take her. And the prestige and influence a magistrate's daughter would add to the Stewart name wasn't to be sneezed at.

Edith rose from her seat, her demeanour a study in control, and the others followed dutifully, taking their cue as always from the formidable woman who controlled each of their lives.

Chapter Thirteen

Connie entered the hotel cold store at the back of the kitchen and quickly checked off the items delivered late the previous night from the list in her hand, before retracing her steps into the relative warmth of the scullery and then the kitchen beyond.

New Year's Eve. She couldn't believe the old year was ending and another was about to begin. This time last year she had still been working in the laundry and preparing to apply for training as a nurse, and now . . . She breathed in a deep sigh of satisfaction as she glanced round the almost deserted kitchen, it still being too early for most of the day staff to have arrived. She had decided to come in to work at this time as the day was going to be a busy one and the evening even busier, there being various functions booked, and she had found in the last months she could accomplish twice as much work in half the time in those precious minutes before the workforce appeared en masse. She had been there almost an hour and got through all the jobs she'd intended to do, so a nice cup of tea and a couple of slices of toast were in order.

She was seated at one of the small tables where the second kitchen maid prepared the vegetables each day, a steaming mug of tea at the side of her and her mouth full of toast, reading a few more pages of Sir Almroth Wright's anti-women's suffrage book, which claimed women were inferior to men, when she heard footsteps just behind her. She didn't look up – the staff would dribble in in their ones and twos now but there was still another twenty minutes to go until the day began officially – being engrossed in the inflammatory book which Connie considered to be the worst sort of bigotry. What with Asquith's 'cat and mouse' bill – the latest strategy in the Government's clash with the suffragettes which enabled temporary discharges to be given to suffragettes in prison undergoing hunger strikes, only for the women to be re-arrested when it pleased the magistrates – and male mobs attacking suffragettes in Hyde Park and Wimbledon and other parts of the country, was it any wonder women were taking the law into their own hands?

Not that she could agree with the actions of the Northumbrian martyr, Emily Davison, who had tried to stop the King's horse at Derby in June and been killed, or all the bombings of property this year, but with public meetings by suffragettes banned by the Government and other restraints aimed at muzzling free speech by the female of the gender in place, women were getting more and more militant. There were men in every strata of society who considered women inferior mentally, physically and spiritually, and half of them were frightened to admit they might be wrong.

And then, as though to prove the last thought, Connie felt a hand stroke the back of her neck as a male voice behind her said thickly, 'Reading, m'dear? You don't want to bother your pretty little head with books, now then.'

'Colonel Fairley.' Connie managed to keep the groan out

of her voice as she spun round and rose quickly, but it was an effort. Colonel Fairley was a distant relation of Harold Alridge and always stayed at the Grand when he visited Sunderland, which fortunately was infrequently, but since Connie had first met him on his arrival at the hotel three days before, the portly, bulbous-nosed military man had made numerous advances to her, all of which she had politely and firmly rejected. It didn't help that the Colonel had free run of the hotel, often sitting for hours in the office with Harold or appearing in the kitchens or elsewhere at the oddest moments. He seemed to appear like a rabbit out of a hat when she least expected it, but that wouldn't be so bad if he would just keep his hands to himself.

Connie forced herself to smile coolly as she turned from slipping the book into her cloth bag which had been hanging over the back of the wooden chair, and her voice was circumspect as she said, 'Is there anything you require, Colonel Fairley? I trust the early morning housemaid brought you your tea?' She had actually seen Agnes preparing the tea-trays when she had first arrived that morning so the question was rhetorical, but it gave her the opportunity to get things back to a more formal footing.

'It arrived on the dot m'dear, on the dot.' The Colonel's pale-blue, pink-rimmed eyes were moving all over her as he spoke, their expression lascivious. 'You young gels know how to look after a fellow, no doubt about it.'

Ugg, but he was a revolting man! Thank goodness he was only staying for two weeks; hopefully they wouldn't see him for another twelve months after that. For Lucy's sake she didn't want to cause any unpleasantness by complaining, but Mary had told her that all the girls were wary of the Colonel, and

217

even Mrs Pegg was distrustful of the manager's relation after he had nipped her backside. 'Mind you,' Mary had continued, her eyes brimming over with laughter, 'I said to Biddy he deserves a medal for that one, either that or a strong pair of glasses. The man's got to be desperate or half sharp.'

Connie looked at the Colonel now and aimed to make her voice brisk as she said, 'Well, if you'll excuse me, Colonel, I've things to do.'

'Of course, m'dear, of course, but how about a little drink later, eh? I enjoy a little tipple before my dinner, don't you know.'

'We haven't even served breakfast yet, Colonel.'

'True, but the day'll be galloping away before you know it.'

'I'm sorry, but I thought I had made it quite plain yesterday that the hotel does not encourage the staff to liaise with the guests socially.'

'Ah, I see your point, m'dear, but no one will know if you come to my room now will they. I always keep a bottle of this and that by me, and we can get to know each other a bit better.' He was sweating slightly, and as a crumb of something or other from his moustache fell on to his bottom lip a thick red tongue flicked out and took it into his mouth.

Connie just managed to suppress a shudder. 'I don't think so, Colonel,' she managed evenly.

'Now that's where you go wrong if you don't mind me saying so. A high-spirited little filly like you needs a bit of fun now and again, and I know how to treat a gel. Got quite a name for meself in some quarters.'

She didn't doubt that for a minute. 'I'm sorry but I have to adhere to hotel policy.' Her voice was cool now, with an edge to it, and something in the florid face in front of her hardened before the Colonel swung round on his heel and marched out of the kitchen.

Had she offended him? She hoped so, she thought wryly. Perhaps he'd leave her alone now. She had more than enough on her plate without worrying about a lecherous old goat like him. She reached across for the fast cooling tea and drained the mug as her thoughts made a beeline for the thing that had occupied them for days. Dan Stewart. Would he try and see her again? Did she *want* him to try and see her again? She wasn't that stupid, was she? The answer to that one made her shut her eyes for an infinitesimal moment but she couldn't deny the pounding of her heart.

Oh he wouldn't anyway – not after she'd been so antagonistic and rude. And that was for the best, absolutely and definitely for the best, she assured herself stolidly. He was part of a family that had treated her and those she loved shamefully; she wouldn't *let* herself harbour any romantic inclinations towards him. It would be like consorting with the enemy. And there was Stewart blood running through his veins just the same as there was through his brother's, that John, and if ever there was an evil so-and-so John Stewart was one. Although Dan wasn't like his brothers . . .

Here her thoughts were cut off by the exclamation in her mind that yelled, Enough! Enough of that. The last thing she wanted was anything at all to do with any of the Stewart clan.

So why had he been on her mind every minute since that evening just before Christmas? Whatever she had done since, even when she and Mary had taken the huge hamper along to Mary's parents on Christmas Eve, and when they'd gone to Midnight Mass and it had been so beautiful, and . . . oh, just all the time, he had been there. And she had to claim victory over this, she had to. Her thoughts were bursting to have free rein again but she forced them under lock and key, jerking her chin upwards and narrowing her eyes. She could do this, it was simply a matter of will. Everything in life boiled down to that really. She knew what she wanted in the next few years – a home of her own, bought and paid for, and the fulfilment of her dream of a little business where she, and others, could work in harmony and really make a go of something.

She liked her work here, she did, and she was so grateful to be out of the workhouse, but she *ached* for more. She supposed she was ambitious. Her chin moved higher. And she was blowed if she was going to apologise for that, even if it was frowned upon by a society that still insisted women should know their place. Well, she knew her place – or she knew where she wanted it to be at least – and she aimed to get there, however long it took. The sweet jar was getting fatter, and although it might be a slow birthing, she would get there.

And then, as Wilf and Mary walked into the kitchen, Connie's expression changed and she called, her voice teasing and light, 'Come on then, come on! The day's half gone already.'

They returned her smile, Wilf grinning as he snapped to attention and raised his hand in a mock salute. Since the evening before Christmas when she had prompted Wilf to take her friend home he had started calling for them on the way to work, ostensibly to escort them both, but they knew where the real object of his desire lay. He had been bolder since he'd realised she was for him, Connie reflected now as she smoothed her hair and prepared for what was going to be a hectic day. It was as if he'd needed an ally to convince him he could penetrate the formidable armour Mary had in place against the male sex in general. But his boldness was not of the swaggering kind, he was a gentle soul behind all the banter, and if Mary gave herself half a chance she could be happy with Wilf Gantry. And he wasn't for rushing her which was good. She needed time, did Mary.

Two hours later Harold Alridge was sitting in his leather chair in the office staring unseeingly across the room into the flickering flames of the fire, a piece of paper held loosely in his limp hand. He had had a shock, a bad shock; what he really needed was a good strong tot of brandy, but it was a bit early in the day for that, he thought dismally, the words of the letter burning in his mind.

'Dear Sir,' it had started, the writing small and precise and the ink very black. 'It has been brought to my attention that the Grand Hotel is at the moment employing a Miss Connie Bell in a position of some authority, namely that of assistant housekeeper. I feel it is my Christian duty to enquire whether higher management have been alerted to this young woman's sordid beginnings, namely that of her mother, Sadie Bell, being a woman of easy virtue who was well known to the police before her death some years ago. The Grand has a reputation second to none, and I feel this lowering of its normally impeccable standards – especially in view of the fact that children and respectable young women of estimable character are entrusted to its care – is inexcusable. Connie Bell's mother sold herself on the streets of Sunderland, and I have good reason to believe that the daughter partakes of the same inherent weakness when it suits her to do so. I know of at least one young man this girl has approached on the hotel's premises in the guise of doing her job, and of the unfortunate liaison that has resulted from this procuring. I am sure you will appreciate that it distresses me greatly to have to acquaint you with these facts, but once enlightened I trust you will act accordingly.

'I remain, Sir, your obedient servant.'

There was no signature.

The start Harold gave as the door opened in the next instant was noticeable, and as he stuffed the letter under his big blotting pad Colonel Fairley's voice brought his head jerking upwards, whereupon Harold expelled a long slow sigh of relief.

'What're you looking so guilty for, m'boy?' the Colonel enquired genially, his small eyes moving to the corner of the paper which was poking out of the side of the blotter. 'You've got to do better than that if you want to fool the wife, you know.'

'It's nothing like that.' Harold was flustered and it showed. 'Good gracious, I'd as soon . . . No, it's nothing like that. It's just – well, I've got the dickens of a problem to tell you the truth, and I'm not sure what to make of it.'

'Lucy know?' The Colonel wasn't overfond of Harold's wife; she was one of those women who had a mind of their own, in the Colonel's opinion, and subsequently were more trouble than they were worth. But Harold thought a bit of her and so the Colonel kept his thoughts to himself.

'Well that's the thing you see, that's what makes this all the more difficult. Lucy likes the girl, she likes and admires her very much, and I have to say I thought the same way myself until . . . But I have to think of Lucy though, I can't have her exposed to any sort of unpleasantness, can I?'

'Are you going to continue to talk in riddles or show me that damn thing you're hiding?'

'Oh, oh yes, of course. I'm sorry.' Harold thrust the piece of paper at the stout figure by the side of him as though it was something unclean, which in a way he felt it was. What sort of person wrote something like this without signing their name at the bottom of it? he asked himself grimly. This was malicious and nasty, very nasty, but he couldn't ignore it. Much as he would like to, he couldn't ignore it.

There was silence while the Colonel surveyed the neat words covering the fine linen paper, and when the Colonel broke it his voice was casual, even unconcerned, as he advised Harold to do the very thing the younger man had been telling himself was impossible. 'Ignore it.' The Colonel narrowed his eyes as he inclined his head to emphasise the words. 'If you want my opinion, ignore it. You can bet there's a jealous woman behind this, m'boy, a girlfriend or even a wife who's had her nose put out of joint in some way. Women can be the very devil. Have you had any cause for concern with the little filly in question?'

'No, none. She's never put a foot wrong.'

'There you are then. Storm in a teacup, m'boy, storm in a teacup. Give it a day or two and you'll have forgotten all about it, eh? No sense in upsetting the gel or Lucy with something like this now then.'

'But . . . but if I don't do something, at least have the girl in here and ask for an explanation, and something happens . . .'

'What could happen? Ask yourself that, there's a good fellow. The bounder who wrote the letter isn't going to come forward now then, not if they haven't signed it in the first place, and who's to say you've ever received it? If you show it to the gel and she gets all upset like women do, Lucy isn't going to appreciate it, and if you say the gel's a good worker . . . Burn it, boy, eh?' The Colonel walked across to the blazing fire, extending his arm as he raised his eyebrows enquiringly. 'Eh? Burn it and forget about it, that's my advice.'

'Well . . .' Harold hesitated. 'If you really think I should.'

'No question about it, m'boy. Good advice, what?' So saying the Colonel dropped the piece of paper into the fire where it flared briefly before being consumed by the flames. 'That's the ticket. Nasty business but all forgotten.'

Harold nodded, his face clearing. 'Yes, I'm sure you're right.' And then more strongly, 'Yes, I'm sure you are. Thanks, Reginald.'

'Pleasure, m'boy. Pleasure. Glad to have helped.'

The Colonel seated himself in the other leather chair after bringing it close to the fire, as Harold went back to his paperwork. He lit his pipe and took a few puffs before reaching down to the hearth and picking up a magazine, *Good Hounds and Hunting*, which he had placed there the day before. But although he had it open on his lap he wasn't reading it. Who would have thought it? The cunning little baggage! And her so hoity-toity with him too. But if she'd bigger fish to fry . . . Oh, she was a crafty one all right, but fetching. Very fetching. He felt his body stir and breathed in deeply. And he would make sure she knew what she owed him. He expected her to be grateful to him – very grateful – for saving her bacon. The bulge in his trousers was as hard as a rock and he moved slightly, adjusting his position in the chair. Yes, he was looking forward to this. There was something about Miss Connie Bell that got hold of a fellow.

* * *

'You think I'm mad, don't you, saying I want to see her again after all that's happened? Be honest, Gladys. You do, don't you.'

'Dan, of all people you should know Art and I understand. Look what we had to go through when we first started walking out. Your mam went mad, clean mad, I tell you.'

'Aye, I know you had a time of it and I'm not making light of that, but this is a bit different, isn't it. At least you wanted Art, it wasn't one-sided.'

Yes, this was different. Gladys turned from the parlour window where she and Dan had been standing looking out into the square which was shadowed and still in the winter afternoon. The lamplighter would be round soon and the square looked beautiful when it was lit up. It was her favourite time of the day – twilight – since they had moved to this lovely house next to West Park off Park Road a year ago.

'You can't blame her for feeling the way she does, Dan,' Gladys said softly as she walked across the room and busied herself poking the fire into a blaze. It was bitterly cold outside, the frost already glittering on the snow which had fallen earlier and the pale light of the dying day turning the bare trees into something beautiful against the silver/gold sky. 'It must have been a terrible experience for a young lass like she was then to have seen such violence, and it sounds like everything went from bad to worse from that point on.'

'Aye, I know, lass. I know.' Dan flung himself into a plumply stuffed armchair, raking back his dark hair with an impatient hand. He knew all that, of course he did, but that didn't exactly help *now*, did it!

And as though she had picked up on the thought, Gladys said quietly, 'Go and see her if that's what your heart is telling you to do. You're going to do it anyway, I don't know why we're even having this conversation.'

'Am I that transparent?' He grinned at her, and Gladys smiled back as she said, 'Aye, you and your brother an' all. How were things before you left the works today?'

'Strained,' said Dan cryptically. He had known it was going to be awkward when he and Art went in to work on Monday and he hadn't been wrong. His father's will had left the controlling share of the business to Edith, with the rest distributed equally between the five brothers, and to give his mother her due she rarely came to the works or interfered in the daily running of the business. But that didn't stop John from acting as though he was in control of it all, even though he hadn't got the business head their father had had. Art was much better in that respect. The specialities of the firm, which met with a continually extending sale, embraced high-class marine engine, cylinder and burning oils, and these were constantly in use by some of the most important steamship lines in the kingdom. Art had arranged that deliveries to any port were greatly accelerated by special railway arrangements to secure speedy shipment.

In addition to their oil specialities, their father had set things up so that the firm held heavy stocks of white lead, zinc white, coloured paints and varnishes, and so on, so that prompt delivery could be guaranteed to the various large works in the district at all times. All in all a most extensive trade had been established together with a well-earned reputation for honourable dealings, although more than once since their father's demise Dan and Art had had to prevent John taking 'short-cuts', which were not only illegal but dangerous and unnecessary. This applied particularly to the heavy goods and ships' provisions stored in the warehouses, and when one considered that Henry Stewart & Co. were on the Government list and held a contract for the War Office, it was sheer foolishness to attempt to sail too close to the wind. But you couldn't tell John anything. It was confrontation all the time with his eldest brother, and he knew Art was as weary of it as he was.

'Well you two hold on in there.' Gladys's voice was urgent now. 'John would just love it if the pair of you threw in the towel and let your mam buy you out, and that wasn't what your da worked all the hours of the night and day for, was it. He wanted the business for all of you.'

'Aye.' Dan stretched out his legs and sighed deeply. 'He was a good man, my father, Gladys. A canny businessman but a nice bloke too.'

'I know that. You and Art are like him.'

'Oh aye?' Art had just entered the room and caught the last piece of the conversation and now he grinned at his wife, his eyes twinkling. 'Well, if we're so perfect and such a good pair of blokes, why isn't the tea on the table, wench? Eh? You answer me that.'

'Oh you.' Gladys pushed at her husband as she spoke, but she was relieved at his bantering tone. He was carrying a heavy load and it was weighing him down, and she didn't really know how to help him except to be there for him. What with all the talk of the build up of arms in western Europe – 'organised insanity' as Lloyd George called it – fuelling fears of possible war, this last altercation with his mother, which had reached new heights once Art had learnt from John his mother was holding him mainly responsible for Dan not returning home, the constant pressure of the business and the hundred and one other problems connected with life in general, Art was not himself. And although she would never let on to Dan, she knew that this lass, Connie Bell, turning up again had brought all the guilt from the past surging back too. Art had never forgiven himself for what had occurred at the house in the wood all those years ago, or the ramifications of the attack which had led to his father's death and Jacob's suicide. She knew now it would haunt her husband to his dying day.

Gladys shivered suddenly, in spite of the warmth of the room, but her voice was ordinary sounding when she said, 'We're not having much the night so I warn you two. There'll be plenty to eat later and I want everyone to tuck in then. Art' – she paused, reaching out her hand and touching her husband's arm as she passed – 'you are absolutely sure you don't want to go to your mam's do tonight? I've only asked the neighbours and Ray and Martha and their brood to come in, so I can easily call it off if you've changed your mind?'

'We're staying put, lass. The others'll go to Mam's, and she'll have all her fancy friends like she normally does, but I couldn't stomach being there and neither could Dan. Right, lad?'

'Too true.' Dan's voice was as grim as Art's face, and Gladys nodded at them both as she said, 'All right then, if you're sure. David and Catherine will love having Ray and Martha's bairns to play with, they've been beside themselves with excitement since I said we were seeing the New Year in here with a little party.'

'Aye, well we should have done it years ago,' said Art bitterly. 'The times I'd have preferred to stay by me own fireside, but out we've trotted to answer the royal summons. No more, lass, I'm telling you, no more. That's all done with, whatever you say about family harmony and the rest. Christmas and New Year, and Easter too, we're staying here.'

'All right, all right, don't go on.'

As Gladys bustled out of the room the two men exchanged a wry smile, and when the door had closed behind the big, thick-set woman, Art murmured quietly, 'She's one of the best and no mistake.'

'Aye, man, I'd agree with you there.' Dan had always been aware of the special relationship between Art and his wife – special within the folds of his family anyway – but it wasn't until he had come to live with them a week ago that he had realised he deeply envied them too. They loved each other. And it wasn't just that they were well set up; if Art was a docker or a miner up to his eyes in filth and muck all day and sweating to provide bone broth or scraps of pot stuff, Gladys would still worship the ground he walked on. And that was what he wanted. That feeling, that emotion that they had. He wanted that with the woman he married and he wouldn't settle for anything less, even if he had to remain single for the rest of his life. And as though the two things were entwined in his mind, he found himself saying in the next moment, 'I'm going to go and see her the night, Art. I can't go in to the New Year without knowing if I stand any chance at all.'

Art didn't have to ask to whom his brother was referring, but what he did say, his voice low but purposely expressionless, was, 'You know what it will mean? If she agrees to take up with you, that is. Are you prepared for the backlash?'

Dan was silent for a moment and then he nodded, his voice faintly embarrassed as he said, 'I can't get her out of my mind, Art, and not just because she's bonny. It's more than that. I can't explain it but from the minute I saw her again it was like I'd been waiting for that moment for years without recognising the fact, but then I knew. In an instant I knew. Oh' – he rubbed his face, his tone irritable – 'I can't put it into words.'

'You did a pretty good job of it I'd say. You tell her what you just told me and I can't see any lass not falling on your neck, lad,' said Art drily.

'But she's not just any lass, is she. That's the trouble.'

Aye, that was the trouble all right. Art glanced once more at the bowed figure of his brother holding his head in his hands, his elbows on his knees, and gave a hard silent sigh. Damn it all, how was this going to end? And then, as though to refute the deep unease he felt whenever he considered his brother and Connie Bell, he found himself saying, 'Aye, well when you see her, and if she's amenable, you can always bring her back here to see the New Year in, and any of her pals she'd like to bring along, you know that. 'Course, she's likely to have made plans already, but you never know, with her working in the hotel trade and all.'

'Thanks, man, but I doubt she'll look the side I'm on.'

Art doubted it too, and he felt a sense of betrayal as he realised he was praying that would be the case. Life was complicated enough at the moment without what would virtually amount to a live grenade being thrown into their midst.

Chapter Fourteen

When Connie emerged from the back entrance of the Grand Hotel at eight that same evening, Mary and Wilf just a step or two behind her, her mind was full of nothing more uplifting than Colonel Fairley. The man had been a source of great irritation all day, trying to waylay her several times and hinting that he had something to say to her of supreme importance. If it hadn't been for the fact that they were rushed off their feet and every minute was precious, she would have made the time to take him somewhere secluded and tell him in no uncertain terms to leave her alone. But tomorrow should be quieter – most folk were battling with thick heads and upset stomachs after drinking and eating too much the night before on New Year's Day – and she would definitely have a word with him then, whether he be a relation of Harold Alridge or King George himself. The last time he had stopped her on the stairs between the second and third floor, he had had the nerve to press himself against her in a most suggestive way, and she wasn't putting up with that kind of behaviour from anyone. Disgusting, horrible man . . .

'Miss Bell?'

The start she gave as a tall dark shadow appeared out of the side of the building almost caused Connie to land flat on her back on the icy, snow-packed ground, and her hand was still pressed to her throat when Dan said, 'I'm sorry, I'm so sorry. I didn't mean to startle you, but I just wanted to make sure I didn't miss you and they said you usually leave this way.'

'Who said?' It was all she could manage as her heart continued to pound.

'The lady I spoke to earlier. A stout lady in a blue dress.'

Mrs Pegg. Of course it would have to be Mrs Pegg of all people he had spoken to. The housekeeper already had ears like cuddy-lugs, and they'd be flapping all the more now she'd got wind of a young man asking for her. A young man . . . Connie swallowed hard, but as Mary and Wilf joined her, one on each side, she felt sufficiently composed to be able to say, 'I don't understand why you are here, Mr Stewart.'

She wasn't going to make this easy but he had expected that, hadn't he? Damn it, he was hot and sweating in spite of nearly having frozen to death in the two hours he had been skulking out here waiting. What should he say? He had been rehearsing enough variations on opening lines to fill a book. And then, strangely, he knew what he was going to say, and it was scattering to the wind all his previous ruminations. 'I couldn't stay away.' It was quiet but steady and Connie's heart flipped over.

This was impossible. She knew it was impossible for more reasons than she could name. She had to nip it in the bud *now*. And then she looked into the dark-brown eyes that appeared black in the dim light and heard herself say, 'Does . . . does your family know you are here?'

'The ones that matter, yes. The others . . . I moved out of my mother's home a week ago, Miss Bell. I'm living with one of my brothers now, Art. I think I mentioned him to you before.'

Art. The brother who supposedly felt sorry, like him, for what had happened. Had there been a family row of some kind?

Dan was staring now, he couldn't help it. She was so incredibly lovely. He could drown in the blue of her eyes. And then he caught his racing thoughts, bringing them under control, and speaking softly, vitally aware of the two silent – and he felt condemning – figures either side of her, as he said, 'My brother and his wife are having a few friends in to welcome the New Year. There . . . there won't be any other members of my family present. They wondered – I wondered – if you would care to join us? Your friends too, of course,' he added quickly, glancing once at Mary's set face. 'As Gladys would say, the more the merrier.'

There *had* been a family split. Connie hesitated before saying, 'Gladys?'

'My sister-in-law.'

So he wasn't married or courting. She had wondered about that once or twice, although she had assumed from the way he had behaved and the fact that there had been only four other women with his mother and brothers at the hotel that Dan was free. But you couldn't always tell, she reminded herself silently. Still, he was hardly likely to invite her to his brother's house if he was spoken for.

She hadn't said no straight away. Dan felt almost drunk with relief. But she might be going to refuse, and he'd never have the courage to go through this again. That little lass at the side of Connie was looking at him daggers. Had he made himself clear enough? They did understand that this was all above board?

233

'Please don't misunderstand me, Miss Bell,' said Dan hastily. 'The invitation is perfectly genuine. Really. It's just that . . . Well, with it being New Year's Eve and all, I thought . . .' Damn it, he couldn't say he had hoped it might be a time for new beginnings, she'd likely hit him. 'I would be honoured if you would come,' he finished weakly, knowing she was going to refuse him. He was on the brink of a chasm, and he could do nothing to prevent himself being cast into endless darkness. Because if she refused him, if she would not countenance having anything to do with him, that's what his life would be from this point on. Oh hell, what could he *say*?

She must answer him, Connie thought feverishly; they couldn't just stand here. She was aware she'd reached a crossroads in her life and that her head was urging her to do one thing and her heart another, and right until she said, 'There's more than just three of us, we're having a little get together with the four ladies at our lodgings,' and Dan said eagerly, 'Oh bring them, please, do bring them. We've masses of food and drink and everything,' before falling silent, clearly hotly embarrassed, she hadn't thought she'd known what her reply was going to be. But as soon as she'd spoken she had known that she'd already made the decision to see him again the moment she had realised it was Dan waiting in the shadows. *He had sought her out.* Her pulse leapt at the thought and she looked into his red, bashful face as the blood sang in her veins. A man like him, a man who could have any lass he wanted, he had come back and waited to see her.

She took a deep breath, her voice betraying just the slightest echo of her inward turmoil as she said, 'Thank you, Mr Stewart. I'll have to check with the others of course and make sure it's all right with them, but hopefully we'll be able to come to your brother's party for an hour or two later. If you would care to give us the address?' And she smiled at him.

'I think you're loopy. I know you don't want to hear it, but I'm goin' to say it all the same. Blood's thicker than water, lass, an' in the end it's blood that'll out. An' lettin' him walk you to the house weren't none too clever either.'

'Oh, Mary.'

'An' don't "Oh, Mary" me in that voice, now then. If it was anyone else you'd be sayin' exactly the same as I'm sayin'. This just isn't like you, lass. I don't understand you.'

She didn't understand herself either.

Connie stared at Mary for a moment across the room, the dress she was going to change into and which she had bought just a few days ago hanging limp in her hands. It was a nice dress, bonny, and if she was honest with herself – really honest – she had bought it with the secret hope that one day, somehow, Dan Stewart might see her in it so that he could picture her in something other than her blue work dress and the apron she had been wearing that night before Christmas. 'You heard what he said, Mary,' she said after a long pause. 'He's left his mam's house and all that side of the family, and he's living with the other brother now. Dan was only fourteen that night, you know.'

'There's plenty bin workin' for a good year or two at that age, he was no bairn.'

'He tried to stop them, and he came back and saved me from the snowdrift. I'd have died that day without him, don't forget that.'

'You might not have.'

'Oh aye, I would. And I owe him something for my life,

don't I? One evening isn't too much to ask.'

'One evenin'?' Mary's tone was sceptical. 'You really think he's goin' to be content to leave it at one evenin'?'

'Probably.'

Aye, and probably not. But what really worried her was that Connie herself didn't want just one evening with Dan Stewart, Mary told herself glumly. She'd been different since she had seen him again. Oh, she'd been right upset the night it had happened, and with that John – the callous so-an'-so – it wasn't surprising, was it, but when she'd got over that side of it she'd been . . . Mary searched for a word to describe Connie's state and found it. Skittish. That's what she'd been. And that just wasn't like Connie. She deserved better than to be taken up for a time with the likes of that scum and then dropped when he'd had what he wanted. And that's what would happen. A man in his position didn't get serious with a lass whose mother had worked the streets. He'd have his fun and off he'd skedaddle.

'I'm going, Mary.' Connie had watched the play of emotions on her friend's face and now her voice was steady and low. 'Even if I have to go by myself, I'm going.'

'Don't be daft, lass! As if me an' Wilf'd let you go by yourself.'

The other four lodgers had plumped for staying at Walworth Way when they had told them about the invitation on their arrival home some minutes before, and had appeared perfectly happy to settle down in the kitchen amongst the food and drink Connie had bought the previous day, Wilf joining them while Mary and Connie changed their working clothes.

'I'd be all right. I'm sure someone would see me home.'

Aye, she didn't doubt it, and she knew his name an' all,

and that was enough to make her go to this blooming party if nothing else. 'No, we're comin', lass, 'course we are.' Mary watched her friend hold the lovely, thick linen dress in a delicate shade of gold against herself for a moment as Connie glanced in the oak-framed mirror hanging over the fireplace. The dress was circumspect by any standards, the sleeves long and ending in a V on the wrists, the bodice fitted but with a high collar, and plenty of material in the skirt which fell to just above the ankles, but on Connie it became, well, alluring, Mary admitted anxiously. The more so because Connie was completely unaware of just how beautiful she was. Looking at her friend now, at her warm, glowing face, her mass of thick golden hair and trim figure and the intrinsic freshness that was part of Connie, Mary felt afraid, and her voice was all the more strident as she repeated, 'We're comin'.'

St George's Square was under half a mile from Walworth Way but it could have been the other end of the world. The misery and hardship that went with disease, unemployment, injustice, grinding poverty and class-consciousness had not touched the square's tranquil borders. Here children still had hot homemade bread, a comic and a bag of dolly mixtures and juju's on a Friday night when their da got paid, but it was without the spectre of the dreaded words 'being laid off' entering into their consciousness. Life was secure here. There was wallpaper on the walls and it was bug free, the pawn shop wasn't part of their vocabulary – neither was the dread and humiliation that went hand in hand with it – and the workhouse was just a building on the other side of St Michael's Ward.

It had seemed to Connie and her two companions that half

of Sunderland was out on the streets as they had made their way down Crowtree Road and into Park Lane, passing Stone Yard on their left as they walked on to West Park. The public houses were doing a roaring trade, and although it wasn't yet ten o'clock there was more than one bleary-eyed reveller lurching along under the starry, icy sky or hanging shakily on to the solidity of a lamp-post or sitting, half propped, on a friendly stone windowsill as they surveyed the world with an inane happy grin.

The three of them had been giggling and infected with the inexplicable thrill that accompanied the seeing in of a northern New Year when they had left Walworth Way, but by the time they had passed Higher Grade School they had become more subdued.

The square was bordered with trees and it was elegant; there was no other word for it, Connie thought apprehensively, as they turned into its gracious confines. And the houses were bonny. By, they were. She could imagine their occupants might well be the sort of liberated folk who would read D.H. Lawrence's *Sons and Lovers*, a new book recently published which had raised a few eyebrows being all about the sentimental education of a miner's son, as the author himself had been. However, Connie couldn't help feeling that few of these homeowners had experienced a working mine. Here it was as though they were a thousand miles away from the grimness of the narrow mean streets of the growing town, and the cesspool of the docks.

'This is it then.' Mary's tone was – if not solemn – definitely repressed, and Connie glanced at the pair's sober faces before she said, a gurgle of laughter in her voice which didn't sound at all like the prim and worthy Miss Bell, assistant housekeeper of daylight hours, 'Just remember, me bairns, they use the privy the same as we do. All right?'

'Connie!' That Mary was shocked was transparent, and her eyes, wide and startled behind her spectacles, sent Connie and Wilf into helpless laughter, the three of them ending up clutching each other as they slithered about on the glassy pavements.

'Oh, lass! Oh, I needed that.' Mary was wiping the tears from her eyes, the three of them still gasping with the remnants of what was mainly nervous hilarity, when a deep male voice from the direction of a house some few yards away said, 'I thought I heard someone out here. You made it then, I'm so glad. Come in, come in all of you.'

The amusement wiped from their faces, Mary and Wilf followed Connie as she made her way towards Dan Stewart where he stood outlined in the lighted doorway.

Had she guessed that he'd been pinned to the upstairs window ever since he'd got back to the square just under an hour ago? Dan asked himself silently as he watched Connie's approach. He just hadn't been able to bring himself to believe she would actually come. But she had. She was here. And 1914 was going to be a wonderful year, the best year of his life. He felt the beating of his heart was going to suffocate him, and because he was out of his depth – a feeling hitherto unknown to him – his voice was all the more hearty as he said, 'That's right, come in. It's bedlam but then it's New Year's Eve, isn't it. Everyone can go mad on New Year's Eve.' And then, realising his words might be misinterpreted, he added hastily, 'Not that a sense of propriety shouldn't still be upheld of course, it's not a licence for . . . Well, what I mean is . . .'

'Everyone should be allowed to enjoy themselves at least once a year?' Connie's voice was soft and she was smiling.

'Aye, yes. Exactly.'

Mary stood irresolute, before darting a worried glance at Wilf as the three of them moved forward and into the house. She liked this less and less. A leopard couldn't change its spots and this was going to end in tears.

The interior of Dan's brother's house was a surprise to Connie. She had expected— Well, she hadn't known quite what she'd expected, she admitted silently. Elegance probably, grandeur even. She had never forgotten the day she had stood in the drive of his mother's house in Ryhope Road or the terrible scene that had followed. She hadn't thought of herself as poor or not good enough before that day, but the look on Edith Stewart's face – even more than what she had said – had buried itself deep into the fertile regions of her brain from that point on. Dan's mother had thought them base and contemptible, she had been disdainful and repelled by them even before she had realised who her mother was. She had thought they were begging.

Connie breathed deeply, suddenly very tense. She shouldn't have come, Mary was right. She had nothing in common with any of these people. And then, as though to prove her wrong, a big woman appeared from the far end of the hall, probably from the kitchen if the plates of sandwiches in her hands were anything to go by, and this woman's voice was reassuringly ordinary and warm – like the cluttered hall – when she said, 'Eee, now don't tell us, you must be Connie. Is that right? You don't mind me calling you Connie, do you, lass?'

'No, no of course not.'

'This is Gladys, my brother's wife.' As Dan went hastily

into more formal introductions, drawing Mary and Wilf forward a moment later, he was silently blessing the day Art had married Gladys. There was no side to his sister-in-law and she was as open as a daisy in the sun, and her voice, thick with its northern accent, was just what was needed to break the ice.

'Now give Dan your coats, that's right, and come in and meet everyone.' Gladys's smile included Mary and Wilf as well as Connie. 'The bairns are playing dressing up in another room at the moment but they're all dizzy with excitement and dashing about like mad things, so I warn you. Martha has already had sloe gin all down the front of her.'

Gladys continued to talk as she led them into the large, pleasant parlour which, together with two other reception rooms and a small kitchen and scullery next to the indoor privy and washhouse, made up the downstairs of the house. There was a huge fire burning in the beautiful ornate fireplace, the furnishings were of good quality and the massive square of Persian carpet which covered most of the floor was splendid, but the atmosphere was homely, the furnishings worn in places and the general ambience was one of unpretentious comfortableness. Gladys had immediately sensed the tension between Dan and the trio when she had walked into the hall, and, having now seen Connie, she could understand how her youngest brother-in-law was feeling. The girl was quite unusually lovely – she didn't think she had ever seen eyes of such a deep violet-blue before – but she was very contained, almost aloof. Although that was probably nerves of course. This must be something of an ordeal for her, and after all that had happened in the past . . . She'd got some guts to be here at all.

Art thought along similar lines a moment later when he braced himself to walk across and shake Connie's hand. 'I'm very glad you could come.' He shook Wilf and Mary's hands, saying the same thing, before turning back to Connie and adding, 'I don't know what to say. Sorry seems too inadequate a word, and far too late, but I can assure you from the bottom of my heart it is genuine. I deeply regret my part in the incident which had such disastrous results for us all.'

Connie nodded, her embarrassment tying her tongue for a second, but then, as she looked into the soft brown eyes that were so like Dan's she was able to say, 'It . . . it's all right. I know you and . . . and your brother weren't like the others, Mr Stewart.'

'Art.' Art smiled at her even as he was thinking, This is the start of something between her and Dan, even a blind man could see it, and what'll happen if Dan starts courting her the Almighty alone knows. Mam'll go mad, stark staring mad, but she's only got herself to blame. She's all but thrown him at her by taking the attitude she has.

'And I'm Connie.' It was said shyly, and accompanied by a smile that didn't quite manage to hide her apprehension, and suddenly Art found himself thinking, Damn Mam and all her manoeuvrings! He wouldn't have had Gladys if his mother had had her way, and why shouldn't Dan have his chance too? His mother wasn't going to like it but they'd all weather the storm if they stood firm.

'What would you like to drink?' Dan was speaking to the three of them but his eyes and ears and all his senses were full of only Connie, and when Art said, 'Oh everyone's helping themselves, lad, that's easier on me and Gladys. You look after Connie and—' he turned to Wilf, his eyebrows raised, and as Wilf said hastily, 'Wilf, Wilf and Mary,' Art continued, 'Wilf can look after Mary, all right?'

Very neatly done. Mary's face was straight as she surveyed them all. The brother had already got Dan and Connie paired off and she didn't trust any of them as far as she could throw them. The wife seemed all right – Mary had to admit that Gladys had been something of a surprise – but she had married the brother, hadn't she, so she couldn't be all she seemed. Well, this lot weren't going to pull the wool over *her* eyes. For some reason Connie had a weak spot where Dan Stewart was concerned, but she hadn't, and she would make sure she kept her eyes and ears open. There were some nice men in the world – she glanced at Wilf out of the corner of her eye at this thought, her mouth softening for a moment – but actions speak louder than words, and it would take more than a bit of soft soap to convince her that Dan Stewart wasn't playing some game of his own.

'Mam, if you take my advice you'll leave 'em to stew in their own juice. They're not daft, they know which side their bread's buttered and they'll be back with their tails between their legs right enough.'

What a stupid individual this particular son was. Edith Stewart looked at John, her cold face with its flat features betraying none of her thoughts. He wasn't like her or Henry – Henry, for all his faults, had been an intelligent man and had possessed excellent business acumen – but John was positively cretinous at times. He was a constant irritation, but never more than when he was presumptuous enough to dare to give her advice, like now.

'The matter is not open for discussion, John.' Edith spoke

quietly, glancing round her drawing room which was full of various pillars of Sunderland society, including the Rotheringtons and their mousey daughter. She liked this room. She had spent a great deal of time and thought on its furnishings and decoration when they had first moved to Ryhope Road two years after Dan was born, and she felt this room was a true reflection of herself. The walls were of an eggshell blue and the paintwork two or three shades darker, and the gold-framed pictures which covered a great deal of their surface had been bought for their size and grandeur rather than their content. The two sets of windows were draped in long folds of dove-grey velvet and exactly matched the carpet, and the heavy mahogany chairs and chaise longues which were dotted about the room, along with the china cabinets and two bookcases, had cost a small fortune. Either side of the enormous fireplace, draped in a mantel-border of the same material and fringing as the curtains, stood two four-foot matching figures of young negro girls worked in black marble and carrying baskets of fruit on their heads. The aesthetic beauty of the statuettes was quite lost on Edith – she had purchased them simply because they had been expensive and impressive.

Edith breathed in deeply, drawing on the satisfaction and sense of power the room always gave her, before she turned to John at her side, and said, her manner dismissive, 'I've told you what I want you to do, John, so go and do it. It's' – she glanced at the enormous gold and black marble clock which took up most of the mantelpiece – 'half past ten now, that will give you plenty of time to convey my message and have them back here before twelve o'clock.'

Damn it all, he didn't believe this. John worked his jaw

for a moment, his teeth clenched and his eyes angry. New Year's Eve and she expected him to go running round to Art's place like an errand boy. 'What if they won't come?'

'What?' Her voice was sharper now and she must have realised this because she had moderated her tone when she said, 'Of course they will come if you tell them I've specifically asked for their presence.'

Them! All this was for Dan, she couldn't give a fig for Art and Gladys. He wetted his lips, then dug his teeth deep into the flesh of the lower one before he said, 'Aye, well that's what you say but I've got my doubts.'

'Really.' The tone was icy.

John's lips moved but whatever he had been about to say he thought better of it as he glanced at his mother's tight face, and after another moment he swung round and made his way across the room.

'John?' Ann had been watching Sidney attempting to make conversation with one of his grandmother's councillor friends and his daughter – a stuck-up little madam if ever she'd seen one – and inwardly commiserating with her son, and now her voice was abrupt as she caught hold of her husband's arm and asked, 'Where do you think you're going?'

'She wants Dan and the other two bringing here.'

'And you offered to go and get them I suppose?' said Ann cuttingly. She had known, within weeks of getting wed, that there were three in her marriage and that Edith was the strongest of them all, and she bitterly resented what she considered her husband's spineless attitude with his mother, especially in view of the fact that he was the devil incarnate with herself.

She had known Edith most of her life – Ann's parents

owned a string of drapery shops in Sunderland and Newcastle and were in the Stewarts' social circle – and Edith had always treated her with some warmth, so when John had started courting her she had known she had his mother's approval. What she hadn't realised, and had only discovered during the first acrimonious weeks of her marriage after a particularly violent altercation with John, was that their courtship had been purely his mother's idea. Edith had demanded a daughter-in-law of some social standing and one who wasn't inclined to be difficult, and Ann had fitted the bill. She had been tricked – and that wasn't too strong a word for it – into marriage with a debauchee who had never had the slightest pang of love towards her to soften his harsh treatment.

If it wasn't for Sidney – who was totally hers and a balm to her soul – she knew now she would have braved her parents' horror and the wrath of her mother-in-law, and even the inevitable ostracism of their social circle, and left him sometime in the last long eighteen years. As it was, three years after Sidney had been born, when they had been wed for six years, she had made a stand against John's rapacious sexual appetites and insisted on separate bedrooms with a determination which had surprised them both, and since that time a little peace had come into her life.

'I didn't offer to go and fetch them as it happens,' John now growled under his breath, 'but she won't listen to reason.'

'And so you are going anyway.'

'Don't start.'

Don't start! Ann glanced across the room and saw Sidney making his way over to her, a look of concern on his young face which was habitual when his father was anywhere near. It disturbed her but she had long since accepted there was nothing she could do about it. Her son was shy and sensitive and clever – everything his father was not – and Sidney had always seemed to sense how things were between his parents, even though she had been careful to avoid any unpleasantness in front of the lad when he was younger.

But at least she had won her fight to allow Sidney to follow the desire of his heart and continue his education with a view to attending university and then medical school, rather than be drawn straight into the family business as John had demanded. But she didn't fool herself that her husband had given in to her wishes or those of his son. Surprisingly Ann had found an ally in Edith when the matter had been brought to the matriarch. A medical man in the family? Possibly even a surgeon or a consultant? Edith had weighed John's desire to have his only son working alongside him and under his control against the prestige connected with her grandson's ambition, and there had been no contest.

'Mother?' The expensive private school Sidney was now attending on the outskirts of Newcastle had taken 'mam' from his vocabulary, but Ann didn't mind. She knew her son loved her.

'It's all right, Sidney.'

John knew what the exchange had meant and he stared at them both for a moment, resentment and deep bitterness burning inside him. She had been determined he would have nothing to do with his son from the moment the child had been born, damn her. She'd fed him poison along with her milk, a toxin which had warped the normal feeling a son should have for his father, until now the lad had an aversion to him. If he could have had his way a year ago – got him away from his mother's skirts and working with him in the business – he might still have been able to reach him. But not now. Sidney was as good as dead to him now. He didn't want it to matter – the lad was a milk-sop, a weakling with all his namby-pamby, mawkish ideas of working for the good of humanity, 'the good of humanity!' what was that? – but it did matter. Damn them both, it did matter.

'I'll be back before twelve.' He was speaking directly to Ann and when she merely shrugged, lifting her eyebrows as she turned away, the desire to strike her was strong. She'd push him too far one of these days with her airs and graces, the mealy-mouthed dried-out bitch. She'd always been skin and bone from a young girl and as plain as a pikestaff; she ought to be down on her knees thanking him for being prepared to take her on in the first place.

He glanced at them both one last time – or at their backs to be more precise as they walked across the room – and then turned on his heel, walking out without looking to left or right or returning the salutations that one or two of the distinguished company sent his way, and his face was as black as thunder.

Connie was sitting in the corner of a comfortable chesterfield sofa, a plate of food on her lap and a glass of wine on the small occasional table at her side. She was beginning to feel more at ease. This was partly due to the fact that the sofa was in an alcove, and the recess engendered a feeling of privacy, although it was still on view to the rest of the room, but she could see Mary and Wilf – who at first had stood stiffly to attention – chatting to another couple and laughing and smiling, and this pleased her.

'They're fine.' Dan had followed her glance and now he brought her attention back to himself as he continued softly,

'Don't worry about your friends.'

'I'm not.' And then Connie smiled self-consciously as she added, 'Well, perhaps I am. They don't know anyone and they only came to keep me company.'

'She doesn't like me, your friend, does she.' It was a statement not a question and followed with, 'Not that I blame her of course.' He gave a short laugh.

'She doesn't know you.'

'No, she doesn't.' There was an awkward pause and then Dan said, his voice so low she could scarcely hear it, 'That's all I'm asking you to do, Connie. Get to know me a little.'

It was the first time he had said her name and she shivered. The silence was longer this time, and after a moment or two she forced herself to turn her head and look at him, and she knew his eyes would be waiting for her.

'Connie, listen to me.' He rubbed his hand tightly across his mouth. 'I know what you're probably thinking and you have every right to think the worst. I can't undo the past, or what happened to your mother and brother and grandmother in the fire, but if I could I would. Do you believe that?'

She stared at him and felt the colour sweeping over her face. She had the urge to jump up from the couch and leave the house, quickly, before either of them said another word. But she couldn't do that. Neither could she sit here and let him say anything else without getting a few things straight. 'My mother wasn't killed in the fire,' she said flatly. 'She died the week before of a heart attack.'

'Oh.' He looked faintly surprised. 'I'm sorry.'

'She was worn out, physically, mentally and emotionally, and that was partly due – *mainly* due – to the work she did. She'd had a choice, you see, after the baby died, to put us all in the workhouse or to try and get a job. But there were no jobs.'

'Connie, you don't have to say anything else.'

'I do.' Her voice was quiet but intense. 'And I tell you now that I'm not ashamed of her. She was a good mam, wonderful, and she did what she had to do to keep the family together. She hated it and it killed her, but she did it for us, for me and Larry and my grandmother. And it was only after Jacob had gone, not before. She was married to my father but he left us before I was born . . .' She went on talking, telling him everything, and he said not a word. The party flowed on in the perimeter of their vision, but their world was narrowed down to the sofa and Connie's low voice.

And then she was silent, and the silence continued for a long moment before Dan said, 'I should say something but frankly I don't know what to say.'

'That's all right.' It was finished before it had started and that was probably the best thing, she told herself fiercely, willing herself with every fibre of her being not to cry. She should have known how he would react – she *had* known she insisted silently, refusing to acknowledge her hope that he would understand, really understand. But it didn't matter, she wouldn't let it matter. She was not going to hang her head in shame – society could make its judgements and snap decisions but she *knew* what her mam had really been like. She hated him. She hated him and his whole rotten family. She had to get out of here . . .

'Connie?' It was the timbre of his voice that raised her drowning eyes to meet his, and what she saw there overwhelmed her for a second. 'I'm sorry your mother was driven to do what she did, and that Larry and your grandmother

250

died like that. I'm sorry you had all those years in the workhouse and for the struggle—' He stopped abruptly, taking an audible breath. How did you express the inexpressible? How did you tell someone you had only met five times in your life – and two of them thirteen years ago – that they filled you with such a raw and painful and ecstatic feeling that you felt you didn't know yourself any more? He was twenty-seven years old and he knew now he had never been alive until that moment twelve nights ago when he had glanced across the restaurant and seen her. And if he told anyone that they would either laugh their heads off or think he'd gone mad. Perhaps he had gone mad? Maybe that was why he was eating and drinking and sleeping her every second of the day and night?

He was still looking at her and she was returning his glance, and when his hand moved over hers she blinked once and then became very still, and it was in that moment, with their senses heightened to breaking point, that Connie became aware of a figure standing close to the edge of the sofa behind Dan and raised her eyes.

'Very touching,' said John softly.

At the sound of his brother's voice Dan spun round and rose swiftly to his feet, and as though they were connected by a wire Art was there in the next instant, his voice low as he said, 'Why are you here? I thought you were all at Mam's?'

'We are.' John took his gaze from Connie's white face long enough to cast his eyes on his brother and then take in the crowded room before he looked at Connie again and said, 'Mam wanted you to come round, that's all, but of course she didn't realise you were having a . . . get-together of your own.' The hesitation was deliberate and covertly insulting and he still didn't raise his gaze from Connie.

His face straight and his voice flat, Art said, 'Aye, well we are as you can see, so you can tell her that, can't you.'

'And more besides.' This was from Dan, and as Connie rose to her feet he reached out and drew her close to him with his hand at her elbow.

'You're encouraging this, you and Gladys?' John was speaking to Art and his voice was derisory.

'This?'

Connie was aware of one or two glances coming their way, and a sick agitation was adding to the deep shock that had first filled her when she had glanced up and seen the man she loathed and detested staring at her with those devilish eyes.

'Dan consorting with the likes of her.'

'That's enough. You shut your filthy mouth.' The words were wrenched up from Dan's stomach, and they were dark and ominous.

'Me filthy?' A mocking smile spread over John's face as he looked at his youngest brother. 'By, there's none so blind as them that can't see. Saint Dan! Holier than thou, Dan. I've had you rammed down me throat since you were a bairn by our mam, perfect you were. But your halo's slipped now, lad, it has that. She's fooling you and you can't see it, can you. She's got you tied up in knots—'

'I'm warning you, John. If you don't shut your mouth I'll shut it for you.'

'Do you know what her mother was? Do you? The last time I saw Sadie Bell she was whoring in a bar down in—'

'*You're not fit to say my mother's name.*' For a moment all three men thought Connie was going to spring at John, and John actually took a step backwards before he checked himself, facing the woman whose flashing eyes were on a level with his. 'You are scum, *real* scum,' Connie hissed quietly but in a voice which vibrated with the depth of her emotion. '*You*, you to call my mam after the damage you've caused, and all because you wanted her. It was jealousy of Jacob that brought you to the cottage all those years ago, wasn't it. You might fool the others but you don't fool me. You wanted my mam but she didn't want you. No woman in her right mind would want you.'

To say that Dan and Art were flabbergasted was putting it mildly. This wee slip of a girl with the face of an angel and the poise of a lady had just voiced what both of them had thought for years but never had the nerve to articulate. And the effect on John was riveting. The blood had surged into his face; even his eyes were coloured with it.

By now most of the room had realised there was some sort of disturbance going on although they had been unable to hear anything clearly, but as Connie finished speaking Gladys appeared on the other side of John, taking his arm as she said, 'Come away out of it, John, this is New Year's Eve for crying out loud. Trust you to spoil it for everyone,' and Wilf and Mary were pressing close to Connie and forming a triangle with Dan, enclosing her.

'One day.' John wasn't shouting, in fact his voice was eerily low, but it had the same effect as if he were shouting on the group clustered around him, causing them to wrinkle their faces against its content. All of them except Connie and Dan, whose countenance was like granite. 'I'll see you brought low one day, you see if I don't, you dirty little baggage—'

No power on earth or beyond could have stopped Dan's fist from shooting out and making crunching contact with

John's jaw, and as a woman somewhere in the background screamed, Connie was conscious of thinking, Oh no, no, for this to happen! Everything's been spoilt, before the room seemed to erupt as Dan and John were at each other's throats.

It was over in seconds as Art and two or three of his friends yanked the two men apart and then held on to them, and as Gladys shouted, 'Get him out of here! Go on!' in John's direction, her brother-in-law shouted back, 'I'm going, don't worry! I wouldn't stay here with the scum you've invited if you paid me a hundred pounds,' which made Dan tense against the hands constraining him and struggle to get free.

Connie stood as though turned to stone, and even after John had gone she still didn't move even though Mary was fussing for her to sit down. It wasn't until Dan's sympathetic captors released him and he drew her down beside him on the sofa that she came out of the whirling confusion of her thoughts. She could feel herself diminishing and shrinking, even though everyone was studiously not looking her way. How much anyone had heard she didn't know, but one thing was for sure, they all knew she wasn't like them. She was different.

She shut her eyes for an infinitesimal moment and then opened them as Dan said, 'He's mad, he always has been, and my mother makes him worse. They're . . . they're unbalanced, the pair of them.'

She couldn't bring herself to reply for a second, and then she said, with Mary's hand pressed comfortingly on her shoulder, 'Perhaps, but . . . they're your family, they have more right to be here than I have.'

'No, it's not like that, really. You don't understand, this has been brewing for years.'

Connie stared at him dry-eyed, but she was drenched with tears inside. Mary had been right and she had been wrong. This had been foolish, worse than foolish, and she should never have come. She had tried to pretend to herself that she could fit in and look what the result had been. 'I have to go.'

'No, no, don't go, Connie. Please, not like this.'

'I've ruined your brother's party.'

'Of course you haven't.' He was patting her hand in his agitation and now he tried to make a joke and lighten the proceedings as he said, a smile on his face, 'We provided a bit of entertainment to brighten up the evening if nothing else.'

It was the wrong tack to take and he knew this immediately as the words registered in her eyes like a blow.

'I really do have to go now.'

'I'll see you home.'

'*No.*' And then more quietly, 'No, Dan. I – I don't want you to. I'll be perfectly all right with Mary and Wilf.'

'But I can see you again? I mean, we could go for a meal, or to the theatre? I hear *The Merchant of Venice* at the Empire is very good, or if you prefer there's a moving picture show at the King's Theatre.'

She didn't reply for some five or six seconds and then it took all her control to say quietly, 'I think we both know that would not be a good idea.'

'On the contrary, I think it's an excellent idea.'

'I'm sorry, Dan.' Connie rose quickly. She really couldn't take any more of this, not with him sitting there with that bewildered look on his face and his cheek showing the mark of one of John's blows. It could never work. She knew it and he knew it really, he was just trying to be a gentleman now.

He'd perhaps even feel relief when she had gone. That thought stiffened her back and enabled her to say quite steadily, 'Goodbye, and . . . and thank you for asking me to come.'

'You aren't even going to stay and see the New Year in?' Dan asked desperately as he too rose to his feet.

'No, I'm sorry.' She turned from him and made her way towards the door. She didn't turn round to see if he was following her, but when she reached the hall there was only Mary and Wilf behind her, their faces strained and concerned.

Art and Gladys and the two men who had ushered John out were standing whispering in a huddle by the front door, and as the two men nodded to Connie before making their way back into the sitting room, Gladys came forward saying, 'You aren't leaving? Not yet? Oh, lass, stay. Don't let our John spoil things.'

'We really do have to go, but thank you for a lovely evening.'

It was a ridiculous statement in the circumstances but no one commented on it, and as Wilf collected their coats from the large mahogany hall-stand Art joined them, looking enquiringly at his wife but asking no questions.

The goodbyes were hasty and awkward, but then they were outside in the bitingly crisp air and walking quickly out of the square, not a word passing between them.

And it wasn't until they were nearly home and just about to enter Walworth Way from Crowtree Road, and the sudden din of the ships' hooters in the docks and the muffled shouts from the public house they had just passed told them they'd entered 1914, that Mary stopped and drew Connie's stiff figure into her arms. She glanced at Wilf's worried face over her friend's shoulder, and her voice was quiet and not at all as one would expect on New Year's Eve, as she said, 'A happy New Year, lass. A happy New Year.'

Chapter Fifteen

It was half past seven on Thursday morning, New Year's Day, and Connie hadn't slept at all. It was strange; she didn't even feel tired. She hadn't done since they had got back to Walworth Way the night before, and Mary and Wilf had joined the others in the kitchen. She had come straight into her room intending to blot the events of the evening out in the soporific escape of sleep.

She had felt tired at that point – bone tired, exhausted – but then she had opened the top drawer of the oak chest-of-drawers she had bought a few weeks previously, and her eyes had fastened on the small engraved box next to her clean nightdress. It was a beautifully carved little thing decorated with animals and birds, and it housed the most precious thing she possessed. She had taken it out of the drawer, walked over to her bed and sat down before she opened the hinged lid. The piece of rag was just as Larry had given it to her, and as she took it out of its resting place and held it against her cheek the pain in her heart became unbearable.

She had still been sitting there rocking to and fro, the rag clutched between her fingers, when the lodgers had gone to bed and Mary had said goodnight to Wilf over an hour later, and the agony of loss and guilt and regret and a hundred other emotions besides hadn't subsided. It had been nine years since her baby brother – and he would forever stay in her mind as her baby brother – had died, but it could have been yesterday such was her anguish. John's venom and the violence of the scene that night had resurrected all the misery that the opiate of day-to-day living normally kept under wraps, and Connie felt desolate. Desolate and confused and alone.

She had pretended to go to sleep for Mary's sake, but once her friend's faint rhythmic snores had rumbled the air waves she had sat up in bed and pulled the curtain nearest to her slightly to one side, peering out of the chink into the dark cobbled street of grim terraced houses. She had remained like that until the night sky had changed to silver grey and it was time to get up, but by then her mind was more at peace.

She hadn't been responsible for the accident which had taken her loved ones, although she would always regret that she hadn't started work a day or two later. If she had been there she knew she would have saved them that night. Whatever it had taken, she would have saved them.

But she *was* responsible for the travesty of the night before and she had to shoulder the blame for this. She had known it was foolish to see Dan Stewart again. It was his kinsfolk who had destroyed her own family, and whatever way you looked at it it was wrong to let her attraction for him – and she was attracted to him, she had to face that – overrule her conscience. Dan, and Art too, weren't like the others, and she had felt their remorse for what had occurred was genuine, but they had made their personal apologies and she had accepted them and that was that. It was settled, and it had to remain that way. For all their sakes.

She rose quietly, pulling her coat over her nightdress and

thrusting her feet into her ankle boots before creeping out into the kitchen. There had been a half-hearted attempt to clear the debris from the jollifications of the night before, and at least someone had had the sense to bank down the fire in the range so it hadn't completely burnt away, although the kitchen was still icy-cold.

Connie soon had the fire blazing and once the kettle was boiled she had a hasty wash before making a cup of tea for herself and Mary and carrying it through to the other room. They would have to get a move on if they weren't going to be late for work, and it was work she was going to concentrate on in this new year. She knew where she was with her job – it was orderly and controlled and there were no nasty surprises – and it was the means of the sweet jar growing fatter. And the sweet jar held the key to the future. A future in which she would be working for herself within the next few years if she had anything to do with it.

The image of a tall dark man with soft brown eyes and a handsome, somewhat autocratic face, swam into her mind for a moment and she brushed the shadow of Dan Stewart aside irritably, angry it had surfaced again. Last night had proved how futile any thoughts in that direction were, and no doubt within a couple of days he would have forgotten about her completely. And she would forget about *him*. She nodded to the thought purposefully, and such was her determination that she marched into the bedroom like a small virago, causing Mary to awake with such a start that her heart didn't stop galloping for a whole minute.

New Year's Day. The year was starting like this and she knew exactly who was to blame for the current state of affairs between herself and her son. Edith brought the fragile china cup, held between her finger and thumb, to her lips and sipped at the tea before placing the cup gently back on the saucer and glancing round the breakfast room. She always breakfasted alone in here now that Dan was gone. Kitty had suggested she might like a tray in her room but she wasn't starting any of those slipshod habits and she had told Kitty so.

She breakfasted light – she was aware that her stout, chunky build was not conducive to large cooked breakfasts – and normally confined herself to one poached egg, a slice of toast and two cups of tea. Moderation in all things led to a long life. She nodded to the thought. And she intended to live for a long, long time.

Her breakfast complete, Edith sat back in the chair and dabbed her mouth on the linen napkin, her hard black eyes fixed on the pair of Spode urn-shaped pot-pourri vases which stood alone on the windowsill, so as to bring all eyes to them. But today her possession of the fine porcelain gave her none of the normal satisfaction, in fact she didn't even see the vases.

She hadn't been able to believe what John had related last night. That Art and Gladys had allowed Dan to bring that girl – that whore's ragamuffin brat – into their home as a guest was beyond the bounds of comprehension. Of course Gladys was a low, raucous-mouthed woman, likely she had seen a kindred spirit in the Bell creature. She hadn't forgotten or forgiven her daughter-in-law's attitude that Sunday in October over the accident in the mine at Sengenhydd in the Aber Valley. Gladys raising her voice to her like that – virtually shouting – and just because she had said that the explosion and fire which had taken the lives of over 400 men was a natural hazard and to be expected. Of course there was a whole branch of Gladys's family that were miners and so she was bound to blame the employers and mineowners; she would never rise above her squalid beginnings, that one. But Gladys, common and unrefined as she was, was one thing. Connie Bell was quite another. She couldn't bear, couldn't *bear* to think of Dan touching that . . . that contaminated person.

Edith admitted to herself that she had been foolish, very foolish, to react as she had on Christmas Day. Of course it was John's fault springing it on her like that and she had told him so, but knowing Dan as she did – his penchant for the underdog and overdeveloped social conscience – she should have played it differently. She sat forward in her chair again, biting her lip with vexation.

She knew the Rotheringtons had expected Dan to be present last night, and if they were to catch any whisper of him consorting with the likes of Connie Bell . . . She stood, her lips folding into a thin line. Something must be done, and at once. Somehow her methodical, well-organised plans had gone haywire and things were getting swiftly out of hand. And she wouldn't have it. She wouldn't tolerate this.

The first step would be to make discreet enquiries as to how her letter had been received by the management of the Grand Hotel, and what they intended to do about the trollop they had working for them. Of course the manager was a man. Edith's eyes narrowed. And he may well be the sort of individual who thought with a lower part of his anatomy than his brain when it came to creatures like the Bell chit. Edith made no apology in her mind for the vulgarity, and it didn't occur to her that the lady she now professed to be would not have thought in such a way.

But pressure could be brought to bear, she told herself tightly. She wanted Connie Bell dismissed, and she would also keep a careful eye on the baggage to make sure she didn't acquire another post like assistant housekeeper. John would come in useful there. She wouldn't rest until that girl was back where she belonged, in the gutter, and Dan saw the daughter of Sadie Bell for what she was: the cunning, conniving little madam.

But her enquiries would have to wait until tomorrow. Edith walked to the door and opened it quietly. She was hosting the New Year luncheon for the Christian Women's Guild of Fellowship – a society drawn from the town's most influential women which had first begun in 1895 when the *Sunderland Daily Echo* had run an appeal to 'Feed the Poor Bairns', and the money raised had provided breakfasts for the town's poor school children – and she wanted to make sure Kitty had the five-course menu under control. The luncheon had been held at the Rotheringtons' last year and they had a cook *and* a maid. However, there had only been four courses and one of those had been a somewhat uninteresting soup.

Edith stepped into the hall, taking a few moments to adjust the blooms in the large flower display standing on a small, walnut veneered table enhanced by herringbone inlays, either side of which stood a pair of superb Queen Anne chairs. Once the roses were to her liking she raised her eyes and glanced around the beautifully decorated surroundings. Her Dan with the scum of the streets! Never. Never would she allow such an abomination. *She would rather see him dead first.*

It was almost eight o'clock in the evening and it had been a long, long day. Connie had just been checking the clean linen in the laundry room – normally her last job of the day – but she had been drawn to the sashed window in the last few moments, where a border of snow was mounting against the bottom pane. It had been snowing all afternoon, and would be quite deep again by now. She stared out into the whirling thick flakes, her hands full of fluffy white towels, the weariness of a heavy day following the emotional turmoil of the evening before and then a sleepless night evident in her bowed shoulders.

What was Dan doing right at this moment? Was he thinking of her? Had he thought of her at all today or had he determined to put her out of his mind following the scene of last night? Men were different to women with regard to emotion, she knew that. They were more logical, sensible she supposed, their codes and values were tied up with the head more than the heart. And yet . . . She didn't feel Dan was like that.

Oh don't talk daft! It was sharp and irritable. How on earth did she know what Dan Stewart was like? Here she was yammering on like a whining bairn and about someone who was virtually a stranger. Where had all her gumption gone?

She found out where it was in the next second when the door to the laundry room opened and Colonel Fairley stepped furtively inside, his manner changing once the door was shut behind him and he saw her standing with her back now to the window.

'There you are, m'dear.' He was smiling as he approached her. 'I thought I might find you in here.'

Colonel Fairley! This was all she needed. When she had arrived at the hotel that morning it was to learn the Colonel had left a few minutes earlier to spend the day with an old army colleague, and Connie had been hoping she could escape without seeing him. Even after a good night's sleep when she was bright and breezy the Colonel was hard to take, but right at this moment . . . 'Colonel Fairley.' Connie forced herself to speak quietly and firmly and she didn't return his smile. 'Is anything wrong? Do you need fresh towels or bed linen? I thought the housemaid had seen to all that this morning.'

'No, it's nothing like that, m'dear. Wanted a little word, don't you know. Something to your advantage if you get my meaning?'

'I'm afraid I don't.'

Her body was like a ramrod now. He was close, too close, and she could smell whisky on his breath.

'Thing is, m'dear, you've got to tread carefully. They're on to you.'

'On to me?' She didn't have the faintest idea what he was talking about, and her bewilderment must have shown in her face because he said, his voice overly surreptitious, 'Harold, m'dear, Harold. He knows. Had a letter – anonymous of course – but I fancy you've upset one of your gentlemen friends, eh? But I'm broad-minded. You're a working girl when all's said and done.'

She stared at him, her magnificent blue eyes open wide, and as the blood surged in his body and desire made him hard, he said thickly, 'Don't play games, m'dear. No need for that with old Fairley. I'll treat you right, always have done with me fillies in the past.'

Connie ignored this, along with the sickening panic that was knotting her stomach, and said, 'Colonel Fairley, you have been misinformed in some way. I have no gentlemen friends, none, and I have done nothing wrong.'

'That's what I told Harold so don't worry, you're quite

safe. Got him to burn the damn thing, all right? And like I said, I'm broad-minded, I don't mind. Had all sorts, don't you know. Travelling the world like I have you can't stand on ceremony.' His tongue curled out, moistening his lips. 'Now you just be kind to old Fairley, eh? 'Cause I've been kind to you, m'dear. Don't want you upset, do we.'

He was between her and the door and she would never make it past him by brute force. He was a stocky man, solid. Connie took a deep breath and said as coldly as she could, considering the state of her quivering insides, 'Colonel, I don't know what this letter said but I can assure you if any allegations were made of an improper nature they are absolutely without foundation. Now if you don't mind I have things to do before I leave.'

What was this? She was trying to wriggle out of it now, was she? And after all he had done for her. Poor dos – this wasn't playing the game at all, but then what could you expect from her class. Didn't know the meaning of the word gratefulness, any of 'em. 'Now look here, m'girl, I've played fair with you and I expect it to be appreciated. And I'm a generous man, I'm very generous. You do right by old Fairley and he'll do right by you. Understood?'

Connie's face was scarlet now and her nails were digging into the palms of her hands as she warned herself not to go for him. She couldn't win in a fight with this man, she had to talk her way out of this room. 'I don't mean to be unappreciative,' she said stiffly, 'but all I can say is that this letter seems to have been a pack of lies and it's given you quite the wrong impression.'

'Is that so?' Now his whole manner was insulting as he leant slightly forward, his body almost touching hers as he

said, 'So your mother wasn't a *fille de joie*, is that what you
are saying? A harlot? A whore?' And as her face spoke for
her, 'I thought so. Well, my money is as good as the next
man's, m'dear.'

'*How dare you.*' All pretence at reasonable persuasion was
gone as Connie shouted at him. 'You get out of here, you
disgusting man.'

'Disgusting?' The Colonel blocked her path as she made
to push round him and he swore, the profanity of the most
base kind, before he pushed her back against the wall causing
her head to crack with a resounding thud against the window.
And then he slapped her, very hard, across the face.

It was so unexpected and so shocking that for a moment
Connie was frozen, the towels scattered about her feet, but
then as she felt his hands tearing at the bodice of her dress she
opened her mouth to scream, only to find herself felled to the
floor as he hit her again. And then he was on top of her and
the wind was completely knocked out of her, and his hand
was across her mouth clamping it shut.

The buzzing and whirling in her head told her she was on
the verge of fainting and she knew she mustn't; all hope would
be gone then and he would have her, like this, on the floor.

He was muttering to himself, one hand still over her mouth
and the other struggling to hoist up her dress and petticoat,
and his gasps were saying, 'Ten a penny, your sort, ten a penny.
Been at it for years I don't doubt, and you try to come the
innocent with old Fairley. Take me for a fool would you.
Would you?'

And then her skirt was up over her thighs, and she felt his
hand roughly probing at the mound between her legs and she
felt she would die, that nothing that could happen to her would

ever be as bad as this. She could feel his hot mouth at her breast where her clothes were gaping wide, and as a consuming revulsion filled her it enabled her to gather every last shred of strength left in her body and bring her knee up with all the force she could muster into Colonel Fairley's groin.

His groan was long and high and he twisted on her, his hands coming up between his legs, causing the breath to further leave her body, but she knew she hadn't a second to lose. She heaved and pushed him off her, crawling to one side as he continued to whimper, his head bent to his knees, and then she was standing up and the door handle was in her fingers. She felt sick, so sick. She wrenched open the door and staggered into the deserted corridor beyond, her senses swimming from the ravenous assault but the need to put some distance between herself and her attacker paramount.

'*Connie?*'

The relief of seeing and hearing Mary brought the feeling of faintness strongly again, but she fought it with all her might, sinking down on to the floor but keeping her head up and taking great gulps of air in-between gasping, 'He . . . Colonel Fairley . . . he tried to . . . in there.'

'Oh, lass, lass.' Mary was on her hunkers at Connie's side with her arms tight round her, and Connie's shaking was vibrating through both of them. 'I've got you, lass, I've got you. You'll be all right. Connie, Connie, come on, lass.'

'Mary . . . he tried to . . .'

'I know, lass, I know. You were late, it's gone eight, an' so I come lookin' for you, an' one of the lasses tipped me the wink that Mrs Pegg had told the Colonel he might find you in there. Give him her keys so I understand tell, 'cos he said he wanted a private word with you afore you went home, but she knew what he was about all right. Didn't know Violet had her lugs flappin' though, did she, the rotten old sow.'

'Oh, Mary.'

'Did . . . did he . . . ?'

'No.' And then more strongly, 'No, no he didn't. But . . .'

'I know, lass, I know.'

'He . . . he was so strong.'

'Aye, they are, lass. The blighters are.'

And then the murmurings were cut off as Colonel Fairley appeared in the doorway, his face beetroot red but his clothing in place. He stood there for a second watching them as they sat huddled together on the floor some two or three yards away but he said not a word, turning and stumbling down the corridor in the opposite direction and disappearing out of sight.

'Help me up, Mary.'

Once on her feet Connie's shaking and the extent of her dishevelment became more obvious, and as Mary attempted to fasten the few remaining buttons that were left on her bodice, Connie stood breathing deeply, trying to control the tremors, before she said, 'He . . . he said Mr Alridge had received a letter, a nasty letter that wasn't signed, Mary. He knew about . . . about my mam. Who would do something like that?'

'I don't know, lass, but the so-an'-so wants stringin' up. Here.' Mary had been dressed ready for the outdoors, and now she pulled her woollen shawl from under her coat, wrapping it round Connie as though she were a child. 'That's better, lass, no one would know now. You can't see where the buttons are off.'

'My . . . hair.'

The normally neat, shining bun was hanging in tangled

golden coils down her back – the pins scattered all over the laundry room floor – and although Connie tried to tidy it, her hands were trembling so much she was making it worse. Again Mary provided the answer, taking most of the pins out of her own hair and fixing Connie's, before bundling her brown locks back under her green felt hat.

'We'll go out the back way, lass, an' if you wait near the cold store I'll get your things.' Mary took Connie's arm, her voice low and encouraging as though she were dealing with an injured child or a fragile invalid.

'Go?' Connie had begun to walk along the corridor with her friend, but now she jerked to an abrupt halt. She stared into Mary's concerned face before she said, her body shuddering but her voice flat, 'I'm not going anywhere, lass, not until I've seen Mr Alridge or Lucy. I want something done about this, he's not getting away with it.' She raised her hands to her aching face, the heat from her burning skin telling her she was going to be black and blue in the morning. 'He hit me and he tried to force me, those are the plain facts.'

'Aye, I know, lass, I know. But . . .'

'What?'

'It's Colonel Fairley, isn't it, an' he's related to the Alridges.'

'What's that got to do with it?' Connie was wondering why she didn't want to cry. She was shaking all over, she didn't seem to be able to stop the quivering that was turning her bowels to water and sending her muscles into spasm, but there was a strange numbness where there should have been tears. Was that shock? She had heard people talk of shock before. Was that what this was? Whatever it was, she blessed it. Tears could come later.

'Oh, lass, you know as well as I do, now then. He's a guest here an' he's gentry. They won't take your part against him what with—' Mary stopped suddenly, aware she was in danger of being unforgivably tactless. But it was too late.

'What with knowing about my mam?' For a moment Connie's head drooped and then she forced it up with savage determination. If Mary could say that, Mary her friend who was closer than a sister and who knew more about her than anyone else in the world, then what would the others say? What Mary was implying was that Mr Alridge and Lucy, and anyone else who heard about this, would assume she had led the Colonel on, that she had invited him to . . . Like mother, like daughter. Brazen huzzies, the pair of them. Bad blood outs. Oh aye, she could hear them. She had already been labelled an upstart, even by the staff who liked her, she knew – she wasn't stupid. And human nature being what it was this would make the gossip all the more vicious.

So what should she do? Keep quiet and put it down to experience? Be grateful that he hadn't actually managed to take her down?

She'd rather put her head in the gas oven!

'I'm going to report him, Mary.'

'You can't, lass, listen to reason. You've worked so hard to get where you are now an' you'll never get another job like this one. An' they won't give you a reference, not if you go with a cloud over your head.'

'Everyone knows what the Colonel's like.'

'Whey aye, they do, but they won't stick their nebs out for you an' you know it.'

'I don't care.' Connie crossed her forearms tight against her waist, the marks of the Colonel's hands standing out in vivid contrast against the lint whiteness of the rest of her face.

'Aye, you do, an' you're not like them with a pretty face an' nowt up top either. Least said, soonest mended. It might stick in your craw – it sticks in mine an' all if you want to know – but it's best in the long run.'

'Best for whom?' Something was happening to the numbness. She had never felt so alone in her life, not even when she had first heard the news about her granny and Larry, or last night when John Stewart had treated her as less than the muck under his boots. But she couldn't give in to the weakness that had her wanting to run away and hide like a small wounded animal. She couldn't. She'd never be able to look at herself in the mirror again. Colonel Fairley had assumed she was a common strumpet, and if she didn't say something it would be like agreeing with what that letter had said about her mam, about them both. It must have been bad, awful, for the Colonel to presume he could crook his little finger and she'd come running.

Connie's eyelids blinked and she swallowed deep in her throat. The two women stared at each other for a matter of seconds, before Connie said, 'With you or without you, I'm going to see Mr Alridge, and right now, Mary. I understand perfectly if you don't want to come, in fact I don't think you should. There is no reason why you should put your job on the line.'

Before answering Mary drew in a long breath. 'Aye, well I thought you'd do what you think best whatever I said but I had to try. I'm just grieved a muck hut like him will win out in the end, an' he will. He will. But I'm with you, lass. You know that.'

Connie nodded. Yes, she'd known that, and she was

grateful, very grateful for it. But it didn't allay the terrible feeling of aloneness that had gripped her. Nevertheless, she reached out and gripped Mary's hands for a moment, squeezing them hard before she started walking again.

They met no one on the way to the office for which Connie was eternally thankful, and when they reached Mr Alridge's door she squared her shoulders, pulling Mary's shawl more tightly around her before saying, 'You wait out here. I'll be all right.'

Mary looked at the beautiful face. It was like a piece of alabaster fired through with dark claret, and suddenly the years rolled away and she was a little lassie again, running home to her mam with the pain in her belly ripping her apart and the blood trickling down her legs. What were these men? They weren't human beings and they weren't fit to be called animals – even animals had boundaries they didn't cross. But when the natural hunger that should be satisfied between a man and a woman within the bounds of wedlock got distorted and perverted the result was frightening. Aye, frightening, and putrid and obscene.

'I'm comin' in, lass.' It was flat and heavy, and after one glance at her friend's face Connie didn't argue.

It was a moment or two before Mr Alridge answered the knock at the door, and then his voice was restrained when he called, 'Come in.'

Colonel Fairley was in there with him. Connie didn't question how she knew. She just knew.

The Colonel was standing looking down into the glowing fire, his legs slightly apart and his hands clasped behind his back as they entered, and he didn't turn round or move a muscle. After one swift glance at the portly figure which caused her stomach to rise up into her mouth, Connie kept her eyes on the stiff face of her employer as she said, 'I need to talk with you, Mr Alridge. I think you know what about.'

Harold Alridge inclined his head slowly, his glance moving from Connie to Mary – standing militantly beside her – and then back to Connie again. 'The Colonel has just related a most distressing series of events, Miss Bell, but I was hoping this could be dealt with when my wife was present. Mrs Alridge is indisposed and has gone to bed early.'

'I'm sorry.' She was. Connie felt her friend might have been some sort of ally against the Colonel, although if Lucy had seen the letter – and worse, believed it – she had to admit that might not be the case. 'But this won't wait. Colonel Fairley attacked me tonight and—'

'What did I tell you?' The Colonel swung round, looking at his relation as he fairly spat, 'The chit's trouble, it's written all over her and—'

'*Reginald.*' Harold Alridge was out of his depth. One moment he had been sitting there with his mind half on the mountain of paperwork in front of him and the other half on Lucy – this was the third dizzy spell she had had in two weeks and he was worried about her – and the next Reginald had burst in as though the devil himself was after him. And the tale he'd told . . . Mind you, it wouldn't be the first time a girl had tried to trap a fellow into marrying her with a bit of slap and tickle, and Reginald was worth a bit. He looked into the older man's face, and his voice was sharp as he said, 'I've told you, it's best I deal with this and you say nothing for the present.'

So that was the line they were going to take. But she'd

known, she had known, hadn't she? Connie asked herself bitterly, nausea and a deep raw anger pulling her mouth taut.

'Colonel Fairley has admitted his . . . unwise response to your encouragements, Miss Bell, which he now heartily regrets in view of the present sorry situation. I tell you frankly I would have found difficulty in believing this of you some weeks ago, but – painful though this is for me to say – I think we both know you have been less than completely truthful in your dealings with my wife and myself.'

'I disagree. I have been totally honest in everything I have said and done whilst in your employ.' The shaking which had begun to subside was taking hold again, but Connie was fighting it with all her might. She had to make Harold Alridge *see*. She had to.

'*Ha!*' The Colonel swayed on his heels and it was evident he was about to say more before he caught Harold Alridge's eye.

'Then there is nothing you feel you should have told us at your initial interview, Miss Bell? Something which would have had a bearing on your success or otherwise of securing the position of assistant housekeeper at the Grand Hotel?' asked Harold.

'No, there is not.' She wasn't going to be put off like this, she wouldn't let them get away with it. 'I am aware you have received a libellous letter about me, Mr Alridge, and I find it difficult to believe you and Mrs Alridge haven't given me the chance to defend myself against what was written.' Connie watched his face stretch a little, and it was clear he was finding her stance surprising, but she went on quickly before her teeth began to chatter. 'But I'm not here to discuss the letter, not now, and you know it. Colonel Fairley used Mrs Pegg's keys to come into the laundry room tonight when he knew he would catch me unawares, and he used brute force on me.'

'You are saying you were not willing?' Harold Alridge had continued to look at Connie all the time she had been speaking and she could read the disbelief on his face, although his voice was quite dispassionate.

She swallowed deeply, bringing her head forward with the effort it took to swallow her spittle, and then she moved the shawl aside deliberately, lifting her chin as she said slowly and distinctly, 'Does this look as though I was willing?'

'She's done that herself.' Colonel Fairley flapped his hand disparagingly at Connie's torn dress. 'Good heavens, Harold. Do you think I would be so foolish as to do something like that? I told you, the gel is trying to trap me. One minute we're having a bit of fun and the next she's talking about marriage and what she'll do if I don't jump to. Not on, old man, not on at all and I told her so.'

'And the scratches?' For only the second time since she had come into the room Connie faced the man who had touched her more intimately than any other human being ever had, and now her eyes were blazing blue fire. 'I suppose I've scratched myself as well?' she hissed painfully. 'You attacked me and I shall prove it. I shall go to the authorities.'

'You must do as you please, but I wouldn't recommend it, Miss Bell.' It was Harold Alridge talking and now he was every inch the public school aristocrat, his tone icy as he surveyed the trembling girl in front of him. 'I have made certain enquiries of my own during the last few days and it has been confirmed you are the daughter of a Sadie Bell who lived a promiscuous and dissolute lifestyle, and also that you have had men asking for you and waiting for you outside the hotel. This is a hotel, not a place of procurement, and for you to approach guests such as Colonel Fairley—'

'*I didn't!* How dare you say that!'

'For you to approach guests such as the Colonel, who incidentally has a military record second to none, is unforgivable, and a total betrayal of the trust my wife and I had mistakenly placed in you.'

'Come on, lass, you won't do any good here. The blighters have got it all sewn up.'

'Oh no they haven't.' Mary had meant well, Connie knew that, but she had seen the flicker of satisfaction in her employer's eyes as her friend had spoken, and she was filled with rage and hurt. The strength of her anger had the effect of banishing the weakening physical consequences of the Colonel's violent assault and firing her with a hatred that brought her ramrod straight. She took a step forward, and there was no hesitation in her tone – neither did it quiver – as she said, 'I don't care about his military record or anything else except the truth.' And then, facing the Colonel, 'You're a dirty, filthy swine, that's what you are, and you know it. A disgusting old man who thinks he can force bit lasses to get what he wants. But you made a mistake with me, Colonel, because I'm not like the rest and I'm not frightened of you. Or you!' She swung back to Harold Alridge who was standing dumbfounded, clearly unable to believe that this fiery young woman was the cool, sedate assistant housekeeper he had known for the last eleven months. 'I'm going to the police station come the morrow, and they won't be able to prove I've known men, or even walked out with a lad, 'cos I haven't.'

She turned so swiftly that she left Mary standing there for a second, and then they were both outside in the corridor, and Mary was saying, 'You wait outside, lass, an' I'll get your things, all right?' as she trotted along at Connie's side.

'I'll get them. I've done nothing wrong and I'm not going to hide away.'

Connie's forcible entrance into the kitchen brought the normal buzz of conversation and clatter of pans to a standstill, and she was almost through to the staff cloakroom when Mrs Pegg's stout figure emerged from the adjoining door.

'Waiting for your keys?' Connie's eyes were blazing. 'You're going to pay for what you did tonight, Mrs Pegg, because I shall make sure you do.'

'Wha— What?'

'You were seen giving Colonel Fairley your keys and you knew exactly what you were about, didn't you. How one woman could do that to another is beyond me, but you're not getting away with it. You'll be lucky to get a job scouring the privies by the time I've finished with you.'

There was absolute silence in the kitchen now, even the bubbling and hissing from the enormous copper pots and pans seemed muted, but as Mrs Pegg began to bluster disjointedly Connie brushed past her, using such force the other woman almost fell on her back.

'By, lass, you gave 'em all what for an' no mistake.' As Connie pulled her coat and hat on Mary was almost gleeful. 'That Mrs Pegg thinks she's the cat's whiskers but she's as common as clarts an' everyone knows it but daren't say. But you told her! Did you see her face? She was bustin' her corsets, the evil old biddy.'

She had to get out of there. Connie found she couldn't

answer Mary, she needed all her remaining strength to walk out of the hotel with some dignity. The shaking was returning and it was much worse. There had been something in the housekeeper's eyes when Mrs Pegg had stared at her – a flash of something so spiteful and nasty – that had caused Connie's breath to catch in her throat. She was amazed to be the focus of such resentment. What had she ever done to Mrs Pegg to receive such hatred? But that Mrs Pegg did hate her was in no doubt. All this because the other woman's daughter was refused the post of assistant housekeeper? She didn't understand human beings, she told herself silently. If Mrs Pegg and Colonel Fairley were created in the likeness of God then where had He gone wrong?

Immediately the thought came she felt inclined to cross herself for protection against what she perceived as blasphemy, but she restrained the impulse. She hadn't been to mass for weeks, if not months, except for Christmas Eve and you couldn't count that. Was this God's punishment? No, no, He was a loving God. Father Hedley always emphasised that. But then there were more than a few Father McGuigans and their God was one of fire and brimstone. Even the best of the priests were just men, they were, and if the truth be known she dared bet that more than one good Catholic had been secretly relieved when Father McGuigan went to join his Maker some time back. And then, despite her previous assessment, Connie did make the sign of the cross, even as she berated herself for the conditioning of twenty years in the next instant.

'Connie?'

Mary had noticed the gesture and now Connie said, pushing open the door of the staff cloakroom, 'Don't fret, lass, I haven't gone doo-lally, not yet leastways,' in answer to the concern in her friend's voice. Although if she were being honest she really wasn't sure how much more she could take . . .

Chapter Sixteen

At eight o'clock the following morning Connie had a visitor.

She had had a surprisingly good night, although considering the events of the last forty-eight hours it perhaps wasn't so surprising that she should sleep the sleep of the dead brought about by utter exhaustion.

Once she and Mary had reached home, Connie had pulled out the tin bath in the kitchen and stoked up the glowing embers under the big iron kettle on the hob, refilling it several times until the bath water was almost to the edge of the bath and as hot as she could stand it. After wedging the door knob with a hard-backed chair – the normal indication to anyone trying to enter that someone was inside having a strip-down wash or bath – she disrobed swiftly, throwing the clothes to the far side of the kitchen as though they were contaminated, which indeed she felt they were. She had scrubbed at her skin at first, over and over until it was too sore to continue, and then she had washed her hair and cleaned her nails until there wasn't a speck of dirt anywhere on her. And her face had been awash with tears the whole time.

It had helped, a little. Enough to enable her to swallow a bowl of broth, made the day before with a ham shank and split green peas, before falling into bed at just after ten. She had expected to lay awake for hours, and it had been with a sense of amazement that she had opened her eyes at seven the next morning. She felt rested, she told herself, and – and here she had to admit to an even deeper amazement – curiously at peace considering how wretched she had felt before she'd gone to sleep with her world turned upside down yet again.

Perhaps everyone experienced periods of ordinary, mundane living which were savagely rent apart when it was least expected? Or perhaps not. Whatever, when she looked back on her life: the tranquil years before the attack on Jacob; then more years of calm before the horror of her mother's heart attack and the devastating fire which had taken the last of her family and her home; the monotonous repetition of the years in the workhouse followed by the bitter disappointment when the door to nursing was banged shut with a vengeance; then the last eleven months of composed order and advance, it definitely had followed long controlled plateaus interspersed with explosive highs of such ferocity that each chapter became like a new beginning.

And that was how she had to look at the caustic events of the last two days and all the ugliness they had held – as a means of prompting her to a new beginning. John Stewart, Colonel Fairley, Mrs Pegg – they weren't going to win, and neither was the sick mind which had written the fateful letter which had led to the Colonel's actions. How often had she woven her dreams of some kind of little business of her own? Hundreds, thousands. And now her bridges at the Grand were well and truly burnt and it was abundantly clear she would not be receiving any kind of reference.

She sat up in bed, hugging her knees as she glanced across the shadowed room to where Mary was still fast asleep. It was bitterly cold in spite of the faint glow from the banked-up fire in the grate, but Connie was quite unaware of the chill as she let her thoughts travel on. Even if Mary went into work today it would only be a matter of time – days, weeks maybe – before Mrs Pegg found some trumped up excuse to get rid of her. And as for her, she wouldn't set foot in that place again for all the tea in China.

She shivered, her stomach turning over as she attempted to force the image of Colonel Fairley and what he had tried to do to her out of her head.

The sweet jar held just over forty-five pounds now, that was half the cost of a modest three-roomed cottage in Hendon or the East End or Monkwearmouth. She had been planning, in the back of her mind, to save enough over the next few years to buy a little place and then convert the living room to a shop. A sweet shop maybe, or one selling hot pies and chitterlings and such. But even with the four lodgers upstairs paying the rent on Walworth Way, she needed to be earning a good wage to save enough each week to make sure she wasn't going to be an old, old lady before she realised her dream. What should she do? She turned her head to the side and looked towards the window, pulling the drapes back an inch or two and staring out into the swirling snow outside.

She felt a moment's pleasure that she hadn't got to leave the house and brave the elements for work that morning, and for a second the temptation to snuggle down and sleep the morning away was strong. It would be so easy to do nothing about Colonel Fairley. He had the weight of the establishment behind him and he would use it to his advantage – the upper classes did what they liked, everyone knew that. But . . . she couldn't bear the idea of creeping away like a small whipped dog either. And that's what it would boil down to if she went quietly. Colonel Fairley, Mrs Pegg, all the others who had been secretly waiting for her to fall flat on her face for the sin of attempting to make something of herself, they'd have a field day. Aye they would, and no mistake.

Her shoulders slumped, and again the urge to nestle down in the warmth of the covers and pretend the rest of the world didn't exist was strong.

No, none of that! She threw back the covers as she bounced her head in agreement with the admonition. If she started that now it would never end. She had come this far hadn't she? And by gum, she was going to go a good way further before she was finished. But for now she'd get dressed and get the breakfast going – a cup of tea and a bowl of hasty pudding would serve to keep the worst of the weather at bay, and there was a pint jug of milk to go with the oatmeal and boiling water. Aye, and the cupboards were full an' all. There was a feeling beyond words that went with having full cupboards . . .

For no reason that Connie could explain she was suddenly back in her granny's cottage; Larry was crying and blue with cold as he yammered for something to eat, the newborn baby as white and cold as the porcelain dolls in the big shops in Fawcett Street and High Street West, and her granny huddled in her old shawl like a tiny wizened gnome. And her mam, oh, her mam – she had thought her mam was breathing her last. And then the door had opened and the farm boys had brought in food, armfuls of food, and coal and wood. Dan had done all that. And he'd brought the doctor too.

She made a sound like a little moan and on hearing it she said again, out loud this time, 'None of that. You're going to get through this, this is nothing. And he was always just a dream. At the bottom of you you knew he was just a dream.'

'Eh? What?' Mary emerged from under her covers like Neptune from the deep, and at the sight of her friend's face – her eyes blinking like an owl's and her hair sticking up in all directions – Connie couldn't help smiling as she said, 'Nothing, lass. I was talking to myself.'

'Eee, Connie, first sign of madness, that is, as me mam used to tell me da when he was mutterin' an' carryin' on when he'd got his linins on back to front after a night's drinkin'.'

Mary was doing that more and more now, Connie thought to herself, returning her friend's grin before pulling her coat round her and making her way to the kitchen. Reminiscing about her family, laughing and talking about the good times they had shared before her childhood had come to such a brutal end and the court case had ripped them apart. It seemed Wilf was working like a healing balm on the deep secret wounds, and the nice things – the warm, happy memories – were coming more and more to the fore. It was good to see. It was very good to see.

And then, as a flustered Mary came padding behind her, her bulky bedspread wrapped round her and trailing on the floor, her friend said, 'Oh, lass, lass, I'm sorry, I am that. I dinna know what I'm thinkin' of. It should be me lookin' after you with yesterday an' all. Now you get yourself back to bed an' I'll bring a sup of tea, all right?' Connie found herself smiling again.

'No one is going back to bed, Mary. You're going to work – they can't get rid of you just 'cos you're my friend – and I'm going to pay a visit to West Wear Street later.'

'You're not?' Mary's eyes were wide. 'You're not goin' to the police station?'

'I am.' Connie was determined Mary wouldn't see how terrified she was by the prospect of entering the grim brick building with its narrow windows and forbidding exterior. 'I'm going to report him, lass. I'm going to make sure I'm a sharp thorn in Colonel Fairley's side if nothing else.'

'Eee.' Mary was lost for words for a moment and then she clutched at her stomach, her face unconsciously comical as she said, 'Oh, I've got to go to the lavvy, lass. It's givin' me the skitters just to think about it. You're one on your own an' no mistake.'

Connie was doubly glad of the resolve which had had her up and breakfasted and the living room tidied and put to rights by eight o'clock, because it was then that Lucy Alridge had called.

Mary had been gone some fifteen minutes when Connie heard the knock at the front door, and for a moment, realising she was all alone except for the old lady upstairs who was as deaf as a post and none too steady on her legs, she hesitated to answer it. It was then that she was made to appreciate fully just how much the Colonel's attack had unnerved her, and she didn't like the feeling of fear which had flooded her limbs making them weak. She took a deep breath, unconsciously raising her chin and narrowing her eyes as she walked into the gloomy hall, made even darker by the atrocious weather outside, and she didn't hesitate as she opened the door.

'Lucy!'

'Can I come in, Connie?' And then, as she saw Connie's

gaze move up and down the street, 'I'm alone, there's no one with me.'

Connie's heart was thumping against her ribs at the sight of the woman she had come to think of as a good friend in the last eleven months. Had Lucy come to add her weight to that of her husband and Colonel Fairley? Or maybe she had been sent as a mediator to persuade her to quieten down and accept the status quo? It seemed likely and Connie really didn't feel up to another battle so soon, but she had noticed the other woman was looking peaky and remembering that Lucy had been ill the night before Connie opened the door wide. 'Come in.' She stood aside to let Lucy pass her before closing the door, and then she indicated towards their living room with a wave of her hand.

'Thank you.' Lucy preceded her into the room, glancing swiftly at the blazing fire in the shining, blackleaded grate and the warm rosy glow from the curtains and cushions, before she turned to Connie saying, 'This is lovely, so bright and cosy.'

'Thank you.' Connie's voice, like her face, was stiff, but then in the next moment she was blinking hard, her face suffused with colour, as Lucy put out a gentle hand and touched her bruised cheek, saying, 'Did he do that? The beast! Oh, the beast. I wish Harold was here to see it, but I made him stay at home. I thought after yesterday that he was one of the last people in the world you would wish to see this morning.'

'You . . . you believe me then?' Connie couldn't accept what she was hearing and her face reflected this.

It caused the older woman to take both of Connie's hands and draw her over to the saddle which had been placed at an angle before the fire; Lucy pulled Connie down beside her before she said, her voice husky, 'Of course I believe you, dear. And I told Harold so when he relayed what had happened.' Here Lucy paused.

She loved her husband, she loved him very much and she couldn't quite bring herself to tell Connie of the fierce quarrel that had taken place when she had heard of his cavalier treatment of their assistant housekeeper. Of course the trouble was that Harold had a blind spot where Reginald was concerned. It came from the Colonel's kindness to him when Harold had been suddenly orphaned at the age of twelve. Although left financially secure Harold had found himself alone in the world save for one aged grandmother and spinster aunt and Reginald – a second cousin twice removed or some such thing on his mother's side. The women had been chary of taking on a lively youngster in the holidays but Reginald, having recently left the army and with time to kill, had made a home for the grieving boy as well as visiting him in term time, first at boarding school and then at university. She couldn't deny that Reginald Fairley had been good to Harold, but that didn't blind Lucy to the Colonel's shortcomings. The man was a lecher. She had had occasion to think so in the past and this with Connie confirmed all her worst misgivings.

'Connie, dear, I have to ask – as a friend and not in my position as Harold's wife – did the worst happen?'

'The worst?' And then Connie's face turned a bright scarlet. 'No, no. I managed to get away before . . . No, he didn't . . .'

Lucy gave a great sigh of relief, slumping slightly in her seat as she fiddled with the silk scarf at her neck before saying, 'Could I have a glass of water please, Connie? I confess to feeling a little faint.'

'Of course.' Connie fairly flew into the kitchen, returning

almost immediately, and it wasn't until Lucy had taken several sips of the water that Connie said, her voice concerned, 'You shouldn't have come, you're not well.'

'I'm a little indisposed, that's all.' Lucy hesitated. She had only told Harold the news last night. And that in a fit of rage when she had shouted at him – yes, she had actually shouted that she wouldn't be able to bear giving birth to a child whose father had been responsible for such a severe miscarriage of justice. She had regretted that later. Especially when Harold had actually wept with joy that she was going to have a baby at last after their ten years of marriage. 'I'm expecting a child,' she said shyly.

'Oh Lucy, that's wonderful. I'm so pleased for you.'

'Yes, it is rather wonderful but a little frightening too.' Lucy suddenly leant forward, gripping one of Connie's hands and her voice no longer sounded like that of a thirty-year-old woman but of a young, nervous girl as she said, 'That's one of the reasons why I don't want to lose your friendship, but only one. There are many more. Connie, I don't presume to judge your mother—'

'She did what she had to do.' It was short and final and indicated that Connie wasn't going to apologise for her mother now or at any other time.

'Yes, of course.' If Lucy had been truthful at this point it would certainly have heralded the end of their friendship, because what she was thinking was, No one has to do that, no one, there are always other means to make a livelihood. However, she was wise enough to keep such thoughts to herself, and she said instead, 'But whatever happened with your mother is in the past after all. Harold told me about the letter last night' – and as Connie raised her eyebrows – 'I didn't know until then, he had kept the matter from me because I've been feeling unwell. It . . . it accused *you* of certain impropriety too. It was hateful.'

'I gathered that.' It was somewhat dry, and their eyes held for a moment before Lucy rose distractedly, placing the glass of water on the mantelpiece before turning back to Connie.

Lucy was feeling awkward, very awkward, and more than a little guilty. Although Harold had been aware of her friendship with their assistant housekeeper he had thought it much more impersonal than it was, and there she had deliberately misled him. No, not misled exactly, Lucy corrected in the next moment. She just hadn't divulged the depth of it, that was all. Harold was a stickler for convention and she had known it would trouble him if he'd thought she was making a confidante of one of their staff. But Connie was different. She was, she was different, but it would have been difficult to explain that to Harold with his prejudices. But she was making excuses for herself here. The plain truth of the matter was that if she had imparted some of the things Connie had mentioned in the past – her love of books and her literary knowledge and intelligence, her strong ethics and moral beliefs, and the specific fact that she had never had so much as a gentleman caller or man friend in the whole of her life – her husband might have reacted differently when he had first received that dreadful letter, or at least questioned its validity with regard to Connie herself. Of course there was Connie's mother – she had to confess she had found that shocking, she could still hardly believe it – but she had never approved of the bigoted axiom of the sins of the fathers. Or in this case the mothers . . .

Lucy breathed in and out deeply twice before she said,

'Connie, I have spoken to Harold and he now understands how wrong he was. Truly he does.'

'Does he?' Connie would have liked to have been able to accept Lucy's words at face value, but a part of her – she wasn't sure if it was intuition, cynicism or quite what – was saying, No, he wants *you* to believe he feels that way because you're expecting his bairn and he doesn't want you upset about me. The damage had been done as far as Harold Alridge was concerned. He would always be waiting for her to fall, to show herself in what he considered were her true colours.

'Yes, yes, dear.' Lucy now reseated herself on the saddle before continuing rapidly, 'After Harold and I had spoken last night he went to the Colonel's room and told him he was no longer welcome at the hotel. I understand Reginald, Colonel Fairley, is going to leave for Europe later this morning. He was going to go anyway at the end of the month, he's just brought the date forward a few weeks. He . . . he won't be returning. And the matter of Mrs Pegg and the keys has been dealt with. She has received her notice this morning and she won't be given a reference. Harold would like you to assume the position of housekeeper if you feel able to return to the hotel?'

The last was spoken in the form of a plea, and it moderated Connie's tone, putting what could be described as a sad note in her voice when she said, 'You're asking me to keep my mouth shut, to let the Colonel get off scot free.'

'No . . . No.'

Aye, she was right enough, even if Lucy didn't realise it herself. Mr Alridge was fond of his relation, everyone knew that, and that's why the female staff had put up with the sly nips, suggestive remarks and familiar slaps on the backside the Colonel had indulged in on his visits. There were fifty – a hundred – ready to step into each pair of shoes should anyone be dismissed, and all the cards were stacked on the side of the gentry. The hotel wasn't different to the rest of the world in that respect, Connie thought bitterly. The poor were expendable.

Look at what had emerged from the enquiry into the terrible loss of life when the *Titanic* had sunk over twenty months ago now. It wasn't the wives and bairns of the millionaires and upper crust lying at the bottom of the North Atlantic, was it. And the verdict of negligence didn't explain why the managing director of the owners, White Star Line, got away in the first lifeboat when only twenty of the hundred and eighty Irish passengers were saved. She could remember a Southwick man who had been visiting his granny in the workhouse at the time saying, his tone morose, that the owners had been Argus-eyed in making sure they got the best deal from the Sunderland Forge and Engineering Company who had supplied the electric winches to the doomed liner, but his neighbour who lived in Vena Street and who'd worked as a greaser in the engine room had told him – being one of the few working-class men to survive – that they hadn't been so vigilant in kitting the ship out with adequate lifeboats.

'Connie, please, I want you to come back.'

'I can't. I really can't, Lucy.' Whatever happened now her time at the Grand was finished, she had known that when she'd awoken that morning.

'The housekeeper's job is yours, I mean it, and it would be twice the wage you are getting now.'

'I don't want it.' Had she just said that? Connie asked herself with something akin to amazement. She had just turned down over a pound a week – she must be mad.

Lucy Alridge didn't speak for a moment, but she held out her hand to her and when Connie took it she said quietly, 'I have no right to ask this of you, no right at all, but . . . but I'm going to ask it anyway. Colonel Fairley is going away this morning and Harold has made it abundantly clear that there is no question of him returning at any time in the future. It hurt Harold very much to have to do that. Oh, I know' – she flapped her other hand as Connie straightened and went to speak – 'I know the Colonel has brought all this on himself, but he was very good to Harold at a time when no one else was there for him. He really isn't all bad, and this, you standing up to him, has taught him a lesson, Connie.'

'You'll have to forgive me if I find that hard to believe just at the moment.'

Connie's voice had been tight, and Lucy nodded. 'You have every reason for saying that of course, but—' She stopped, and then said in a rush, 'I'm asking you not to take this matter any further, for Harold's sake.'

She had known that was what Lucy was going to say but it still hurt and Lucy must have been aware of this because she continued quickly, 'I'm sorry. Oh, I am sorry, but Reginald is the only family Harold has and . . . But that's not a good reason, not for you after what the Colonel put you through.'

Had she purposely chosen those very words? Connie stared at the beautiful face in front of her and Lucy's eyes, luminescent in their appeal, gazed back. 'The only family Harold has.' How could she fight against the shaft of pain that had penetrated her heart at those words? She had suffered enough from losing everyone she held dear. She didn't want to be the means of making another suffer. But this was different, oh, it was. And the Colonel and Harold were two grown men, not bewildered little bairns. Nevertheless, the empty desolation she had felt standing at the graveside and knowing they were gone from her as she heard the clods falling on the coffins was as real in this moment as when it had happened. She could actually smell the fresh hewn earth, feel the scented warmth of the bright summer's day and hear a bird singing high in the thermals.

She wanted to bend forward, to wrap her arms round her waist and squeeze tight, but instead she swallowed deeply and her words were precise and to the point when she said, 'I'll hold my hand, but for you, Lucy, not Mr Alridge. I can't pretend.'

'Oh, Connie.' Lucy had no voice with which to continue, and after gulping in her throat she lowered her head for some twenty seconds before she raised it to say, 'In case . . . in case you felt you couldn't return Harold has made some financial provision. It might take you some time to find another position and this is the least, the very least, we can do. He will write a reference today and you'll receive it tomorrow. I'm sorry, I'm sorry, my dear. I wouldn't have had this happen for all the world.'

'I know.' Lucy's words, said with such deep sincerity, eased the pain in her heart and brought a lump to her throat, but it was all too much. She just wanted to be left alone now.

'We can remain friends?'

There was urgency in Lucy's tone and Connie forced a smile, taking the sealed envelope Lucy proffered as she said, 'Of course we can.'

'I don't have many friends. My childhood was not conducive to it, and although I have social acquaintances—'

Lucy's voice ended abruptly and she rose from the saddle, turning blindly towards the sitting room door and, after opening it, walking the two or three steps which took her to the front door. Here she turned, saying, 'Next week? Could we meet for tea next week? Perhaps Tuesday afternoon at say three o'clock at Binns?'

Connie moved her head in an uncertain movement. 'Won't Mr Alridge mind?'

'No, Harold won't mind.' Lucy's face was straight and determined. 'If we are going to remain friends he will have to get used to my seeing you, won't he. Till Tuesday then.'

Connie watched the tall slim figure treading carefully along the snowy pavement until Lucy turned, raising her gloved hand in farewell at the corner of Walworth Way and Union Street before disappearing from view. Then she closed the door, leaning against it for a few moments before she glanced down at the pale lilac envelope in her hand.

Had she been foolish to allow herself to be swayed by friendship? Probably. She continued leaning against the door for some seconds and then walked through to the sitting room. But she couldn't have done anything else feeling as she did. She hadn't wanted to be able to put herself in Harold Alridge's shoes, nor to appreciate the pain and concern Lucy was feeling for her husband, but she couldn't help it. She shook her head at what, at this moment, felt like weakness and sat down heavily on the saddle, staring into the red glow of the fire for some time before she roused herself to tear open the envelope. Mind, she had always known there was virtually no chance of the police accepting her version of events against Colonel Fairley's once they knew she was Sadie Bell's daughter. The prospect of having to explain in intimate detail to strangers what had happened was bad enough, but knowing that her story would be treated with scepticism . . .

It was a moment before Connie's eyes focused on the bank draft in her hand, and when they did she remained absolutely still for a full thirty seconds; she didn't know whether she wanted to laugh or cry. Twenty-five pounds. Oh Lucy, Lucy. Twenty-five pounds. Even if she had accepted the housekeeper's position there was six months' wages here, a small fortune. And with what she already had in the sweet jar . . . Her heart began to gallop so fast she pressed her hand against her chest.

Would Lucy still have given her the envelope if she hadn't agreed to say nothing about the Colonel? And then in the next instant she told herself sharply, That doesn't matter. You'll never know one way or the other now so don't waste time thinking about it. Seventy pounds. *Seventy pounds!* She, Connie Bell, had seventy pounds. Seventy pounds' worth of power. Her mother, all of them, had been trampled on and used and treated like scum because they had lacked money and prestige. The only way she was going to be safe was to protect herself with these things. And money made money. By, it did that; she'd proved it herself when she had been able to put the deposit down on Walworth Way and enable them to live for the last months rent-free. And perhaps that was the way to go now? To rent a place to start off her business? She had been thinking small in buying a tiny cottage and then converting the front room to a shop or something similar, but why not rent a much larger building she could use for tea-rooms too?

The surge of excitement brought her up from the saddle and pacing the floor, the envelope still clutched in her hand.

She could do it – she knew she could do it – but where did she start? She didn't even know how to go about cashing the bank draft. And then, as they had done so often in the past during her childhood, her thoughts turned to Father Hedley. He would know, the Father would know how to go about things; he would advise her. She hugged the envelope to her, closing her eyes tight as she swayed for a moment with her chin lifted high. She'd go and see him this very day, he'd be getting ready for his sermon on Sunday tomorrow so it was best she went today. And then, careless of the bruises and scratches that marked the soft flesh of her breasts and inner thighs under her clothes she twirled round the room a few times, doing something she would never have thought possible after the events of the evening before – laughing out loud.

Chapter Seventeen

Kitty had ceased to compare her Aunty Ida's house with that of Edith Stewart long ago.

Her aunty lived close to the White Swan in High Street East which lay above the old riverside houses in Low Street, and which was connected by narrow alleyways and passages to the dockside. In the summer the smell from the outside privies and the small lanes linking the streets could be overpowering on occasion, but today it was snowing and freezing hard and the white blanket covered over a multitude of sins.

But in spite of the dirt and insanitary conditions, and the step which hadn't seen a bathbrick for a decade, Kitty always felt a sense of peace envelop her when she walked through the battered, paintless door that led into the dwelling which housed her aunty's copious brood.

Kitty was fifty years of age but looked ten years younger and this seemed to be a family trait because Ida Pearsley could have passed for a fat fifty-year-old in spite of being sixty-two. Her husband had died some years before, but the three-storeyed house was filled to overflowing with two of her married sons and their families, totalling ten grandchildren in all, her other nine sons and five daughters and their prolific

families living in rented accommodation all over the East End
and Bishopwearmouth. Ida was a devout Catholic and proud
of it, and as Kitty looked at her now, in the sympathetic light
of the dark winter's day, Ida said, 'You trust your instinct,
lass, it's never done you down afore. If ever there's an upstart
swine she's one. Aye, she is, an' worse an' all. But she'll get
her come-uppance. You can't mock God an' get away with it,
now then. You was right to tell the lad to hold out for what he
wants.'

'You don't think I was adding fuel to the fire?'

'By tellin' a grown man of twenty . . . What?'

'Twenty-seven. Dan's twenty-seven.'

'By tellin' a grown man of twenty-seven to go his own
road? Come on, lass, you're canny, you always have bin, but
you don't need to be canny to know he should've bin weaned
from the breast nigh on twenty-five years ago.' Ida hitched
up her own enormous bosom – which hung to below her waist
like two pendulous melons – with her forearms before she
continued, 'An' it strikes me your Dan's a canny lad himself,
comin' back to clear out his togs an' all yesterday when Lady
Muck'd got one of her blessed dinners on. Knew she wouldn't
play up in front of all the fancy wives, didn't he.'

Kitty nodded. 'He was in and out in five minutes. Not that
he's gutless, Aunty Ida, not Dan, but he knows there's no
reasoning with her, that's the thing.'

'An' you say he's fair gone on this bit lass, the one John
went for, at Art's?'

'He's fair gone on her all right,' said Kitty flatly. Would
that he wasn't. Oh, she'd got nowt against the lass herself –
how could she have? The last time she'd seen Connie Bell
she'd been a ragamuffin bairn with the face of an angel and a

spirit that had been all at odds with her small stature. The way she'd taken Edith Stewart on had been something to see that day thirteen years ago. But it wasn't in Edith's nature to forget or forgive the slightest slur – imagined or otherwise – and the fact that the lass had dared to lay hands on her . . . She'd been beside herself for days, weeks.

'Well, what will be will be, lass, but now the young 'un's skedaddled the same as the rest the offer of a home here still holds good. It's not Ryhope Road, I grant you that, an' when my lot are stuffin' their kites come an evenin' it's more like feedin' time at the zoo, but compared to what it was like in the old days when all the bairns were young it's not so bad. You could share the front room with me, there's the desk bed already in there, an' if nothin' else we could have some right good cracks, eh, lass?'

'Thanks, Aunty Ida, but I can't leave.'

'Why not? It's about time you had a bit of a life, now then. She'd soon get someone else an' you'd pick up somethin' if you weren't too fussy, enough for your wants leastways. Money isn't everythin', lass.' And then as Ida glanced at the two bulging bags of groceries Kitty had brought, she added, her voice suddenly uncharacteristically soft, 'Not that I'm not grateful, you know that. There's bin times in the past when you've kept this family goin', lass. I'm just thinkin' of you, that's all.'

'I know.' How could she explain that it wasn't misguided loyalty to her mistress or even her comfortable lifestyle that still tied her to the Stewart household? The Stewart children were *her* children, that's how she felt about them, even poor Mavis who now didn't know a soul and lived in a world of her own in her institution down south. And the person they needed protecting from more than anyone else was their mother, and she wouldn't be able to deflect Edith's wrath or tip them the wink when necessary or steer them through troubled waters – things she did as naturally as breathing – if she wasn't at the hub of the family. She had thought it would be different once the children were older and had left home but it wasn't, it was worse if anything. And now this latest with Dan, her bonny lad . . . But then Kitty was saved from having to try to explain, the conversation being cut short when what appeared to be a whole throng of children came bursting into the none too clean kitchen where they were sitting, followed by Ida's daughters-in-law, big blowsy women in the same mould as their respective husbands' mother.

'Eee, Mam, it's enough to freeze your lugs off out there.'

'Granny, I spent me penny on bullets an' scenty mixtures an' now our Charlie wants one 'cos he's ate his.'

'Our Josie kicked me, Gran.'

'I didn't, Gran. He's a dirty liar, he is.'

There was more, much more, and when Kitty left the house an hour later she had had two cups of strong black tea and three of her aunty's hot girdle scones doused with butter, and had laughed more than a little. But by the time she had made her way to the tram stop the brightness was fading from her face. They might not have room to swing a cat back there, and the smell and general dirt hit you backwards when you first walked through the door, but they were happy and cheerful and normal. *Normal.* What did any of the Stewart children know about normal?

She bit hard on her lip, blinking her eyes a little in the bitingly cold air in which desultory snowflakes were drifting haphazardly in the keen wind as she recalled Dan's parting words the day before.

'I shall never forgive John, Kitty – not if I live to be a hundred. And her, she's made him what he is.' Strange, very strange after all the humiliations and hurts she had suffered under Edith Stewart, but the 'her' had pierced her through. But then it was her lad she was thinking of rather than his mother, Kitty thought now. The 'her' spoke of deep pain and resentment. 'But they aren't going to spoil this for me. We were getting on fine until John came in. She likes me, I know she does.'

'She couldn't do anything else.' She had been smiling as she had spoken but he hadn't responded in like, his face straight and strained as he'd said, 'She's the one, Kitty. Whatever it takes.'

Whatever it takes. Kitty drew in a numbingly cold breath as the tram rumbled to a stop in front of her, the conductor's voice cheerful as he said, 'It's a raw 'un, lass. You're best in than out the day.'

Well, whatever it took she would be there for her lad, to act as a buffer between him and the joint forces of Edith and John. Kitty stared unseeingly out of the window as she sat on the long, wooden seat with a little plop. But John was a wily and hard-bitten adversary, and his mother . . .

As the tram jerked and stuttered on Kitty found herself praying, something she hadn't done in many a long day. Pray God she was strong enough to see Dan and the little lass through, aye, pray God. Because there was more to come. She could feel it in her bones.

'And who shall I say is calling?' Mrs Clark was at her most

officious. Since Father McGuigan's death the year before a young priest had joined Father Hedley and as yet he hadn't won the hearts of the flock. Consequently Father Hedley's workload had doubled, if not trebled, and the good Mrs Clark was worried about him. This was the third visit of the day by a parishioner – why did they have to bother him at home? What did they think the confessional box was for anyway? No wonder he had caught one cold after another this winter. Run down, that's what he was.

'Connie Bell.'

'And it won't wait until Sunday?' Mrs Clark asked frostily.

'No, it won't.'

'Hmm.' Mrs Clark ran disapproving eyes over the beautiful young girl standing on the doorstep. Bonny is as bonny does, and this one was a mite too pushy for her liking. Mind, when she'd first opened the door she had half expected the lass to ask for Father Brody. On the rare occasions the young priest did have any parishioners call to see him it was usually bit lasses fluttering their eyelashes. Brazen some of them were.

'Wait here.' Mrs Clark stood to one side to allow Connie to enter the hall and pointed to a spot inside the front door. 'I'll see if the Father can be disturbed.'

Sixty seconds later Connie was sitting in Father Hedley's study in front of a roaring fire, her body filled with the gratification the warmth of the old priest's greeting had engendered. He was so nice, Father Hedley. He was. And she should have tried to get to mass much more often. It wasn't fair she only went to church once in a blue moon now, and he'd think she only came to see him when she was in some trouble or other.

If Father Hedley was thinking along those lines he gave no

sign of it as he said, his eyes twinkling, 'So you managed to get past Mrs Clark, eh? Don't mind her, she's a good woman, none better, but she worries about me. Now, what can I do for you, Connie?'

Her previous thoughts made her face red as she said, 'I want some advice, Father, about . . . about some money I've saved.'

'Advice about money?' Father Hedley sat up straighter, and there was a moment's silence before he said quietly, 'How much money?'

'Seventy pounds, Father.'

'*Seventy pounds?*'

'I didn't save all of it, the last twenty-five was from Mrs Alridge. Well, Mr Alridge really but he wouldn't have given me anything if it wasn't for her.'

He could remember this acute sense of disquiet from the past and it had only ever been this child who had caused it, but she wasn't a child any more. She was a beautiful, a very beautiful young woman. And seventy pounds was a lot of money. Father Hedley was bolt upright now and there was no shred of laughter left in his face when he said, 'I think you had better start at the beginning, Connie, all right?'

And so she did, and she told him it all, even the incident concerning Colonel Fairley, although she stuttered and stammered a bit over that.

There was an even longer silence when she had finished, and just when she was thinking she would have to say something to break it, Father Hedley spoke, his voice filled with something approaching awe. 'You mean to say . . .' He stopped, cleared his throat once, and went on, 'You mean to say you saved forty-five pounds out of your wages over the last years? Didn't you want to spend it on yourself? Buy things?'

'Oh, I did sometimes.'

'And you've got this money in a *sweet jar* in your home?'

Connie nodded. 'But Mr Alridge's is here.' She handed the Father the lilac envelope which he opened slowly, staring at it for a few moments before raising his eyes to her waiting face.

'This man, this Colonel Fairley? He didn't . . .'

'No, no, he didn't, Father.' She was brick-red now and sweating slightly, but it was more to do with embarrassment than the heat from the big coal fire.

'Glory be to God for that, child. And you are content to take the matter no further?'

Connie nodded. She didn't know about content but her mind was made up. That part of her life was over with, finished, and it was time to move on. 'He's already left for Europe, Father.'

'He could be brought back.'

'No.' She couldn't repress an involuntary shudder. 'No, I prefer it this way.'

'So be it. Well, God works in mysterious ways. Aye, He does that.' Father Hedley stared at her for another moment before he shook his grey head, glancing at the elaborately decorated clock on the mantelpiece as he said, 'I usually have my tea and biscuits at this time. Do you like shortbread and ginger nuts?'

'Aye, yes I do, Father.'

'Then we'll have a sup and a bite, and see what's to be done, eh? I've a mind you'd better start with a visit to my bank manager in Fawcett Street.'

* * *

The next morning saw Connie – armed with the name and address of Father Hedley's bank manager, who was also the priest's friend and a patient man as his dealings with the church roof fund proved – walking along a noisy, bustling Fawcett Street. She was carrying the sweet jar, now wrapped in brown paper and tied with string, in both hands, and she had the lilac envelope in her pocket. Somehow, and she couldn't have explained the whys and wherefores even to herself, she hadn't wanted to place the envelope with the silver coins and notes she had saved with such painstaking devotion.

Fawcett Street was grand and spacious with its three- or four-storey houses and shops, the Gothic building which housed the offices of the Gas Company and the imposing frontage of the Athenaeum – minus its classical Greek columns which had been removed some years before because it was considered they were causing an obstruction – among them, but it was the beautiful Town Hall with its magnificent clock tower which dominated the sky line.

Connie was feeling very small and very insignificant as she trod the wide pavements in what was the heart of Sunderland's business world, her breakfast sitting heavy in her stomach and her nerves taut as she reached the bank's handsome building.

It would be all right, she could do this.

She bent down and placed the sweet jar on the pavement which some conscientious bank employee had cleared of packed snow and ice, and took a deep breath as she straightened, adjusting her blue felt hat and smoothing down the lapels of her grey winter coat. She had cleaned her hat with salt and flour that morning, brushed down her coat and

309

shined her black boots; she was as neat and well turned out as she could make herself, she told her quivering stomach bracingly.

All she had to do was to ask for Mr Bainbridge. Father Hedley had promised he would let the bank manager know she would be arriving some time after ten o'clock. And then once she had shown him the contents of the sweet jar and the envelope they could discuss the possibility of her renting premises with a view to starting up a little business. A shop, tea-rooms too, whatever.

A shining black motor car drew into the kerb to one side of the tram lines, and as Connie watched a smartly dressed man help an equally smartly dressed lady to dismount, she caught the woman's eye. And it was in that moment, as the cool gaze moved over her from head to foot in a scrutiny that was both haughty and disdainful, that the impulse to pick up the sweet jar and take to her heels almost overwhelmed her. But then the couple had passed her, sweeping into the bank without looking to left or right and leaving only the faint whiff of expensive perfume behind them.

By, she thought she was the cat's whiskers all right. Connie stood for a moment longer before she bent down and retrieved the sweet jar. Lord and Lady Muck as Mary would say. Mind, she couldn't help feeling that a real, honest to goodness lady – like Lucy – wouldn't need to prove their superiority by being so hoity-toity as that fancy piece. *Anyway, she would own a car like that one day.* She stood for a moment more looking at the gleaming vehicle with its great brass headlights and leather seats. Aye, she would, and she'd live in a house that was bought and paid for too and hold her head high. But not like that lady had just done. No, not like that.

The interior of the bank was more than a little intimidating and she had to sit and wait for some ten minutes after she had stated that her business was with Mr Bainbridge. But then she was being ushered through to the manager's office at the back of the building, and as she stepped into the large and pleasant room the lingering fragrance told her who the previous occupants had been. So, she was following in Lord and Lady Muck's footsteps, was she? Wouldn't that upset madam if she knew! Her mouth curled up at the thought and it was like that that she came face to face with the bank manager.

Twenty minutes later she was outside on the pavement again, minus the sweet jar and envelope and clutching the name and address of a solicitor in Stockton Road that Mr Bainbridge had recommended. There were others, he had told her with a nice smile, in the High Street and Bridge Street, but being at the hub of the town centre they'd likely charge five shillings for walking through the door. Watson and Son were reasonable and personal friends, she wouldn't go wrong with them. And now she was off again to keep the appointment Mr Bainbridge had arranged for her on the telephone, her head whirling with facts and figures and her feet seeming to float as she made her way into Holmeside and then Vine Place before turning into Stockton Road some ten minutes later.

Watson and Son were situated on the opposite side of the road from the large three-storey brick building of the Eye Infirmary, and the office looked like an ordinary house from the outside. The premises were tucked away behind a high iron-railing fence which cut some few feet of overgrown front garden off from the street, and when Connie reached the front door it was slightly ajar. The reason for this became apparent when she entered a dark hall and saw a sign which said, 'Newcastle & District Insurance Society, ground floor; Fowler R. Emigration Agent, first floor; Watson & Son Solicitors, second floor'.

After climbing the two flights of stairs Connie came to a door which again read, 'Watson & Son, Solicitors. Please knock and enter'. After doing as she was bidden she found herself in a room which, although comparatively large, seemed small because of the amount of paper, books and files piled high in boxes on the floor, on the top of filing cabinets and on two tables on the far side of the room. There was a high desk with two high stools in the middle of the room, and a thin white-haired man had just slid off one of the stools and was now coming across to greet her. 'Miss Bell?'

'Yes.' Never had she felt so out of her depth. 'Mr Watson?'

'No, no. I'm Mr Watson's chief clerk, Miss. Please be seated and I will tell Mr Watson you have arrived.'

It was hardly worth seating herself on the hard-backed chair he'd pointed out because no sooner had he walked through the interconnecting door than he was back saying, 'Mr Watson will see you now, Miss Bell.'

If she had thought the chief clerk looked old his employer seemed positively ancient, being tiny and gnome-like and quite dwarfed by his enormous chair and desk. A huge bookcase took up all of one wall and stacked against a second were named deed-boxes of prominent local families, but otherwise this room was quite orderly and tidy and lacked the overpowering fusty smell of the former.

'Miss Bell.' The voice matched the appearance being almost a trill. 'Do please be seated. Would you care for a cup of tea? Mr Smeathe and I were about to have one.'

'That would be very nice, thank you.'

Once she was seated in a cavernous leather armchair opposite Mr Watson – who was the son of Watson & Son, he took great delight in telling her, his father having retired only eight years before at the age of eighty-seven – and Mr Smeathe had handed her a steaming cup of tea in a fine bone china cup and saucer before disappearing back into the outer office, Mr Watson stared at her for a few moments before saying, 'Mr Bainbridge tells me your nest egg is now safely deposited within his four walls. Is that correct?'

'Yes, it is.'

Connie thought she had detected a note of admonition in the reedy treble, and this was borne out when Mr Watson shook his head twice, tut-tutted a few times and said, 'Miss Bell, as your solicitor I have to advise you that it would be unwise, very, very unwise, to trust such a sum to the questionable security of a – ahem! – a sweet jar again. When I think of it . . .' He shook his head again, and then his voice lost its doleful tone as he continued briskly, 'I understand you are interested in securing property, Miss Bell?'

'I . . . That is . . .' Connie searched for the right words to begin and then said quickly but quietly, 'I was thinking of renting somewhere to get a little business going, but Mr Bainbridge seemed to think it was wiser to buy. With my money as a deposit' – she wasn't sure if she was saying the right words here, her time with the bank manager had seemed like a confusing dream – 'he said I could purchase a building of some substance, with the bank's help of course, and then when the business allows I can pay off my debt . . .' Her voice trailed away. She thought that was what Mr Bainbridge had said anyway.

'Quite so, quite so. Mr Bainbridge is a very astute business-man, Miss Bell. You can trust his advice.'

'And he said it would be better if you dealt with the agents for me. That you could negotiate . . . I thought I could do that myself but Mr Bainbridge did not favour the idea.'

Mr Watson shut his eyes for an infinitesimal moment. This mere slip of a girl, who had innocence written all over her in big capital letters, thinking she could conciliate with some of the hard-bitten individuals in that field? He didn't know who or what had steered her in Ned Bainbridge's direction but she should look on it as God's providence. Ned was a good judge of character – he had to be in his profession – and between them they should be able to look after her best interests and set her on the right road. And he would enjoy doing that. There was something about this young woman that was most pleasing.

'May I ask the nature of the business you are thinking of venturing into, Miss Bell?'

'I thought a shop at first – just a shop,' Connie said nervously, 'but now I think a baker's shop with tea-rooms too?'

'And you would bake your own produce?'

'Certainly.' It hadn't occurred to her before but it would make sense not to pay through the nose.

'Capital, capital.' Mr Watson was nodding energetically as though the undertaking would be the easiest thing in the world, but then he disabused her of that idea when he said, 'You do understand this will require a lot of planning and forethought followed by hard work?'

'I am used to hard work, Mr Watson.' And now Connie's voice was firm and she looked the small wizened man straight in the face as she said, 'But this will be different, this will be working for myself and I shall make a success of it.' And the name above the shop would be Bell, Bell in great big letters, and if that stuck in anyone's craw and they didn't want to avail themselves of the shop and tea-rooms, so be it.

Mr Watson inclined his head towards her, his voice courteous but with a genuine note of warmth which was not typical of the shrewd, tough little solicitor, and his answer was, 'I have no doubt about that, Miss Bell, none at all, and neither has Mr Bainbridge because I can assure you he does not offer to lend the bank's money lightly. In fact to my knowledge he does not normally *offer* to lend it at all. No, the boot is usually firmly on the other foot, if you get my meaning. I have actually heard complaints which would lead me to believe he is most chary in that regard.'

'Really?' Connie smiled. She liked this funny little elf of a man with the bright, artful eyes and sagacious manner, and she had liked his friend, Mr Bainbridge, too. She believed they both liked her, and felt a warm glow inside which was nothing to do with the tea. It was ironic that the dreadful letter Mr Alridge had received and which had been intended for her downfall should have been the means of sending her down this road which was so promising. It was up to her now. She had the means of fulfilling her dreams, she did, and she had to grasp the opportunity with both hands. Someone had wished her harm – it could have been Mrs Pegg, John Stewart, even Colonel Fairley himself, or one of many who viewed her endeavour to better herself as the bumptious aim of an upstart. But it didn't matter who it was, she couldn't waste time dwelling on that, and she would master the sick disgust which engulfed her every time she remembered the feel of the

Colonel's hands and mouth on those most intimate parts of her body too.

Do you hear me, John Stewart?

She sent a silent message winging into the air, and it wasn't until that very moment that she admitted she believed it was Dan's brother who had written such evil. You won't crush me and you won't beat me. I'm stronger than you. *I'm stronger than you.* It was strange, she had never thought of herself as daring or bold. All her life she had simply followed what her heart had told her to do in the difficult situations in which she had found herself, and thousands, millions, did the same after all. But she had been terrified this morning before she had walked into the bank, and nearly as nervous in facing another prestigious member of the establishment in the form of this solicitor. But she had made herself do it and what had she found? That they were just men, nice men, men who wanted to help her. Aye, she felt that. They wanted to help her.

Her smile widened. She was on her way up and nothing – and no one – was going to stop her. She simply wouldn't let it. And then she straightened her face and listened to Mr Watson's advice.

On leaving Watson & Son, Mr Watson having promised to get on to the matter of finding a suitable property first thing on Monday morning, Connie made her way home, doing a little shopping in Holmeside on the way. J. Piper's grocer's shop, with its choice smell of coffee beans, barrels of butter and blue-bagged sugar, provided most of what she needed, and she also called in to Maynards Sweet Shop on the corner of Holmeside and Waterloo Place for a box of toffee to share with Mary later that day by way of celebration. Consequently her arms were full of packages as she approached home, and she was finding she had to concentrate on where she placed her feet on the snow packed pavements, some of which were lethal. But it was her buzzing mind that was the main obstacle to staying on her feet. It was full of images – wonderful, intoxicating images of a bustling shop and crowded tea-rooms – and every time she slid a few inches or felt her feet slip she would warn herself to stop day-dreaming, but it was no good.

She was walking down the thin cobbled street, a new flurry of snow already dancing in the keen wind, and she had just reached her doorstep when a voice – a voice she would recognise anywhere – spoke from the dubious shelter of the slightly recessed arched doorway next door, and most of the packages went flying as she whirled to face it. 'Dan!'

'Hallo, Connie.' Hallo, Connie. The simplicity of the words mocked him after all he had imagined himself saying when he first saw her again. Man, but she was beautiful. But no, that was too ordinary a word, too well used, to describe the inner radiance that lit up her eyes and turned her skin to pure silk. And then he came to himself, glancing at the strewn pavement as he said, 'Oh, I'm sorry, I startled you. And the sugar bag is split.'

'It doesn't matter.' He was here. *He was here!* She couldn't believe it.

'Here, I'll see to them.'

Connie had made a move to retrieve the packages but he stopped her, going down on his hunkers as he crouched to gather them to him. He was wearing a bowler hat and heavy thick overcoat today, clothing which denoted his distance from the flat caps and cloth jackets of the working class and took him up into the bracket of employers and the upper classes, but then, as he raised his head and glanced up at her, she forgot everything but the fact that he had again sought her out.

And then he was standing up, towering over her by a good seven or eight inches, and she felt a little shiver flicker down her spine and right into the core of her and it was neither unpleasant nor unwelcome.

They stood looking at each other for a moment, their arms equally full of her purchases, before Dan repeated the words he had first spoken when she had been unaware of his presence. 'I had to come and see you, Connie.'

His face was unsmiling and his voice had been deep in his throat, and now she swallowed twice before she said, 'You shouldn't have,' and then – as a flash of something raw showed in his eyes – she added hastily, 'I mean because of your family, Dan. They . . . they won't like it.'

'They aren't important.' It wasn't said lightly but was a declaration of intent. They continued to look at each other for a few seconds more before he continued, 'Do you mind me coming, Connie?'

If she sent him away now he would not return. The words hammered in her head. And then a light would go out of her life that, once extinguished, could never be relit. But it would be the sensible thing for both of them, aye, it would. Different classes didn't mix, how often had she heard that said? But then her mam had said Dan's father had been an ordinary working-class man who had made good so it wasn't as if he'd been born into generations of money, was it? But there was his family, she couldn't forget that. They had hated her mother and they probably hated her. Oh, what should she do?

And then in a second the thing was settled for good or ill when Dan said, his voice husky, 'Do you, Connie? Do you mind me coming? Because if the answer is yes I have to tell you I couldn't have stayed away, and I'm not sure I *can* stay away in the future.'

Their eyes were still locked, and now her voice had the faintest gurgle in it when she said, 'Then my answer had better be no, I don't mind, hadn't it.'

They were close now, their breaths mingling.

'Do you mean it?'

'I never say what I don't mean.'

And then he grinned, his smile lighting up his whole face and turning his eyes to warm chocolate as he said, 'That might well make things a sight uncomfortable in the future but I can live with it.'

'That's very gracious of you.'

And then they both laughed before becoming silent again, and it was some moments until Dan said, 'Would you care to go to a variety show at the King's Theatre tonight?'

The King's Theatre. Connie had never been to a show there since the theatre in Crowtree Road had opened on Christmas Eve just over seven years ago, but she understood that this most beautiful of theatres added a whole new meaning to luxury.

'That . . . that would be very nice. Thank you.'

'It will be my pleasure.' He wanted to laugh and shout and jump up and down, and it was with the greatest restraint that Dan managed to say, the snow whirling about them in ever greater swirls, 'Would you like me to carry these in for you?'

'No, no I can manage, thank you,' Connie said hastily. She could just imagine what Mrs Fraser across the road would make of a gentleman caller being shown admittance when the rest of the house were at work – well, everyone except Mrs McRankin that was, but it was common knowledge that she was virtually bedridden. And if she wasn't much mistaken Mrs Fraser's curtains were already flapping. Nosy old biddy! But she had a vicious tongue, and an army of cronies who liked nothing better than a good gossip in the backyards.

'Till seven o'clock then?' Connie had turned and opened the front door and now he piled the rest of the packages into her arms as she stood on the step. 'I'll call for you here.'

'Till seven.' She nodded and then smiled at him and his blood sang, bringing the colour into his face so that his cheeks felt on fire as he slowly backed away while she shut the door.

She had agreed to go with him to the theatre this very night. The refrain was singing in his head as he made his way into Union Street before turning into High Street West. It was more than he had dared to hope for. But she had, she had. A surge of feeling swept through him and he felt like a young lad again. He wanted to whoop loudly, to slide along the icy pavements – anything to express his burning elation. He would buy her chocolates, a huge box of chocolates! No, not too big, he checked himself in the next moment. He didn't want her to think he was showing off. And for the same reason he wouldn't book a box, not with it just being the two of them. She might feel uncomfortable with the other three seats unoccupied, although he would pay ten times more than the £1.11.6d the boxes cost to have her to himself for a few hours. But it would be the next best seats, the orchestra stalls at three shillings. He'd call in at Ferry and Foster's in Bridge Street and book them now before he carried on to work, but he'd have to be quick, his lunch break was nearly over and the mood John had been in since the New Year he wouldn't miss a chance to get some snide dig in.

'Course, he'd wasted nearly ten minutes at the Grand before

they had told him she didn't work there any more, but as it happened it had worked out to his advantage when he'd followed his inclination to call at the house. If he had been a couple of minutes earlier she wouldn't have been back from her shopping and he'd have missed her. As it was he'd spotted her at the far end of the street just as he'd got to the house and had been able to nip in the doorway next door.

Dan was humming a popular refrain from a couple of years back – 'Alexander's Ragtime Band' – as he entered the premises of Ferry and Foster's, and he was still humming when he left some two or three minutes later, but within a second the humming was cut off as he came face to face with John on the pavement outside.

'Hallo, little brother.' It was a term John had taken to using since the family altercation on Christmas Day and was always spoken with a covert sneer. 'Bright-eyed and bushy-tailed the day, aren't we? Lost sixpence and found a shilling?'

Dan looked straight at him but he didn't answer. He had no intention of telling John his business and they both knew it.

'You on your way back?'

Dan nodded but he still didn't speak. John, of all people! He had wanted to hold on to the magic a few moments longer before he stepped into the office and lost the glow. There were a hundred and one ways to make life unpleasant at work, and since Christmas Day, and even more so since New Year's Eve, John had used them all. If it wasn't for Art he'd have thrown in the towel days ago. He had always been sensitive to atmosphere, and with John and the twins on one side and Art and himself on the other, each day had taken on the quality of walking blindfolded through a minefield.

They had turned into High Street West and had just passed Lambton Street before John spoke again, and then his words were spoken in such a casual, almost pleasant tone, that the full import didn't register with Dan for a moment or two. 'Has she got a whoremaster or does she please herself who she opens her legs for?'

'What? What did you say?' Dan's voice seemed to be torn from his throat and his big fist came round like a shot, stopping just an inch or so from John's face. And then his fingers opened and he grasped the collar of John's overcoat, hauling his brother on to his toes as John endeavoured to prevent himself being strangled.

'Let up, let up, man.'

'Let up?' It was a slow growl and now Dan, careless of the horrified glances of the lunchtime shoppers, shook John like a rat, his eyes narrowed and emitting a black light as he said, 'You ever, you *ever* talk about her again like that and I'll kill you, I swear it. Do you hear me, John? I'll kill you.'

'All— All right . . . Man, you – you're strangling me – Give over, man.'

'I'll kill you, John, and take whatever comes.'

'All – right.'

John was turkey red now and choking, and after one final shake Dan let his brother drop back down on to his feet while still keeping his hand on his collar as he said, his face thrust close, 'You're a dirty-minded little runt, you always have been. You come within six feet of her and I'll do for you.'

Any reference to John's lack of inches normally brought his hackles up and had him as aggressive as a fighting cock, but there was something in Dan's face today that tempered John's reply, although his teeth were clenched and his eyes slits as he bit out, 'Don't be daft, man, I don't want her. More trouble than they're worth, the lot of them.'

He wanted her all right. The knowledge was a burning coal in the pit of Dan's stomach. And Connie had been right on New Year's Eve – John had wanted her mother too. He had seen the truth of it register in his face when Connie had spoken. 'You stay away from her, John.'

'I told you—'

'Aye, you told me.' And now there was no vestige of the easy-going brother or long-suffering son in Dan's countenance as he ground out, with quiet certainty, 'I'll make you wish you'd never been born, so think on, John. Think on.'

They stared at each other for a moment more, their mutual hate a live thing, and then Dan turned, walking swiftly round the corner into William Street and leaving John where he was, his body pressed up against a shop wall and his eyes as cold and hard as black marble.

Part Four
1914
Love And War

Chapter Eighteen

The first eight weeks of the New Year were trying and troublesome ones for England. The grim prospect of war enveloping Europe was looming larger, Ulster was teetering on the brink of its own civil war, militant suffragettes burned down two Scottish mansions and a parish church as the women's campaign to be heard grew more aggressive, and strikes were sparking all over the country.

It was a time of unrest, uncertainty and dissatisfaction, and over it all were brooding the darkening storm clouds of 'the war to end wars'. But for Connie and Dan, caught up in the wonder of their burgeoning love, it was a season of ecstasy and weightlessness.

That first evening at the King's Theatre, when they had laughed and talked and Dan had dared to draw her arm through his – ostensibly because of the difficult progress along the pavements coated in ice and snow – on the short walk home from Crowtree Road to Walworth Way, had been but the first of many such outings together. January and February had seen them visiting the antiquities gallery and art gallery in the museum just off Borough Road; wandering among the tropical plants and cages of foreign birds in the Winter Garden at the rear of the museum; enjoying more excursions to the King's

Theatre, along with the Palace and the Empire, and the Villiers Electric Theatre – Sunderland's first purpose-built cinema.

Connie felt as though she had known Dan always, that there had never been a time when he hadn't filled her thoughts and her vision with breathless excitement, and yet . . . She was frightened too. Frightened that the bubble would burst, that the dire warnings of Mary – frequently expressed – might just come true.

But when she was with him, his hand clasping hers, oftentimes her arm entwined through his when they were walking and his body so close she could feel his hip moving against her, on those occasions she felt nothing could ever separate them.

He hadn't kissed her for weeks – five whole weeks – and although she knew that that was how gentlemen behaved when they respected the lass, she had begun to think he perhaps didn't care for her the way she did him, in spite of all his attentions which seemed to indicate otherwise.

And then, one Saturday evening in early February, when they were strolling home in the bitterly cold frosty air after an afternoon of fun and laughter spent skating on the frozen lake in Mowbray Park and eating roast potatoes and hot chestnuts purchased from the brazier man, Connie had almost fallen headlong on the icy pavement. She had slipped several times during the afternoon too, but then they had been surrounded by myriad whirling figures and noisy bairns skimming over the frozen lake, and it had been different. Now there was just the two of them in the glittering darkness that turned even Union Street into something magical, and as his arms went round her he pulled her into him, crushing her against him until she could feel his pounding heart as though it were her own.

She had dreamt of this moment for weeks, lived it, tasted it, but the reality – as his lips took hers in a kiss that was fire and passion – was a million times better.

How long they stood there, her head flung back against his arm and their mouths straining for deeper intimacy, Connie did not know. All she knew was that when eventually they drew apart something had been said that could never have been voiced by mere words. He had touched each contour of her face, his fingers gentle as he had said, 'Oh, my love, my love. Do you care for me even a quarter as much as I love you? Do you know what these last weeks have meant to me? Do you? They have been beyond my wildest dreams,' and then they had kissed again, tenderly this time, and he had held her as though she was precious and priceless.

Yes, he had said all that, Connie told herself on the first Monday in March when she awoke in the early hours and lay snuggled beneath the bed covers with just Mary's snores disturbing the silence, and she believed he had meant it – she did. So why, *why*, hadn't she been able to bring herself to tell him about the second most important thing in her life after him – her fledgling business? She had wanted to. A hundred times it had been on the tip of her tongue to tell him about the property in Holmeside which, on Mr Watson's advice and with the bank's substantial backing, was now hers. But if she had there would, of necessity, have been further explanations. Explanations that would have had to encompass the letter, Colonel Fairley's degrading treatment of her, everything. And she didn't want to talk about such ugliness.

She had discussed the matter once or twice with Lucy during their Tuesday afternoon teas which had now become a regular occurrence, but her friend had been careful to venture no opinion as to whether she should inform Dan of the full facts relating to her decision to leave the Grand. Dan had accepted her account that she wanted a change and was looking for something new, and, in the meantime, helping out a friend of a friend who had required the services of a temporary housekeeper. She had told him this in the first week of their acquaintance and the subject hadn't risen again except for the odd casual remark easily deflected.

She hadn't felt so bad about it all when Mr Watson had still been negotiating on her behalf, but since the matter had been signed and sealed some five weeks before she had become increasingly disturbed. She should have told him then, the very day she had become the mistress of the rundown three-storey property which had been operating as a somewhat seedy café for years. Connie twisted under the covers and drew in her breath on a long hard sigh.

And she couldn't pretend to herself any longer that her reason for not doing so was purely because of the repugnance she felt at mentioning the circumstances of her departure from the hotel. It was more than that. Oh, Dan . . . His name was laden with self-recrimination. How could you love someone and yet not trust them? She was horrible, she was. She should trust him; he was fine and upright and honourable, and yet . . . She didn't, not wholly. He was a Stewart, wasn't he. The Stewarts had hated her mother, the name Bell had been like a profanity to them, and if she told him about the letter and what the Colonel had tried to do he might just believe she was . . . loose. Immoral. Following in her mother's footsteps. Even that she had encouraged the Colonel to behave as he did. And she wouldn't be able to bear it, she wouldn't, if the look on his face changed and the light in his eyes died.

But she was going to have to tell him her true position soon, once the baker's shop and tea-rooms opened. Mary had left the Grand on the day Connie had signed the contract, and since then both girls – along with Mary's two oldest brothers who had been laid off from the pit since Christmas and were desperately glad of the existence wage Connie paid them each week – had been hard at work renovating the dilapidated interior of the premises. Mary's brothers had been invaluable in ripping out all the old furnishings and taking up the rotten wooden boards on the ground floor, whilst Connie and Mary had cleared the basement and painted the walls and ceiling before scrubbing the dirt and filth of years from the huge flagstones that made up the floor.

The two upper floors had been filthy but empty, having been used as living accommodation by the former owners, and beyond stripping the walls of layers of faded wallpaper and then scrubbing them – along with the grimy floorboards – they had left them alone. It was imperative to get the basement – wherein the proposed bakery would be housed – and the ground floor – which would consist of the shop and tea-rooms – ready first. She was having nightmares about the expenditure to date and they needed to start making money.

Once cleared, they had found the basement and ground floor quite spacious, being some 65 feet in depth and 25 feet wide, and once the plumber had made a hole in the existing lead pipe and wiped the new joint into place with his moleskin, fixing a brass tap on the other end of the new pipe in the basement, the supplementary water supply was established. Similarly, the gas man extended the gas pipe from the small kitchen to the rear of the ground floor down into the basement, and once everything was established Mary's brothers built several provers – cupboards with a little gas jet at the bottom – out of wood for the bread and tea-cake dough, and the big ovens were brought in along with the other equipment.

The ground floor, Connie had decided, would be arranged and furnished in recherché style, the well-stocked shop at the front leading to a pretty tea-room, very tastefully fitted, and beyond that the kitchen. The scheme of decoration in each portion was artistic and harmonious, the counters being fitted with white marble slabs and the walls panelled with the same material to a certain height, whilst the floors throughout were laid with an effective design in red mosaic tiles. It was clean and bright and modern, Connie thought now as she saw it all in her mind's eye, and with the tables and chairs for the tea-room being delivered in two days' time everything was nearly ready.

She was slightly apprehensive regarding the wisdom of asking Mary's mother, Ellen, a thin, shrivelled-up little mouse of a woman whose numerous pregnancies seemed to have sucked her inwards, to stand in as temporary cook. However, she couldn't afford the wages an experienced cook was asking, and as Mary insisted her mother's cooking was second to none, she had capitulated to her friend's request that her mother be given a chance to prove herself. Ellen had agreed to start work each morning at 4.30 a.m., Connie and Mary joining her at 6.30 a.m. when they would all work in the bakery until the shop opened at eight. At that time Connie would retire upstairs to the shop with Mary helping both her mother and Connie as circumstances dictated. The tea-rooms would open at ten o'clock and at that point Mary would remain upstairs. By the time Ellen left at mid-day she would have baked enough produce to keep the tea-rooms and the shop supplied until they closed at 6.30 in the evening. At least that was the plan. Connie wriggled under the covers again. How it would all work out was another matter. In the meantime the two brothers would repoint and whitewash the outside privy and washhouse in the large backyard, repave the yard which was a sea of mud and broken paving stones, before turning their attention to decorating and making good what was to be Connie and Mary's living quarters on the two top floors. But at least the roof was sound. Connie allowed herself a wry smile. Mr Watson had been most emphatic about that.

And then the smile faded as thoughts of Dan invaded again. She would tell him tomorrow evening when he called to escort her to Art and Gladys's for tea. It was the first time she had accepted an invitation to return to his brother's house – although they had asked her twice before – since the disastrous episode on New Year's Eve, but she was suddenly quite sure she couldn't go unless she had told Dan everything. She gnawed at her lower lip and squeezed her eyes tightly shut. Tomorrow night would have to be the night. And he would understand, Dan *would* understand. He loved her, didn't he?

Dan's love was about to be put to the test.

'Read that.' Edith Stewart thrust the sheet of paper at Dan with some force, her small body rigid. 'And before you ask it has all been verified.'

'By him?' Dan's voice was scathing as he jerked his head towards John.

'No, not by him. By an independent personage,' Edith snapped tightly.

'An independent personage? What does that mean?' And then, as his mother continued to gaze at him with unfaltering black eyes, 'I don't believe it, you've had her investigated haven't you! You've actually dared to authorise some dirty little gossipmonger to make up stories about her.'

'Mr Simmons is not a gossipmonger; he is a reputable and experienced private detective with an excellent reputation,' Edith said icily, 'and you ought to be thanking me for preventing you from making what would be the biggest mistake of your life. The chit has hoodwinked you, Dan, and if you weren't so infatuated you would see it yourself.'

'*I'm warning you, Mam.*'

They were all standing in Art's parlour – Dan, Art, Gladys, Edith and John. Over the last eight weeks Edith had demanded Dan's presence at the house in Ryhope Road at regular intervals and he had refused just as regularly, maintaining that if she wanted to see him she could come to him. And now she had done just that. But she was far from defeated, and John was positively cock-a-hoop. As soon as Dan had set eyes on his brother's exultant face he had known it didn't bode well.

'You're a fool.' The cutting tone in John's voice didn't mask his jubilation. 'She's taken you for a monkey and you're too proud to admit it, that's it at bottom, but you won't be able to do anything else when you read that.'

'*Get out.*'

The darkness in Dan's face caused John to take a step backwards, but it was Edith's indignant voice as she said, 'Get out? By, it's come to this, has it? You're telling your own brother to get out because of that trollop's bastard?' that checked Dan's advance on his brother and brought him swinging round to face his mother, and now, as Edith watched the blood flow into her youngest born's face, she knew immediately that she had gone too far.

Dan's eyes were unblinking as he thrust his face down towards his mother's and his words were forced out through his clenched teeth as he said, 'All my life I've held my hand with you because you are my mother and as such deserving of respect. I watched you make Da's life a misery from when I was old enough to take note of what went on in the house, and you've ruined the twins' lives, and his' – here he pointed to John without taking his eyes off his mother – 'and Art only escaped because he had the guts to stand up to you. You're a tyrant, you always have been. An egotistical tyrant, but you aren't ruining my life like you've tried to do to all the others.'

'Dan, Dan man, that's enough, come away.' Art had his hand on his brother's arm, Gladys standing to one side of them with the fingers of one hand pressed over her mouth, but Dan shook him off, and none too gently, as he continued, 'You're dangerous, do you know that, Mam? Dangerous.' He paused here for a few seconds before adding, 'Get out, and take your lap dog with you.'

'You'll live to rue this day.' Edith was spitting in her fury and John, bristling like the small dog Dan had accused him of resembling, looked all set to make a fight of it.

Dan hoped he would. His glittering gaze moved from his mother to his oldest brother, and the two men stared at each other for some moments before John moistened his lips and said, 'Come on, Mam. You could talk till you're blue in the face and it'll do no good. He wants to play the big fellow so let him, let him.'

'She's the named owner of a property in Holmeside, did you know that, eh?' Edith was determined to have the last

word. 'A workhouse brat, and she's bought a place and doing
it up? I ask you! She's got a fancy man, and a wealthy one by
the looks of it, who's not averse to putting his hand in his
pocket if it keeps her happy. She left the Grand at the beginning
of the year and the next thing she's in clover and playing Lady
Bountiful.'

'That's not true, she's been doing a temporary
housekeeping job.' Even as he spoke the words Dan knew he
didn't believe them. She never spoke about her work and every
time he had asked anything – simple things, like what sort of
day she had had or how long they wanted her to stay on – she
had deftly changed the subject. It hadn't seemed important,
in fact he hadn't even known he'd registered it, until now.

'Temporary housekeeping job?' Edith gave a bark of a
laugh and her voice was full of contempt as she said, 'I've
heard it called some things in my time but never that, and
while we're on the subject you might like to have a chat with
the ex-housekeeper at the Grand, her name and address are
on that report. She's a mine of information. Not content with
servicing the owner the Bell girl looked after his uncle who
was visiting at Christmas, and when Mrs Pegg objected to the
goings-on she was dismissed without a reference. Years of
faithful service and that was her reward. Mind, it was the
wrong sort of service as far as Harold Alridge was concerned!
And then when Alridge's wife got involved and demanded
the Bell chit be got rid of he paid her off, handsomely no
doubt, but of course he wasn't the only string to her bow. Not
by a long chalk as present developments prove.'

'I don't believe any of it.'

'No?' Edith drew back a little, her small eyes gimlet hard
as she surveyed the stricken face of her beloved son, her

Danny-boy as she had referred to him when he was a little lad. And then she delivered her parting shot straight for the heart, allowing herself a scornful smile, her thin lips curling back from her strong white teeth as she said, 'Then why don't you ask her why she's kept quiet about her good luck, eh? Someone's pouring money in, lad – maybe she's got a rich relation she's shy of mentioning but I wouldn't hold your breath about that.'

'You've said enough, more than enough.' Art now committed the unforgivable sin of taking his mother's arm and manhandling her to the parlour door, jerking his head at John as he added, 'You. Out.'

'I won't forget this, Art.' Edith's voice was a low hiss but she still had the presence of mind to turn at the door, her gaze seeking Dan's deathly white face as she said again, her voice insistent, 'Ask her, Dan, and look into her eyes when she gives you her answer.'

When the door had closed behind the other three Gladys looked at Dan, who hadn't been able to prevent himself from sinking on to the sofa, his head in his hands, and she said, 'I don't believe the lass I met on New Year's Eve is capable of what your mam has just accused her of, Dan. You know your mam. I don't like to say it but she's a devil at times, a real devil. She's jealous of the lass, that's what this is all about.'

Dan didn't answer, but as he raised his head, his eyes skimming over the crumpled paper in his hand, Art came back into the room and he and Gladys watched Dan's face slowly stiffen. They looked anxiously at each other and then back to Dan before Art said, 'What is it? What does it say?'

Dan didn't reply for some moments and then he seemed to have to drag his eyes from the so-called report. He stared at them both for a second or two more and then shook his head slowly. 'I don't believe it, any of it. This Mr Simmons must have the wrong girl.'

'Let's have a look.' Art now scanned the single sheet of paper, Gladys peering over his shoulder, and when he had finished he said, 'Apart from this Mrs Pegg's allegations there is nothing to suggest Connie has done anything wrong, even if it turns out she does own this shop or whatever in Holmeside, and reading between the lines this housekeeper seems to have her own axe to grind. Who knows why she was dismissed from the Grand other than what she's said to this half-nowt Mam's dug up? Folk always have a whinge when they get the push from somewhere, you know that as well as I do, Dan. Look at the trouble we've had at our place with one or two who turned nasty.'

Dan stared at his brother. Art was avoiding the main issue. If, *if*, this report was true and Connie's name was on the deeds to some kind of business or other, who had put it there? And more importantly, why? He suddenly felt sick. He had to go and see her.

He wasn't aware that he had spoken the last thought out loud until Art said, 'Think about it, man. Think over what you're going to say. You're seeing her tomorrow night; take her out somewhere instead of bringing her here, somewhere quiet, and have a long calm talk. Don't go about it like a bull in a china shop.'

It was good advice but Dan knew he wasn't going to take it. He could no more have spent the rest of the evening sitting in Art and Gladys's parlour or working on the stock report for the William Street warehouse he'd brought home than fly to the moon. He needed to talk to her, now, tonight. He'd be stark staring barmy by morning if he didn't.

His face must have spoken for him because Art sighed heavily, his tongue coming over his lips before he said, 'Aye, well maybe I'd do the same thing in your shoes, but go easy, eh? Mam's a cunning so-an'-so and John's as bad, and anything they've had a hand in will have more muck under the surface than Jarrow slake.'

Dan nodded. He knew that. Aye, he knew it full well and that was one of the reasons he had to see her tonight. If she could look straight at him and say it was all lies he would believe her word over that of his family any day.

It didn't occur to him until later – much later – that the 'if' in his mind had been a seed planted by his mother, and that it had already taken root.

John was hard put to keep the smile off his face as he drove his mother home to Ryhope Road. They could easily have walked the short distance to Art's place, but since Edith had acquired her small Ford – at the exorbitant cost of some £500 – she liked to be seen in it whenever possible. He didn't blame her. Apart from the Rotheringtons and one or two other leading lights in the town no one he knew owned an automobile, although he had read in the paper a few nights back that some 130,000 cars had been registered in the United Kingdom. His mother was a canny body. He nodded mentally at the thought. She knew what was what all right. It wasn't enough to acquire wealth, you had to display it – it had to be seen if you wanted respect. That was something his father had never fully understood.

He couldn't remember how old he was when he had first started eavesdropping on his parents when they had thought he was abed, but their rows had been bitter. His mother had had to push and push to get them where they were now; his father had been too soft, that had been his trouble. Too bothered about the workers and their rights and such. Rights! They had no rights except those they were allowed by management, and if he had his way they'd be running a tighter ship right now, but it was a constant fight with Art and Dan putting in their twopennyworth.

The thought of his younger brother deepened the secret glow of satisfaction. He had spent the last few weeks – ever since his mam had got wind of what was afoot from Mr Simmons – keeping an eye on the Bell piece a few evenings a week, and the number of times his brother had made an appearance and they'd gone off somewhere or other had made his blood boil. A milksop like him with her! Dan would never know how to handle a red-blooded female like Connie Bell and he'd never satisfy her either. Her type needed it hot and strong and none too gentle. Oh aye, he knew how to treat her sort all right. A whore was always a whore however they tried to pretend otherwise. And there was Dan, with his holier-than-thou ideas, having been led right up the garden path. He had to give the baggage credit where it was due. But now she'd been rumbled; he'd seen the dawning knowledge in his brother's stunned eyes and nothing had ever given him greater satisfaction.

He shifted in his seat, glancing swiftly at his mother sitting rigidly at his side, a tartan car-rug over her knees and her eyes fixed straight ahead, before concentrating on the road ahead again.

Dan had blotted his copy-book with their mam all right, and not before time. He had waited years for something like this. And it was all the sweeter for knowing that what had occurred tonight had left the road wide open for him with the Bell chit. His eyes narrowed on the wintry scene ahead. He was going to have her, and in the having of her he'd be sure to teach her a lesson she'd never forget. Her and her strumpet mother with their airs and graces; by, if anyone had it coming to them she did. The mother was out of his reach but Sadie had been used and worn out anyway. The daughter was still young enough to be everything her mother had been when he'd first seen her, aye, and then some.

All good things come to those that wait. As he drove the car through the big gates they had left wide open and on to the front drive of the house his crotch was damp with anticipation. And he had waited long enough.

'Dan, this is a surprise.' Connie's voice was eager as she saw the big figure in the doorway to the living room, Mary – who had answered the knock at the front door – standing just behind him. 'I thought we weren't seeing each other until tomorrow evening?'

'I need to talk with you.'

'Of course, come in.' Her voice was less delighted now; she had noticed his body was as stiff as a ramrod and that his face was set. Something was wrong, badly wrong. And she spoke the last thought out loud as she said, 'Is anything the matter?'

'I'll make a cup of tea.' Mary closed the door behind her a second after she had spoken, leaving them alone, and for a moment Connie wanted to call her back as Dan came fully into the room and she saw the look in his eyes. But that was stupid, she chided herself in the next instant. She had nothing to fear from Dan. Not Dan.

She had risen when she had first seen him, and now she indicated the saddle with a wave of her hand as she resumed her seat in the rocking chair without going to him and raising her face for his kiss which would have been normal. 'What is it?' she asked quietly as he stood in front of her without taking up the invitation to be seated.

'It has been brought to my attention—' Dan stopped abruptly. That was too pompous, too ridiculous. He wet his lips, looking down into her lovely face and feeling his heart thud to the point where it was painful as he said, 'Connie, I have to ask you . . .'

'Yes?'

'Have you recently bought a property in Holmeside?'

There was a silence, a long silence, and then her voice came, small but surprisingly firm, as it said, 'Aye, I have. I was going to tell you about it.'

Dear God, dear God. Dan had never been a praying man but he found himself praying now and he was entreating the Almighty that somehow, *somehow*, she would have a believable explanation for her new-found wealth. He continued looking at her for another moment and then stepped backwards, sitting down on the saddle with his hands resting on his knees as he forced himself to say, calmly and quietly, 'How did you come by the means to purchase it?'

She should have told him before; oh, *why* hadn't she? Her guilt made Connie's face flush as she said quickly, 'I saved quite a lot. I started years ago, when I first went to the workhouse.'

'You saved quite a lot.' The words barely moved his lips. 'How much does a property like that cost, Connie?'

She stared at him, her stomach churning and her joined hands pressed into her lap. 'One hundred and seventy pounds.' And as the amount registered in Dan's eyes, 'But Mr Watson said it was a bargain, being where it is and all, and it's a big place. We . . . we're turning it into a shop and tea-rooms, and there's a bakery in the basement.'

'We?'

And now his tone made her stiffen as she said, 'Mary and I. And her brothers.'

'And the housekeeping job?'

Connie raised her chin, but there was a pleading note in her voice as she said, 'I left the Grand in January and I've been working on the place in Holmeside ever since. I wanted to tell you, Dan, and I was going to. I swear it.'

There was only a matter of some two or three feet separating them but they could have been worlds apart, and now Connie's voice was rushed and high. 'Listen to me, Dan, please listen. I went to the bank with the money I'd saved, seventy pounds, and saw the manager, Mr Bainbridge. He said the bank would help me—'

'Who is Colonel Fairley?'

'What?'

The name was like a blow right between the eyes, and as Dan saw her face change, her skin blanch, he stood up in one savage movement and walked over to the mantelpiece, resting one arm on it as he stared down into the glowing fire and said again, his back to her, 'Who is Colonel Fairley? Or perhaps I should say, what is he to you?'

'He is nothing to me.'

'Then let me rephrase the question,' said Dan harshly as he swung round again. 'What *was* he to you during the time he was staying at the Grand? You don't deny he stayed at the Grand?'

'Of course I don't deny it.' Anger was replacing the sick horror and apprehension. The worst had happened; he had heard something and drawn his own conclusions and she was being hung, drawn and quartered. He hadn't come here tonight for an explanation, Connie thought bitterly. He'd already made his mind up about her long before he'd stepped through the door. She rose now, her head back and her violet-blue eyes as hard as sapphires as she said, very clearly and loudly, 'Colonel Fairley is a relation of Mr Alridge's and he made improper advances to me which I reported.'

'To the police?'

'To Mr and Mrs Alridge.'

'And they did what? Asked you to leave? Isn't that a little odd with you being the innocent party? Oh come on, Connie, what do you take me for?'

'You don't really want me to answer that, do you?' she said cuttingly. 'I don't know what you've heard about me or from whom, but obviously you'd rather believe them than me. You think I'm bad, don't you? That's what this is all about. Well, don't you?'

He stared at her in silence for what seemed a long, long while and then his voice was flat without the harshness of before, but the words terrible-sounding to her, as he said, 'I don't know what to think and that's the truth of it. Look, read this and then tell me it's all lies.'

When he thrust the piece of paper he had drawn out of his pocket at her he thought for a moment she wasn't going to take it, but then her hand reached out, her eyes still holding his for a good ten seconds, before she lowered them to the neatly typed words, asking immediately, 'Who is Mr Simmons?'

'That's not important.' And then, as her eyes met his and held, 'He is an investigator, a private detective.'

'Hired by?'

'My mother.'

Connie nodded slowly. She might have guessed. And then, her heart racing, she read down the paper. Oh this was clever, it was, it was clever. There was just enough truth here to make the lies perfectly believable. That horrible old woman had actually hired someone to poke and pry into her private affairs. How dared she. *How dared she*. And then running to Dan with the tittle-tattle and him soaking it all up. She hated him. She hated the lot of them. She had been stupid, so, so *stupid*, to think Dan was different. He was just like the rest of them.

'This is not *all* lies.' She thrust the paper back into his chest so hard he was caught off balance and took a step backwards. 'I do own a property in Holmeside and I did leave the Grand because of Colonel Fairley, but it was as *I* said, not this Mr Simmons or Mrs Pegg. Mrs Pegg was a hateful woman and she always resented me. But I am not going to say any more and you can think what you like. If you had really' – she couldn't bring herself to say loved – 'cared for me you wouldn't have believed such wicked lies.'

'I didn't say I believed them—'

Connie interrupted him with a mirthless laugh. 'Oh aye, you did. Not in words maybe, but words are nothing. Actions speak louder than words. Just go, Dan, and please don't come back. Not ever.'

Again they were staring at each other and nothing in Connie's proud, tight face betrayed the fact that she was bleeding inside. He would ask her to forgive him, say he had been wrong, that he loved her and couldn't possibly believe what this Mr Simmons had written. Right up until the moment Dan turned, her heart was telling her that he wouldn't really go, it couldn't end like this.

The minute the front door banged Mary was back in the sitting room, and as always her friend came straight to the point. 'What on earth was that about?' She stared at Connie who was again sitting in the rocking chair, her face as white as a sheet. 'What's up, lass?'

Connie couldn't answer for a moment, and then, her arms crossing her stomach and her hands gripping her waist, she told her. She went on talking while Mary gazed at her open-mouthed, and when she ended, 'So I sent him away,' Mary closed her eyes for a second and turned her head to the side.

Then, looking at Connie again she said, 'You played right into her hands, the pair of you. By, lass, I thought you'd got more sense.'

'Me?' If Father Hedley had suddenly materialised with two horns and a forked tail, Connie couldn't have been more astounded. Or hurt. And it was her hurt that made her say, 'How can you say that when you've never liked him? You've been on and on at me from day one to finish with him now then. I'd have thought you'd be congratulating yourself you were proved right.'

'Don't be daft.'

'I'm not.'

'Aye, you are, an' I'll tell you somethin' else while I'm about it. I don't blame him for thinkin' the worst the way he found out. He's only human, lass.'

She didn't believe this. First Dan and now Mary. Connie's

great saucer eyes had always been mirrors for her soul, and now Mary dropped her head back on her shoulders and looked up to the ceiling, and what she said was, 'Don't look at me like that, lass. I don't mean to have a go but you've always seemed to have a screw loose where he's concerned,' and, her head lowering, 'I suppose everyone's got a weak point an' he's yours.'

'So you are saying this is my fault?' Connie asked with painful restraint.

'Aye, I suppose I am, a bit leastways.'

'I see.' The urge to cry had left her; Mary's defection on top of Dan's had sent the hurt too deep for tears. And now Connie stood up slowly, her manner strained as she said, 'Well, you're entitled to your opinion of course but it doesn't make any difference. He has gone and I'm glad, *glad*, do you hear? And I don't want you to mention his name again, all right?'

'If that's the way you want it, lass.'

'It is.' And it was the way it would remain. She was finished with love and fancy promises and sweet words that meant nothing. Bricks and mortar were solid and substantial and real, and they didn't have the power to break her heart, Connie told herself fiercely. She wouldn't forget that again. Like Mary had said, she'd had a screw loose where Dan Stewart was concerned, but oh . . . The lead weight in her chest was pressing down, grinding her heart to pieces. How did you stop loving someone just because they had stopped loving you?

Chapter Nineteen

At midnight on 4th August, 1914, Britain declared war on Germany, and cheering crowds surged through London to gather in Downing Street and outside Buckingham Palace, where thousands of people sang the national anthem amid scenes of great jubilation. News of the commencement of war reached Sunderland shortly after midnight, and was related to a bellicose crowd gathered outside the *Echo* offices.

The flood of patriotic fervour temporarily washed away the bitterness of the builders', mine workers' and railway workers' strikes which had laid two million men idle in the preceding months and caused whole families to starve and become destitute, and young men waved their hats and cheered all the way to the recruiting offices, eager to take part in the war which was predicted to be over by Christmas.

For Connie, the last few months had been a composite of back-breaking hard work and nail biting tension as she, along with Mary and Ellen, had struggled to make enough to even cover their meagre wages, and then euphoria in July when suddenly the bakery and tea-rooms were crowded every day. But overall it had been a time of waiting. At least that was how Connie felt deep inside.

She couldn't believe, she just couldn't *believe* that one

day Dan wouldn't come knocking on the door. She told herself it was ridiculous to continue hoping, and she was eternally thankful for the exhausting days and nights that meant she fell into bed each night too tired to think, but nevertheless, buried deep, deep in the core of her, the last remnant of hope refused to die completely.

At the beginning of May she and Mary had moved from Walworth Way to the four rooms above the premises of the new 'Bell's Bakery & Tea-rooms'. With the assistance of a plumber friend Mary's brothers had turned the first floor into a neat little parlour leading through to a kitchen, and the second floor consisted of their two bedrooms. It had taken them a full week to get used to the space. With their old room also rented out, Walworth Way was making Connie a handsome little profit each week, which had been very useful whilst things were tight and had provided for their groceries and fuel more than once when the cupboards had been bare.

Connie had been glad to leave Walworth Way for reasons other than merely the splendour of their new living accommodation and the convenience of being above the shop and bakery however.

Exactly two weeks to the day from the confrontation with Dan, John Stewart had knocked at the door asking to see her. She had refused him entry, and when he had made it plain – with a brazenness which had shocked and amazed her – why he had called, she had slammed the door in his face after warning him that if he came again she would inform the constable he was bothering her. The incident had upset and unnerved her, and twice in the weeks leading up to the move she had glimpsed sight of him in the vicinity of Walworth Way, although he had made no attempt to approach her, possibly because Mary had been with her. She told Mary nothing of this, nor Lucy, who was now heavy with child and confined to her bed most days with severe swelling of her limbs and face. Connie visited her frequently and they spoke of most things, but she found she couldn't mention John Stewart to anyone. It was too humiliating, too debasing, the fact that he thought he could suggest . . . She didn't like to dwell on what he had suggested.

But on the evening of 5th August Connie wasn't thinking of John Stewart or even Dan; she was concentrating on keeping the customers in the tea-rooms happy. She and Mary had been rushed off their feet all day – it seemed everyone wanted to be out and about and talking about the splendour of Britain's ultimatum calling on Germany to respect the neutrality of Belgium which Germany had patently ignored – so when she saw Harold Alridge at the door of the shop she waved gaily at first, before she took in his desperate expression.

'What is it?' She had reached his side in seconds. 'Is Lucy all right?'

'Can you come?' Harold glanced round the crowded tea-rooms. 'Lucy is asking for you. The baby is coming early.'

'But she is all right?'

Harold looked at her, gulping spittle into his dry mouth. 'She is tired, very tired,' was his reply, but the manner in which it was spoken prompted Connie to call to Mary as she untied her apron, and after explaining the circumstances to leave at a run.

Lucy's labour pains had started in earnest at four o'clock in the morning and it was now nearly six in the evening and still the baby showed no signs of emerging. When Connie entered the luxurious bedroom in the manager's suite she was shocked at the sight of her friend. Lucy was barely recognisable as the beautiful elegant creature she had always known. Her hair was wild, her poor swollen body straining against the pain racking it, and she appeared oblivious to the ministrations of the midwife who was with her.

'The doctor is on his way.' Harold had approached his wife, stroking her forehead with a tender hand as he added, 'And I fetched Connie as you asked.'

As Harold moved to one side Connie took his place at the other side of the bed to the midwife, and when Lucy's tortured eyes turned to her she said softly, 'I'm here, Lucy. I'm here.'

'Connie?'

'Yes, dear.'

'Watch . . . watch over my baby, won't . . . you. Help . . . Harold care for it. My mother, she might try to take it . . . and she mustn't. My father . . . It mustn't grow up with my father, Connie.'

'Lucy, don't talk like that, dear. Your baby will grow up with you and Harold.'

'Promise me, Connie.' And then, as another spasm gripped her, 'Oh no, no, not again.'

Connie reached out and took her friend's hand in her own and Lucy held on to it with all her might as she strained and stretched against the contraction, but it was obvious to each one of them that Lucy had no strength left.

At the same moment as the spasm finished and Lucy sank back into the rumpled pillows, the door opened to show the doctor, but when Connie tried to leave Lucy's grip on her hand became vice-like. 'P . . . promise me, Connie. I want my child to be free and . . . unfettered, not caged. My home was like . . . a prison. I couldn't breathe. Help

Harold, he'll need you. You understand?'

'Yes, I understand.' From all Lucy had confided about her life as a child Connie had often thought the constrictions not unlike the workhouse. 'But you'll be taking care of your baby, Lucy, as soon as you are well enough. But I promise, dear. Of course I do. I'll help in any way I can.'

'Harold knows, and he . . . he's promised.' Lucy was gasping against the forthcoming contraction. 'My parents don't understand children, they never have.'

'Don't worry any more.'

Connie would have said more but the doctor and midwife were waiting for her to leave, and she could do nothing other than join Harold on the landing after bending down and holding Lucy close for a moment.

It was another hour before the child was born. It was very small and barely alive, and it was a girl. Lucy Alridge died twenty minutes later.

'Lass, I know what you promised, an' it was to *watch over* the bairn, not take it on full-time. You'll never manage it, not an' run this place an' see to everythin' else. He can afford a nurse-maid, now then. An' there must be other friends he can call on?'

'They didn't have friends as such. Social acquaintances maybe, and Harold has his associates at his gentlemen's club, but not friends. Lucy used to say she always felt an outsider here, coming from the south, and what with running the hotel and all it left little time for getting to know people. Besides, she wasn't like that, you know she wasn't. She kept herself very much to herself. It . . . it was the way she had been brought up. Her father had stifled that part of her and she was only just . . . just beginning . . .'

'All right, all right, don't take on, lass. You know I'll do what I can, an' me mam an' all, it's just that lookin' after a bairn is a full-time job at the best of times an' what with it bein' sickly an' all . . .'

Connie swallowed deeply in her throat. Mary was right, she knew she was right, but it didn't make any difference. From the first moment she had seen Lucy's child last night she had loved her. The tiny screwed up face, the minute hands . . . This wee scrap of nothing *had* to live, it had to. And Lucy wouldn't have wanted her daughter to be entrusted to a nursemaid, not at first anyway. Her friend would have wanted her to be with someone who loved her. But not her parents. She had been adamant about that. And poor Harold . . . Connie had never really taken to Lucy's husband, but seeing him last night had made her realise his whole world had revolved around Lucy. He had been utterly broken, lost. And he hadn't even held the child . . .

'Lass, why don't you just let things settle for a week or two an' see what he sorts out, eh? He's not short of a bob or two.'

'This isn't about money, Mary.' Money was the last thing it was about. This was to do with paying back the deep faith in her which Lucy had always shown, a faith which had been tried and tested over the Colonel Fairley affair when Lucy had even gone against her beloved Harold in Connie's defence; it was about a wretched little cottage and that other tiny fragile child who had been born too soon into a world that had no time for her; it was about Larry and her granny and her mam. They had all gone and she missed them so much, and she couldn't hold them and tell them how much she loved them. But she could Lucy's child. That she could do.

Mary had been watching the play of emotion over Connie's face and what she said now, in a tone of resignation, was, 'So, you goin' round there now then?' It was half past five in the morning and they had been sitting at the kitchen table for half an hour, neither of them having been able to sleep much since Connie got home the night before.

Connie nodded. The midwife had agreed to stay and nurture the infant through the night after the doctor had spoken to her, but the woman had made it clear she would have to leave at seven o'clock, having her own family to see to. 'If he's still the same' – and she didn't doubt Harold Alridge would still be beside himself; it was more his attitude with the child that had worried Connie the night before – 'I'll have a chat with the midwife about bringing her back here until Harold's more like himself and can think straight.'

'Aye.' Mary inclined her head but her voice was taciturn as she said, 'But you bring it back here now an' you'll be makin' a rod for your own back, lass, you take it from me. It's human nature to flog a willin' horse. You'll be stuck with it an' he'll take advantage.'

Oh, she hoped so. She did so hope so. Connie stared at her friend's small, bespectacled face, and whatever Mary read there suddenly caused her to grin as she pushed her glasses further up her small snub nose. 'Well, lass, I've said it afore an' no doubt I'll say it agen, there's never a dull moment. If nothin' else, there's never a dull moment.'

Harold Alridge was more than willing for Connie to take his daughter until he was able, as he put it, to marshal his thoughts and make appropriate plans for the child's future. He couldn't have described how he felt about the child to a living soul, but even to look at it made him want to be physically sick. He had planted that thing in his Lucy and in the bearing of it it had killed her. After hours of torture, terrible, terrible torture, it had killed her. It was an . . . an abomination.

He watched now as Connie went about gathering all the paraphernalia Lucy had bought so happily over the last few months, and after a full minute of silence he had to force himself to say, 'I am deeply in your debt. My . . . my wife was insistent her parents mustn't have her child, but I'm really not in a position to have it here.'

That was ridiculous and they both knew it; a nursemaid would have fitted in easily at the hotel. But Connie merely nodded as though it was perfectly natural before she said, 'I promised Lucy I would help, didn't I, and there is plenty of room at home now we have moved. You must come every day if you like and as soon as you feel able to have her home please say, but in the meantime I'm happy to keep her as long as you want. I mean that.' And then she straightened and stopped her buzzing about as she looked him full in the face and said, her voice soft, 'Lucy would have wanted this so please don't worry; I will take good care of her child.'

If it occurred to either of them that the child had been referred to throughout as purely Lucy's, neither of them mentioned the fact, but when Connie carried the baby out to the horse-drawn taxi carriage Harold had arranged, two sober-faced housemaids following with the crib packed full of clothes and blankets and the two pap-bottles the midwife had sent out for, Harold didn't ask to kiss his daughter goodbye and Connie didn't suggest it.

And so it was that during the month of August, when more

and more nations declared war on each other and the human casualties began to rise with alarming swiftness, culminating in the blood-bath at Mons when British, French and Belgian troops fell beneath the oncoming German cavalry, one little Sunderland bairn slept the month away surrounded by love and gently soothing arms.

Little Hazel – the name Lucy had wanted for a girl – rarely cried, but then she was rarely allowed to. From the moment Connie brought her down to the bakery at six-thirty in the morning until she went back upstairs with Connie and Mary any time after nine in the evening when they had finished cleaning and clearing away for the next morning, there were several pairs of arms reaching out to her if she so much as raised a squawk.

Ellen's first job of the morning was to mix ten stones of flour with salt and yeast in five bath tins, and then, once the first bath tin dough had risen, to weigh out just over one pound two ounces for each loaf to be baked before working the loaves and then putting them to rise again. This was followed by brushing the bread with raw lard before putting the first batch, now duly risen, into one of the huge ovens. Once the ovens were full Ellen would prepare the tea cakes and fancy cakes, and until little Hazel's appearance at Holmeside this stage of the morning proceedings had taken place at about half past six, when Connie and Mary had first come down. Now, however, Ellen had taken to arriving at the bakery at 4.00 a.m. and taking a break at six-thirty, which meant she was just in time to give the baby her bottle whilst the first quantity of tea cakes rose in their prover.

Mary, in particular, found this desire of her mother's to hold and pet the infant more than a little surprising, due to the fact that Ellen had never shown a pronounced maternal streak with her own brood.

'That's different, lass.' When Mary had voiced her feelings her mother had been quite unrepentant. 'You can't give 'em back when they're yer own, an' when ye're workin' yer fingers to the bone an' knakky-kneed with exhaustion it's enough to keep 'em fed an' watered.'

'Aye, I suppose it is.' Mary had stood staring at the thin, scraggy figure who looked twenty years older than her forty-seven years and then she had gone across and hugged her mother for the first time in a long time. Her mam had been through it an' all, and her da, bless them, and they had tried to do the best for all their bairns in their own way, she thought soberly. And since she'd started to take Wilf round for an hour or two some weeks they had made him so welcome – you'd think she was being courted by royalty rather than a porter who barely earned enough to keep body and soul together. How they would ever afford to get wed she didn't know, not on Wilf's money; not that he'd asked her anyway. But she had the feeling he would if his prospects were a bit brighter. And what would she say if he did? She had asked herself this more than once lately, and the answer was always the same – she'd face that when it happened. Wilf was a canny body, aye, he was, and she ought to be thanking her lucky stars he was so keen on her, but . . . that other side, the side that came with marriage. It scared her to death. But then so did the thought of Wilf going away to war and her never seeing him again.

There were more and more young men joining up to 'teach that damn maniac, the Kaiser, a lesson he'd never forget'. Thinking he could go cocking a snook at the British and knocking hell out of them poor Belgians; he'd learn, he would, by the time they'd finished with him. It was the universal opinion of Britain's working man and frequently expressed in the pubs and working men's clubs, inciting more and more lads, who didn't know one end of a rifle from the other let alone what it took to kill a man, to 'show what they were made of'.

What men were made of was spread all over the battlefields, from Belgium in the north to Alsace and Lorraine in the south. In under a month the Germans had swept over most of Belgium, crossing the Sambre and Meuse and forcing a French retreat to the Somme, the last barrier before Paris. At the end of August the Russian army suffered a terrible defeat on the Eastern Front in a battle at Tannenberg, which raged for days in heavily wooded country along the borders of East Prussia.

Angry and shocked northerners read in their newspapers that General Samsonov's Second Army had been cut to pieces in a hail of German shellfire. Something like 300,000 men were believed to have taken part in the titanic struggle, it was reported. Cavalry swept through the villages under a blazing sun whilst white-bloused Russian infantrymen recklessly charged emplacements to use the bayonet against the grey-clad German machine-gunners.

It made the British with their sense of fair play mad – fighting mad – and by the beginning of September almost as many men were joining the army in a day as were normally recruited in a year, and still Herbert Asquith, the Prime Minister, was asking for some 500,000 more. Lord Kitchener had ordered the number of training centres to be rapidly expanded, and those recruits without rooms in barracks would receive two shillings a day board and lodging in addition to their one shilling pay. And who could say fairer than that? And so the youth of Britain – and some not so young – continued to enlist. And the slaughter went on.

It was in the second week of September that Kitty McLeary paid an impromptu visit to her Aunty Ida in the East End. She was upset, she was very upset, and she needed the warmth and comfort of family and her Aunty Ida in particular. So when Vera, one of the daughters-in-law, met her at the door saying, 'Eee, Kitty, it's not your usual day, is it, lass? Anythin' wrong?' before continuing, 'Mam's bad in bed, she's got the Father with her,' she felt somewhat deflated.

'What's wrong with her?'

'Had a fall comin' out of church last night of all places, I reckon that's why the Father's here this mornin', likely feels a bit responsible,' Vera whispered back, before adding, 'Go on in, lass.'

'Oh no, I won't bother her now, Vera.' She hadn't been inside a church in years and the guilt weighed heavy on her at the best of times; the last thing she needed was to have to sit and make small talk with one of Ida's priests!

But then the decision was taken out of Kitty's hands as her aunty's voice, as full-bodied as ever, called from inside the front room, 'Vera? Who is it, lass?' And at Vera's reply of 'Kitty, Mam,' – 'Tell her to come in then, we don't stand on ceremony here.'

When Kitty pushed open the door she saw the priest was Father Hedley; she remembered him from her first days in Sunderland when she had stayed with her aunty and accompanied her to church. He was sitting in an armchair by the bed, drinking a cup of tea with a plate of well-buttered hot girdle scones resting on his lap, and his opening words were meant to put Kitty at her ease as he said, 'Ah now, just what was needed. You'll help me eat a couple of these scones, won't you now?'

Kitty forced a weak smile as she said, 'I've not long had me breakfast, Father.' She had liked this priest, he'd been kind, had had the human touch – not like the other one who had constantly preached of the dire consequences of going against God's holy will and of the tribulations and horrors that would fall on them all when they ignored His holy mass.

'Aye, I said the same, and look where it got me.'

And then Father Hedley's attempt at tactfulness was brought to nothing when Ida, ensconced in a knitted bed-jacket in an alarming shade of pink, said cheerily, 'You remember me niece, Father? Me sister's child from over the water? Good little Catholic she was afore she went to work for the Stewarts in Ryhope Road.'

Oh, her aunty!

'Yes, I remember Kitty.' Father Hedley's voice was quiet as he stood and offered Kitty his chair despite her embarrassed protests, bringing another for himself from across the crowded, smelly room and putting it a foot or so away as he continued, a note of amusement in his voice, 'I could hardly do anything else when you talk of her so often, could I, Ida? You've been very good to your aunty over the years, Kitty,' he added softly.

He *was* nice, this priest. Kitty stared back into the gentle face watching her and this time her smile was more natural as she said, 'She's been very good to me an' all.'

'I don't doubt it.'

They continued to talk for some time, and Kitty was just on the verge of taking her leave when, in reply to her aunt's lamentations about the bairns all over the world who would find themselves orphans due to the madness of one man – the Kaiser – Father Hedley said something that stayed her hand. 'Aye, it's a wicked thing, a wicked thing right enough,' the priest said sadly, shaking his greying head. 'There's enough heartache in the normal way of things for any soul to carry. Mind, it's the tragedies that bring out the greatness in folk, we mustn't forget that. It's done me heart good just this last week to hear of such a case.'

'Oh aye?'

'Aye. A young lass, one of the flock, Ida. You might know her. Connie? Connie Bell? She's taken in a wee one when the mother died in childbirth, tragic, tragic. And the father gone all to pieces, so I understand.'

'Connie Bell?' It was Kitty who spoke and her voice was sharp. 'You did say Connie Bell, Father? Her mother wasn't called Sadie, was she?'

'Aye, aye that's the one. You know her maybe?' It was Father Hedley's turn to feel uncomfortable. He had just remembered Sadie's connection with the family this woman worked for.

'Not exactly.' Kitty hesitated a moment before saying, 'This girl is a little young to be looking after a child, isn't she?'

'Young?' Father Hedley considered the word. 'No, I don't think so. She must be over twenty now and there's plenty had one or two of their own by that age, besides which Connie was born with an old head on her shoulders, some bairns are like that.' Father Hedley could feel a slight flush creeping over his face but he still said what he wanted to say. 'The child had a rough start in life but she's a survivor, is Connie, and a good girl too. Saved up for years and started a little business of her own and that takes some doing. No, I'd say she's more than able to take care of a bairn.'

Kitty stared at the elderly priest for some moments, then bit on her lip. Dan was tearing himself apart over this lass; he had been for months and nothing would convince her that this latest – him joining up this morning – was because of Connie Bell. She'd been privy to the ins and outs of what had occurred; she'd had the story from all sides, Dan, Art and Gladys, even John, and she had felt all along that this report by the private detective Edith had hired was mostly conjecture. She had said as much to Dan after he had been to see the lass and he had agreed with her, whilst stating that it was too late now. He had acted like a jealous fool; he had accused her of all manner of things and Connie had made it plain she didn't want to see him again. She hated him now and he didn't blame her.

The look on Kitty's face told Father Hedley something was afoot but he surmised Kitty didn't want to talk in front of her aunty, so now he rose from the chair, dusting his black coat free of crumbs as he said, 'I shall have to be making tracks, Ida, but I'll look in again in a few days if you're not up and about.'

'Oh I shall be, Father, I shall be. You know me, tough as old boots.'

'I've got to be going too.' Kitty got to her feet, tidying her hair and adjusting her straw hat more securely on the top of her head. 'I'll . . . I'll see the Father out, Aunty Ida.'

'Aye, all right, lass, an' thanks for callin' in.'

Once outside in the street they both unconsciously lifted their noses to the summer air and breathed it in; the dank unwashed smell of humanity had been strong in the house, and it was Father Hedley who broke the silence as he said, 'You seem troubled, Kitty, or am I wrong?'

They were standing looking at each other on the hot pavement, and now Kitty's eyes dropped as she said, 'No, you're not wrong, Father.'

'Can I be of help in any way?'

'Oh, Father.'

It was an answer in itself, and Father Hedley said briskly, 'Let's walk a way. I always find walking helps me think, clears the mind. So, you talk and I'll listen and think, eh?' And he smiled.

She hadn't meant to tell him all of it, of the lads' part in the attack on Jacob, but Kitty found she had to start at the beginning and work through, and when she was finished Father Hedley was silent for some ten seconds before he said, 'So the lad is going away and neither of them knows how the other feels, not really. That's it at bottom? Well, for my part I can tell you that Connie saved every penny of the deposit she put down for the business, Kitty, and that this man, this Colonel Fairley, was someone she loathed and detested.' He could feel Father McGuigan turning in his grave. Here he was, encouraging the liaison between a heathen and one of the flock, and blatantly. Dear God, dear God . . .

Kitty nodded, but her voice was very quiet and tentative as she said, after a quick darting glance at the black-clothed figure at the side of her, 'The thing is, Father, I know how Mrs Stewart feels about Connie Bell. She—' Kitty stopped abruptly. She had been going to say, 'She is unbalanced about the lass', but that was the wrong word to use. It suggested an unstableness, someone who was irrational or deranged, and Edith's obsession with Connie Bell was frighteningly cognitive in spite of the dark emotion at the root of it. There was nothing rash or impulsive about Edith, her hatred of the girl would be channelled into carefully considered and premeditated attacks if she thought there was a chance Dan might resume his pursuit of her.

'Yes?' Father Hedley had stopped walking and now he turned Kitty to face him with a light hand on her elbow. 'How does Mrs Stewart feel about the girl?'

'She hates her, Father.' Father Hedley watched Kitty swallow and her eyes blinked before she said, 'Dan is her favourite you see, always has been, and I really don't think she'd stop at anything if she thought there was a chance they might get together. She's very cold, Dan's mother, and calculating. Aye, calculating and clever.'

They looked at each other for a moment and something clicked in the priest's brain. 'Calculating you say?' He nodded thoughtfully. 'And clever. Are you aware that this Colonel Fairley attacked Connie and that she feels his assault was precipitated by an anonymous letter the hotel manager received?'

Kitty McLeary's round handsome face had a blank expression for a moment, then her eyes stretched wide and her mouth opened slightly before she shut it with a little snap, only to open it again to say, 'I've known she's been up to something, her and John, but I thought it was just the private detective.'

'You think your employer is capable of doing something like that?'

'Oh aye, Father.' It was bitter. 'And much worse.' And now Dan was going away to fight and she knew it was to put as much distance between himself and everything that reminded him of Connie as he could. The last few months it had been as if he didn't care whether he lived or died. Something froze in Kitty at the thought, a chill going down her spine. *He had to be made to care.* A man going into battle with nothing to lose and nothing to hope for had little chance of seeing another day.

'Are you all right, Kitty?'

She came back to herself to see Father Hedley staring at her, and the look on the priest's face told Kitty her own face was reflecting the sick panic she was feeling. 'Aye, aye I'm all right, Father,' she said dully. Oh, Dan, Dan, what have you done? Why couldn't you have waited one more day before enlisting? She could have told him about the letter then, encouraged him to go and see the lass and try to sort things out. But then if Dan hadn't told her last night he was going to join up this morning, she wouldn't have come to see her Aunty Ida and met Father Hedley.

But perhaps it wasn't too late? Dan might have changed his mind or delayed things maybe? There were always panics at the works; something might have cropped up to prevent him following through? She had to go and see him, and right now. 'I have to go, Father.' Her voice was urgent and she was already backing away as she spoke. 'I've . . . I've an appointment, I'm sorry.'

'Aye, you run along, Kitty, and don't you worry. Bring everything to God in prayer now.'

'I will, Father. Goodbye.'

Father Hedley stood watching the plump, well-dressed figure of the Stewarts' housekeeper hurrying down the street but he wasn't really seeing her; his mind was grappling with a memory – a feeling – from the past, which the expression on Kitty's face had brought to his remembrance. But it wasn't possible. As he turned away he put his hand to his head, the scones suddenly becoming lead weights in his stomach. Not that. A letter was one thing, but to torch a place knowing there were folk inside. No, no it wasn't possible. And yet . . . He recalled his unease at the time, which he had been unable to explain, even to himself. But a woman couldn't have done that surely? Although Kitty had spoken of the son, John, in the same breath as the mother.

It was all too complicated he told himself in the next instant, and he only had his own gut feeling to go on anyway. The past was the past. But what was evident – here, now, in the present – was that someone, be it Edith Stewart or persons unknown, had meant to do Connie harm with that letter. And he had the notion, and strongly, that the Stewarts were at the bottom of it.

He would pay Connie a visit in a few days' time. He nodded at the thought. He had been intending to call anyway, to remind her that the church door was always open and she would be needing more help and guidance from the Almighty than ever with the heavy responsibilities she had taken on. And while he was there he would mention that two women living alone, above a little business – small as it may be – needed to be careful about such matters as security and good strong bolts on the doors and windows. Aye, he'd do that.

He passed a group of small children playing with a skipping rope one of them had tied to the jutting arm of a lamppost, their faces merry beneath the dirt despite the fact that the two little girls were in filthy rags and the boys had no backsides in their trousers. They were all barefoot and crawling with lice, but at least they looked well fed; they were the lucky ones.

One of the little mites smiled shyly at the old priest as he glanced down at them and he returned the smile, fishing in his cavernous black pocket for one of the bags of bullets he always carried around with him. He left the children sitting in a huddle sharing out the sweets, and as he walked away, the sun beating down on his face and causing a shimmer in the road ahead, the little girl's smile stayed with him.

There was no need for consternation, none at all, but he wouldn't wait a few days. He would go and see Connie tomorrow and just tell her to watch out for herself.

Chapter Twenty

It was exactly half past six when Dan walked through the door of Bell's Bakery & Tea-rooms, and when he came face to face with Mary he steeled himself for a fight, only to have the wind well and truly taken out of his sails when she said, after looking him up and down, 'Well, it's taken you long enough an' all.'

'What?'

'You heard.' And then she further surprised him when she said, 'I'm just closin' up. She's upstairs feedin' the bairn. You know about the bairn?'

'Yes, yes I do.'

'She'll be down in a minute, we've another two hours' or so work to do down here, but if I was you I'd go up.'

'Go up?' He stared at her a trifle vacantly, and then pulled himself together enough to say, 'Yes, I'll do that, Mary, and . . . thank you.'

'It's the door off the tea-rooms, an' Dan' – she caught hold of his arm as he made to pass her – 'you *have* come to tell her you were a bloody fool, haven't you?'

They stared at each other, both of them perfectly still as the last of the customers sidled past them and out of the front door of the shop, and as the little bell above the door tinkled and then became quiet, Dan looked down into Connie's friend's plain little face, and what he read there made his voice subdued and even humble as he said, 'Yes, Mary. I've come to tell her I was a bloody fool.'

'Aye, that's what I thought.' And then she grinned at him – the first time he could remember her doing so – and said, 'Go on then, what are you waitin' for?'

Yes, what was he waiting for? Why had he waited all these long weeks? Mary was right, he was a fool, a blind, ignorant, faithless fool. He should have come to see Connie weeks ago, the day after their quarrel when he had woken up in Art's little study and had known – without a shadow of a doubt – that she could never have done the things that foul report had suggested. She might have sent him packing – she might send him packing today – but at least he would have told her how he felt. Hell, he'd been a fool all right. But pray God Kitty's feeling was right and Connie felt enough for him to forgive him. He'd do anything: beg, plead, grovel . . .

He didn't have to grovel.

Connie was sitting in a rocking chair, rosy-red cushions behind her back and wisps of golden hair about her face as she nursed the sleeping baby in her arms, a half full bottle held limply in one hand. She didn't look up as she said, 'She won't have any more so ten to one she'll be playing us up in another hour. Is that the last one gone?'

And then, when there was no reply, she glanced up and saw him standing in the doorway.

She made no sound but her lips formed his name, and all the things he had meant to say went out of the window at the look on her face.

'Forgive me? I don't deserve it and I will never forgive

myself, but . . . forgive me, beloved.' He had moved across the room as he'd spoken, dropping down beside the rocking chair and taking her free hand, carrying the palm to his mouth as he said, 'I've been in hell, worse than hell. I knew you were incapable of those things, as soon as I'd had time to think about it I knew, but I thought you hated me and I'd ruined everything. Have I?'

He had come. All the last months of bitter pain and anguish were gone in a breath. She hadn't been alive these last months, she knew that now. She had stopped living the day he had left and her heart had started beating again a few seconds ago when she had seen his face. He had come. *He had come.*

He remained still now, her hand held against his cheek as he waited.

'I love you,' she whispered, and then, as his lips took hers and the sleeping child made a little hiccuping sigh, the sight and smell and the feel of him was overwhelming and it made her head spin.

'I'm a fool, Connie.'

'No, don't say that.' As he drew away to look into her face her voice was tremulous.

'It's true. Mary called me a *bloody* fool,' he added with a touch of wryness, and as they stared into each other's faces they both found themselves smiling and then laughing.

'Oh, I'm sorry, Dan, she shouldn't have said that.' Connie was shaking her head, and then, as they became still again and their eyes held, Dan reached forward and very gently lifted the baby off her lap and into the crib at the side of the chair before drawing her to her feet.

'I love you my darling, you do know that, don't you? I love you more than any man has ever loved a woman, and it's the only thing that matters, I know that now.'

And then they were in each other's arms, their lips clinging and their bodies endeavouring to merge as they swayed together in an ecstasy that was part pain, part pleasure. When at last Dan released her she leant against his chest, limp and trembling, before she drew back a little to look up into his face. 'We need to talk, I have to tell you—'

'No.' He put a finger to her lips, his other hand caressing the back of her neck. 'You don't have to tell me anything, my love. I was a stupid, jealous idiot, I knew that the next morning. I thought . . . I thought you'd washed your hands of me and I couldn't have blamed you.'

'As if I could.' And then they were kissing again until Connie pulled away saying, 'I do have to tell you, Dan, I must. And it wasn't all your fault, I should have told you about this place right at the start. Mary said I had a screw loose in not telling you, she said you were my weak point.'

'Am I?' He looked inordinately pleased. 'Pray God I'll always be your weak point, my darling, because you are certainly mine, in the nicest possible way. Oh, Connie . . .'

'No, no you have to listen.'

And so she told him and he listened, and when she had finished he gathered her close in his arms and held her there. And it was some moments before he said, 'You remember me mentioning Kitty, my mother's housekeeper? Well, she met a friend of yours today, Father Hedley . . .' And now it was Dan's turn to talk, and he sat down with Connie on his knee and told her the series of events as he knew them. And when he had done, neither of them mentioned the letter again or vocally surmised who had sent it.

'I love you with all my heart, Connie.' They had been sitting entwined in heart and body for some ten minutes without speaking; their lips, which were drawn together time after time, saying all that needed to be said.

'Your family won't like it if we start seeing each other again,' she warned him softly.

'Damn my family.' And then, as though he realised the mention of his family had struck a discordant note, Dan continued, 'Beloved, I have to tell you something and I want you to be brave.' He gripped her hands as he told her what he had done that morning, and for a moment, after he had become silent, she just stared at him with great saucer eyes full of anguish.

'Tomorrow? You have to leave for training tomorrow? Oh, Dan, Dan.' He was going away, and who knew when they would see each other again? *If* they would see each other again?

'I will write, every day, I promise.' His voice was urgent. 'The training centre is in Scotland; will you come to the station tomorrow morning and see me off?'

'Yes, yes.' She fell against him again, her throat working. *He was going away.* He had joined up. He was a soldier.

'It won't be for ever, sweetheart. It won't be for ever.'

Dan said the same thing the next morning. They met just inside the main entrance to Sunderland central station – the north end off High Street West – and Connie's heart leapt at her first sight of him. He came striding up to her, his face alight as he saw her standing to one side of the machine, much beloved by children, that enabled one to punch one's name on a tin strip, and as he took her hands his dark eyes said a hundred things which were unutterable in a busy railway station.

'Come and have a coffee, I've another half an hour before I have to leave.'

'Half an hour? Oh, Dan, is that all?'

'It won't be for ever, sweetheart.' As he led her into the buffet room with a hand tucked under her arm, Connie had to resist the impulse to cling to him and beg him not to go. He had to go, she knew that, and she had to make this as easy for him as she could. He had already said the night before how bitterly he was regretting enlisting, now it meant he was being sent away from her.

And then the buffet room vanished, together with its occupants, when ensconced at a small table with two cups of coffee in front of them Dan leant forward and took her hands again, his dark eyes hungry as he said, 'Oh, darling, darling, how am I going to leave you? You are so beautiful, so fine, and through my foolishness we've wasted so much time. Oh, Connie!' He bent over the table, murmuring words that gave her a warm inward glow and made her heart race, before he cupped her face tenderly in his hands. 'We have to get married, you know that don't you? And soon, very soon. I can't wait to hold you, to make you really mine.'

'I am yours, I am.'

'Will you marry me, Connie?' He let go of her face as he spoke, fishing in one pocket before bringing out a small velvet box which he placed on the table in front of her. 'Will you be my wife?'

She tore her eyes from his, lifting the lid of the box to see three exquisite diamonds on a half loop of gold, and at her, 'Dan! Oh it's beautiful, beautiful, and yes, of course I'll marry you,' he pulled her to meet him across the tiny table, his lips exultant as he kissed her, careless of any onlookers.

'Here.' He took the ring from its snug box, slipping it on to the third finger of her left hand. 'You're mine, you're promised to me. You wave that at any other fellows who come calling! Oh, darling, I love you, I love you. I can't believe so much has happened in twenty-four hours.'

Neither could she. And now she did cling on to him, her eyes bright with unshed tears as she said, 'Be careful won't you.'

'It's only training camp, sweetheart.'

For now. Yes, for now, but she had heard stories of men being shipped overseas swiftly from training with just a telegram or a letter to say they were going. The whole world had turned upside down in the few weeks since war had been declared, everything had changed and was still changing.

She sat back in her seat, forcing herself to take several sips of coffee. The ring felt heavy on her finger, alien, and as she glanced down at the sparkling stones, again the urge to weep and beg him not to go almost overcame her, and to combat the weakness she said quickly, 'Your family? Are they not coming to say goodbye?'

'You are the only one I wanted this morning.' He touched her mouth with one finger, tracing the contours of her rosy-red lips before he added, 'I said goodbye to Art and Gladys at the house.'

'And . . . and your mother?' And then, at the look on his face, 'You did tell your mother, Dan?'

He stared at the sweet, young face in front of him. How could he tell her he hadn't dared go to see his mother because he had known he wouldn't be responsible for what he might do to her? He had known, the second he had heard about the letter, that his mother had written it. She would deny it of course, she had always been very good at making black white, but he *knew*. He knew. And recognising the depth of his fury he had realised he must not see the woman he now knew he had disliked all his life. But the dislike had changed into something deeper and darker, something he did not want to examine because when all was said and done, she was his mother.

He smiled at Connie now, and kept his tone light as he said, 'I had no need to tell her, not when John knows all about it. All our lives my brothers and sister and I have known that it's the equivalent of shouting in Mam's ear if John gets a whisper of anything.'

'They're close then, your mam and John?'

'No, they're not close, Connie, not in the way you mean anyway. It's more . . .' He paused, unable to explain the twisted threads that wove his family together. 'They think alike,' he finished quietly, before shaking his head and adding, 'But what are we wasting precious minutes for talking about my mother and John? I love you, I love you, my darling. Tell me you love me.'

'I do, I do love you.'

'And you won't forget me or look at anyone else?'

'As if I could.'

'Oh, dearest.'

In the time that was left before the train came they sat close together, their hands tightly joined as they willed the minutes to pass slowly. And then it was time to show their tickets and pass through the barrier and Connie felt desperate. 'Promise me, promise me you'll be careful,' she whispered frantically as the train pulled into the station. 'Don't take any chances, promise me.'

'I promise, sweetheart, but this is just training, remember.'

He smiled at her, the chocolate brown of his eyes tender, but as he put his arms about her, his lips touching hers, Connie was seized by a dread which was all the more painful for being unutterable. Her mother, her grandmother and brother, Lucy, they were all gone. And now Dan was going too, and to war. To war. Never mind the training, the end result was war. And they were beginning to hear such awful, terrible things . . .

They were holding one another tightly now, but in spite of the bustle and scurry all about them on the crowded platform their kiss was hungry and urgent in a way which would have been unthinkable in such a public place just months ago. But times were changing, and fast. It was no good standing on ceremony now was it? more and more folks were saying, when you didn't know if you and yours were destined to see the morrow. And you're a long time dead, aye, you are that. Live for the day, the hour, the minute – it might be your last.

The train had slowed down and stopped, doors were opened and Connie walked with him to the carriage. There was no more intelligible conversation, just disconnected, inarticulate murmurings until Dan said, 'I've wasted so much time the last months, my darling, but you're promised to me now and there'll never be anyone but you. Believe me on that, dearest. Look, I've got to go.'

He got into the carriage and a large, stout man who was sitting near the window closed the door somewhat abruptly, only for Dan to open it again and, reaching down, kiss her passionately one more time. 'I love you. Remember that always. It won't be long till I'm home.'

But then he was back in the carriage and the train was

moving away and in the blink of an eye – or so it seemed – he was gone. Gone.

Connie stood for more than a minute staring after the train and her mind, her senses, her whole body was with Dan. And then she turned, slowly and deliberately, to leave. It was only training and he would be home for a weekend in a few weeks or so, she told herself feverishly. Hundreds, thousands of women were going through this every day and managing to hold together, and she was luckier than most. She had the business to occupy her mind and Hazel to keep her from brooding. There's plenty would give their eye teeth to be in her position. And she wasn't going to cry. She wasn't. She had just got engaged to the most wonderful man in the world, that was nothing to cry about, was it?

Nevertheless, she was blinking hard, her eyes bright and glittering as she left the platform, and consequently she paid little attention to anyone else, which was a mistake.

Edith was finding it difficult to accept what she had seen, and as her eyes followed the slim young figure of 'that trollop's chit' – as she had labelled Connie in her mind – the fury and jealousy were like corroding acid.

Since John had called in to see her on his way home from work last night with the news about Dan, she had waited all evening in a state of high expectation for her youngest son to make an appearance at the house. She had known he would come. Sure he wouldn't leave Sunderland without making his peace with her and putting things right. She had been horrified at his foolhardiness in voluntarily enlisting, but at the back of her mind – and barely acknowledged – there was an element of relief too. He would be far away from the defiling possibility that one day he might be tempted to seek out the Bell chit.

She'd known the affair had come to an abrupt end after she had challenged Dan with Mr Simmons's findings – John had kept an eye on both of them for weeks past – but when men's passions were stirred they didn't always think with their heads, and she wouldn't have been surprised if the strumpet had tried to get her hooks into him again. They knew plenty of tricks, women of that calibre, and when you considered where she came from . . . But as the weeks had gone by it had seemed the thing was over, and when John had reported the Bell woman had taken on the offspring of Harold Alridge after his poor wife had died, Edith had felt a lot happier. She had known she was right about him and Connie all along and this only proved it, didn't it. You don't take on a man's bairn for nothing; he was obviously the one who had set her up in her own place and no doubt the huzzy was hoping that by taking the bairn she could get him to marry her and probably when his wife was barely cold. By, men were such fools!

Edith's eyes narrowed as she watched Connie disappear from view and her face was stiff. To think that baggage was sitting pretty and no doubt revelling in the fact that she had her lover to pay the bills and Dan as her bit on the side. And Dan might not be the only one, oh no, but it was as clear as the nose on her face that she'd managed to talk him round to accepting anything. That a son of hers could fall so low.

Edith started to follow Connie, her small stocky body ramrod straight. She had swallowed her pride in coming here this morning, and for what? For what! The trollop's chit had turned Dan against her and poisoned his mind, that much was plain. Had Kitty known that this had all started up again? Her large nostrils flared and her mouth tightened. She'd make her suffer for it if she found out that was the case. Soft as clarts, that woman, and always had been.

It was not in Edith's nature to either consider or appreciate the loyalty and hard work Kitty had shown the family over the years. She knew Kitty had always been underpaid and that no other servant would have given of themselves so unstintingly, but this was explained away in Edith's eyes by the fact that the 'great lump of an Irishwoman' – as she termed her housekeeper – had thought she wouldn't be able to get a job anywhere else, an idea Edith had always encouraged whenever she could. She didn't value the other woman, and if someone had asked her whether she liked Kitty or not she would have looked at them in amazement. The woman was her housekeeper, a paid servant, liking or not didn't come into it. But she was a convenient whipping boy, and over the years Edith had often used Kitty to verbally vent her frustrations on when something had gone wrong.

Once out in the street Edith stood to one side of the pavement by the tram terminus and found she was trembling with the force of her rage. She would make that little chit wish she had never been born; she was her mother all over again. Not only did she look remarkably like that whore but she had inherited her bad blood too. Well, she'd rue the day she ever crossed swords with Edith Stewart! Edith nodded to herself grimly. And Dan? There was none of the usual softening in her face at the thought of her youngest. He'd do penance for putting that piece of scum before his own mother, she'd make sure of that. She'd have him squirming before he was finished, but only when she'd dragged the name of Connie Bell through the mud.

The first letter came just two weeks after Dan had left and

twenty-four hours after John had paid a visit to the tea-rooms and got short shrift from an incensed Connie. It had been lunchtime and the tea-rooms had been busy, but in spite of all the interested onlookers Connie had refused to serve John Stewart, and the manner in which she had ordered him to leave had brought his hand up to strike her – as he had once struck her mother – before he had controlled the blazing fury.

Mary had been at Connie's side in an instant and two khaki-clad soldiers, who had been sitting with their girlfriends in one corner, had risen, adding their twopennyworth to the scene which had erupted out of nowhere.

'Here, man, what's up with you? We're havin' none of that mind.'

'You want to knock hell out of someone get a uniform on yer back an' get across the water to old Kaiser Bill.'

'Did you hear what she just said to me? I've as much right to eat here as anyone else.' John's voice was a snarl.

'Aye, well that's as maybe, but if she wants you out, you're out, man.'

John had stood glaring at them all for a moment, his stocky body leant slightly forwards and his hands clenched fists at his side, and then he had swung round and left the shop without another word, but the look in his eyes had made Connie pay a visit to the privy in the yard where she was physically sick a few minutes later.

And then the letter had come. She had been receiving letters almost every day from Dan – wonderful, thrilling letters that had her blushing as she read them – but she hadn't recognised the handwriting on this particular envelope, and, thinking it was a communication with regard to the business, she had opened it quickly, without really concentrating. And then she had sat as though turned to stone, the blood draining from her face.

'What is it?'

Connie tended to open the post when she gave Hazel her mid-morning bottle in the parlour upstairs – Ellen emerging from the bowels of the building for half an hour or so to help Mary in the shop and tea-rooms before disappearing back into her subterranean kingdom once Connie reappeared downstairs – but this particular day had been hectic and the post had been left until Connie had locked up and the two girls had gone upstairs with Hazel.

'It's . . .' Connie couldn't continue, handing the letter to Mary as she pressed her hand over her mouth.

'Oh, lass, lass. Look, you've got to take this to the police, this is nasty. An' the blighter didn't have the guts to sign it!'

'No, no I can't do that.'

'Why the dickens not?'

'Because it's from him, Dan's brother, isn't it. He's trying to cause trouble. He probably knows by now that Dan asked me to marry him and this is his way of being spiteful.'

'Spiteful?' Mary shook her head as her eyes scanned the venom splattered over the paper in her hand. 'This is a darn sight more than spiteful, lass. He wants lockin' up if you ask me. And to say those things about you an' her da . . .' They both glanced at Hazel lying fast asleep in her crib to one side of the rocking chair. 'If you showed this to Mr Alridge he'd get to the bottom of it – aye, an' sort the blighter out by usin' the law an' all.'

'I can't, Mary.' Connie held out her hand for the letter and once Mary had given it to her she ripped it into tiny pieces. 'I'll ignore it, that's best in the long run. If Mr Alridge thought people were talking about us he might . . . he might take Hazel away and I promised Lucy. John's had his say, he'll consider he's got his own back for yesterday. It's finished with.'

But was it? She had seen John in action; he was unbalanced, vicious, and this was the second time he had written a series of lies about her. But he *was* Dan's brother, and to report him to the police . . .

The second letter was more loathsome than the first, but it came some weeks later on the weekend Dan got twenty-four hours' leave before he was shipped to France. He reached Sunderland in the morning and had to leave in the evening, and the day was so precious, so tender, Connie couldn't spoil it by mentioning such obnoxious filth.

She saw Dan off at the station again, but this time they clung to each other in an agony of pain and longing, and Dan's face was grey and stiff as he waved to her as the train departed. He was going across the water, into mayhem and confusion and death – but no, no, it wouldn't be death, not for Dan, Connie told herself as she walked home in a maze of numbed misery. Dan would live. He would, he would live, and he would come back to her. He had to come back to her – anything else was unthinkable.

It was the middle of November when Connie and Mary were roused at four in the morning by a frantic Ellen to find the words 'whore's house' daubed in whitewash on the pavement outside.

November had not been a good month. The letters had become weekly affairs that went straight into the fire without being opened, but their sinister content was nevertheless oppressive.

In the meantime, as Kitchener called for yet more

volunteers and Queen Mary appealed to the women of the Empire to knit 300,000 pairs of socks for the troops, dysentery and other diseases were adding to the death toll inflicted by the battles, and more especially the trenches, on England's manhood. Connie hadn't heard from Dan in over a month and she was quietly desperate at what it meant. Men were dying in their thousands, often immersed in muck and freezing water so that their flesh slowly rotted on their bones. There was a stalemate amid the mud and barbed wire of the trenches, with reports from the front talking of little else but 'alternate advances and retirements'; nobody had developed a tactic to break the deadlock.

Mary's two brothers had joined up with the local regiment, the Durham Light Infantry, at the beginning of the month, the eldest just scraping in at an inch above the minimum height of 5 feet 3 inches, and Mary was living in fear that Wilf would do the same and was not at all her normal cheerful self. To cap it all, Harold Alridge was talking of moving away down south and engaging a full-time nanny to take charge of Hazel. This had come about just a few days ago, and Connie suspected from her ex-employer's somewhat stiff stance when he had called to see her that he had got wind of something – a morsel of gossip, a rumour, whatever – concerning her supposed relationship with him, and moving away was the result. He had never actually got over the unease about her that the first letter had engendered and although he, of all people, knew these present rumours were untrue wouldn't risk any slur on his good name or that of his beloved Lucy. But at least he had promised her he wouldn't give the child to Lucy's parents, that was something she supposed.

Connie stood, staring at the pavement, but through the

shock and disgust a fortifying rage sent hot adrenalin into every nerve and sinew. Enough was enough; Dan's brother or no, she was not going to be intimidated by scum like John Stewart for one more day.

'I'll clear it, lass.'

'No, I'll do it.' She took the scrubbing brush and pail of hot soapy water from Ellen, her face grim and her mouth set. And she would do something else this evening once the tea-rooms had closed. She would go and see Art and Gladys and acquaint them with what had been happening. She had been holding her hand thus far because, for Dan's sake, she hadn't wanted to be responsible for hauling the name of Stewart into a police court. But that finished right here and now. She was going to fight this wicked and execrable persecution with every means at her disposal.

She didn't have the power to change what was happening – or had happened – to Dan; neither did she have the legal right to prevent Harold Alridge taking Lucy's daughter away to another part of the country, but this victimisation was different.

There was a great swelling deep inside her chest and she knew what it meant. All the worry and hurt and, yes, fear, of the past months was striving to burst forth in a flood of weeping, but she gritted her teeth as she told herself she wasn't going to let John Stewart make her cry.

She would cry for Dan if she had to, aye, she would, and that wouldn't be weakness. And if Hazel was taken away she would grieve for Lucy's child because she loved the little bairn like her own and she couldn't bear the thought of the infant growing up in a loveless environment, but John Stewart? He was scum – filth – the worst of society couldn't hold a candle to that man, and she was blowed if he would break her. He was a devil, that's what he was, but she was going to rise above this, and him. Or die in the attempt.

Chapter Twenty-One

The warmth of the greeting which Connie received at Art and Gladys's that same evening went some way to easing the ache in her sore heart. She arrived at the house just as the door opened to emit a group of chattering women, and as she stood to one side to let them pass she almost turned and walked away. Almost. But she couldn't weaken now, she told herself firmly. This thing – nasty and unpleasant as it was – had come to a head and it had to be sorted.

'Connie?' Gladys was right at the end of the stream of women, and as Dan's sister-in-law caught sight of her Connie saw the blunt, good-natured face light up. 'Connie, it *is* you! Oh, come away in, lass, come away in. It's enough to freeze your lugs off out there.'

Connie found herself borne into the warm, bright parlour which was dotted with piles of material and clothing, and Gladys waved her arm at them as she said, 'Excuse the mess, lass, it's the sewing guild I belong to. We're making clothes for the servicemen. You never know, it might be Dan that gets one of our pairs of trousers or a jacket. Now, can I get you a cup of tea, lass?'

'No, no please don't go to any trouble.' Connie was feeling acutely embarrassed in view of the nature of her visit and she stood in the middle of the room awkwardly, her cheeks flushed. 'I just need a word with Art if he's in?'

'He's took the bairns round me mam's to escape this lot,' Gladys said with a rueful glance at the bundles scattered about the room, 'but he won't be long. Sit yourself down, lass, and take the weight off and I'll get that tea.'

'Gladys?' Something in Connie's voice stopped the other woman's bustling, and as they stood staring at each other Connie said quietly, 'I've come about John, Dan's brother, and . . . and it's not very nice, Gladys, but first I wanted to ask you if you'd heard from Dan at all? He was writing every day until the middle of October, but the last few weeks I haven't heard a thing.'

'Oh, lass.' Gladys took Connie's hands in hers and squeezed them as she said, 'Don't worry, lass, don't worry, I'm sure he's all right, but we haven't heard nothing neither. Mind he wasn't writing every day to us' – she said this with a smile and Connie smiled weakly back – 'although it must be difficult depending where they are. Likely they had to move or something.'

'Aye, I suppose so.'

'An' this is the ring then? By, it's a beauty, lass. Me and Art were tickled pink when we heard.'

'Were you?' There was the faintest edge to Connie's voice, and in answer to it Gladys said, her face solemn now and her hand still holding Connie's left hand up in front of her eyes, 'Aye, we were, I'm telling you straight, lass. You're the one for him, there's no mistaking it. Fair worships the ground you walk on, does Dan.'

'Oh, Gladys.'

And then it all came pouring out in a flood of emotion

which wasn't at all how Connie had planned to impart the matter of the letters and the incident of the morning, and she found herself divulging far more than she had intended – the manner of her departure from the Grand, John's visits to her at Walworth Way and the shop, the way he had spoken to her.

At some time during the discourse Gladys drew her over to the sofa and they sat down, and then, when Connie finished speaking, there was silence for a moment or two before Gladys said, 'And you didn't tell Dan about the letters when he came home on leave that time, or John bothering you?'

'How could I, Gladys? There he is miles and miles away; it'd just worry him sick, and his brother, his own brother . . .' The two women stared at each other for a moment or two.

'By, he wants seeing to, that one,' said Gladys. 'He's always been that way inclined with women, the dirty so-an'-so. Art's told me a few things about when they were sharing a room back in Ryhope Road and I bet he don't know the half of it. Pity they can't do the same operation as they do to the bullocks on blokes like him.'

Gladys had spoken perfectly seriously but her indignant expression combined with her naturally comical face brought a smile to Connie's solemn countenance, and then both women were laughing helplessly for some long moments.

'Come on, lass, come on through to the kitchen and we'll have that cuppa,' said Gladys when they had both dried their eyes. 'There's something I need to put to you and it'll be better with a cup of tea inside us.'

'His *mother*?!' They had drunk two cups of tea and eaten a shive of sly cake each, and now Connie sat back in her seat at the kitchen table and stared at Gladys who was nodding her head.

'Aye, aye that's my theory for what it's worth. The words on the pavement is John to a T, mind, and him trying it on figures; his poor wife has had a raw deal all her married life from what I can make out. His lad hates him leastways, it's as plain as the nose on your face. But the letters . . . Now that smacks of a woman to my mind, and it'd be just up Edith's street. She's a nasty piece of work is their mam.'

When Art arrived home half an hour later he agreed with his wife and his voice was both ashamed and weary. 'I'd say it's the pair of them involved in this, Connie,' he said quietly. 'My mother can be a mealy-mouthed woman when it suits her, but other times she's worse than a fish wife. I don't understand her and John, I never have, but there's something in both of them . . .' His voice trailed away and then he straightened, his hand going across his face as though to brush something away. 'Do you want me to talk to them and sort this out?'

Connie looked away from them both for a moment before she said, 'If I'm being honest, Art, there's nothing I would like more, and if it was just John I would ask you to come with me to see him, but . . .' She paused, then taking a deep breath said, 'I have to go and see your mother myself, she needs to know I mean business, and if things are as you and Gladys suspect then John will do what he's told, don't you think?'

Gladys had made a quick urgent movement of protest as Connie had spoken, and Art glanced at his wife before he said, 'You don't know what she's like, lass,' his tone expressing far more than the actual words.

'I'm beginning to.'

'Well, let me come along with you then, eh? For moral support. Dan would expect that.'

'I think it's better I go alone,' Connie said gently.

Gladys's face was very troubled. 'Connie, she's got a tongue that would cut steel.'

'I know. I have had some experience of her in the past, remember?'

'Oh, lass.'

Connie spent another hour with Gladys and Art and she left promising she would return the following Sunday afternoon with Hazel. It was only a ten-minute walk from St George's Square along Park Lane to Holmeside, but the November night was raw and cold with a stinging icy rain and keen wind, and when Art insisted on accompanying Connie home she protested until she realised he and Gladys were not going to take no for an answer.

'Dan would do the same for Gladys.'

'But I'll be fine, really.'

'Aye, that's as maybe.'

There was genuine warmth in the goodbyes of the two women, and once she and Art were walking along Park Lane, Connie said, 'Gladys is a grand lass, Art. You're a lucky man.'

'Aye, I know it, and the same could be said for our Dan.'

'Thank you.'

'I mean it, lass, and don't you worry, you'll be hearing from him someday soon and then you can set about making your wedding plans, eh?'

Connie glanced at the big figure next to her. 'Do your mother and John know he has asked me to marry him?'

'Put it this way, lass, I haven't told 'em. It's up to you and

Dan to tell who you want to, and as far as I know he's said nowt to anyone but Kitty and me and Gladys. Speaks volumes about our family, doesn't it,' he added a trifle bitterly.

Connie nodded but said nothing; there was nothing to say after all, and as Art glanced at the slim young girl at the side of him he found himself praying he was right about them hearing from Dan, and it wasn't all to do with concern for his brother. This young lass had had a raw deal – whichever way you looked at it she'd had a raw deal and his family had started the ball rolling; it was time she had a bit of happiness. Although happiness and his mam didn't go together. He frowned at the thought. He didn't like the idea of her going to see his mother – it smacked too much of sending a lamb to the slaughter – but he had to admit there was a well of strength in Connie Bell that you didn't suspect when you looked at the ethereal beauty of the outside, and maybe she'd be a match for the woman who tried to rule all their lives. He hoped so. He did hope so.

It was another three days before Connie made the visit to Ryhope Road.

She had returned home from Art's house on the Tuesday evening determined to go first thing the next day, but on walking into the parlour she had found Mary in floods of tears and Wilf sitting in abject misery at the side of her, his head drooping.

'He's enlisted.' Connie had barely got through the door when Mary flung the words at her, her face blotchy and red. 'Just because one or two have bin makin' remarks he's had to go an' enlist.'

'Remarks? What sort of remarks, Wilf?'

''Bout him bein' lily-livered an' gutless an' the like,' Mary said before Wilf could open his mouth. 'It's her that lives next door to him that started it; her lad bought it first week he was in France an' now she's determined every other poor devil'll get the same.'

'It wasn't Mrs Trotter, not really,' Wilf protested, a trifle weakly. There had been feelings of patriotism there too, along with growing frustration about his relationship with Mary. It was one step forward, two steps back all the time as far as he was concerned; he'd lost count of how many times he'd asked her to marry him since that first time at the beginning of September when he'd decided – what with the war and all – that he couldn't wait until he was well set up as he'd originally planned. She had made every excuse under the sun except the real one – that she was frightened of him. That was it at bottom. Oh, he knew she'd gone to hell and back with what her uncle and his friend had done to her when she was a little bairn, but surely she knew him well enough now to know he would never do anything to hurt her? At least he'd thought so, before the war had prompted him to find out different. And he'd been getting more and more angry and confused, and he didn't want to feel like that, not about Mary, so . . . he'd escaped the situation, he'd enlisted. It might not have been the brightest thing he'd ever done but it would have had to have happened sooner or later; this war clearly wasn't going to be the short, hard slam at Kaiser Bill that they'd all been led to believe. So, with things as they were, it might as well be sooner. That's how he felt about it.

By the time Wilf had left that night Connie had persuaded Mary to spend the next day with him before he departed for training camp, and to try and get things sorted out, and then the two girls had sat up half the night talking.

'You'll never find anyone else who loves you like Wilf does,' Connie had said gently when Mary had poured out her fears about marriage and commitment.

'I know, I know.'

'And with him going away to fight . . .'

'Oh, Connie.'

'You were going to have to say yay or nay one day, lass, so it might as well be tomorrow. It's only fair for the lad to know where he stands and he's been patient, you've got to admit that, Mary.'

'I *know*.'

The end result had been Mary coming back flushed and happy the next day with the cheapest ring the jeweller's shop had boasted, which she wore with touching pride.

And then the next day Ellen had been unable to come to work due to her youngest being ill so again they were short manned, and it was the Friday morning, when the papers were full of the news that German and Austrian civilian internees had rioted at a detention camp on the Isle of Man, having been part of the national round-up of aliens at the end of the previous month, before Connie could get away.

She caught the tram to the top of Ryhope Road, and although the icy rain and bitter wind of the last few days hadn't let up, Connie was oblivious to the weather as she alighted at her stop. All her thoughts were on the forthcoming confrontation with Dan's mother.

Ryhope Road had changed little in the last fourteen years, and as Connie walked briskly down the wide and pleasant road, her three-quarter-length mink-coloured coat and hat in thick good cloth bought at a fraction of the original cost from the old market in the East End at the beginning of the autumn effectively keeping out the worst of the cold, the hard knot in her stomach became tighter.

In her mind's eye she could see three little ghosts – one a slim and beautiful golden-haired woman, the others a boy and a girl – walking down this same road, and for a moment the desire to go back in time was so acute she could taste it. Fourteen years ago they had been here, her mam and Larry, alive and warm and breathing. She had been able to touch them, to see them, to hold them . . .

Stop it, stop it. The voice in her head was strong. Deal with *now*, you can't go back, and she'll seize on any weakness she senses in you. Think about what you are going to say, concentrate on that and that alone. You are a respectable businesswoman, you *are*. She can't intimidate you or frighten you because you aren't going to let her.

The house was exactly as she remembered it as she opened the fancy wrought-iron gate set in the high stone wall, and the pebbled drive just as immaculate, even the giant oaks – their gnarled limbs devoid of leaves as they had been that morning fourteen years ago – appeared frozen in time.

Connie's heart was thudding as she mounted the seven horseshoe-shaped steps to the front door, but after she had pulled the bell she remained on the top step with her head held high and her back very straight.

'Good morning. I'd like to see Mrs Stewart please.'

It was Kitty who answered the door, and as Connie spoke the Irishwoman's face stretched a little before her head jerked and she said, her voice quivering, 'Eh lass, lass, it's you, isn't it. What have you come here for?'

The words themselves could have been presumptuous, but

spoken as they were, in a gentle, pleading fashion, they took on a quite different connotation, and now – knowing how fondly Dan thought of this woman – Connie said, 'I have to see Mrs Stewart; there's been some unpleasantness and I have to clear it up but I'd prefer to do it without Dan being upset. Could . . . could you tell her I'm here?'

'Lass, are you sure? She's bin in a right two-an'-eight since she found out about you and Dan and there's no reasoning with her. Dan knew that.'

'It's not about our relationship. There's . . . been letters, nasty letters. I can't let it continue.'

'Aw, lass, no. No, not that. Oh, it's heart sorry I am, lass. What are things coming to?'

Connie swallowed before she could answer – the other woman's understanding and warmth was welcome but it undermined the anger she needed to feel to empower her to take on Edith Stewart and win. Finally she managed to say, her voice low, 'I do need to see her, Kitty.'

And then, in a repeat of that morning fourteen years ago, an autocratic voice demanded from inside the house, 'Kitty? Who is it?'

Kitty didn't answer, she just continued staring at Connie and it was a moment or two before the door opened fully and Edith Stewart stood framed in the aperture, her manner abrasive as she said, 'For goodness sake, woman, I was speaking to you. I asked you—' And then her words were cut off as though by a knife.

'Good morning, Mrs Stewart. I need to talk with you and I'm sure you know what about.'

If Edith was taken aback by the cool authority in Connie's voice and manner she didn't betray it by so much as the flicker of an eyelash. She seemed to rise in stature, her small, thick body bridling, and Connie watched the invective fill the chunky frame before it spewed forth in spitting rage, her eyes flashing as she said, 'Get off my property, you trollop you! How dare you come here!'

'Oh I dare, Mrs Stewart. I most certainly dare.'

'I'll have the police on you.'

'I think not.' Connie's voice was controlled and steady, in stark contrast to that of Dan's mother, and no one looking at her would have guessed her insides had turned to water. She kept her head high and her gaze directed full on Edith's furious face as she said, 'In fact I think that should be more my line than yours in the circumstances.'

'You're mad, unhinged! The life you lead has unbalanced you, you filthy—'

'That's enough of that.' Connie was aware of Kitty's fascinated gaze on the perimeter of her vision but her focus was concentrated on Edith's countenance which looked evil. 'You wrote some letters to me, disgusting, horrible letters, and the police have a way of checking handwriting, Mrs Stewart. I think they would be very interested in what I have to say.' She was bluffing, she had destroyed each letter as it came – most unread – as the thought of keeping such poison had been insupportable, but Dan's mother didn't know that, and she knew she was on the right tack as the other woman's face changed. 'There was another letter too, in the same handwriting, and I feel sure Mr Alridge would be only too pleased to show that to the police. I wonder how your fine friends would view such behaviour, Mrs Stewart? Or perhaps they wouldn't mind associating with someone who was in court answering such charges?'

'You wouldn't dare!'

'As I've already said, Mrs Stewart, I would most certainly dare.' There was a definite note of authority in Connie's voice now and it seemed to incense the woman in front of her, because Edith Stewart suddenly cast all caution to the wind and fairly shouted at her, 'Every word was true! Every word! And you'll rot in hell before you're finished, you dirty little strumpet.'

'No, no I won't, Mrs Stewart. When I die I shall go to join my mother and she is certainly not in that place.' At the mention of her old enemy Edith looked as though she was about to have a seizure, her face turning a more vivid shade of scarlet and her eyes seeming to pop out of her head, and now Connie continued coldly, 'If you write one more letter or your eldest son bothers me one more time I shall take every scrap of correspondence to the police station so I warn you.'

'*You* warn *me*?!' The words were deep and guttural. 'And what's this about John bothering you? What are you suggesting?'

'I'm not *suggesting* anything, I'm telling you. He has tried to make advances to me several times and I know he was responsible for daubing obscenities outside my property a few mornings ago.'

'*John* making advances to *you*? He wouldn't touch you with a bargepole, girl! And Dan will see through you, don't think he won't. You might be keeping him sweet at the moment but he's only after one thing and you know it at heart. He'll use you for his pleasure and then throw you back in the gutter where you belong.'

'Dan and I are engaged to be married, Mrs Stewart.' It was quiet but deadly and for a moment Edith stood as though turned to stone, her eyes as round as buttons as she stared at the hand Connie was holding out, Dan's ring flashing bright, and then she let out a cry of fury and raised her doubled fist at Connie.

That the blow would have hit Connie full in the face but for Kitty catching her employer's arm and wrestling her away was in no doubt, and the action revealed as much about Edith's origins as the spate of obscenities that followed.

It was a full thirty seconds before Edith became limp in Kitty's grasp but Connie hadn't moved, and what she said now, her voice trembling slightly was, 'I will do as I have said, Mrs Stewart, so don't think I won't. And Dan will be with me on this. But then you already know that, don't you. He has made his choice and that's what sticks in your craw.'

'I'll see me day with you, girl, you see if I don't.'

'You don't frighten me, Mrs Stewart, and you didn't frighten my mother, do you know that? She despised you, and that sick individual who is your eldest son. He wanted her – John wanted my mother – but she didn't want him and that's what caused everything that happened. John was jealous of Jacob, *jealous*. You haven't got the faintest idea what he is really like.'

Edith was trying to wrestle herself free of Kitty who was holding on to the furious woman with a grip of steel, and now Dan's mother's enraged face turned to her housekeeper as she cried, 'Can you hear her? The lies she's telling?' before her eyes flashed back to Connie and she spat, 'You'll never have Dan, not legally, I'll kill you both first.'

'And ruin everything you have worked for all your life? You would really drag the name of Stewart into the very gutter you accuse me of coming from?' Connie retorted scornfully.

'I think not. You might think you love your son, Mrs Stewart, but the only person you really love is yourself. Well, you've got what you wanted – a beautiful home, influence, prestige and the rest. But you haven't got Dan, and you probably haven't got the love of your other children either. You are going to be a very lonely and bitter old woman, Mrs Stewart.'

'Get out! *Get out!*'

'I'm going.' And now Connie's lips curled back from her small white teeth, and she could have been surveying something repulsive as she said, 'I wouldn't stay here for all the tea in China.'

It was gone mid-day when Connie returned to Holmeside, and Gladys and Art came into the shop over an hour later. It was clear Gladys had been crying, and when she handed Connie the printed, dull-yellow card it was another few seconds before Connie could force herself to lower her eyes and read it.

'He's a prisoner?' Mary had come to stand by her, and now Connie took her eyes from Dan's brother and sister-in-law and turning to Mary, gripped her friend's arm as she said again, her voice shaking, 'He's a prisoner, Mary.'

'Oh, lass.'

'I thought . . . I thought he was . . .'

'I know, so did we.' Gladys was nodding her head and wiping her eyes again. 'He gave us as his next of kin when he joined up, he's living with us as you know, and when that card came . . . Oh, lass, I thought I'd die, I did straight. It took me a good couple of minutes afore I could look at it.'

'But he's a prisoner, he's safe, he'll be coming home.'

'God willing, lass. God willing.'

Aye, God willing. Connie stared at the three faces in front of her but her mind was praying, Please, God, please keep him safe, please. You know how much I love him, I can't live the rest of my life without him, I can't. Watch over him, protect him, please, and I'll never ask You for another thing as long as I live. Just bring him home.

Part Five
1918
Retribution

Chapter Twenty-Two

The weeks turned into months and the months into years, and the years were full of mixed blessings for the mothers, wives and sweethearts, and their loved ones, of Sunderland. There was plenty of tragedy and the occasional shaft of joy, but every thinking man and woman was aware they were experiencing a turning point in history, not least the beginning of the emancipation of women. Women had taken the place of their absent menfolk in the shipyards, the factories, the banks and on the railways. They were acting as postmen, window cleaners, cabbies, and the first female conductors began to serve on the trams; but chiefly women were ammunition workers, thousands of them. And men – to their surprise, and in some cases agitation if not downright alarm – found women were excellent workers and well worth the good wages they were receiving.

Connie had a double cross to bear in the first year of the war when, added to Dan's internment, Harold Alridge followed through on his resolution to move down south and take Hazel with him. For a time she felt her sorrow was insurmountable and she cried herself to sleep each night, but gradually she did what she had always done – she coped with what had to be coped with and got on with life. Mary and

Wilf's friendship eased the soreness a little.

Wilf's war had been a short one. After only eight months he had been an early victim of the greenish-yellow, choking chlorine gas – the Germans' terrible new weapon – and on fleeing from his dugout with his comrades, coughing, half-blind and panic-stricken, he had been injured by shrapnel as the Germans attacked. The end result was that he was invalided home into Mary's arms, and they were married some three months later. Connie provided him with a job in the bakery helping Ellen, which Wilf took to like a duck to water.

On 1st April 1916, on the same day a Zeppelin's deadly cargo killed twenty-two people and injured over one hundred in Sunderland – some of the casualties being as a result of one of the bombs landing at the Wheatsheaf and wrecking the tram office – they learnt that both of Mary's brothers had been killed, leaving the two men's young families without breadwinners.

This sad occurrence prompted Connie into an undertaking she had been thinking about for some months. Her business was booming, due, in part, to several bakeries going out of business as men were conscripted, and even basic requirements like flour rising drastically in price, but also to the hard work Connie, aided and abetted by Mary, Ellen and now Wilf, was putting into the venture. Their clientele was growing daily and they now had a healthy crop of regulars.

So in May 1916, large new kitchens were built in what had been the original backyard of the premises, with an allowance for extending upwards at a later date, and the tea-rooms and baker's shop were enlarged.

Once the work was finished, Mary's sisters-in-law were employed by Connie on a part-time basis, each woman working on alternate days with the second looking after the children of both families. The arrangement had worked out very well for all concerned, and by the end of the following year Connie was in the happy position of following through on her original plans and building – with the assistance of Mr Bainbridge and the bank – a handsomely appointed first-floor restaurant above the new kitchens, approached via the tea-rooms, with a two-bedroomed flat above that for herself. This left Mary and Wilf to the privacy of their own home in the original rooms over the shop.

The middle of 1918 saw a full restaurant each night and queues outside the shop every morning, when folk would stand and wait for bread, spice cakes, flapjacks, pies and sausage rolls – all hot from the oven – and Mary and Wilf, Ellen, and Gladys too, were forced to admit that all their pessimistic predictions of financial disaster were unfounded. Indeed the war, which had crippled so many businesses, had actually worked to Connie's advantage, due to her foresight, business acumen and entrepreneurial flair. In October 1916, when the price of a loaf reached record levels, of ten pence, Connie had kept her prices well below those of most of her competitors, and people didn't forget such things.

The tighter call-up net for married men had snared both Art and John, but it was found that the twins had weak hearts – hitherto unrecognised – and they were rejected for active service and carried on running the family business in the absence of the other brothers.

Both Art and John were involved in the third Battle of Ypres in August 1917, which unfolded to the accompaniment of ceaseless bombardments and remorseless rainstorms according to Art's letters home to Gladys. 'I can't decide whether it's the German machine-gunner or the Flanders mud that's worse,' he wrote, 'but I think the mud has it. They tell us the launching of the offensive was preceded by the firing of the heaviest load of shell yet unloosed in the war, and this, coupled with double the average rainfall, has wrecked the network of streams and dykes upon which the Flanders drainage system depends. All I know, my darling, is that the fields around Passchendaele ridge have been turned into a quagmire the like of which I've never seen, where men are being sucked to their deaths if they should slip from the duckboards. This is hell, Gladys. A wet, glutinous hell and still the rain comes. I think of you all the time' – all the time was underlined several times – 'and don't forget to kiss the bairns for me. This won't last for ever and then I'll be home.'

It was the last letter Gladys was to receive.

In October she was formally notified of Art's death, and the shoulder she chose to cry on was Connie's. The women's friendship had been growing steadily over the last few months but with Art's demise it strengthened still further, and Gladys – lonely and miserable for the first time in her life – spent most Sundays, accompanied by David and Catherine, with Connie and Mary and Wilf.

Six weeks after they heard about Art, John was shipped home to England, minus both legs and with severe burns to his upper torso and face. His wife was told he wouldn't last until Christmas, but John did survive, and the day after Ann was informed by a bright-faced nurse that her husband would be allowed home within the week she took the biggest decision of her life. She left him.

Her flouting of convention was something to do with the new confidence and belief in herself she had gained from her wartime job as section manageress in one of the elegant show saloons for the display of stylish millinery in Binns Store, but more from what she had pieced together from John's ravings whilst he had been delirious. However, apart from one caustic and explosive visit to her mother-in-law -- which effectively ended any further communication between the two women -- Ann said nothing of what she had discovered.

The stir the separation created in Sunderland's still narrow society was considerable, but the shock waves were not as intense as they would have been before the war, and the resulting furore was relatively short-lived.

The older inhabitants of the town shook their heads and commented that life had changed for the worse -- from former soberness and propriety to the new 'fast' mode which cocked a snook at age-old morals and the sanctity of marriage. Still, they gossiped, what could you expect when silly bits of lasses barely out of school were earning £3 and £4 a week at the munitions factories? Spending all they earnt on fur coats and the latest fashions in dress and the like; there was no way they were going to know their place after the war, now was there! Upset things good and proper, this war had.

However, there were a few people -- John's own sisters-in-law among them -- who refused to ostracise Ann when the dust had settled and John was back home, installed in Ryhope Road with Edith, and this resulted in further fragmentation within the Stewart ranks.

During the years of the war Connie's life, by and large, had run smoothly, but it was overshadowed by a deep and consuming fear, which surfaced in regular nightmares when she would awake sweating and wide-eyed, that Dan wouldn't be coming home.

They had had no word since the first communication to Art and Gladys stating that he was a prisoner of war. Connie knew other women who heard from internees, admittedly spasmodically, and it was clear the brief postcards were heavily censored, but from Dan there was just empty silence.

From Edith too there had been silence since the day they had received notification about Dan's capture, and although in the early days, before he had been conscripted, John had taken to strolling along the pavements outside the shops at Holmeside several times a week, often pausing to look in the Bell's Bakery Shop window for a moment or two, he had never ventured into the shop or spoken to Connie.

And now it was the 15th of November, 1918 – Victory Day – and the country had gone mad. Peace had fallen on a war-weary Britain, and all over the country there were unprecedented scenes of public revelry and rejoicing, like a giant school let out for the day.

The morning had begun quietly under sombre, granite skies, but at eleven o'clock precisely – when the armistice took effect – giant maroons were fired throughout the land, church bells began ringing, boy scouts cycled through villages and towns sounding the 'all-clear' on bugles and sirens, and the entire population – or so it seemed – rushed out on to the streets.

The factories closed, street lights were unmasked, blackout curtains ripped down and shop windows became ablaze with light. The rigid wartime licensing laws were ignored and the pubs packed until they ran out of beer, and all over the jubilant country street parties, with fireworks and dancing and hastily improvised flagpoles sporting flags of every Allied nation, were taking place.

Connie and her neighbours organised their own gathering

in Holmeside. Long trestle tables, groaning with food and decorated with flags and potted plants, were brought out into the street. The men played their accordions and harmonicas and the excited children kept time by banging dustbin lids and anything else they could find that made a noise.

And Connie smiled and chatted and joked with the best of them. She fussed over Mary – now heavily pregnant and looking radiant – and she danced the evening away, even drinking a couple of glasses of Mr Bailey's – the local butcher – homemade elderberry wine. But all the time her heart was heavy. She wondered if Dan was able to see the same night sky, and if, *if* he was still alive, what sort of state those monsters would have left him in? And Hazel, precious little Hazel, where was she this night? She would be four years old now. *Four*. And apart from one brief letter a month after he had first taken the child to Kent, she had heard nothing from Lucy's husband in spite of repeated requests for news.

Would she ever hold her own baby in her arms? And then, in the next instant, she berated herself sternly. This wasn't a night to be thinking such thoughts – it was an evening for celebration and rejoicing and living for the moment. That's what it was.

Gladys had left the square's get-together in the late afternoon and made her way to Holmeside with David and Catherine, and Connie felt comforted by the other woman's presence and the fondness with which the fifteen-year-old Catherine and thirteen-year-old David greeted their 'Aunt' Connie.

All three of them, she knew, were thinking of the fourth member of their family, whose ultimate sacrifice – along with over three-quarters of a million men from Britain – had made it possible for them to sing the song of victory, and towards the end of the evening when David – who was the shining star of his church choir and the possessor of a pure, clear, perfectly toned voice – was called upon to perform, he reduced most of the women present to tears.

'This is for my da,' he said loudly, before giving a heart-rending rendition of 'Till We Meet Again', and then, as he sang the last note, he added, 'And I want to finish with a quote by Siegfried Sassoon. In the war they called him Mad Jack because of his solitary expeditions into No Man's Land, but he is a brave man and he's the sort of poet my da would have understood. I like him.' The last was a touch defiant – it wasn't usual for a thirteen-year-old lad to confess to a liking for either poets or poetry.

He looked at them all, his eyes swimming with tears. 'He went where my da died, and this is what he said. "I died in hell, (they called it Passchendaele)". I shan't forget my da.'

It effectively finished the evening for everyone.

Rationing was still biting hard as Christmas approached, and the black market was doing a roaring trade among those who could afford to buy.

The local economy had also been badly hit by the effect of the most lethal epidemic ever to hit Sunderland's shores; that of the dreaded Spanish flu which had first reached Britain in September, and, as always, the poor had been affected the most.

So many men, women and children had died when the deadly strain of influenza was at its worst that the undertakers could not cope with the number of bodies. Hundreds were left for days in what had been their homes, and there were many instances – certainly in the East End and Monkwearmouth – of the dead actually lying in the same room with the living for seventy-two hours or more.

Schools had been used as temporary mortuaries, and joiners in shipyards and engine works had helped make coffins for Sunderland's stricken community. It had devastated some families – especially those where the men were away fighting and mothers were caring for large numbers of children by themselves – but now, as the year limped towards its close, the northern people were gathering together as they always did when adversity hit. Some folk had taken to keeping rabbits or hens in the backyards during the war, and those fortunate enough to have small gardens had turned them into vegetable plots; consequently, as Christmas Eve approached, a great deal of bartering, as well as open-handed acts of generosity, went on.

There had been a number of families close to Holmeside that Connie had heard were in difficulties during October and November when the plague was at its height, and during those weeks Connie, accompanied by Wilf or one of Mary's sisters-in-law, had delivered food parcels to the worst afflicted.

But now it was almost Christmas and, according to Gladys, Edith had sent out the usual imperious summons for the family to assemble at her house despite Gladys having made it plain she would not be reconsidering the decision made when Art was still alive; namely that Christmas Day would be spent in their own home. The last was stretching the truth a little; Gladys and the children had spent last Christmas at Connie's, and they would be doing the same this year – along with Mary and Wilf, and Mary's two sisters-in-law and their children. It made a party of thirteen in all, unless Mary's baby decided to surprise them all and come early.

Christmas Eve dawned bright but bitterly cold, and by midday the sky had changed to one of heavy pewter, with the tangy smell of snow in the air. Connie had gone upstairs to the flat at lunchtime; she needed the afternoon to get things ready for her guests of the morrow. She had filled starched white pillowcases with gaily wrapped parcels for each of the children – including David and Catherine who still considered themselves young enough for such a treat – and had bought gifts for all the adults, and she had been cooking for days.

She was very fortunate. Connie stopped wrapping a thick fleecy dressing gown she had bought for Mary for when her friend would be getting up to feed the baby at night, and gazed about the bright and attractive room that was her parlour. All the furniture was of good quality and in a warm shade of deep mahogany, and the pale-blue rose brocade curtains, cherry-red square of carpet and chintz sofa and chairs were all new. The two bedrooms were furnished equally well, and the kitchen was well equipped and a joy to potter in. This was her own home, furthermore she had acquired her own business and now employed nine people – a cook, waiter and two kitchen helpers having been engaged in May to help Wilf who ran the restaurant at night. The business was going in leaps and bounds; she was one of Mr Bainbridge's favoured clients, and she knew she would be able to clear the latest loan long before the period stipulated on the agreement.

Aye, she was very fortunate all right. Her mam and Larry and her granny would be tickled pink if they could see her now. She sighed deeply, gathering the folds of the dressing gown into her arms and burying her face in it for several moments. But she would give all this up like a shot and count

it as gain if Dan was here. Dan, oh Dan, please don't be dead
. . . The pain she kept under wraps twenty-four hours a day
surfaced briefly and she shut her eyes tight before opening
them wide and staring across the room again. Enough of this
– *he wasn't dead.* She wouldn't let him be dead, and if she
didn't let him he wouldn't be. It was what her granny would
have termed a heap of blather but it helped nevertheless. She
took a deep breath, straightened her back and carried on
wrapping the presents she had bought for everyone.

Gladys and the children arrived at four in the afternoon –
they were staying with Connie until the day after Boxing Day
– and as soon as Dan's sister-in-law walked in the flat Connie
sensed an air of suppressed excitement about her. Gladys was
carrying armfuls of presents, and David and Catherine were
loaded down with a big cooked ham, a precious bag of sugar
which had taken weeks of Gladys's ration coupons, a huge
slab of corned beef and some other groceries Gladys had
insisted on bringing.

'I told you you shouldn't,' Connie scolded gently as she
took the offerings with a warm smile. 'It's lovely to have you
and the bairns here. You didn't need to bring anything.'

Gladys deposited her parcels on to the sofa and then she
said, her voice throbbing slightly, 'I've got an early Christmas
box for you. Sit down in that chair, lass, and hold out your
hands.'

'An early Christmas box?'

'Go on, Aunt Connie, go on.' David and Catherine's faces
were bright. 'Sit *down*.'

'All right, all right.' Connie was laughing as she seated
herself, duly shutting her eyes and holding out her hands. And
then she felt a piece of paper placed in them and she opened

415

her eyes to see it was a telegram.

'It came this morning, lass.'

'Gladys?' Connie's voice was a faint murmur.

'Go on, lass. It's all right.'

'Oh, Gladys.'

Connie slowly lowered her eyes and for a moment the printed words swam and danced and then she read them. And she read them again, and again, before raising her swimming eyes to Gladys's glowing countenance.

'He's coming home, lass, he's coming home,' said Gladys softly. 'We don't know the ins and outs; these official communications tell you nowt, but there it is in black an' white. He's alive an' he's coming home.'

And then, as Connie rose, the two women were hugging and crying, Catherine joining them a moment later and howling fit to burst. How long the mêlée would have continued is uncertain, but after a minute or two David's voice was heard to say, 'Women! I'll never understand them as long as I live. You all oughta be laughing not crying,' and the three parted, their faces wet, to look at the young lad at the side of them. And then they were laughing, one after the other, David included, and as Connie gathered them all close again she was thinking, Thank you, God, thank you. He's coming home. I don't care what condition he's in, I'll make him better. *He's coming home*. Oh, this was the most wonderful Christmas ever.

Mary went into labour the Saturday after Christmas, the same momentous day that women voted for the first time in a United Kingdom election.

Connie stayed with the midwife throughout, and Mary's

short labour and easy birth was something of a healing for her. She hadn't realised how seeing her sister stillborn and Lucy's tragic confinement had affected her until this point, but she found it something of a revelation that Mary was able to smile and talk and exchange wisecracks with Mrs Drew, the very able midwife, right up until the last hour when the hard work really began.

'It's got to be a girl, Mary, coming on this day.' It was two o'clock in the afternoon and the birth was imminent. 'A brand new little suffragette.'

'I don't care what it is as long as it gets a move on.'

Ellen had joined them once she had finished her stint in the bakery, and now she smiled as she rubbed her daughter's hand and said, 'Ee, lass, you're doin' fine. You're like me, you'll have 'em as easy as shellin' peas. One every year from now on, eh?'

The look Mary cast her mother spoke volumes.

Martha Ellen Gantry was born at half past two, and considering Mary's slight build and small stature she was a big baby at seven pounds. She had a shock of brown hair and a loud and raucous cry, and the way Mary cradled her after the cord had been cut, and the love in her eyes, brought a lump to Connie's throat. She was nothing like little Hazel, and in a way it was a relief. Connie had faced the fact that Harold Alridge had ruthlessly cut all ties with Sunderland and the past, and the fewer reminders she had to prod the ache in her heart for Lucy's daughter the better. But she thought of her often; she always would.

And now it was four o'clock in the afternoon. Outside the house was a white frozen world – the snow was packed hard on the ground and more was forecast – but inside Mary and

Wilf's quarters above the shop there was warmth and comfort and the smell of the pot roast Connie had put on earlier.

Wilf, who had been like a jack in the box up and down the stairs from the bakery since Mary had gone into labour at nine that morning, had held his daughter and cuddled his wife and was now organising things in the restaurant so he could have a night off with Mary. Ellen had gone home to tell her husband he was a grandfather again and to spread the news amongst the family, and the midwife had left. Connie and Mary were alone with the tiny arrival, and Connie was sitting by Mary's bed, having just made a cup of tea for them both, holding little Martha Ellen in her arms.

'Thank you, lass.'

'Thank you?' Connie glanced up from her rapt contemplation of the miracle of new life. 'What for?'

'Everythin'. I don't know what I'd have done all those years ago if I hadn't met you.' And then, as Connie shook her head and opened her mouth to object, Mary said, 'No, let me say it, lass. I need to say it just the once. I was all locked up in meself over what had happened when I was a bairn, you know that as well as I do. Oh I put on a good front, acted the part – I can't abide them as wear their hearts on their sleeves – but that's all it was, a front. Good old Mary, always game for a laugh, nothin' ever gets her down – that's what they all used to say. But inside I was hurtin', lass, an' talkin' to you, an' you listenin' over and over again, it sort of released somethin'. An' I've you to thank for Wilf an' all, I needed a push there, didn't I?'

'You'd have got there yourself in time.'

'No, no I wouldn't, lass,' Mary said soberly. 'An' now we've this place an' a good job goin' on an' I'm right with

me mam an' da again. Life's good, lass, right good, an' I want
to say thank you.'

'Oh, Mary.' They held each other close, the baby
sandwiched between them, and both their faces were wet when
they drew away.

Dan had found there were many different kinds of fear. There
was the gut-wrenching sort when you were given an order to
go over the top into the midst of bursting shells that blew
men either side of you into smithereens, so that the tortured
ground the officer had been told to take was a mass of broken
bodies and mutilated limbs and blood. Rivers and rivers of
blood.

Then there was the flesh-crawling, sickly kind – the fear
that came when you were walking through a town or village
of ruined houses and factories and you never knew when the
next sniper with a machine-gun was going to fire. You could
feel the dread of those bullets peppering your back mounting
up until it was almost a relief when someone got hit, even if it
was a comrade in arms.

There were the trenches, thick with choking mud and
flooded with water that – with every shell that exploded –
could so easily become a tomb for those who still lived. He'd
seen the look on the faces of some they had pulled out too
late – the horror, the stark terror as they realised how they
were going to die.

Then there was the dread of falling asleep; that was yet
another kind of bogey-man. The things he saw in his
nightmares . . . .

They had first come in the prisoner-of-war camp in
Germany, the dreams about his dead compatriots. Sergeant

419

Forester, Micky Thompson, Geoff Cole, Jock – by, he didn't like to think of how Jock had died – but they had all come, burnt, limbless, covered in blood and mud, and they had pointed accusing fingers at him and demanded to know why he was still alive. There had been times when he had wondered if he *would* live through the hell of that camp, mind. He'd been a bloodthirsty psychopath, their camp Commandant. He'd since heard from other released prisoners from different camps that the international agreements covering the care and treatment of prisoners of war had been mostly adhered to, but not in his camp, not by Commandant Moltke. Each day had become a macabre game of Russian roulette, and then, when they had gleaned that the war was drawing to a close, had come the harrowing craven fear that now, right at the last hurdle with the end in sight, he would be the next one to be tortured or executed for some trumped-up misdemeanour.

Aye, he knew all about fear. He'd lived with it and slept with it, ate and drank it for years. It had infested his bones and it crawled in his stomach until he barely recognised himself any more. He had seen men who behaved lower than the animals and others who – confronted by horrors unspeakable – rose nobly to whatever the occasion demanded. He had watched men give their lives for their friends, and others betray their own brothers and become Commandant Moltke's spies to preserve their own lives.

Dan sat back in his seat in the train and wiped his hand across his sweating face, forcing his thoughts back to the present. A young man, no more than eighteen or nineteen, sitting opposite him in the carriage caught his eye and smiled sympathetically, and Dan inclined his head as he thought, Aye, you've been to hell and back an' all. It was in the eyes.

But now he was facing a new fear, and he was finding this one was the worst of all. It had been four years since he'd been gone and for most of that time Connie hadn't heard anything. It had been eighteen months before they had discovered that Moltke had destroyed every letter written for outside, although, with the lack of incoming mail, they'd suspected it long before then. Four years. She must have thought he'd died.

He found he was grinding his teeth together and stopped abruptly when the little old lady sitting next to the young man eyed him disapprovingly from under her felt hat.

And she was beautiful. Connie was so, so beautiful. The fear gripped his bowels and he had to steel himself not to twist in the seat. He wouldn't blame her if she'd found someone else. And then, in the next instant, yes he damn well would. He'd want to tear the man limb from limb, he admitted harshly. He turned to the train window against which he was sitting and shut his eyes for a moment at the reflection that stared back at him through the murky twilight. Walking scarecrow he looked; fifty if a day and his hair almost completely grey now. He had weighed nearly twelve stone when he was captured, but was less than nine now, but he was lucky compared to some of the poor devils. Aye, he was, he was lucky all right. He had his arms and his legs and his sight. What would he have done if he'd been blinded?

The train was approaching Sunderland central station now and the fear became so thick as to be paralysing. He knew the authorities had contacted Art and Gladys – they were down as his official next of kin – but he had purposely spoken to no one. He had wanted to come home quietly, without anyone knowing the day or time of arrival. He needed to see her first, alone. Once he had done that . . . He breathed deeply, his heart racing. It could start then. Feelings, emotions, learning to live again – it could all start. Whatever he found.

'Home for the New Year then, are you, lad?'

It was the little old lady who had spoken, and Dan nodded and smiled as he reflected, wryly, that only a wrinkled and ancient little body like this one would ever call him lad again. He had stopped being a lad after he had killed his first German.

'Aye, well it'll be a better year than the ones afore it, that's for certain,' the gnarled little woman with cheeks like rosy-red apples said busily. 'Ten million dead in this war, an' they call it the "Great War". Nothin' great about it if you ask me. Four grandsons an' one son gone; by, they talk about a lost generation an' they're right an' all. You got any bairns, lad?'

'No. No, I haven't.'

'Aye, well there's still time, eh? Now you're home.'

Pray God there was. Aye, pray God. Dan nodded again but he didn't speak as the train shuddered to a halt.

It was New Year's Eve – that was portentous, wasn't it? He hadn't planned to arrive home on this particular day but it was the way it had worked out. Surely that meant something?

Stop clutching at straws. The words in his head were caustic, but then the young man opened the carriage door and passengers began to alight. He was home. He was here. His head swam for a moment and he breathed deeply, aiming to get a grip on the dizziness that still assailed him at odd moments. But it was getting better; he'd put on nearly half a stone in the last weeks in the hospital. By, that hospital. Half of them with their minds gone and the other half with their bodies shattered and maimed. What was Britain going to be left with after this lot? Lost generation didn't even begin to cover it.

Dan reached for his kitbag and stood to his feet. This was it. In a few more minutes he'd know. His face was as grey as his shock of hair as he stepped on to the platform and began walking.

He couldn't get over the fact that nothing seemed to have changed at first and yet . . . yes, things were different. It was a woman in the ticket office at the south end for a start.

After leaving the station he walked briskly along Union Street and Waterloo Place before turning into Holmeside, and there he stood for a moment gazing down the busy street. Most of the shop awnings were up – the day had been a stormy one – and a tram was laboriously making its way towards him, passing a horse and cart as it came. There were one or two gentlemen on bicycles, a whole bevy of busy shoppers and the inevitable bairn wailing its head off as it was hauled along the pavement by an irate mother. A woman with a perambulator passed him, one of the huge wheels rolling over his toes, and at her harassed apology Dan smiled and said it didn't matter but he didn't move. He was feeling strange, very strange. All these people and they knew exactly where they were going and what they were about. And it was normal. It was so, so normal. But he didn't feel normal inside; in fact he didn't think he would ever feel rational and well adjusted again.

But he was rushing things once more; he wasn't giving himself time. It was the one thing the nuns in the hospital had tried to drum into him – he had to give himself time.

He began to walk along the street but his step wasn't as brisk now and he was sweating again. He noticed the glances of one or two passers-by and he thought, I must look terrible. Well, he knew he looked terrible, didn't he, but that was something else the nuns had said time would rectify. And he had to count his blessings; Sister Bernadette had drummed that into all of them. But his future, his *life*, hinged on one blessing and one alone – if Connie had waited for him, if she still wore his ring and intended to be his wife – he stopped suddenly, leaning against a shop window as he took great draughts of the bitter northern air – then all the rest would fall into place.

When he came to the shop he stood looking at the sign above the new smart entrance and his eyes questioned what they were seeing for a moment. 'Bell's Restaurant, first floor; Tea-rooms and Bakery, ground floor'.

He felt a sharp surge of pleasure that was separate to what the next few minutes might hold. She had done well for herself, more than well by the look of it. She had extended the property; it looked a right bonny place now and a restaurant no less. He found he was smiling and it came as a surprise – he hadn't felt like smiling in a long, long time.

He stood a moment more, gathering his frayed nerves, or what was left of them after the last four years had taken their toll, and then he opened the door of the shop.

It had been a hectic day. Connie glanced over the crowded tea-rooms and flexed her shoulder blades wearily. The whole world and his wife had wanted to eat out today, or so it had seemed, and the restaurant was booked to capacity tonight. Not that she should complain, she chided herself in the next instant, and she wasn't, not really. It was just that she was feeling a touch blue, she told herself silently. It was New Year's

Eve – the old year with all its heartaches and unfulfilled dreams was nearly gone and a bright untouched year stretched before old and young alike. It was a time of new beginnings, new promises, hope, faith and love . . . She *ached* to see Dan. She couldn't think of anything else now the furore surrounding little Martha Ellen had settled.

Why hadn't he written? A letter, a postcard even? Her heart began to thud as it had done every morning since the day after Boxing Day when she had searched the post frantically for that special writing. He was ill, was that it? Or badly injured? Disfigured even? She wouldn't care; surely he knew she wouldn't care? Or perhaps his feelings had changed. It was a thought that had come to haunt her over the last day or two when there had been no news, and now she brushed it aside angrily. No, she trusted him. She hadn't trusted him once before and it had driven them apart; she wouldn't make the same mistake again. But *why* hadn't he written?

And then she turned and saw him.

She stared at this person who was Dan and yet not Dan, and then she shut her eyes and opened them again and he was still there. He was real.

The length of the shop was between them but she seemed to reach him in one ecstatic moment as she breathed his name into the air, and as his arms opened and he enfolded her into him she knew what heaven was like.

'Dan, oh, Dan. Dan . . .' She wasn't aware she was whispering his name as he covered her face in little frantic kisses, she wasn't aware of anything but him, his smell, the feel of him, his arms holding her close. He was here, he was alive. He was alive and whole. He had come back to her. *He had come back.*

Chapter Twenty-Three

They sat and loved and talked into the early hours of the New Year in Connie's little home. They joined Mary and Wilf briefly at twelve o'clock before withdrawing to the flat again as soon as they could without appearing rude.

Connie cooked them a meal, but interspersed with everything they did they would kiss and hold each other close, their arms locked about each other and their passionate murmurings inarticulate half of the time.

Connie was shocked at the change in him, although she made no reference to his appearance, but his prematurely grey hair, unnaturally pale face in which the bones showed prominent beneath the drawn skin, and his sunken eyes, created in her an inexpressible desire to make him better.

At two o'clock they were sitting quietly, so close as to be inseparable, with their fingers interlocked and Connie's head resting on his shoulder. Every so often Dan would nuzzle the soft silk of her golden hair, shutting his eyes as he inhaled the sweet, fresh fragrance that was reminiscent of apples and orchards and hot summer days. He couldn't believe Art had gone. He felt the pain stab him again. And John, *both legs*. He had been shocked when Connie had related that Ann had left his brother, although on reflection he supposed he wasn't surprised – neither could he altogether blame her. John had made Ann's life hell for years, they had all known it. But to leave him in that state . . . Anyway it was none of his business and he'd call and see Ann some time to tell her she was still his sister-in-law as far as he was concerned; he didn't want to lose touch with her and his nephew.

And then, as though she had sensed the direction of his thoughts, Connie stirred and raised her head to look into his face as she said, 'You *are* intending to go and see your mam and John, aren't you? After everything that's happened, this war and all, it's time to make peace don't you think?'

Peace. Peace with his mother. He took the words into his mind and considered them and he knew they were futile. He had done a lot of thinking in the camp, and veil upon veil had been lifted from his understanding. His mother was an unnatural woman; cold, virtually without conscience, unloving and unlovable, and part of her obsession with Sadie Bell – and now Connie – was that she recognised in them a drawing power. They drew and held men to them like bees to a honey-pot, and not through fear or emotional blackmail or any of the other tricks his mother used. Women like Sadie and Connie had an elemental warmth, something soft and tender and flowing that made men want to envelop them and in turn be enveloped. It was a voluptuous thing, inexplicable, like the redolence given off by a flower when it was ripe with pollen. He had made his choice – he had made it four years ago – and peace with his mother was not an option. Neither was any form of understanding with John.

'I shall go and see them, Connie.' He stroked a wisp of hair from her forehead as he spoke. He intended to sell his share of the family business; he wanted out. And he wanted to tell them he was marrying Connie as soon as it could be arranged; it needed to be said face to face.

'Don't say it like that.' She straightened now, taking his emaciated, dear, *dear* face in her hands as she turned towards him. 'They might have mellowed, Dan. Four years is a long time and they've suffered too.'

'Do you believe they've mellowed?'

She looked at him and the answer was in her eyes.

'No, neither do I, but I will go and see them after I've got Gladys to call Kitty to the square so I can say hallo to her first. She's such a dear soul, Kitty. How she has stood my mother all these years I don't know.'

'You're all her family I suppose.'

'Aye.' He nodded. 'Aye, that's it sure enough.'

But family or no the ties had been irrevocably broken with his mother and John and there was no turning back. Even if things had turned out differently and Connie had found someone else there would have been no meeting point. Perhaps there never had been.

He settled Connie back in his arms again, tucking her head under his chin. He was going to book into a hotel tomorrow, there was a small one at the end of the street which would serve him very well, and it would mean he was just two or three minutes' walk away from Connie. Any further and he wouldn't be able to bear it. She had already said he could stay in her spare room but he wasn't going to have any gossip about her – this was going to be done properly, he loved her too much for anything else. But tonight, tonight was a night apart. Tonight they would hold each other, like this, so close they could feel each other's heartbeat and they would watch the dawn rise. And tomorrow he would go and see her old friend, Father Hedley, and arrange for them to be married as soon as the priest could arrange it – Connie wanted that as much as he did. They had waited too long as it was . . . He was asleep on the last word and it was a deep, dreamless sleep, like a bairn's, and there were no nightmares that night.

The next day Connie and Dan went to St George's Square and there was an emotional reunion with Gladys and the children, followed by an equally poignant one with Kitty later in the morning after Gladys had sent Catherine to tell her the good news.

There were flurries of snow showers that could at any time turn into the blizzard which was forecast for New Year's Day, but inside Gladys's snug house all was warmth and light and wet faces as Kitty hugged Dan as though she would never let him go.

'Oh, lad, lad.' The plump Irishwoman was incapable of saying anything else for a good few minutes, her eyes streaming as she held on to the tall, painfully thin, bony figure of this, her favourite 'bairn'. 'Lad, lad, lad.'

'He's home, Kitty. He's home.' Kitty's naked joy had touched something very tender in Connie's heart, and her voice was soft and understanding as she put her arms round the other woman. 'We're going to get wed as soon as we can, and we want you to know that there will always be a place for you with us if ever you want to leave Mrs Stewart. And of course you'll be welcome to call any time, any time, Kitty.'

Connie knew Dan thought of this woman as his mother, and it was as a mother that Kitty now said, her face close to theirs as the three of them remained joined, 'Thank you, lass, thank you, but I'm a great one in believing a married couple should start off on their own where they can. But I'll remember the offer, aye, I will, lass, an' it's thanking you I am for it. And I won't be a stranger to your door, I can promise you that. You're a good lass, aye, a good lass.' The last words held an inflexion that made them a statement. This young woman Dan had fallen for was no strumpet, whatever her mother might have been.

Silently now, Kitty gripped Connie's hand that was resting on her arm, and then her voice was purposely bright as she said, 'Aye, well I'd best be getting back. I had to make some excuse about seeing me Aunt Ida after Catherine had tipped me the wink in the kitchen afore she went in to see her granny, but she didn't like it. Not that she could say much considering I haven't even had the sniff of a day off in weeks.'

'How . . . how are they both?'

It was noticeable that in the time Kitty had been with them Dan hadn't mentioned his mother or John, and now Kitty looked directly at him as she said, ''Bout as you'd expect, lad.'

'Why do you put up with it, Kitty?' This was from Gladys. 'You could easily get another job with your experience. What with all the big houses and such having to give up their' – she almost said servants – 'staff in the war, there's a shortage of housekeepers and the like. Half of them who have come out of service won't be going back, you can bet your life on that; you could be sitting pretty somewhere else.'

'Better the devil you know, lass, better the devil you know.' Kitty was smiling as she spoke and Gladys smiled back, but once the goodbyes had been said and Kitty was hurrying back along Burdon Road in the direction of Ryhope Road, she came back to the question Art's wife had asked. Why did she put up with what Edith Stewart dished out? Better the devil you know, she had said to them back there. She gave a small, mirthless laugh to herself. And Edith was a devil all right; since she'd been obliged to take John in when Ann went life hadn't been worth living in that mausoleum of a house. She had never thought to see the day she'd feel sorry for John, but she did. Aye, she did, wretched piteous individual that he was now. Was it for him that she stayed?

The sky was low and heavy, the wind cutting through her like a knife, and she put her head down as she scurried along the pavement.

It was partly for John, but only partly, she admitted silently. The rest of it she couldn't explain to herself, let alone anyone else. It was all tied up with guilt and regret and love and hate, and, not least, familiarity. And being needed. Now her mouth twisted bitterly. The greatest snare there was, the knowledge that you were needed. And she wasn't thinking of John here, although heaven knew that poor soul needed her since he'd come home.

She had run the house for years single-handed; there wasn't a nook or cranny that didn't have her stamp and she kept the daily routine as smooth as cream – she was the mistress of the house in all but name. Edith would be lost without her. So was she saying she stayed for Edith? She moved her head in denial of the thought, and then clicked her tongue irritably at herself. Enough, enough of thinking; hadn't Henry always said it was the most dangerous pastime there was and he was right, God bless his soul. She did what she knew she had to do and that was the end of it, but she had put her foot down more in the last few years. She wasn't a stranger to the Church now, not since that time she had met Father Hedley again at her Aunt Ida's, and it helped. Aye, it helped right enough. Everyone else had been living on a knife edge through the war and there she'd been, more at peace with herself than she'd been for years. Life was strange. It was, it was strange. There was that lad back there having been home twenty-four hours and his mother was going to be the last to know. Aye, life was strange all right.

It was exactly half past three in the afternoon when Connie and Dan walked down Ryhope Road. The wind was lashing the bare branches of the trees overhanging the road and it was already quite dark, the leaden grey sky overhead full of the forecast snow which had yet to begin falling. Connie was holding on to Dan's arm very tightly and his face was taut and strained, but their footsteps were brisk and steady as they approached the Stewart residence. This had to be done, they both knew it, and it had to be done right, from the beginning. They needed to present a united front to the formidable woman who was Dan's mother; it might succeed in preventing further mischief-making in the future at least.

Dan opened the gate and Connie stepped through on to the drive, then they were mounting the steps to the front door and the bell was jangling from Dan's pull. Strangely, now the moment she had been dreading all day was here, Connie felt absolutely calm. She had wanted to be at Dan's side to support him through whatever went on; that was the only thing that mattered. She hoped his mother, and John too, would meet him halfway because when all was said and done they were his family, but she expected nothing good from this encounter. Dan had virtually returned from the dead, but he had returned to her – that's how his mother would see it. The woman who had screamed at her with such venom on this very doorstep four years ago was not of a forgiving nature, neither was she conciliatory in any form. And Connie was worried about Dan; he was ill, anyone could see that, and he had a hacking cough and had nearly passed out twice today. They needed to get this over and then she could start looking after him and getting him well again. And she would, and swiftly, she told herself silently.

When Kitty opened the door and saw them standing there she closed her eyes for an infinitesimal moment before saying, 'Come in, come in the pair of you,' her voice shaking. It was clear Kitty had been anticipating the proposed meeting with some distress; nevertheless, she led them to the drawing room door without saying anything else, merely squeezing their arms briefly before opening the door and saying, her voice now bright and excited which Dan thought was the best piece of play-acting he had heard for a long while, 'Madam, oh Madam, look who's here. Oh, isn't it wonderful!'

Edith was alone in the large and imposing room and it was apparent she had been sitting reading, not – as one would have expected from the inclement weather – in front of the roaring fire which was burning in the ornate fireplace, but at some distance across the room on one of the chaise longues.

They watched her raise her head and saw her face change as she took in Dan in the doorway, with Connie just behind him, and then, as Dan walked further into the room, drawing Connie into the side of him, Edith rose slowly to her feet. 'You're alive.' There was no expression in her voice at all; no joy, no vestige of greeting, nothing. 'We thought you had perished when there was no word.'

'No, I didn't perish, Mother.'

'Isn't it wonderful?' Kitty was giving the performance of her life. 'All this time and no news and in he walks, as large as life! I can't believe—'

'Kitty!'

Connie couldn't prevent her hand going to her mouth as the word was barked across the room.

'Madam, it's *Dan*.'

'I know who it is and I can see who he has with him. Would you kindly show my son and that . . . that *person* out, please?'

'No, I won't.'

The words had the same effect as a live grenade on Edith. She virtually sprang across the room, her head bouncing on her shoulders as she hissed, 'Then I'll do it! I'll do it.'

'Mother, *please*. It's been over four years and with a war in-between, can't we at least behave like human beings? We came to tell you we intend to get married and . . . and to ask you to be present.'

Edith was looking straight at Dan and she made a small movement with her head. She was trembling as if consumed with rage, and then her answer came through clenched teeth. 'I don't fraternise with whores.'

'You old devil.' Dan's lips moved away from his teeth as if he was surveying something vile as he stared into the cold, narrowed eyes watching him, and as Connie pulled on his arm saying, 'Leave it, Dan, leave it. Please, come away, dear,' he said, 'She's worth ten, twenty of you and you know it.'

'Get out of my house!'

'With pleasure, but before I go I might as well tell you I intend to sell my share of the business, all right? So you can get the papers drawn up and then I'll be out of your hair for good. You can send them to the Three Tuns at Holmeside where I'm staying.'

'Get out!'

They had stepped out into the hall, a distraught Kitty behind them, when, in answer to his name being spoken from the direction of what had been his father's study, Dan became transfixed by the sight of the man who had just wheeled himself into the hall.

Connie heard his sudden intake of breath and she turned her head just a moment after Dan, and then she too became frozen. There was nothing about the creature in the wheelchair she recognised save the eyes, and these were like chips of black lead in the distorted gargoyle of a face. The exploding shell which had taken John's legs had tried to incinerate all the projections of his face. The nose was almost completely burnt away, leaving a portion of bone and two gaping holes, and his lips, eyebrows and chin had all suffered a lesser fate. Funnily enough the eyelids looked to be intact, although red and scarred like the rest of his skin, and both ears were almost whole. There was no hair above his forehead, but from the long tufts resting on his shoulders it was clear the back of his head was not affected. It was a monstrous face, a face from hell, and Connie had to force herself not to close her eyes to shut out the sight of it.

'So you came through untouched?' The voice was thick, like someone speaking through layers of treacle. 'I might have guessed.'

'They're leaving.'

Edith's voice was like snapping steel jaws but John ignored his mother, the dark piercing light of his eyes moving over Dan before travelling to Connie at the side of

436

him and then returning to his brother.

'Hallo, John.'

Dan's voice was shaking, and in answer to it John said, 'Not a pretty sight, is it? Mam can't bear to look at me, can you, Mam – not that she was ever keen to do so before anyway. I'm locked away in there' – the head gestured towards the half-open door – 'when she has her fancy friends call. She's worried I'll frighten 'em, aren't you, Mam? But she was placed in an awkward position when that bitch of a wife of mine left me, Dan. She could hardly refuse to take in her own son, now could she? What would the Christian Women's Guild of Fellowship have thought of their president then, eh?'

Edith said not a word, but as she looked at John – and he at her – the enmity between them was like a live thing, snaking across the hall and causing the fine hairs on the back of Connie's neck to rise.

'I'm sorry, John.'

'Sorry, are you?' John's gaze snapped back to Dan as he spoke. 'Aye, I just bet you are. And you, are you sorry?' he asked Connie, the terrible face turning to look fully at her. 'Pleases you, does it, to see me reduced to half a man, less than half a man? Sitting pretty aren't you, from what we hear, and they say that whoring don't pay! By, you could tell 'em different, eh?'

'Come on, we're getting out of here,' said Dan quickly as he glanced at Connie's deathly white face.

'Aye, well you've got two legs to carry you where you want, eh, Dan?' Not once in all the time he had been speaking had John raised his voice from the low, almost conversational tone he had been using. 'Two legs, her to supply all your basic needs—'

'Connie is going to be my wife, John.'

'Is that right? Aye, well there was a time when I'd have said you were being taken for a mug, but she's doing all right for herself now, isn't she. The pair of you will be living the high life . . . little brother.'

The Great War might have ended seven weeks ago but not this one. This one wouldn't end until one of them was dead. The thought, coming from nowhere as it did, shocked Connie into action, and now she actually tugged at Dan's arm saying, 'Please, Dan, you can do no good here. Nothing has changed.'

'Nothing's changed?' The words were so weighed down with bitterness that they emerged in a snarl from John's misshapen lips, and were followed by a host of profanities that caused the spittle to collect in white blobs and dribble on to his chin.

Connie was hardly aware of Dan leading her across the hall but when they stepped outside she took great hungry lungfuls of the clean cold air in which the first snowflakes were beginning to whirl and dance.

So much hate, so much resentment and hostility; the house wreaked with it. How did Kitty *stand* it? Connie asked herself now, as she fully understood what had prompted the same question from Gladys earlier in the day.

'Oh, love, I'm sorry, I'm sorry. I should never have let you persuade me to let you come today.' Dan looked as white as a sheet, the dark shadow of the beginning of stubble on his chin standing out in stark contrast to his sallow skin.

'I wouldn't have taken no for an answer.'

They walked down the steps leading from the front door as they spoke, Kitty just behind them, and now the buxom housekeeper said, 'Aye, that's right, lass. You start as you mean to carry on, eh?' and the three of them smiled weakly. 'I'd best be getting back in; John has these seizures, fits, when he gets upset or excited, and she won't give him his medication. Won't have anything to do with that side of things, says she finds it too upsetting.'

They all stared at each other for a moment; Kitty's voice had held a deep and bitter cynicism that was at odds with her easy-going, kind nature.

'Thank you, Kitty.'

Dan stood looking rather helplessly at the older woman as he spoke, and now Connie took his arm – the contours of which were painfully accentuated under the thick cloth of his overcoat. 'Come and see us as soon as you can, Kitty,' she said softly. 'Dan's staying at the Three Tuns until we can get married but he'll be having all his meals with me and just going back there to sleep.'

'Except tonight. I've booked us a table at the Three Tuns tonight so I can have you all to myself,' put in Dan quickly, and then, turning to Kitty he said, 'There's always someone wanting to ask her about something back at the tea-rooms and restaurant; no wonder she's as thin as a rake.'

'Well that makes a pair of you.'

A slight movement on the perimeter of Connie's vision brought her eyes from Kitty's determinedly cheery face to the partly open front door. John was in the aperture; how long he had been there she didn't know. He was staring at her, his flaky lids drooping over the hard black light of his eyes, his hands working at the tartan blanket draped over his waist and hanging emptily to the base of the wheelchair.

The look in his eyes pinned her for a moment and then she wrenched her gaze away from the raw lust, her voice almost a gabble as she said, 'Look, it's coming down thicker, we'll have to go. Goodbye, Kitty.'

'So long, lass. So long, lad.'

They all hugged once more and as they turned to go their separate ways – she and Dan towards the gate and Kitty back into the house – Connie knew without glancing his way that John had disappeared.

They didn't talk much on the way home. The wind was driving the snow before it in stinging gusts and there were few people about. Connie wished Dan hadn't set his heart on this meal at his hotel for the two of them. The dull pasty white of his face and the exhausted pinkness of his eyes bothered her; she would far rather have cooked them a tasty meal in the flat and then – regardless of his noble leanings – seen Dan tucked up in the spare bedroom with a hot water bottle and one of Mary's special herbal night-time drinks that aided restful sleep. John had accused Dan of coming through the war untouched, but the walking skeleton at the side of her had been disabled all right. Maybe not as visibly as his brother, but the physical and mental wounds were still there, and the broken body and mind needed time to heal. And love, lots and lots of love. She wanted to bathe him in her love, wrap him up in it, pour it on the hurt and trauma like a healing balm.

They spent some time with Wilf and Mary before they left for the Three Tuns, and Dan held the baby. His face had worked when Connie had first placed the small infant in his arms, and knowing a little of the horrors he had been through and the abominations he had seen, the other three had chattered away about inconsequentials to give Dan a chance to compose himself.

Dan had sat quietly, his head down. Damn it, he was going to cry! No, he mustn't cry, not here, not now. He had seen some of them that started on that game and once started they'd found it difficult to stop; half barmy some of them had become. No, he could master this. He could. It was just that the sight of the sweet, innocent little face and tiny, tiny limbs had caused something to melt deep inside where the hard core sat, but that was all right, it was. He could let it go a little at a time and it would be all right. Thank God this war had been the war to end wars; if nothing else the suffering and mayhem had had a purpose in teaching men that. But at what a cost. Ten million dead and still more left like John. And Art gone, and most of the men he had joined up with.

'Are We Down-Hearted? No!' That had been the mood of the songwriters when the war had begun. 'It's a Long Way to Tipperary' but 'Your King and Country Want You' so 'Jolly Good Luck to the Girl Who Loves a Soldier'; she must, the songwriters had urged, 'Keep the Home Fires Burning'. And then, by 1916, stoicism had set in, Dan thought bitterly. 'What's the Use of Worrying?' as thousands 'Packed Up Your Troubles' and dreamed of gathering 'Roses in Picardy'. But by 1918 there was bitter irony in carolling, 'Oh, Oh, Oh, it's a Lovely War!' By that time the annihilation had touched every family in Britain, high or low born, rich or poor. Fathers, sons, grandsons, brothers . . .

'Isn't she bonny?'

Connie's voice brought him out of the abyss and he turned his head to see her at the side of him, young, fresh, beautiful and his. *His*. He had everything to live for, everything to strive and work for. He had Connie.

'Aye, she is that,' he said softly. 'She's the dawn of a new tomorrow.' And he wasn't just talking about Martha Ellen.

John had encouraged Kitty to accompany his mother to Gilbert and Doreen's New Year's Day musical soirée. She knew she loved the time with the bairns in the nursery, he'd said, and the bairns looked forward to her going and it was a help to Doreen if she knew the evening wasn't going to be interrupted. He would be perfectly all right; he wasn't a bairn for crying out loud and he didn't need his nappy changed. So Kitty had gone. And immediately the house was empty John had wheeled himself into the drawing room and used the telephone to call for a taxi which had arrived promptly at eight o'clock.

John was waiting for the knock at the front door and he had a wad of notes in his hand to ensure the cabbie's assistance in the awkward task of getting himself and the wheelchair where he wanted to go. And he had his service revolver in his pocket.

He wasn't going to get another chance like this one, he told himself, as the taxi moved slowly through the snowstorm towards the Three Tuns Hotel. He knew exactly where they were and he had surprise on his side; it could be weeks before he was left alone in the house again. Kitty watched him like a hawk, stupid interfering old baggage that she was. She might have pulled the wool over his mother's eyes but he had known she'd been aware of Dan's return before his brother and Connie turned up at the house. Dan had always been her favourite. Seems he was everyone's favourite, but not for much longer. No, not for much longer.

As anticipation and excitement began to make his heart race he warned himself to go carefully. He couldn't afford to have a fit now, although he'd taken as much of his medication as he dared without sending himself to sleep. The muted screaming in his head – which was always with him but sometimes became so loud it caused a red mist in front of his eyes and a pain like knives stabbing into his brain – was shouting two names tonight. *Connie and Dan. Connie and Dan.* He'd show her. Aye, he'd show her all right. She had been the cause of him losing everything. Her and her whoring mother had put a curse on him, that was it.

He would never have her. The lust that had driven him all his life since he had had his first taste of a woman as a lad of fourteen was just as strong as it had ever been, adding to the daily torment of living, and now he felt himself become hard beneath the tartan blanket. But the revenge he was about to take would bring him a measure of satisfaction through the long nights when his body burnt and ached for the release a woman could bring. No, not just a woman – her, Sadie Bell's ragamuffin brat. The whore, the filthy, dirty strumpet . . . The profanities in his head died away as the taxi stopped outside the Three Tuns. He had to concentrate now; everything depended on the next few minutes and he had to keep calm and steady.

The scandal of tonight would bring his mother low, her and her precious social standing. The thought gave him immense pleasure and he savoured it through the task of being transported into the hotel foyer. They had all been sacrificed on the altar of his mother's craving for power and prestige, and in one night he would bring it all to nowt. He just wished he could see her face when they told her the news, that would have been the sweetest pleasure of all. Damn her. Damn them all . . .

* * *

For a moment Connie couldn't believe her eyes. 'John . . .'

'What?' Dan heard the murmur and saw her face turn white, but it was a moment before he turned in his seat and by then the waiter had wheeled John down the two steps into the dining room of the hotel and over to the side of their table in the far corner.

'What on earth . . . John, what do you think you are doing?' Dan had half risen as he'd spoken, but now, at an abrupt gesture from John, he sank back down into his seat again.

'What am I doing?' John's voice was low and conversational as though he wasn't aware of the horrified faces of some of the diners who were less tactful than others. 'I'm here to have a talk with my brother, Dan. Nowt wrong with that, is there?'

'Where's . . .?'

'Mam? Kitty?' John watched Dan's eyes return from the dining room door before he said, 'I'm here alone, Dan. I'm a big lad now, or hadn't anyone told you?'

'What do you want?' Connie's heart was leaping painfully but her voice didn't betray it, and the cool measured tones brought John's eyes fixing on to her face.

'You're a cold, hard bitch at heart, aren't you? Your mam was the same. I'd have looked after her, set her up so she was sitting pretty but she'd have none of it. She'd got her eye on getting Jacob to marry her, that was the thing, and she knew I wouldn't fall for that one.'

'My mother loved Jacob.'

'And the small fact he'd got a wife didn't come into it?'

'Oh don't take the line of morality, John, not you.' Dan's voice was cutting.

John's shoulders visibly stiffened and they watched him

take a few deep breaths. When he spoke again his voice was still quiet. 'We've never got on, have we, Dan. Not even when we were bairns. You were always the favoured one, the blue-eyed boy, simpering and drooling to get your own way. Everything, including her' – he inclined his head towards Connie – 'has fallen into your lap.'

'That's not true.' It was Connie who spoke and her voice was fierce. 'You don't know what he's gone through—'

'Spare me.' Connie's hand had reached across the table to clasp Dan's as she'd spoken and the sight seemed to infuriate the man in the wheelchair. And now John's voice was precise, definite, when he said, 'You were the cause of Ann leaving me. Oh, aye, you were,' he added at her involuntary gesture of denial. 'It was when I was first shipped home. I was delirious most of the time apparently, and I talked a bit. Said things.'

'Things?' Connie asked tautly.

'Aye, things.' And John settled back in his chair, his expression indicating that he was enjoying the anticipation of what he was about to reveal. 'She told me, the day she said she was leaving me, that I'd let on about the night I burnt your brother and granny. About the screaming, the smell, all of it.'

'Dan . . .' Connie's hand was gripping the neck of her dress, but although she spoke Dan's name her eyes were fixed on the devilish face of his brother.

'You swine! You loathsome, filthy swine.' In the same moment that Dan rose to his feet, intending to bodily remove his brother from the restaurant, John brought out the gun he had been hiding under the blanket on his lap.

It was instinct that threw Connie across the table at the

wheelchair as the gun was fired, aimed straight at Dan's heart, and as the momentum of her thrust sent the wheelchair skidding to one side Dan clutched his chest and fell to the ground amid a conglomeration of cutlery, plates, glasses and tablecloth.

The lurching of the wheelchair caused John to drop the gun on the floor where it went spinning under a nearby table, but he didn't mind. He had done what he came to do. He began to chuckle, his face lit up as he gave vent to his glee, and with the laughter went the last shreds of his sanity.

Chapter Twenty-Four

'By, lass! There's me an' Wilf sittin' at home nice as you like an' all this happenin'. I feel like I can't turn me back for a minute.'

It was so typically Mary, and so unconsciously humorous, that despite the dire circumstances Connie couldn't help but smile as she exchanged a wry glance with Dan across his hospital bed, and it was Dan who said meekly, 'I'm sorry, Mary, but it did take us a bit by surprise too.'

'An' you say he meant to do for you, Dan?'

'Oh aye.' Dan nodded, his face straightening as he glanced down at the copious bandages covering the left side of his chest and shoulder. 'If Connie hadn't caused him to miss his aim he'd have done for me all right.'

'Whatever next!' Mary shook her head slowly. 'He must be mad.'

'Apparently the police doctor would agree with you there.' Connie's voice was calm and steady. The doctor who had seen to Dan and the very capable sister in charge of the ward had both emphasised that Dan was in shock – and who wouldn't be with their own brother attempting to murder them! the sister had added – and he needed peace and quiet and the deeper connotations of John's actions playing down for the present.

He had lost a lot of blood, the doctor had explained, but that wasn't really the problem here. He had had a rough time of it in the prisoner of war camp by all accounts, and these things affected the mind even more than the body. Something like this could at best delay his recovery, at worst . . . The doctor hadn't gone on to explain what the worst would mean but he hadn't had to.

'They're sayin' John's gone doo-lally?' Mary asked now.

'I think he always has been, Mary.' Dan glanced across at Connie and they stared hard at each other, their eyes unblinking, and it was in that moment that Connie experienced something akin to a feeling of relief. Dan wasn't in shock, not in the way the doctor thought anyway. Whatever had had to be faced regarding his brother he had faced a long time ago.

It had been pandemonium when they had brought Dan in last night, and the doctor had operated immediately to remove the bullet lodged in the bottom of his shoulder. He had still been heavily sedated when Connie had arrived back at the hospital first thing that morning after leaving a message for Mary with Ellen, and it was only in the last couple of hours that he had been able to converse with her. They hadn't mentioned John's last words before he had fired the gun, but each knew the other believed them. Connie couldn't let herself think about the screaming part – she *had* to believe that was John's spite coming through and that her brother and granny had been overcome with smoke as Father Hedley had insisted at the time – but she did believe he had been responsible for the tragedy. *Murder.* He had murdered her family, and he had probably intended that she die in the fire too.

The police were saying that it was the war that had sent

John over the edge; shell-shock they'd labelled it, and it was a bad case. No hope of recovery. Heartbreaking for all concerned. He'd likely be institutionalised for life, the constable who had come to sit by the side of Dan's bed for a while said gravely, because they understood he was separated from his wife and his mother had said she couldn't have him back to live with her again. Poor devil . . .

Poor devil. Connie had looked at the ruddy, fresh-faced constable and for a moment he had appeared very young to her. John was a monster, that's what he was. And yet, it wasn't him, not wholly. Dan's father dying before his time; Jacob's suicide; Mavis losing her mind and now John attempting to kill his own brother; the family disintegrating – it all had its seed in Edith's obsessional desire for power and dominance. What she couldn't control she destroyed, and she had destroyed her own family as well as Connie's. Dear God. Dear God . . . Connie was praying with her eyes open as she listened to the constable droning on.

It had to stop somewhere, didn't it, this cycle of hate and destruction? She loved Dan and she knew he loved her. Aye, she knew that all right. And she wanted his bairns. There were still times when her arms ached for Lucy's daughter, but when she had her own children that loss would be eased. A new generation, products of love and tenderness not ambition or cold manipulation. Perhaps in their children the past would finally be put to rest.

Connie turned to Mary now, squeezing her friend's arm as she said, 'It was good of you to come but we didn't expect it, not with the baby and everything.'

'Don't be daft, lass. I wanted to.'

'I'm glad you did, Mary. You can do me a favour if you

will.' Dan was lying propped against his pillows and his face was the same colour as the white linen. 'Take this woman home and make sure she has something hot to eat and then goes to bed. She's exhausted.' And then he said to Connie, at her involuntary movement of protest, 'I mean it, dear. They'll be bringing the evening meal in a moment and I shall eat that and then settle down, but I shan't have an easy mind if you don't go with Mary now. You've been here all day and you're worn out.'

'He's right, lass.' Mary stood to her feet with a smile at Dan. 'I'll wait outside until you're ready to go.'

It was another five minutes before Connie joined Mary in the corridor outside the ward, mainly because – as she had leant over to kiss him goodbye – Dan had whispered, 'Darling, what John said . . . It won't make any difference to us, will it?' After her reassurance she had sat on his bed, his good arm holding her close, and they had remained like that for a minute or two until she had kissed him again before rising to her feet.

'I love you, Dan Stewart.' She stared into the dark, chocolate-brown eyes and what he saw in her blue ones caused him to relax back against the pillows again, a slight smile touching his lips as he breathed out very slowly.

'I love you, Connie Bell.'

'Then that's all that matters.'

Connie shared a meal with Mary and Wilf and returned to her own flat at seven o'clock, and at half past, after answering a knock at her front door, she found a red-faced and agitated Wilf in front of her again. 'What is it, Wilf?' she asked quickly. 'Are Mary and the baby all right?'

'Aye, aye.' His voice was low and he was speaking rapidly. 'It's her, Dan's mam. She's down in the restaurant asking to see you.'

'Mrs Stewart?'

'Aye, I got a right gliff meself, lass, and the old biddy was all for pushing past me and making her way up here until she realised the door was locked.' For safety reasons it had been decided, when the extension was being built, that the door leading up to the flat would have its own set of keys of which Connie had one, Mary and Wilf another, Gladys the third and now Dan had been given the spare. 'Got right uppity she did an' all, ordering me about like I was a servant or something.' It was clear Wilf was not enamoured of Edith Stewart.

'Oh, I'm sorry, Wilf, but did she say what she wants?'

'Just that she wants to see you.'

They stared at each other for a moment, and then Connie smoothed a few tendrils of hair that had come adrift from the bun on the top of her head back behind her ears and jerked her chin upwards, her eyes narrowing as she said, 'Then would you mind showing her up, Wilf?'

'Lass, Mary'd skin me alive if I left that wicked old so-an'-so alone with you up here.'

'I'm not frightened of her, Wilf.' The chin went up a notch higher. 'And I wouldn't give her the satisfaction of thinking I am. I will be perfectly all right.'

It was an order, and after a long moment of hesitation Wilf nodded. Connie remained standing just inside the front door as Mary's husband turned and made his way down the steep, narrow stairs leading to the door which opened into an alcove at the side of the restaurant, but he was only halfway down when the sound of shouting brought her on to the small landing. Wilf turned and looked up at her, motioning her with his hand to stay where she was, and then continued swiftly down the remaining stairs, shutting the door securely behind him.

Surely . . . Yes, that was Kitty's voice she could hear. Connie was down the steps in a trice, and as she opened the door that Wilf had just closed it was to see Edith Stewart in front of her, her profile all but snarling, and Kitty, pale-faced but unmoving, standing a few yards away with Wilf between them.

'What is it?'

They all turned at the sound of Connie's voice, but it was Wilf who said, before either of the two women could open their mouths, 'This 'un' – indicating Edith with a jerk of one thumb which caused the bristling woman to expand still further – 'is telling this lady to get out.' The terminology left no one in any doubt as to Wilf's standpoint. 'And she's refusing to leave.'

'This is Kitty, Wilf.' The two had never met but she had spoken of Edith's housekeeper and the fondness Dan held for her several times. 'And she knows she is welcome in my home at any time.'

'She followed me here!' Edith was beside herself, her small body thrusting forward in her rage. 'How dare you! How *dare* you follow me, Kitty, and don't say you didn't. Get back to the house and we'll speak of this later.'

'Aye, I did follow you here.' There was no vestige of the menial in Kitty's stance, nor yet in the tone of her voice when she continued, 'And it looks like it was just as well I did. I'd have thought you were satisfied by the trouble you've caused without plotting further mischief.'

'What? *What did you say?*' Edith stared at the plump

woman in front of her. She had known the warm-hearted Irishwoman for most of her life, and taken advantage of her for just as long, but she would have sworn on her own life that Kitty didn't have the gumption of a bairn. Soft as clarts, that's how Edith had always thought of her, and now here Kitty was openly defying her. But what was worse, much worse, was that it was in front of that baggage who had brought such shame to their name, and from the sound of it the two weren't unacquainted. By, Kitty would suffer for this little lot.

'The restaurant is due to open in a few minutes and I won't have a disturbance,' Connie said coolly. 'If you wish to speak with me you had better come upstairs. You too, Kitty.'

Edith Stewart looked fully at Connie, and the younger woman's poise and calm had the effect of making her want to leap at the lovely face, to tear and gouge at it with her fingernails. The strength of the desire shocked her; it suggested a lack of control that wasn't to be borne, and to combat the weakness she breathed deeply, inclining her head in a stiff nod of acquiescence.

Connie led the way upstairs, and once the two women were standing in the parlour she indicated the sofa, saying, 'Please be seated,' her heart thudding with the force of a sledgehammer.

'I haven't come to sit and chat,' Edith said sharply. The interior of the flat had surprised her – it showed great charm and taste which further increased the anger and irritation she was trying to master. That this little chit, that whore's flyblow had risen to this! By, the devil looked after his own all right. And Kitty, standing there as though she had every right to force her way where she pleased. Well, she still intended to say everything she had come to say – that would give her great lump of a housekeeper something to think about! She had always suspected that Kitty had been sweet on Henry and that the silly woman had thought he had a soft spot for her; this would teach the insolent baggage a lesson. No one crossed her and got away with it.

'Then perhaps you would like to tell me what you have come for?' said Connie steadily, her face betraying nothing of her inward turmoil.

'Very well.' Edith suppressed the rage that Connie's refusal to be intimidated was causing and allowed a pause, while they stared at each other, before she said, 'The scandal you have caused will take some living down, you are aware of that I suppose? But it will be explained that John is suffering from shell-shock and that his injuries have turned his mind; people can understand that with our war heroes.'

War hero? John had risen to war hero status now?

'And of course once Dan is sufficiently recovered to leave the infirmary he will return home to live with me. I understand from the doctors that he is a sick man. All this will be made easier if you leave the district, or perhaps I should say *when* you leave the district. With you gone people will forget very quickly, and once Dan is well again he can resume his relationship with Miss Rotherington; the two were very close at one time.'

She was as mad as John. Connie found her mouth had fallen open in a little gape and she shut it quickly, blinking twice before she said, 'Dan was never close to Miss Rotherington and he wouldn't consider coming to live with you again; you must know that surely? We are going to be married.'

'Over my dead body.'

'Now look, Mrs Stewart—'

'No, *you* look!' The constraint had gone; Edith's true colours were flying with a vengeance, and as Kitty stiffened at the side of them Edith's face was contorted with hatred as she spat, 'You'll do as I say, girl, or I'll destroy you, and Dan with you. Do you want that, eh? He's not marrying gutterscum, not while I've breath in my body.'

'You can't hurt us.'

'No?' Edith stepped back a pace and Connie watched her fight to gain control. Then she gave a short, bitter bark of a laugh as she said, 'If he marries you it's as good as dragging the Stewart name through the mud and I've fought too hard to get where I am today to let that happen. I'm sure the police would be interested to know a few facts about you and Dan, like the little matter of you being brother and sister?'

Connie stared at her, her face bloodless, as she said, 'That's a lie and you know it.'

'Do I? Prove it. I shall tell them you are my husband's bastard, and that he had a stroke the night his other children went to the house of his fancy piece to force her to finish the relationship that was splitting their home and hurting their mother.'

'It was Jacob.' Kitty took hold of Edith's arm, spinning the other woman round to face her. 'You know it was Jacob; Henry was a fine, upstanding man. You can't sully his reputation now.'

Edith shrugged. 'John will verify every word I say even now if I want him to,' she said with dangerous quiet, 'and even if he can't, I shall say the knowledge of his brother committing incest is what sent him over the edge and caused the attack on Dan. That will put a different complexion on things, don't you think? And Matthew and Gilbert will stand by me in this; they are greedy, those two. If I offer them enough, perhaps even my share of the business split between them, they will do as I say.'

'You can't prove this, it's not true,' Connie said numbly.

'Maybe not.' Edith's eyebrows rose upwards but her voice was cold. 'But enough mud will stick to soil any union you might have, I shall make sure of that. If you marry him you're ruining us anyway, I have nothing to lose. And think of any children you might have; something like this would be a dark cloud hanging over them for the rest of their lives.'

'You would do that? To your own grandchildren?'

'Nothing that's part of you has any claim on me. And I swear I shall do all I can to bring you down. If you love my son as you say you do then you will wish to spare him the indignity of a court case with all the ballyhoo that will follow. And it will, I promise you that.'

Connie stared at the small woman in front of her and she found it impossible to understand how her Dan, her generous, warm-hearted, wonderful Dan could have come from such a person. Edith Stewart would do everything she had threatened, Connie had no doubt about that. She and Dan would have to sell up and move far away – if not for themselves then for the future of the children Edith had spoken of – and even then the tentacles of this woman might reach out to wind round their lives again. But they would do it; she would take Dan far, far away, because one thing was for sure – she would never let him get enmeshed in his mother's clutches again. If Edith thought her threats and omens would make her relinquish Dan then she was wrong. It had only made her all the more determined that

Edith would have no place in his life ever again.

'You dreadful, dreadful woman.'

Connie's voice was low, and for a moment Edith didn't seem to take in the softly spoken words, but then she stood stiff and staring as Connie continued, in the quiet, even tone which was more weighty than any screaming, 'You are a truly low and common woman, do you know that? My grandmother used to say you can't make a silk purse out of a sow's ear and you are living proof of it. Well, you can do your worst, Mrs Stewart, your very worst, and do you know what? Dan and I will laugh at you! Aye, we will. Because we'll have each other and that's all that matters. We're going to have a good life, Dan and I.'

'You'll live to rue this day.' Edith's voice was quivering with rage. 'By all that's holy you'll be sorry, girl. You'll be crawling in the gutter before you're finished, like your mother before you.'

'No, I'll be living with your son, Mrs Stewart, and we shall watch our children and our grandchildren grow up free of any knowledge of you.' Connie's stomach was trembling, and as Edith took a step towards her and raised her hand, Connie had no chance to avoid the ringing slap Edith delivered across her face.

Connie's head jerked back so hard her neck gave a loud crack, but other than raise her hand to her face Connie remained still. 'Truly low and common,' she repeated contemptuously, 'but you can't win. *You can't win*, Mrs Stewart.'

Kitty had sprung forward, grabbing Edith's arms and yanking them back so hard the other woman's bust was thrust forward like an obscene offering, and as Connie finished speaking Kitty said, 'Are you mad? Stop this! Stop it, I say.'

There was something of a tussle before Edith wrenched herself free, and through it all Connie was fighting the urge to throw herself on Dan's mother and beat her fists into the small squat body. She wanted to hurt her, really hurt her, and the force of the destructive hate was so strong her ears were ringing with it. Only the knowledge that her mental and physical control had to be seen to be superior to that of her enemy prevented her from acting worse than any woman of the streets. She wanted to be sick; she felt chilled inside and out, and through it all every fibre of her being was calling Dan's name.

Edith was half leaning against the edge of the elegant chiffonier now, steadying herself against the polished wood, and Connie's voice didn't falter as she looked at Kitty and said, 'Would you mind seeing Mrs Stewart out, Kitty?' for all the world as though the other woman was her housekeeper and she was asking her to show a guest out after a social call.

It was plain that her attitude was further salt in the wound – Edith actually ground her teeth as she straightened herself, slapping at Kitty's hand which had gone out to help her – and her voice was a low hiss as she said, 'I'm going, don't worry, but you'll be hearing from my solicitors once I get the ball rolling and we'll see how all your fine words hold up then, eh? You might not mind the filth flying, you were born into it when all's said and done, but a man's pride is a different thing. You'll break him if you go through with this, you know that, don't you? And the result of it will be on your conscience for the rest of your life.'

Connie knew she dare not speak – one word and all her good intentions would fly out of the window and she would pummel the vicious little woman in front of her to the floor –

and so she remained standing quite still in the middle of the room as Edith glared at her one more time before turning and walking to the door, Kitty on her heels.

When was it going to end, all the striving and contending and fighting against the havoc Edith Stewart had incited – and still intended to incite – against her? Connie asked herself as the front door closed behind the two women.

And then, almost in answer, she heard the shrill, drawn-out scream that froze her to the spot for a terrified moment, the fine hairs on the back of her neck standing up in protest. And then she was leaping across the room, wrenching open the front door and coming to an abrupt halt on the small landing to see Kitty – her hand to her mouth and her eyes staring – looking down at the crumpled body at the bottom of the steep stairs.

'Kitty?' Connie grabbed at the other woman's arm, shaking it slightly.

'She went from top to bottom, lass.' Kitty didn't look at Connie as she spoke but continued to lean slightly against the wall, her eyes on the ominously still and twisted figure of her employer. 'I always said her temper would get the better of her one day; just missed her footing and down she went.'

As they started down the stairs, Connie leading the way, the door to the restaurant opened and Wilf stood framed in the aperture. He took in the situation at a glance, and as he looked upwards there was mingled horror and relief on his face as he said, 'By, lass, when I heard that scream . . . I thought it was you.'

Edith was lying sprawled across the bottom stair and the floor and from the unnatural position of her head there was no doubt she was dead. Connie looked down at Dan's mother from two or three steps up. Edith's head was bent backwards so her face was uppermost, and her features were contorted in an expression which looked to be of shock rather than pain.

'Dear God . . .' As Kitty spoke she slumped down on the step on which she was standing, and Connie turned away from the sight of the distorted face to take the other woman in her arms, saying, 'Come back upstairs, come on, you can't do anything here. Wilf will see to things, won't you, Wilf?'

'Aye, lass. You take Kitty upstairs and make her a nice cup of tea.'

Connie could feel Kitty shaking as they entered the flat again and the sensation was reflected in her own body. It wasn't that she was sorry Edith Stewart was dead; she wasn't, she couldn't be, and she wasn't going to be hypocritical, but the suddenness of it . . . One minute here in this world and then the next . . . And whatever had gone on in the past Kitty's whole life had been wrapped up with Edith and the rest of the family. This must be terrible for her. And the sight of that face . . . Connie found she had to sit down very suddenly as her legs failed her and take several long deep gulps of air before she could rise again and see about making the tea for Kitty.

Chapter Twenty-Five

The wedding took place eight weeks later, and Father Hedley was aware of the opinions of some of the more conservative members of his congregation as clearly as if they had voiced them.

'What have things come to? That lad's poor mam barely cold an' him gettin' wed! Never should the Father allow it.'

'An' did you know the lad wasn't of the true faith even? Admittedly he's not a Hallelujah – even the Father, liberal though he seems to have gone, wouldn't allow that – but a Protestant and a Catholic? Now what sort of marriage will that be?'

'Mind, meself, I blame it on the war. Don't know their place any more, the young. It's all changed. Start of the end this is, you mark me words. Aye, start of the end.'

Connie and Dan were oblivious to the murmurings, but even if they had put themselves in a position where the gossip was repeated it wouldn't have made a scrap of difference. They wanted to be married at once, and they didn't intend to let narrow prejudice or blind convention or anything else stop them. And everyone who really mattered saw it their way – Mary and Wilf, Gladys and the children, Kitty, Ann, even the twins and their wives surprisingly. Funnily enough it had been

461

at Edith's funeral that the twins' wives and Ann – who had become close friends in the aftermath of the separation when Doreen and Ruth had refused to follow Edith's edict to ostracise John's wife – had made it plain where their sympathies lay, and Gilbert and Matthew had been unable to do anything else but follow suit.

The wedding ceremony was conducted by Father Hedley at twelve o'clock, and although it wasn't a grand affair, everyone agreed they had never seen such a beautiful bride.

Connie had expected to be taut with nerves, but instead, once she had entered the church on Wilf's arm and caught sight of Dan, tall and handsome although still painfully thin, waiting for her, she had floated for the rest of the day on a bubble of happiness.

Dan had turned to watch her walk up the aisle, and on his face there showed such joy and naked adoration that there wasn't a dry eye in the place. Connie's wedding dress was a simple, close-fitting, full-length affair, in a fine, delicately woven linen material, the ivory dress covered by a full-length cape edged with fur with a large soft hood that fell about Connie's head and framed her face, and matched the fur muff in which her hands were tucked. The muff had served a dual purpose; to keep her fingers warm in the bitter cold of the February day, but also to conceal the small box she was carrying, in which reposed a tattered and frayed piece of cloth. But it was precious. More precious than all her success and wealth. They were still with her . . . Connie smiled as she approached Dan and took his hand. Her mother, her granny, her darling Larry, and Lucy too – all the people she had loved and lost. They were still with her, their images engraved on her heart and her soul.

Can you see me, Mam? she asked silently as she took her place at Dan's side in front of the smiling figure of Father Hedley. I love you, please know how much I love you. You made it possible for me to stand here today. You didn't give up, you fought every inch of the way for us all. I love you, Mam. And Larry and Gran. Kiss them for me, tell them how precious they are . . . And for a moment, just for a moment, she could almost see them over Father Hedley's shoulder, and they were smiling, her mother's and her grandmother's arms resting on Larry's small, thin shoulders and their faces soft with love and pride.

And then Dan's arm went round her waist and he squeezed her close for a moment, and Connie raised her golden head to his dear face. The intensity of his love reached out to enfold her in a warm protecting shield and she relaxed against him for a blissful moment, before turning and handing her muff to Mary who was her matron-of-honour and looking very pretty in pale pink.

Dan's kiss was swift but passionate as the service ended, and it lit within Connie a desire equal to that of her husband. It continued to burn through all the laughter and fun of the celebrations that afternoon and evening at the restaurant, the tea-rooms having been cleared of chairs and tables for dancing, and then came the moment when all their guests had gone and Mary and Wilf and the baby had retired to their own rooms above the bakery.

Connie and Dan had decided to have their wedding night at the flat before they left for a few days' honeymoon at a very grand hotel in Newcastle. Now they were alone at last, and Dan turned from locking the shop door, walked across to where Connie stood waiting, and took her into his arms. His kiss was hard and passionate and free of all the restraints he had shown thus far, and by the time he led her upstairs she was trembling and moist.

He was gentle, incredibly gentle as he tenderly peeled away her bridal dress and the silk underwear which had cost as much as the dress, and all the time he undressed her and then himself, he was raining kisses upon her upturned face.

'You're not frightened of me, my angel, are you?' he asked softly when, their clothes gone, he drew her over to the brand new double bed they had bought the week before.

Connie was trembling, she couldn't help it, yet it wasn't with fear – at least not any fear she recognised. The sight of his naked body had aroused so many different emotions in her that she couldn't name them. Compassion, as the full extent of his suffering was revealed in the lean angular lines of his body; regret and a touch of erroneous guilt as her eyes took in the angry red scar at the bottom of his shoulder where John's bullet had been dug out; apprehension and not a little awe at her first sight of a fully aroused, naked man; concern that she wouldn't know how to please him, and many, many other feelings all came together to make her briefly stiff and unyielding.

And then he began to stroke her and again shower gossamer soft kisses on her face and throat before slowly working downwards to her collarbones, the exposed peaks of her full breasts, her small waist and flat, taut stomach, and by the time he slid up the bed again to take her mouth she was ready to receive him.

He became still the moment before he entered her, and then he said, his voice a whisper against the hot flushed skin of her cheek, 'Don't be frightened, my angel, I won't hurt you.'

And he didn't.

Instead he took her into a soaring world of love and light and belonging, a world where she was indelibly printed with the knowledge of what it felt like to be loved and to love back. And it was ecstasy.

Epilogue

Father Hedley was tired, very tired. The pews in front of the confessional box were still a third full, and yet he felt he must have seen every one of his flock three times over . . . bless them.

He shouldn't have enjoyed himself quite so much at Connie's wedding reception the other day, he told himself soberly, as he sent Mrs O'Flaggerty off to say the first Joyful Mystery of the Rosary after her act of contrition. He was too old for such high jinks, aye, he was. But it had been a blessed day.

He allowed his mind to rest longingly on his armchair and the vision of a steaming cup of tea and a shive of Mrs Clark's seed cake before the sound of another penitent groping their way into the confessional box brought a long, silent sigh.

'Pray, Father, give me your blessing for I have sinned.'

It was Kitty McLeary. He moved his face closer to the grid to confirm the thought and then leant back again. He had been pleased when Kitty had started attending church again round about the time the war started. It did that to some people, drove them closer to God, but of course there were others that went a different way. Mind, he hadn't seen hide nor hair of her in church for a few weeks, not since Mrs Stewart's accident in fact, after which Kitty had moved in with Ida. Still, the lass had had a lot on her plate and she'd obviously taken heed of his admonition at the wedding.

'Make your confession, my child.'

Make your confession. Kitty shut her eyes tight for a moment. She could have gone into Newcastle or Gateshead to do this, but it had seemed . . . dishonest. But the Father was going to be shocked, horrified, and she valued his good opinion. She hadn't realised how much she had valued it until the last eight weeks. Not that she regretted what she'd done or even thought it was wrong, but still . . . You couldn't expect the Father to see it like that, him being a priest and all.

'Father, I've . . . I've done something . . . bad.'

'Yes?'

'Really bad, Father. At least, most people would say but then they don't know.'

What on earth had she done? Father Hedley settled himself more comfortably and said encouragingly, 'It's only the good Lord Himself, child, that was able to withstand the temptation of sin in this earthly realm. Make your confession.'

'I've . . . killed someone.'

There was an abrupt movement on the other side of the grid and the sound of the Father clearing his throat some number of times before he said, 'You mean literally? You have committed murder?'

'Aye, yes.'

'Are you sure?' That sounded ridiculous and Father Hedley quickly qualified it with, 'We can all feel guilty when someone we dislike dies, and remorse can make us believe all sorts of things.'

'Oh I disliked her, Father, but it was nothing to do with that.

And . . . and I don't feel remorse. At least, if I was faced with the same situation again I'd do exactly the same, so that can't mean I feel remorse, can it?'

Dear God, dear God.

'I . . . I knew she was going to destroy someone I loved, this woman, and she was bad, Father. Really bad. It would have gone on and on, the hatred and the wickedness, and they are young, Father, they've got the whole of their lives before them. Why should she be allowed to go on wrecking lives?'

Connie and Dan. She was talking about Connie and Dan. Father Hedley drew his lips into his mouth and breathed out heavily through his nose before he said, 'You say she was going to destroy someone?'

'Aye, Father, and with lies. Terrible, wicked lies. He . . . he's been through enough, the lad. And so I pushed her. It was just a little push with the flat of me hand, but it was enough to . . .'

Kitty was telling him she had caused the accident which had killed Edith Stewart. Father Hedley sat in stunned silence for a moment before he managed to say, 'You're aware this is the greatest of sins, to take a mortal life?'

'Well, the way I look at it it was one life to save two – no, more than two, because you can be sure she would have hounded their bairns an' all. She was vicious see, you don't know how vicious, Father. It was her that provoked John to set about Jacob all them years ago, and she was behind the firing of the cottage an' all. And she wrote letters, filthy letters, about the lass. She would have followed them and then it would've been their bairns that suffered too, and there's been more than enough of making the bairns suffer for the sins of the parents, if you know what I mean, Father.'

Father Hedley ran his hand about his face. A little while ago his feet had been as cold as ice and he had been feeling chilled to the bone, but the last few minutes had brought on a hot sweat that was causing the perspiration to flow from every pore of his body.

'An' there's my Mavis stuck in that godforsaken place down south and now John's a raving lunatic, worse than her. No, I don't feel sorry, Father, I don't. I can't say I do in all honesty. And rightly or wrongly I feel God understands why I did it. It wasn't for me. I'd have put up with things, I've put up with things for years, but they are young. The future is theirs. He came through the war and I was blowed if I was going to stand by and see him destroyed by his own mother.'

'There is no justification for cold-blooded murder if that is what you are saying happened.'

'It wasn't exactly cold-blooded, Father. I didn't plan it or anything, but after what I heard her say to the lass I knew she was hell bent – sorry, Father – I knew she was determined to hurt them and go on hurting them. And then there she was in front of me and me hand just sort of came out like.'

'You're saying you were momentarily unhinged?'

'Unhinged?' There had been what was almost a pleading note in the priest's voice, and now Kitty considered the word for a second or two before she said, 'Aye, well I suppose you could look at it like that, Father. I've peace about it anyway.'

'You haven't given me the names of the person or persons involved in this . . . crime, and of course I can't force you to go to the police or come to see me out of the confessional.' Was he countenancing murder here? He knew his duty – he should make her see that this terrible act had to be reported and then she must let justice take its course. That was his duty. 'You have confessed to God that in a moment of madness you behaved' – Father Hedley swallowed hard – 'out of character, and now you must seek Him for direction.'

Would he be acting like this if the people involved didn't include Connie? But what would it do to the lass, and Dan, if Kitty came clean to the law and the whole sordid mess was raked up for public gaze? Further heartache, further pain and suffering, and for what? Edith Stewart was dead, nothing could bring her back, and Kitty had confessed her trespass to God. He was the great Judge, the Rock of Ages.

'Aye, I'll do that, Father, but like I said, I've peace about it and I can't say any different. I just needed to get it aired official like, in His house.'

In His house. The coals of fire were beginning to smoulder on the good Father's head. 'Make a firm act of contrition.' His voice was hoarse.

'Oh, my God, I am very sorry that I have sinned against Thee because Thou art so good and by the help of Thy Holy Grace I will not sin again. Amen.'

Kitty waited for a moment. Surely she wasn't going to get off this light? she asked herself silently. She had expected her prescribed penance to go on for hours. She rose creakily to her feet off the wooden kneeler and hesitated again before leaving the box, but there was no further sound from the priest's side.

The church was dimly lit and very peaceful as Kitty gazed around. She felt better now. She had been putting it off for weeks, telling Father Hedley, but it hadn't been so bad. She would light a candle, several candles. She nodded to herself, walking quietly towards the altar. Life was good. It was, it was good, and by God's grace she would be around to see

Dan's bairns born and grow up. She had a lot to thank God for . . .